Dear Readers,

Many years ago, when I was a kid, my father said to me, "Bill, it doesn't really matter what you do in life. What's important is to be the best William Johnstone you can be."

I've never forgotten those words. And now, many years and almost 200 books later, I like to think that I am still trying to be the best William Johnstone I can be. Whether it's Ben Raines in the Ashes series, or Frank Morgan, the last gunfighter, or Smoke Jensen, our intrepid mountain man, or John Barrone and his hard-working crew keeping America safe from terrorist lowlifes in the Code Name series, I want to make each new book better than the last and deliver powerful storytelling.

Equally important, I try to create the kinds of believable characters that we can all identify with, real people who face tough challenges. When one of my creations blasts an enemy into the middle of next week, you can be damn sure he had a good reason.

As a storyteller, my job is to entertain you, my readers, and to make sure that you get plenty of enjoyment from my books for your hard-earned money. This is not a job I take lightly. And I greatly appreciate your feedback—you are my gold, and your opinions do count. So please keep the letters and e-mails coming.

Respectfully yours,

WILLIAM W. JOHNSTONE

HONOR OF THE MOUNTAIN MAN

WILLIAM W. JOHNSTONE

with

FRED AUSTIN

THE FIRST MOUNTAIN MAN: PREACHER'S FORTUNE

PINNACLE BOOKS
Kensington Publishing Corp.
http://www.kensingtonbooks.com

HONOR OF THE
MOUNTAIN MAN

PROLOGUE

Chihuahua, Mexico, sweltered under a brutal summer sun. The temperature was over 110 degrees; dogs, too exhausted by the heat to chase each other, lay panting in what scant shade there was.

Colonel Emilio Vasquez sat in a cantina called El Gato, enjoying its quiet coolness as he downed a mug of beer and chased it with a tumbler of tequila. He was second in command of the Rurales, local law enforcement officers made up primarily of uneducated men too lazy to work at honest labor and too cowardly to steal openly. Sergeant Juan Garcia, a huge bear of a man weighing almost three hundred pounds, was drinking with him. Garcia sleeved sweat off his forehead. *"Madre de Dios, es muy caliente,"* he said. Garcia was called *puerquito* by the other men, but never to his face. The Spanish word meant both little pig and a person who was filthy and disgusting. Vasquez glanced at Garcia, thinking his compadre fit the description, lacking both personal hygiene and any moral sense whatsoever.

Vasquez laughed. "Juanito, if you would not eat everything that did not eat you first, you wouldn't have to complain about the heat so much."

Garcia raised his eyebrows. "But, *mi corlonel,* the food, she tastes so good."

Vasquez sneered, about to reply, when his eyes caught a stain on the floor by the bar, covered with sawdust. "Geraldo," he called to the barman, "do we have to eat in a pigsty?"

Geraldo frowned in puzzlement. "What do you mean, Colonel Vasquez?"

Vasquez pointed at the bloodstain on the floor. "It has been almost a week since I taught those vaqueros how to respect my uniform, and their stinkin' blood still remains." He turned back to Garcia, waving a dismissive hand. "Have someone mop the floor pronto."

"Sí Señor Vasquez!"

As the bartender rushed to find a mop and a bucket, Vasquez thought back to the incident the previous week. . . .

Vasquez, Garcia, and two other Rurales entered the cantina. They were covered with a fine coat of trail dust from their ride in the desert. Three *bandidos* had raided a nearby ranch and Vasquez and his men chased them for two days. They caught them at noon and brought all three men back into town draped across their saddles, riddled with rifle bullets. Vasquez was in an irritable mood, because the men had been killed before he had a chance to work on them with his machete.

"Geraldo, tequila for me and my men," he called to the barman in a loud, obnoxious voice.

Vasquez and his three soldiers walked to their usual table, only to find it occupied by four cowboys. The men had large pitchers of beer on the table and were eating tamales and beans, sopping up the juice with folded-over tortillas.

Vasquez stood with his hands on his hips. "Excuse me, señors, but you are sitting at my table."

One of the men looked up, his weather-beaten, wrinkled face evidence of many years working outdoors under the brutal Mexican sun. He glanced around the cantina, seeing several unoccupied tables nearby. He grinned. "There are many places left to sit, señor." He waved a careless hand and went back to his eating. "Take any of them that pleases you."

Vasquez's face turned purple with rage. He whipped his sombrero from his head and swatted the man across the face with it *"Bastardo!* You will address a colonel of the Rurales with more respect in the future."

The man jumped from his chair as one of his friends at the table tried to restrain him.

"Ernesto, it is nothing. We can move to another table."

Ernesto shook the man's hand off his arm, his eyes narrowed with hate. "We were here first, there is no need for us to move." He leaned his head to the side and spit on Vasquez's boots. "Find another table, you Rurale piece of dog shit!"

Vasquez's lips curled in a sneer. "No one talks to Emilio Vasquez like that," he growled.

Ernesto grinned mockingly. "Not to your face, perhaps, but you should hear what the villagers say about you behind your back."

"Oh? And what do they say, my brave friend?"

"That you Rurales are worse than the criminals you pretend to protect us from. You steal more than you're worth, and they laugh at you and your pompous ways when you're not around to hear them."

Vasquez drew the long-bladed machete from its scabbard on his belt in one lightning-quick move and slashed backhanded at Ernesto. The razor-sharp blade caught the cowboy in the upper right arm just below the shoulder.

Ernesto screamed in pain and grasped at his shoulder with his left hand. Another slash, and the machete nearly severed his neck, killing him and ending his cries of terror.

When the men at the table with him kicked back their chairs and reached for their guns, Vasquez began to flail at them with the long knife as Garcia and his other soldiers drew their pistols and gunned down the men in a hail of bullets.

After the smoke cleared, four vaqueros lay in spreading pools of blood on the cantina floor. Vasquez kicked their bodies out of the way with his boot and sat at their table.

"Geraldo, clean up this mess and bring us our tequila, *muy pronto!*"

A small smile turned up the corners of Vasquez's mouth as he remembered the moment. He loved to kill with the machete, it was so much more . . . personal than using a pistol or a rifle. It was almost sexual in its intimacy, and usually caused Vasquez to become so excited that his first action after such a killing was to find a local prostitute and ease himself within her willing body.

"Garcia, if you are finished eating, it is time to go. General Sanchez has asked to see me." He puffed out his chest. "Probably wants to congratulate me on the swift apprehension of those *bandidos* last week."

He stood, leaving the cantina without bothering to pay for their drinks. He considered free alcohol his right for protecting the ignorant *campesinos* from local *bandidos* and Indians.

When they arrived at the Rurales command post, Vasquez was summoned into the office of General Arturo Sanchez, his commanding officer. Sanchez was looking out his window with hands clasped behind his back.

When he turned, his face was serious. "Emilio, I have received official complaints about your actions last week."

Vasquez's eyes narrowed. "Oh?"

Sanchez consulted a paper on his desk. "It seems that you killed several workers on Don Gonzalez's rancho." He tapped the paper with his index finger while staring at

Vasquez. "Don Gonzalez says that you hacked three of his vaqueros to death with your machete for no reason."

"That is not true, your excellency. His men were drunk and insulted my honor while at the cantina in town. I did not know until later that they worked for Señor Gonzalez."

Sanchez nodded. "Well, El Machete," he said, calling Vasquez by his nickname, "it seems Don Gonzalez has very important connections in Mexico City. He had complained to the governor of this province, and I have been instructed to arrest you on charge of murder."

"What? That is not possible!"

Sanchez shook his head. "Because of our long friendship, I will delay execution of my orders until tomorrow." He looked once again out of the window, turning his back on Vasquez. "If you happen to desert and leave Chihuahua before then, why, the matter will be solved to both our satisfaction."

Vasquez spit out the words *"Sí, mi comandante."* He turned on his heel and stalked angrily from the room. That *bastardo,* he thought, he has always known and approved of my methods. I will make him pay for abandoning me now.

Vasquez left the building in search of the men under his command he knew he could trust. Plans had to be made quickly.

That evening Vasquez and ten of his most trusted men, all as corrupt and vicious as he, broke into the command's stockade—over twenty-five murderers and rapists were housed in the jail, mixed breeds of Mestizo and Mescalero Apache Indians and half-breeds and several notorious *bandidos* Vasquez and his men had captured.

Vasquez paced back and forth in front of their cells, offering them a chance to escape a firing squad and to ride free if they promised to obey his orders and ride for him.

With nothing to lose, the men all agreed, and Vasquez and

Garcia unlocked their cells and provided them with guns and ammunition. While Garcia stole horses and tack from the command post stables, Vasquez slipped into Sanchez's bedroom. He tapped the sleeping man on the shoulder, wanting to look into his eyes while he killed him. Sanchez awakened, his eyes wide and bright in silvery moonlight.

"Adiós, cabrón," Vasquez snarled as he severed Sanchez's neck with his machete.

Vasquez rejoined his group of desperadoes and led them off into the night, headed northwest toward the Rio Bravo and Del Rio, Texas.

Along the way they raided several haciendas for food and money, killing with cold abandon, meeting little resistance. After making a cold camp, they slept until dawn. The Rio Bravo, and freedom from pursuit, was less than ten miles away.

After a short ride, just as the sun was starting its ascent, the riders came upon a *ranchito* a few miles from the river crossing at Del Rio. The land was dry and its corn was withered and not worth stealing, but there were about twenty head of longhorn cattle milling near the adobe ranch house.

Vasquez signaled his men to a halt. "Hey, Juanito," he said to Sergeant Garcia, "I think we can get some money for those cattle across the border. What do you think?"

Garcia nodded. *"Sí.* There is a small town called Bracketville not too far away. I have an uncle who works for a ranch there. He say they always need more cattle."

Vasquez pulled his *pistola* from its holster and yelled, "Ride, vaqueros, ride!" He fired his pistol, and the group rode hard toward the little adobe hut, expecting an easy time of it.

As they approached at full gallop, two men ran from a small corral toward the house, trying to make it to safety. They were knocked off their feet in a fusillade of bullets, each shot several times.

Suddenly, a diminutive figure wearing a wide western

hat and a brace of Colts strapped down low on his thighs stepped out of the doorway. Bullets began to pock the walls of the house, but he didn't flinch or move. He threw a Henry repeating rifle to his shoulder and began to cock and fire a steady stream of slugs into the *bandidos*. When two of the Apaches fell screaming to the ground, blood pouring from their chests, the other riders pulled their mounts around and began to ride in a circle near the house.

Vasquez screamed, "Kill him, kill the gringo!"

His men tried, firing over a hundred bullets at the little man, who remained where he stood, shooting calmly and accurately until his rifle was empty. When he threw the long gun down, the riders again tried to rush the hut, screaming and yelling at the top of their lungs.

Suddenly both the man's hands were filled with iron, and he proceeded to blow four more of Vasquez's men out of their saddles.

Vasquez pulled his men back out of pistol range and had several of the Rurales keep the man pinned down in the doorway while the Mescalero Apaches and half-breeds drove the cattle toward the Rio Grande.

A final shot from one of the riflemen caused a high-pitched scream to come from within the house, and the rancher holstered his pistols and ducked back out of sight. As they rode off, leaving their dead and wounded where they lay, Vasquez said to Garcia, "That hombre had the *cojones del toro!*"

Garcia shrugged. "Or maybe him just plenty *loco en la cabeza.*"

Joey Wells punched out his empties and reloaded both his Colts just in case the crazy marauders returned. Only then did he turn his attention to his wife and son, who lay in a spreading pool of blood on the dirt floor of his house. One quick look out the door to make sure the killers were gone, then he knelt by his wife's side.

She was unconscious, still clasping their three-year-old son in her arms. One of the bandit's bullets had torn through little Tom's right leg and into Betty's chest. The boy was moaning, barely conscious, and his leg hung at a funny angle. Joey whipped his bandanna off and tied it in a tight knot around the leg, slowing the bleeding to a trickle. He rolled Betty on her side, pulled a long, wicked-looking Arkansas Toothpick from a scabbard at the rear of his belt, and cut away her dress.

The bullet had entered her chest just below her left breast, hit a rib, and skidded around her rib cage just under the skin to exit out her back. There was no bloody froth on her lips, and her breathing was rapid but deep, without whistling. Joey knew from close association with gunshot wounds that hers was not immediately life-threatening.

He took a slab of fatback from the cupboard and placed it over her wound to slow the bleeding and tied it in place with what was left of her blouse.

He sat back on his heels, staring at his wife and son and their blood staining the dirt floor of their home, remembering what had happened to his first wife and son. . . .

It seemed almost to have happened to someone else instead of him, that day in 1858. Joey was young, but men married young in the mountains of Missouri in those days. He was a mountain man, as were his relatives who hailed from the blue ridges of Virginia, the peaks of Tennessee, and the broken crags of the Ozarks. The mountains and their ways of life were ingrained blood-deep in him: independence, self-reliance, and strength led to the peculiar code of the mountain man. To rectify a wrong, to seek vengeance for a hurt, was as all-important as returning a favor or keeping one's word once given. It was as strong as religion, and sometimes stronger, and the way of the Missouri Feud lived as long as the man did.

Joey Wells had come to Sutton County, Missouri, and brought forty acres, a quarter section, of bottom land with soil as black and rich as any in the state. His creek was full and his crops were growing as fast and tall as his new baby boy. If things continued to go his way, he'd buy the forty acres adjacent to the ones he now tilled.

That early spring day was cold, with wind swirling through wet pines and making a sound like a widow moaning at her man's funeral. The rain hit with the force of bullets, causing his lead mule to dance and stamp his feet, wanting the warm sanctuary of the half-finished barn.

Joey didn't mind the weather. His life was as full as he could hope, and be needed to get the crops in and well established before the spring rains began to fall and turned his fields into mud holes too wet to work. He hitched his mules to the turning plow while the sun was still minutes away from rising and the temperature only a few degrees above freezing. He cut a plug of tobacco and stuffed it in his mouth, chewing and waiting for the dawn so he could see to plow.

It was midmorning before Joey smelled smoke on the freshening breeze. He pulled back on the double reins and hollered, "Whoa there, mules, whoa there."

He followed his nose and saw the black clouds rising in giant puffs over the wooded ridge between him and his house. As he looked, he heard shots, and his blood turned cold with fear. His wife and son were in the cabin alone.

He left the mules where they stood, running wildly across the three miles to his house through briars and stinging nettle and brush, his face bloodied by branches unfelt in his hurry home. He splashed through his creek, staining the water with blood from his bare feet, clambering up the gully on the far side, pulling at roots and trees and grass to speed his progress.

He screamed in agony at the sight that befell him as he charged into the small clearing surrounding his house. He fell, exhausted and panting, to his knees, his voice a keening wail of sorrow. The timbers of his cabin were fallen in, flames eating what was left of Joey's dream of hearth and home. He scrambled to his feet and charged the fire until he was driven back, his face blistered and burned, his coveralls smoldering from the intense heat. He circled the cabin, screaming his wife's and boy's names over and over, until his voice was raspy and his soot-filled throat closed, as if that would somehow make them appear, alive and healthy.

It was almost nightfall before the flames subsided enough for him to search the ruins. He found them in what had been their bedroom. They were lying next to each other, the fire-blackened arms of his baby boy stretched out, his small fingers searching for his mother's, which would remain forever just out of reach. Sobbing and choking, Joey wrapped their bodies in burlap sacks and carried them to a large oak tree near the creek. He dug a single grave and placed them tenderly in the dirt. As the sun sank to the west and the stars broke through scattered clouds, he recited what he could remember of a Christian burial ceremony. His final words were "An eye fer an eye, an' a tooth fer a tooth."

As tears made furrows in his soot-blackened cheeks, and sobs racked his lungs, Joey turned his face upward toward a slender moon and vowed revenge. It was the last time Joey Wells would cry.

Joey shook his head, snapping his mind back to the present. He had work to do if he wanted to save his wife's and his boy's lives. Walking quickly across sun-baked dirt, he went first to check on Carlos and Ricardo, his hired hands. They were both dead, killed instantly in the first rush of battle.

Joey turned, wearing a death grimace, pulled his Arkansas

Toothpick from its scabbard, and walked slowly to check the six bodies lying in various locations around his house. Four were dead, two still breathing but unconscious.

He knelt next to the first one and, with a rapid back-and-forth motion slapped his face until the man opened pain-filled eyes. Joey leaned close to him, growling, "Who did this? Who is your leader?"

The Apache half-breed grinned, baring bloodstained teeth. "Fuck you, gringo, I tell you nothing!"

Joey didn't say anything, just grabbed the wounded man's collar and dragged him over to where the other man lay. This one, a Mexican, was conscious but unable to move. His spine was shattered where Joey's slug tore through it.

Joey asked him the same question. "Who is your leader, and why did you hit my place?"

The man gritted his teeth and shook his head. Evidently, he wasn't inclined to speak either.

Joey said, "Watch . . ." He pulled the Apache's head up by its hair and quickly sliced off both ears, causing the man to scream until his eyes bulged out. Joey grinned, a grin with no humor in it, at the other man. "Guess it's not true what they say about injuns not showin' any pain, huh?"

When the Mexican bandit again shook his head, Joey shrugged and with a lightning-quick motion moved his knife around the half-breed's head, then ripped his scalp off with a wet, sucking sound. One last scream, and the Apache died.

Joey turned again to the wounded man, who was wearing a dirty Mexican Rurale uniform. He slowly wiped his blade on the bandit's shirt. "Now, we kin do this one o' two ways . . . an easy way an' a hard way." He inclined his head and raised his eyebrows. "My wife an' kid're in that house, both shot by you bastards. I hope ya choose the hard way."

The Mexican licked his lips, his eyes flicking from the bloody knife blade to Joey s eyes, cold as stones. "It was

Emilio Vasquez, El Machete, who bring us here. We just wanted your cattle, for money."

"Where they headin' next?"

"I do not know, señor."

Joey swung the knife down, penetrating the killer's hand and impaling it to the dirt. As he screamed and tried to pull it away, Joey said, "Wanna try thet question again?"

"Bracketville . . . they go to Brackeville to sell cattle. Aiyeee . . . my hand . . ."

"Hurts, does it?" Joey asked. When the man nodded, Joey watched his eyes as he jerked the knife free and swung it backhanded across the man's throat, slitting it from ear to ear.

He didn't turn to watch the bandit die, drowning in his own blood, but walked rapidly to the corral to attach his two horses to his buckboard. He needed to get his wife and son to Del Rio as soon as he could. The Mexican town of Jimenez was closer and on his side of the Rio Grande, but Joey knew there was no doctor there, at least none he would trust with his family.

It took him almost four hours to load his wife and son in the buckboard and make the trip to Del Rio. He was relieved to hear that both would survive, though the doctor couldn't tell if the boy would ever be able to walk on his shattered leg. "It's in God's hands," the man said.

Joey nodded, his face grim. "I'll leave the healin' ta Him, long as He leaves the killin' ta me." He gave the doctor a handful of gold coins. "Take care o' my kin, doc, till I git back."

"But . . . where are you going. Your family needs you. . . ."

The look of naked hatred and fury in Joey's eyes stopped him in midsentence. "I gotta bury my hands and close up my house. Then I'm gonna kill every mother's son who had a hand in hurtin' me and mine. Tell Betty and little Tom I'll be back fer 'em when I'm done. She'll understand." He set his hat tight on his head. "She knows the way o' the Missouri Feud."

1

Three days later Joey rode his big roan stallion, Red, into Bracketville. It was a small cattle town twenty-five miles northwest of Del Rio, and a gathering place where ranchers from nearby spreads bought and sold stock of all kinds.

Joey was loaded for bear. He wore a brace of Colt .44s tied down low on his thighs, a shoulder holster with a Navy .36 under his left arm, his Arkansas Toothpick at his back, and he carried a Henry repeating rifle across his saddle horn and a Greener ten-gauge sawed-off shotgun in a saddle boot.

As he rode down the main street, his eyes flicked back and forth, covering his approach on both sides, including rooftops. It was a habit learned young, when after the Civil War he spent two years hunting and killing Kansas Redlegs until there were none left.

The war and its aftermath had turned young Joey Wells into a vicious killing machine, until he met Betty and tried to change his life. Now he was back on the trail, hunting nature's most deadly animals, other men.

He cut a corner off a slab of Bull Durham and stuck it in his mouth. He felt the familiar surge of adrenaline—a quickening of the heart, a dryness of the mouth, a quiver of muscles ready to act on a moment's notice. A minute later he leaned to the side and spit, thinking, "God help me, but I've missed this," as his mind drifted back to 1858. . . .

It didn't take Joey Wells long to discover who had burned his cabin and killed his wife and son, and why. There had been raids along the Missouri-Kansas border since 1854, but the burning of Wells's cabin had been the first incursion of the Kansas Redleg raids to hit Sutton County. The Redlegs were becoming infamous, leading raiders and killers and rapists into Missouri. Their leaders were infamous as well—Doc Jamison, Johnny Sutter, and a colonel named Waters. These men and the thugs they commanded hid behind a "cause," but they really cared only about killing and looting and burning.

After burying his family, Joey took to the bush, where he found others like himself—men who had been burned out, families either killed or driven off, men who had lost everything except the need for vengeance.

By the time the actual War Between the States began, these men, and Joey, were seasoned guerrilla fighters, men as at home on horseback or lying covered in leaves and bushes in thick timber as they were around a campfire. They could live for weeks on berries and squirrels and birds, and could sneak up to a man and steal his dinner from his plate without being seen. They were also mean and deadly as snakes, and just as quick to kill.

To these warriors there were no rules, no lines of battle, no command structure. It was simply kill or be killed, but be damned sure to take some with you when you shot your final load.

Finally, Union General Ewing made his biggest mistake of the war. He issued an order to arrest womenfolk, burn their homes, and kill everyone along the Missouri-Kansas border. This caused hundreds, even thousands, to join the guerrilla ranks of the Missouri Volunteers. Names began to be carved into history and legend, names written in the blood of hundreds of Union soldiers and sympathizers. Quantrill, Bloody Bill Anderson, Dave Johanson, George Tilden, Joey Wells; mere mention of these men could make grown men blanch and pale, and women grab their children and run for cover.

After Union raiders killed a mother and her young son in one of their many raids, her other two sons joined the ranks of the Missouri Volunteers, to ride with Bloody Bill Anderson. They were Frank and Jesse James.

These Volunteers perfected the art of guerrilla warfare. They used pistols mostly. Riding with reins in their teeth, guiding their mounts with their knees, a Colt pistol in each hand, they charged forces superior in numbers and weaponry time and again, to defeat them by sheer raw courage and fearlessness.

Joey reined Red in before a saloon with a sign over the front entrance lettered THE BULL AND COW. He flipped the reins around a hitching rail, slung his Henry over his shoulder, and stepped through the batwings. He stood just inside for a moment, letting his eyes adjust to the smoky gloom, checking right and left, evaluating whether there was any immediate danger. He saw no group of men who could be the ones he was trailing and relaxed slightly, ambling to the bar, putting his Henry in front of him, its hammer back.

"Whiskey," he growled, watching other patrons behind his back in a big mirror over the bar. None seemed to be taking any great notice of him.

The barman placed a bottle in front of him and a glass so dirty he couldn't see through it. Joey fixed him with a stare, eyes narrow. "You want me ta clean thet glass on yore shirt?"

The bartender blanched and hastily replaced the glass

with a clean one. "An' gimme a bottle with a label on it, I don't want none o' this hoss piss here."

The man nodded rapidly. "Yessir, Old Kentucky okay?"

Joey didn't answer. He took the bottle and poured a tumblerful, drinking it down in one swallow. "Leave the jug."

"Yessir." The bartender took a rag and began wiping down the far end of the bar, as far away from Joey as he could get, head down, eyes averted, as if he could smell danger on him.

Joey took the bottle and walked to an empty table in a corner of the saloon, one where he had his back to a wall, and he sat facing the other tables, drinking slowly, watching and waiting.

At midnight a door slammed on the second story of the saloon and a very drunk, fat Mexican staggered down the stairs, an almost empty bottle of tequila in one hand and his sweat-stained sombrero in the other. He wore a Mexican Rurale uniform still covered with trail dust. At the bottom of the stairs be upended the bottle and drank the last of its contents, then let out a loud belch and stumbled toward the bar.

Joey called softly, "Amigo, over here, *por favor.*"

The drunk looked through bloodshot, bleary eyes toward Joey as he walked toward him. "What you want, mister?"

Joey inclined his head toward his bottle. "I got this here whiskey an' I don't like ta drink alone."

The man glared suspiciously at him. Evidently he wasn't used to Anglo strangers offering him free drinks. Joey whispered, "An' I'd like ta know 'bout the girls here. They worth a couple o' dollars?"

A grin spread across the Mexican's face, and he plopped down in a chair across from Joey. *"Sí, señor.* They not so young, but what you do in town this small?"

Joey signaled the barman for another glass and poured it full when it arrived. The fat man drank half of it down in one gulp, then hiccupped and laughed. "Not so much fire as tequila, but . . ." He shrugged.

Joey grinned. "Yeah, I know what you mean. Still, it'll git the job done, all right."

"My name is Tomás. Tomás Rodriguez." He nodded at Joey and drank the rest of the bourbon without pausing.

Joey sipped his, watching through slitted eyes. "I'm headin' on down Del Rio way. You ever been there?"

He nodded drunkenly. *"Sí.* Much better cantina in Del Rio. *Muchas señoritas, muchas tequila."*

"I'm lookin' ta buy some longhorns. You know anybody down that way might have some ta sell?"

Rodriguez shook his head. "You want longhorns? Too bad. *Mi compadres* just sold ours two days before."

Joey smiled again. "You mean those cattle Vasquez sold here?"

The man looked up quickly, suspicion in his pig eyes. "You know Vasquez?"

Joey shrugged. "Sure, old friend of mine. Used ta call 'im El Machete back when I knowed him."

Rodriguez smiled broadly, showing several missing teeth. "Oh, you been to Chihuahua?"

"Yeah, once or twice."

Rodriguez leaned across the table and put his finger to his lips as if he were about to tell a secret. "Vasquez not in Chihuahua no more." He shook his head. "He goin' to Colorado, and I join him there."

"Colorado, huh? Why's ol' Machete goin' all the way ta Colorado?"

"Big *jefe* in Pueblo named Murdock going to hire us. Need vaqueros good with *pistolas*." Rodriguez held up the empty bottle. "You got more whiskey?"

"Sure, it's across the street at the hotel, in my room. Come on and I'll get us another bottle."

Joey threw his arm around the drunk's shoulders and they stepped through the batwings, the Mexican singing some folksong in Spanish that Joey had never heard before. He walked him around a corner of the saloon and into the darkness of an alley. As the man realized something was wrong and straightened, pulling away, Joey pulled out his Arkansas Toothpick and held the point under Rodriguez's chin.

The fat man slowly raised his hands. "Why for you do this, gringo?"

"The only reason I ain't killin' ya right now, *bastardo,* is I don't want the U.S. law on my trail while I track down an' kill yore murderin' friends." The knife flashed and severed all four of the fingers on Rodriguez's right hand, then, with a backhanded swipe, Joey hit him dead in the middle of his forehead with the butt of the knife, knocking him instantly unconscious before he had time to scream. He dropped like a stone, blood pouring from his ruined hand.

After wiping his knife on the man's shirt, Joey walked around the corner to get on Red and head toward Pueblo, Colorado. As he stepped into the saddle, a voice came from the door of the saloon.

"I thought that was you the barman described, Wells."

Joey's hand was on his pistol butt before he saw who was talking to him. It was Louis Carbone, and standing next to him was his friend and constant companion, Al Martine.

Joey shook his head and grinned. "Looks like they'll let any ol' trash come up to Texas."

Carbone smiled. "You got time for to wet your whistle, killer?"

Joey looked to his left at the entrance to the alley. "Well, maybe just one, then I gotta be on my way."

Martine raised an eyebrow when he saw Joey's eyes flicker toward the alley. "Yore hurry wouldn't have nothin' to do with that hombre you escorted outta here, would it?"

Joey shook hands with the two men and they went back into the saloon. They showed him to their table, where there was a bottle of bourbon, half empty, and two mugs of beer. "Wanna beer?" Carbone asked.

"Naw, like I said, I gotta git goin' here 'fore too long. Whiskey'll do me just fine."

After they all downed a drink, Joey asked, "What're you two doin' all the way up here? Last I heared, you was stuck down there in Chihuahua, entertainin' all the señoritas."

"We came to buy some longhorns from Texas and run 'em back down to Mexico. Those Mexican crossbred cattle ain't worth spit."

"Say," Joey asked, "you boys know anything 'bout a galoot named Murdock ranchin' up Colorado way?"

The two looked at each other and grinned. "Yeah, and I hope the fact that you're askin' about him means he's gonna die real soon," Martine said.

"Oh?"

Carbone chuckled. "Yeah, Al's got a hard-on for the guy. 'Bout a year back, when we was last up here buying cattle, he got in a poker game with Murdock and lost half the money we had for cattle."

Martine scowled. "Later, I heard he ran a crooked game. He cleaned some ol' boy outta everything he had, includin' the deed to a ranch somewhere up in the mountain country. Coulda been Colorado, I guess."

"Last news we had was the Rangers tole him to git his butt outta Texas or they'd make 'im wished he had," Carbone added.

Joey's face turned hard. "Don't worry none 'bout gittin' any revenge, Al. I'm headed up that way ta have a talk with Murdock and some men he's hired." Joey went on to tell the two about how the marauders had shot Betty and Tom.

Carbone put his hand on Joey's arm. "Don't worry none 'bout your family, compadre, Al and I will stay here and make sure they are well cared for while you take care of Vasquez and his men. But watch your ass. I hear Vasquez is crooked as a snake's trail, and twice as dangerous with that long knife of his."

"Thanks, Louis."

The men walked outside to stand next to their horses at the hitching rail.

Al narrowed his eyes. "If you happen to get up near Big Rock, Colorado, there's someone I'd like you to look up for us."

"Who'd that be?"

"Man name of Smoke Jensen. He did Louis and me a big favor a couple of years back, and I'd like you to take him a present from us."

"Smoke Jensen? Smoke Jensen the pistoleer?"

Martine said, "Come on over to my horse. I have something in my saddlebags for you to take with you."

2

Smoke and Pearlie and Cal rode three abreast across the lush meadows of Sugarloaf, Smoke's ranch, keeping their horses at an easy canter. The fields were full of wildflowers, riotous colors not yet muted by the early frost, and the air was crisp and cold with a gunmetal smell of snow on the breezes. The sun was bright in a cloudless sky but brought little warmth.

They were riding the pastures and fields to make sure the spring calving hadn't left any cows down, their calves left to starve. Spring rains had knocked some fences down, and Pearlie and Cal were checking to see which ones needed fixing first, so Pearlie could send the punchers out to repair the damage.

Out of the corner of his eye Smoke saw Cal flexing and swinging his left arm, a grimace of pain on his face. "How's the arm, Cal?"

The boy straightened in his saddle, wiping pain from his face. "Oh, it's fine, Smoke, no problem at all."

Pearlie gave Smoke a wink. "Yeah, it's fine, 'ceptin' I reckon ol' Cal'll be able to tell us when a storm's comin', from the aching in that wound of his."

Cal had only recently recovered from a bullet he took in

his chest while helping Smoke in his fight against the man who called himself Sundance. Smoke sobered, his grin fading as he remembered how Cal and Pearlie had saved his life. . . .

Smoke planned to cover the north part of the trail himself and to slow down, or eliminate that bunch of paid assassins. He directed Cal and Pearlie farther down the mountain to harass and attack a second bunch headed up the mountain along a winding deer trail through tall timber.

By the time Cal and Pearlie made their way down the slopes to locate the gunmen's campfire, it was past ten o'clock at night. The snow had stopped falling, and the dark skies were beginning to clear.

Cal and Pearlie lay just outside the circle of light from the fire and listened to the outlaws as they prepared to turn in for the night.

One-Eye Jordan, his hand wrapped around a whiskey bottle and his speech slightly slurred, said, "Black Jack, I'll lay a side wager that I'm the one puts lead in Smoke Jensen first."

Black Jack Warner looked up from checking his Colt's loads, spun the cylinder, and answered, "You're on, One-Eye. I've got two double-eagle gold pieces that say I'll not only drill Jensen first, but that I'll be the one who kills him."

The Mexican and two Anglos who were watching from the other side of the fire chuckled and shook their heads. They apparently did not think much of their leader's wager, or were simply tired and wanted them to quit jawing so they could turn in and get some rest.

Finally, when One-Eye finished his bottle and tossed it in the flames, the men quit talking and rolled up in their blankets under a dusting of light snow.

Pearlie and Cal waited until the gunnies were snoring

loudly, and then they stood, stretching muscles cramped from lying on the snow-covered ground. Being careful not to make too much noise, they circled the camp, noting the location and number of horses, the layout of surrounding terrain. They crept up on the group of sleeping gun hawks, moving slowly while counting bedrolls to make sure all of Sundance's men were accounted for.

Pearlie leaned over and cupped his hand around Cal's ear, whispering, "I count five bodies. That matches the number of horses."

Cal nodded, holding up five fingers to show he agreed. He took two sticks of dynamite from his pack and held them up so Pearlie could see, then he pointed to Pearlie and made a circular motion with his hand to indicate he wanted Pearlie to go around to the other side of camp and cover him.

Pearlie nodded and slipped a twelve-gauge shotgun off his shoulder. He broke it open and made sure both chambers were loaded, then snapped it shut gently so as not to make a sound. He gave Cal a wink as he slipped quietly into the darkness.

Cal waited five minutes to give Pearlie time to get into position. Taking a deep breath, he drew his Navy Colt with his right hand and held the dynamite in his left. He slowly made his way among the sleeping outlaws, being careful not to step on anything that might cause noise. When he was near the fire, he tossed both sticks of dynamite into the dying flames and quickly stepped out of camp. He ducked behind a thick ponderosa pine just as the dynamite exploded with an ear-splitting roar, blowing chunks of bark off the other side of the tree.

The screaming began before echoes from the explosion stopped reverberating off the mountainside. Flaming pieces of wood spiraled through the darkness, hissing when they fell into drifts of snow.

Cal swung around his tree, both hands full of iron. One of

the outlaws, his hair and shirt on fire, ran toward him, yelling and shooting his pistol wildly.

Cal fired both Colts, thumbing back hammers, pulling triggers so quickly the roaring gunshots seemed like a single blast. Pistols jumped and bucked in his hands, belching flame and smoke toward the running gunnie.

The bandit, shot in his chest and stomach, was thrown backward to land like a discarded rag doll on his back, smoke curling lazily from his flaming scalp.

One-Eye Jordan threw his smoldering blanket aside and stood, dazed and confused. His eye patch had been blown off, along with most of the left side of his face. He staggered a few steps, then pulled his pistol and aimed it at Cal, moving as if in slow motion.

Twin explosions erupted from Pearlie's scattergun, taking Jordan low in the back, splitting his torso with molten pieces of lead. His lifeless body flew across the clearing, where it landed atop another outlaw who had been killed in the dynamite blast.

One of the Mexican *bandidos,* shrieking curses in Spanish, crawled away from the fire on hands and knees. Scrabbling like a wounded crab toward the shelter of darkness, he looked over his shoulder to find Pearlie staring at him across the sights of a Colt .44.

"Aiyee . . . no . . ." he yelled, holding his hands in front of him as if they could stop the inevitable bullets. Pearlie shot him, the hot lead passing through his hand and entering the bandit's left eye, exploding his skull and sending brains and blood spurting into the air.

Black Jack Warner, who was thrown twenty feet in the air into a deep snowdrift, struggled to his feet. As he drew his pistol, he saw Pearlie shoot his compadre. Pearlie was turned away from Warner and did not see the stunned outlaw creep slowly toward him, drawing a bead on his back with a hogleg.

Cal glanced up, checking on bodies for signs of life. He

saw Warner with his arm extended, about to shoot Pearlie in the back.

With no thought for his own safety, Cal yelled as he stood up, drawing his Navy Colt, triggering off a hasty shot.

Warner heard the shout and whirled, catching a bullet in his neck as he wheeled around. A death spasm curled his trigger finger, and his pistol fired as he fell.

Cal felt like a mule had kicked him in the chest as he was thrown backward. He lay in the snow, gasping for breath, staring at stars. In shock, he felt little pain—that would come much later. He knew he was hit hard and wondered briefly if he was going to die. His right arm was numb and wouldn't move, and his vision began to dim, as if snow clouds were again covering the stars.

Suddenly Pearlie s face appeared above him, tears streaming down his cheeks. "Hey, pardner, you saved my life," he said, worry pinching his forehead.

Cal gasped, trying to breathe. He felt as if the mule that had kicked him was now sitting on his chest. "Pearlie," he said in a hoarse whisper rasping through parched lips, "how're you doin'?"

Pearlie pulled Cal's shirt open and examined a blood-splattered hole in the right side of his ribs. He choked back a sob, then he muttered, "I'm fine, cowboy. How about you? You havin' much pain?"

Cal winced when, suddenly, his wound began to throb. "I feel like someone's tryin' to put a brand on my chest, an' it hurts like hell."

Pearlie rolled him to the side, looking for an exit wound. The bullet had struck his fourth rib, shattering it, and traveled around the chest just underneath the skin, causing a deep, bloody furrow, then exited from the side, just under Cal's right arm. The wound was oozing blood, but there was none of the spurting that would signify artery damage, and it looked as if the slug had not entered his chest cavity.

Cal groaned, coughed, and passed out. Pearlie tore his own shirt off and wrapped it around Cal, tying it as tightly as he could to stanch the flow of blood from the bullet hole. He sat back on his haunches, trying to think of something else he could do to help his friend. "Goddammit, kid," he whispered, sweat beading his forehead, "it shoulda been me lyin' there instead of you."

The sound of a twig snapping not far away caught Pearlie's attention, and he jerked his Colt, thumbing back the hammer.

"Hold on there, young'un," a voice called from the darkness, "it's jest me, ol' Puma, come to see what all this commotion's about."

Pearlie released the hammer and holstered his gun with a sigh of relief. "Puma! Boy am I glad to see you!"

Puma sauntered into the light, then he saw Cal lying wounded at Pearlie's feet. He squatted down, laying his Sharps Big Fifty rifle near his feet, and bent over the kid. He lifted Pearlie's improvised dressing and examined Cal's wound. Pursing his lips, he whistled softly. "Whew . . . this child's got him some hurt."

He pulled a large Bowie knife from his scabbard and held it out to Pearlie. "Here. Put this in that fire and get me some fatback and lard out'n my saddlebag."

When Pearlie just stared at him, Puma's voice turned harsh. "Hurry, son, we don't have a surfeit of time if'n we want to save this'n."

Pearlie snatched the knife from Puma and hurried to carry out his request.

Puma took his bandanna and began wiping sweat from Cal's forehead, speaking to him in a low, soothing voice.

"You just rest easy, young beaver, ol' Puma's here now, an' yore gonna be jest fine."

When Pearlie returned carrying a sack of fatback and a small tin of lard, Puma asked him if he had any whiskey.

"Some, in my saddlebags, but . . ."

"Git it, and don't dawdle now, you hear?"

After Pearlie handed Puma the whiskey, the old mountain man cradled Cal's head in his arms and slowly poured half the bottle down his throat, stopped to let him cough and gag, then gave him the rest of the liquor.

Without looking up, he said, "Git my blade outta the fire, it oughta be 'bout ready by now."

Pearlie fished the knife out of the coals, its blade glowing red hot and steaming in the chilly air. He carried it to Puma and gave it to him, dreading what was to come next.

"Pearlie, you sit on the young'un's legs and try an' keep him from moving too much. I'll sit on his left arm and hold down his right."

When they were in position, Puma pulled a two-inch cartridge from his pocket and placed it between Cal's teeth. "Bite down on this, boy, an' don't worry none if'n you have to yell every now'n then. There ain't nobody left alive to hear you."

Cal nodded, fear in his eyes, jaws clenched around the bullet.

Puma laid the glowing knife blade sideways on Cal's wound and dragged it along his skin, cauterizing the flesh. It hissed and steamed, and the smell of burning meat caused Pearlie to turn his head and empty his stomach in the snow.

Cal's face turned blotchy red and every muscle in his body tensed, but he made no sound while the knife did its work.

When he was through, Puma stuck his blade in the snow to cool it, sleeving sweat off his forehead. He looked down at Cal, who was breathing hard through his nose, bullet sticking out of his lips like an unlit cigarette. "Smoke was right, Cal," Puma whispered. "You're one hairy little son of a bitch. You were born with the bark on, all right."

Cal spit the bullet out and mumbled, "Do you think you could move, Pearlie? Yore about to break my legs."

Pearlie laughed. "Shore, Cal. I wouldn't want to cause you no extra amount of pain."

Cal chuckled, then he winced and moaned. "Oh. It hurts so bad when I laugh."

While they were talking, Puma gently washed the wound with snow, then packed the furrow with crushed chewing tobacco.

"What's that for?" Pearlie asked.

"Tabaccy will heal just about anything," Puma answered as he dipped his fingers in the lard and spread a thin layer over the tobacco-covered wound.

Cal looked down at his chest, then up at Pearlie. "Would you build me a cigarette, Pearlie? I think I'd rather burn a twist of tobacco than wear it."

Puma sliced a hunk of fatback off a larger piece, laid it over Cal's chest, and tied it down with Pearlie's shirt. "There, that oughta keep you from bleedin' to death till you git down to Big Rock an' the doctor."

Pearlie handed Cal a cigarette and lit it for him. "How are we gonna git him down to town, Puma? I don't think he can sit a horse."

Puma stood up and walked off into the darkness, fetching two geldings back, leading them into the light. He tied a dally rope from one to the other and then turned to the two younger men. "We'll sit Cal in the saddle, and you'll ride double behind him, with yore arms around him holdin' the reins. That way, if'n he faints or passes out, you can hold him in the saddle. 'Bout halfway down, change horses when this'n gits tired." He glanced up at the stars. "I figure you'll make it to town about daylight."

Pearlie said, "But what about Smoke? How'll he know what happened to us? He's expectin' us back at camp in the morning."

Puma smiled. "Don't you worry none about that. I'll tell him what you done and where you're gone to. Now, git goin' if'n you want to make it in time fer breakfast."

The two men lifted Cal into the saddle, and Pearlie climbed on behind, his arms around the younger man.

"Just a minute," Cal said, feeling his empty holster. "Where's my Navy?"

"Don't worry about it," Pearlie said, "I'll get you another one."

Cal shook his head. "No. That was Smoke's gun when he came up here with Preacher. It means somethin' special to me, an' I won't leave without it."

Puma dug in the snow where Cal had fallen until he found the pistol. He brushed it off and handed it to the teenager. "Here ya go, beaver. You might want to check yore loads 'fore you put it in yore holster." He glanced back, surveying the outlaws' bodies lying around camp. "Looks like you mighta used a few cartridges in the fracas earlier."

Pearlie grinned as they rode off. "That we did, Puma, that we did."

Cal had been as close to death as a man could come and still survive. His wound left him bedridden for three months, with Smoke and Pearlie taking turns sitting by his bedside, feeding him beef stew and later steaks to build up his strength and help replace the blood he had lost. For his part, Cal never complained about the excruciating pain, gritting his teeth and forcing food down when he wasn't hungry so he could heal faster.*

Pearlie chuckled. "He's so proud of that wound, he's even taken to working with his shirt off so's the other punchers kin see that ugly ol' scar. Guess he wants 'em to know he's a genuine pistoleer."

*Vengeance of the Mountain Man

Cal, blushing furiously, said, "Shut yore mouth, Pearlie! I don't neither!"

Smoke grinned to himself. From the way the two cowpokes jawed at each other, you'd never guess they were best friends. Such was the way of the West and of the boys who grew to be men too fast.

"Why," Pearlie continued, unwilling to let the teenager off so easy, "I reckon at the next Fourth of July picnic in Big Rock he'll be parading around bare-chested, askin' all the young ladies if'n they wanna touch his famous scar."

"Pearlie, I swear to God, I'm gonna whup you if'n you don't shut yore trap!"

Smoke's grin faded as he cut his eyes to the side, peering from under his hat brim. He slowed his big Palouse stallion, Horse, to a walk and without saying anything reached down and slipped rawhide thongs off the hammers of his Colt .44s, then leaned forward to loosen his Henry repeating rifle in its saddle boot.

Pearlie noticed Smoke's actions and sat straighter in his saddle, pulling his Stetson down tight. "Trouble, Smoke?"

"Maybe." He glanced right and left, eyes searching the tree line on either side of the meadow they were riding across. "I saw a reflection off a glass in those trees to the right, and something flushed a covey of quail out of that copse of trees to our left. I hope you boys are loaded up six and six."

Cal and Pearlie both began to survey the nearby forest as they loosened pistols in their holsters.

"We need to get to cover. When I give the word, spur your mounts toward that tank up ahead." He inclined his head at a small pond used to water cattle that lay a hundred yards distant. It had been dug by hand and was surrounded by an embankment of earth several feet high on all sides. It wasn't much, but it was all they had.

After a moment Smoke leaned forward and shouted, "Now! Shag your mounts, boys!"

The three men lay over their saddle horns and rode hell bent for leather just as a group of riders broke cover on either side of them, puffs of smoke and distant pops of gunfire ringing out to break the stillness of the morning air.

As their horses strained and grunted, sweat flying from their bulging muscles, hooves throwing clods of dirt into the air, a rifle bullet whined overhead, slapping off Pearlie's hat. "Goddamn son of a bitch," he growled through gritted teeth, blinking his eyes against sweat running off his forehead.

They didn't slow as their broncs jumped the embankment, splashing into the shallow waterhole. They shucked rifles from saddle boots and dove out of their saddles to sprawl against the covering wall of dirt, Smoke on one side, Cal and Pearlie on the other. Small geysers of soil exploded as bullets slammed into the ground around them, stinging their eyes and faces.

Smoke flipped his Henry over the edge of the mound, cocking and firing so fast, the booming of the big gun sounded as one roar. As Cal and Pearlie returned fire, the air filled with billowing clouds of cordite and their ears rang from cracking explosions of their rifles.

Six men rode hard toward Smoke's side, firing rifles and pistols over their horses' heads. Smoke's first shot took the lead rider full in the chest, punching through, blowing out his spine, and catapulting him backward off his mount. Smoke's second shot missed, but his third caught another rider in the face, exploding his head into a fine red mist, killing him instantly. As the other three bushwhackers turned their broncs to the side to escape his withering fire, Smoke blasted two of them out of their saddles to lie writhing among the wildflowers, staining them with blood and guts.

The other two riders finally got their horses turned and were hightailing it for the cover of the trees, leaning almost flat over their saddle horns, trying to get to safety.

Smoke, oblivious to the lead peppering the ground around

him from behind, scrambled to the top of the dirt ridge and took careful aim, elevating the barrel of his long gun until its bead was a foot above one of the fleeing gunmen. Taking his time, he gently caressed the trigger and squeezed off a final shot, grunting as the big Henry slammed back into his shoulder. Three seconds later, the ambusher straightened in his saddle, flinging his arms wide before toppling to the side to lie unmoving in the dirt. The other rider glanced over his shoulder to watch his comrade hit the ground, but didn't slow his mount as it disappeared into the tree line.

Two more explosions rang out behind Smoke before he heard Pearlie growl, "Got ya, ya son of a bitch. That hat cost me two dollars."

Cal said, "That's it for this side, Smoke. We dusted 'em all."

Smoke turned, eyes narrowed against the morning sun. "You boys all right?"

"Well, goddamn!" said Pearlie, looking at Cal, who had a red stain on his left shoulder where a bullet took a chunk out of his left arm. "Cal, I swear, boy, you a regular magnet fer lead."

"It's okay, it's jest a scratch," Cal replied as he reloaded his Colt Navy pistol.

Pearlie stepped to his side and began to tie his bandanna around the wound. "Shit, Smoke, now we'll never git this boy to wear a shirt!"

Smoke punched cartridges into his Henry until it was full. He looked around at the bloody corpses surrounding them. "Pearlie, you and Cal go check those galoots and make sure they're all dead. I'll take this side."

"And if they're not?"

Smoke shrugged. "See if you can find out why they jumped us and who sent them." He eared back the hammer on the Henry and climbed out of the waterhole, walking slowly toward the five men lying nearby. His eyes searched the trees, but there was no sign of the one who got away.

Only one of the gunmen Smoke shot was still alive. He had a bubbly red froth on his lips and a gaping wound on the right side of his chest, indicating a shot lung. Smoke crouched next to him, slapping his face gently until he opened his eyes.

"Goddamn you, Smoke Jensen," he croaked through wet lips. "You done kilt me."

"Not yet, cowboy, but you're close. Why'd you draw down on me and my men?"

"Fer the money." He moaned and touched his wound, then raised his hand to see the blood covering it. Turning fear-widened eyes to Smoke, he whispered, "It's funny, Jensen. I'm hit hard, but it don't hurt much."

Smoke frowned. "It will if you last long enough. What money are you talking about?"

The gunny coughed once, grimacing as the pain began. "Jesse found a paper on you in New Mexico. Said you was worth ten thousand alive er dead." He coughed again, said, "Oh, Jesus . . ." and died, empty eyes staring at eternity.

Smoke reached down and fingered his eyes shut, sighed, and walked over to the first man he shot. He lay on his back, arms flung wide, dead face looking somehow surprised. Smoke pulled a folded paper from the ambusher's shirt pocket. He wiped bloodstains off on the man's shirt and spread it open. It was a wanted poster dated several years before. There was a drawn picture of a younger Smoke Jensen on it and the offer of a reward of ten thousand dollars for his capture, dead or alive.

Smoke shook his head. The fools, he thought, this poster was recalled years ago. It was just after Lee Slater and his gang shot up Big Rock, the town Smoke founded, and wounded Smoke's wife, Sally. Smoke chased them up into the piny San Juan Mountains. A judge back east, related to Slater, issued a phony warrant on Smoke, causing a passel of bounty hunters to go up into the mountains after him. Smoke came down out of those peaks alone—the bounty hunters stayed up there, where they had died. U.S. marshal Mills Walsdorf got the warrant declared null and void, and the papers were supposed to have been recalled.*

Smoke snorted. "I guess they missed of few of those posters. I wonder how many more are out there, drawing bountiers to me like flies to molasses." He walked slowly across the meadow toward the waterhole, detouring slightly to make sure the other three gun hawks were dead. Cal and Pearlie had rounded up the men's horses and were waiting for him when he got there.

"Any survivors?" Smoke asked.

"Naw," Pearlie answered, "they's all dead as yesterday's news."

"You want us to bury 'em, Mr. Smoke?" Cal asked.

Smoke shook his head. "No, winter storm's coming soon. Wolves and coyotes got to eat, same as worms. Leave 'em where they lie." He removed his hat and ran his hands through his sand-colored hair. "Far as I can see, they don't deserve the sweat of honest men."

He slipped his Henry into its saddle boot. "Put dally ropes on those broncs and we'll take them back to the ranch house." He looked at the horses as he swung into his saddle. "They're a sorry lot, but they'll do as spares in the remuda." He pointed at the bodies. "Cal, while Pearlie's getting the horses ready, why don't you round up those outlaws' pistols and rifles and ammunition. No need letting them lay out here to rust."

It was almost dusk when they arrived at Smoke's cabin. Cal and Pearlie saw to the horses and guns and Smoke went into the house. His wife, Sally, wiped her hands on her apron and threw her arms around Smoke's neck, hugging him tightly. She stiffened, stepped back, and wrinkled her nose.

* *Code of the Mountain Man*

"You stink of gunpowder. Did you have some trouble?"

He unbuckled his gun belt and hung it on a peg next to the door. "A little." He handed her the wanted poster with his picture on it. "A few bounty hunters thought they'd get rich the easy way." He grinned at her when she looked up from reading the paper. "They found out it wasn't so easy after all."

Sally's eyes turned toward the bunkhouse. "Are Cal and Pearlie all right?"

"Cal got a minor wound in his shoulder. Pearlie says it'll give him another scar to brag about."

She frowned. "Smoke Jensen, you go get that boy right now and bring him back over here. I'll boil some water and dress his wound so it doesn't get infected." She turned, saying to herself, "If I know you men, you just wrapped a dirty old bandanna around it."

Smoke turned quickly to hide his smile. "Yes, ma'am." He walked out the door to fetch Cal. Over the years, Sally had patched up more bullet wounds than most doctors, a good many of which had been on Smoke himself.

That night, as they got ready for bed, Sally asked, "What are you going to do about those men who died?"

"I'll ride into Big Rock in the morning and report it to Monte Carson. I need to have him wire New Mexico and see if any more of those posters are still out there."

3

It was a typical fall Saturday in Big Rock, Colorado. The town was full of cowboys from nearby ranches come to spend their wages and raise hell. Louis Longmont sat at his usual table in the saloon he owned, playing solitaire and drinking coffee. A piano player with garters on his sleeves was plinking in a corner, and two tables had stud poker games going, with stakes too small to interest Louis. Several hungover cowpokes were trying to force down steak and eggs without much enthusiasm, faces haggard and eyes bloodshot from too much whiskey the night before. Cigar and cigarette smoke hung in the air like morning fog, giving the room a gloomy atmosphere in spite of the bright sunshine outside.

Louis was a lean, hawk-faced man with strong, slender hands and long fingers. His nails were carefully manicured, and his hands clean. His hair was jet black, and he sported a pencil-thin mustache. He was dressed as usual in a black suit, with a white shirt and dark ascot—the ascot something he'd picked up on a trip to England a few years back. He wore low-heeled boots, shined until they glistened, and carried a pistol hung low in a tied-down holster on his right thigh; it was not for show alone, for Louis was snake quick with a short gun. A feared, deadly gunman when pushed, he preferred to make his living teaching would-be gamblers how to lose their money at poker when they failed to correctly figure the odds.

He reached an impasse in his game and threw his cards down in disgust, looking up as the batwings were flung wide. A man entered slowly, stepping to the side when he got inside, so his back was to a wall. He stood there, letting his eyes adjust to the darkened interior of the saloon. Louis recognized the actions of an experienced pistoleer: how the man's eyes scanned the room, flicking back and forth before he proceeded to the bar. The cowboy was short, about five feet nine inches, Louis figured, and was covered with a fine coat of trail dust. He had a nasty-looking scar on his right cheek, running from the corner of his eye to disappear in the edge of his handlebar mustache. The scar had contracted as it healed, shortening and drawing his lip up in a perpetual sneer. His small gray eyes were as cold and deadly as a snake's, and he wore a brace of Colt .44s on his hips, tied down low, and carried a Colt Navy .36 in a shoulder holster. Louis, an experienced gunfighter himself, speculated he had never seen a more dangerous hombre in all his years. He looks as tough as a just-woke grizzly, he thought.

As hair on the back of his neck prickled and stirred, Louis shifted slightly in his seat, straightening his right leg and reaching down to loosen the rawhide thong on his Colt, just in case.

The stranger flipped a gold double eagle on the bar, took possession of a bottle of whiskey, and spoke a few words in a low tone to the bartender. After a moment the barman inclined his head toward Louis, then busied himself wiping the counter with a rag, casting worried glances at Louis out of the corner of his eye.

The newcomer turned, leaning his back against the bar, and stared at Louis. His eyes flicked up and down, noting the way Louis had shifted his position and how his right hand was resting on his thigh near the handle of his Colt. His expression softened and his lips moved slightly, turning up in what might have been a smile in any other face. He evidently recognized Louis as a man of his own kind, a brother predator in a world of prey.

Louis watched the gunman's eyes, thinking to himself, this man has stared death in the face on many occasions and has never known fear. With a slow, deliberate motion, his gaze never straying, Louis picked up his china coffee cup with his left hand and drained it to moisten his suddenly dry mouth, wondering just what the stranger had in mind, and whether he had finally met the man who was going to beat him to the draw and put him in the ground.

The pistoleer grabbed his whiskey with his left hand and began to saunter toward Louis, his right hand hanging at his side. As he passed one of the poker tables, a puncher threw his playing cards down and jumped up from the table with a snort of anger. "Goddamned cards just won't fall for me today," he said as he turned abruptly toward the bar, colliding with the stranger.

The cowboy, too much into his whiskey to recognize his danger, peered at the newcomer through bleary, red-rimmed eyes, spoiling for a fight. "Why don't you watch where yer goin', shorty?" he growled.

The gunman's expression never changed, though Louis thought he detected a kind of weary acceptance in his eyes, as if he had been there many times before. In a voice smooth with soft consonants of the South in it, he replied, "I believe ya need a lesson in manners, sir."

The drunken cowboy sneered. "And you think yore man enough to give me that lesson?"

In less time than it took Louis to blink, the pistoleer's Colt was drawn, cocked, and the barrel was pressed under the puncher's chin, pushing his head back. "Unless ya want yore brains decoratin' the ceiling, I'd suggest ya apologize to the people here fer yore poor upbringin' and fer yore mama not never teachin' ya any better than to jaw at yore betters."

The room became deathly quiet. One of the other men at the table moved slightly, and the stranger said without looking at him, "Friend, 'less ya want that arm blown plumb off, I'd haul in yore horns till I'm through with this'n."

Fear-sweat poured off the cowboy's face, and his eyes rolled, trying to see the gun stuck in his throat. "I'm . . . I'm right sorry, sir. It was my fault and I—I apologize fer my remarks."

The gunman stepped back, holstered his Colt, and glanced at a wet spot on the front of the drunk's trousers. "Apology accepted, sir." His eyes cut to the man at the table, who had frozen in position, afraid to move a muscle. "Ya made a wise choice not ta buy chips in this game, friend. It's a hard life ta go through with only one hand." Without another word he ambled over to stand next to Louis's table, his back to the wall, where he could observe the room as he talked.

"Ya be Mr. Longmont?"

Louis nodded, eyebrows raised. "Yes, sir, I am. And to whom do I have the pleasure of speaking?"

"I be Joseph Wells, 'though most calls me Joey."

At the mention of his name, the men at the poker table got hastily to their feet and grabbed their friend by his arm and hustled him out the door, looking back over their shoulders at the living legend who almost curled him up.

Louis didn't offer his hand, but smiled at Wells. "Pleased to make your acquaintance, Mr. Wells." He nodded at an empty chair across the table from him. "Would you care to take a seat and have some food?"

Wells scanned the room again with his snake eyes before he pulled a chair around and sat, his back still to a wall. "Don't mind if'n I do, thank ye kindly."

Louis waved a hand, and a young black waiter came to his table. "Jeremiah, Mr. Wells would like to order."

"Yes, sir," the boy replied as he looked inquiringly at Wells.

"I'll have a beefsteak cooked jest long enough ta keep it from crawling off'n my plate, four hen's eggs scrambled, an' some tomaters if'n ya have any."

The boy nodded rapidly and turned to leave.

"An' some *cafecito,* hot, black, and strong enough to float a horseshoe," Wells added.

Louis grinned, "I like to see a man with a healthy appetite." He glanced at a thick layer of trail dust on Wells's buckskin coat. "You have the look of a man a long time on the trail."

"That's a fact. All the way from Mexico, pretty near a month now."

The waiter appeared and placed a coffee mug on the table, filled it with steaming black coffee from a silver server, and added some to Louis's cup before setting the pot on the table. Wells pulled a cork from his whiskey bottle and poured a dollop of the amber liquid into his coffee. He offered the bottle to Louis, who shook his head.

Wells shrugged, blew on his coffee to cool it, and drank the entire cup down in one long draft. He leaned back, took his fixings out, and built himself a cigarette. Striking a lucifer on his boot, he lit the cigarette. He left it in his mouth while he spoke, squinting one eye against the smoke. "That's might good coffee." He refilled his cup and again topped it off with a touch of whiskey. "Shore beats that mesquite bean coffee I been drinking fer the last month."

Louis nodded, reviewing in his mind what he had heard about the famous Joey Wells. Wells had been born in the foothills of Missouri. He was barely in his teens when he fought in the Civil War for the Confederate Army. Riding with a group called the Missouri Volunteers, he became a fearless, vicious killer, eagerly absorbing every trick of guerrilla warfare known from the mountain men and hillbillies he fought with. After Lee's surrender at Appomattox, Wells's group attempted to turn themselves in. They reported to a Union Army outpost and handed over their weapons, expecting to be sent home like other Confederate soldiers had been. Instead, the entire group was assassinated. All except Wells and a few others, who were late getting to the surrender site. From a hill nearby they watched their unarmed comrades being gunned down. Under the code of the Missouri Feud, they vowed to fight the Union to the death.

After Joey and his men perpetrated several raids upon unsuspecting Union soldiers and camps, killing viciously to fulfill their vow of vengeance, a group of hired killers and thugs known as the Kansas Redlegs was assigned to hunt down the remaining Missouri Volunteers. After several years of raids and counterraids, Joey was the last surviving member of his renegade group. It took him another year and a half, using every trick he had learned, to track down and kill all of the remaining Redlegs, over a hundred and fifty men. Along the way he became a legend, a figure mothers would use to scare their children into doing their chores, a figure men would whisper about around campfires at night. With each telling, his legend grew, magnified by penny dreadfuls and shilling shockers, until there was no place left in America for him to run to.

After the last Redleg lay dead at his feet, Joey was said to have gone to Mexico and set up a ranch there. Rumor had it the Texas Rangers had struck a bargain with him, vowing to leave him in peace if he stayed south of the border.

Louis fired up another cigar, sipped his coffee, and wondered what had happened to cause Wells to break his truce and head north to Colorado. Of course, he didn't ask. In the

West, sticking your nose in another's business was an invitation to have someone shoot it off.

After his food was served, Wells leaned forward and ate with a single-minded concentration, not speaking again until his plate was bare. He filled his empty coffee cup with whiskey, built another cigarette, and leaned back with a contented sigh. Smoke floated from the butt in his mouth and caused him to squint as he stared at Louis from under his hat brim. "A while back, I met some fellahs down Chihuahua way tole me 'bout a couple o' friends of theirs in Colorado. One was named Longmont."

Louis motioned to the waiter to bring him some brandy, then nodded, waiting for Wells to continue. "Yep. Said this Longmont dressed like a dandy and talked real fancy, but not to let that fool me. This Longmont was a real bad pistoleer and knew his way around a Colt, and was maybe the second-fastest man with a short gun they'd ever seen."

Louis dipped the butt of his stogie in his brandy, then stuck it in his mouth and puffed, sending a cloud of blue smoke toward the ceiling. "These men say anything else?" he asked, eyebrows raised.

"Uh-huh. Said this Longmont would do ta ride the river with, and if'n he was yore friend, he'd stand toe ta toe with ya against the devil hisself if need be."

Louis threw back his head and laughed. "Well, excusing your friends for engaging in a small amount of hyperbole, I suppose their assessment of my character is basically correct."

Wells's lips curled in a small smile. "Like they said, ya talk real purty."

"And who was the other man your friends mentioned?"

"Hombre named Smoke Jensen. They said Jensen was so fast, he could snatch a double eagle off'n a rattler's head and leave change 'fore the snake could strike."

Louis drowned his quiet smile in coffee. "Your friends

have quite a way with words themselves. Might I ask what their names are?"

"'Couple o' Mexes named Louis Carbone and Al Martine. Got 'em a little *ranchito* near Chihuahua." Wells dropped his cigarette on the floor and ground it out with his boot. "They be pretty fair with short guns theyselves, fer Mexes."

Louis nodded, remembering the last time he had seen Carbone and Martine. The pair had hired out their guns to a rotten, no-good back-shooter named Lee Slater. Slater bit off more than he could chew when he and his men rode through Big Rock, shooting up the town and raising hell. Problem was, they also wounded and almost killed Sally Jensen, Smoke's wife. Smoke went after them, and in the end faced down the gang in the very streets of Big Rock, where it all started. . . .

Lee Slater stepped out of the shadows, his hands wrapped around the butts of Colts, as were Smoke's. "I'm gonna kill you, Jensen!" he screamed.

A rifle barked, the slug striking Lee in the middle of his back and exiting out the front. The outlaw gang leader lay dead on the hot, dusty street.

Sally Jensen stepped back into Louis's gambling hall and jacked another round into her carbine.

Smoke smiled at her and walked down the boardwalk.

"Looking for me, amigo?" Al Martine spoke from the shadows of a doorway. His guns were in leather.

"Not really. Ride on, Al."

"Why would you make such an offer to me? I am an outlaw, a killer. I hunted you in the mountains."

"You have a family, Al?"

"*Sí.* A father and mother, brothers and sister, all down in Mexico."

"Why don't you go pay them a visit? Hang up your guns for a time?"

The Mexican smiled and finished rolling a cigarette. He lit it and held it to Smoke's lips.

"Thanks, Al."

"Thank you, Smoke. I shall be in Chihuahua. If you ever need me, send word, everybody knows where to find me. I will come very quickly."

"I might do that."

"Adios, compadre." Al stepped off the boardwalk and was gone. A few moments later, Sheriff Silva and a posse rode up in a cloud of dust.

"That's it, Smoke," the sheriff announced. "It s all over. You're a free man, and all these other yahoos are gonna be behind bars."

"Suits me," Smoke said, and holstered his guns.

"No, it ain't over!" The scream came from up the street.

Everybody looked. Pecos stood there, his hands over the butts of his fancy engraved .45s.

"Oh, crap!" Smoke said.

"Don't do it, kid!" Louis Carbone called from the boardwalk. "It's over. He'll kill you, boy."

"Hell with you, you greasy son of a bitch!" Pecos yelled.

Carbone stiffened, cut his eyes to Smoke.

"Man sure shouldn't have to take a cut like that, Carbone," Smoke told him.

Carbone stepped out into the street, his big silver spurs jingling. "Kid, you can insult me all day. But you cannot insult my mother."

Pecos laughed and told him what he thought about Carbone's sister too.

Carbone shot him before the Kid could even clear leather. The Pecos Kid died in the dusty street of a town that would be gone in ten years. He was buried in an unmarked grave.

"If you hurry, Carbone," Smoke called, "I think you can catch up with Martine. Me and him smoked a cigarette together a few minutes ago, and he told me he was going back to Chihuahua to visit his folks."

Carbone grinned and saluted Smoke. A minute later he was riding out of town, heading south.*

Louis grinned at the memory. Carbone and Martine had been given a second chance at life through the generosity of Smoke Jensen. He hoped they took advantage of it.

"How are Carbone and Martine doing?"

Wells shrugged. "Pretty fair. Ain't much fer ranchin' though. Spend most of their time drinkin' tequila and shaggin' every señorita within a hundred miles, most of the señoras too, I 'spect."

Louis laughed again. "That would certainly be like Al and Louis all right."

"They said they owed you and Jensen a debt of honor fer how you all helped them out a while back." Wells reached into a leather pouch slung over his shoulder on a rawhide thong.

Louis tensed, his hand moving toward his Colt. Wells noticed the motion and shook his head slightly. "Don't you worry none, Mr. Longmont. I ain't here to do you or your'n any harm. I'm jest deliverin' somethin' fer Carbone and Martine. A token o' their 'preciation, they called it."

He opened his pouch and took out a set of silver spurs with large, pointed-star rowels and hand-tooled leather straps, and a large shiny Bowie knife with a handle inlaid with silver and turquoise. "The knife's fer Jensen, the spurs are fer you."

Louis was about to tell Wells thanks, when the batwings opened and two men cradling Greener ten-gauge shotguns stepped through the door.

*Code of the Mountain Man

4

Wells straightened and half rose from his chair, his hands hovering over his Colts until Louis put a hand on his shoulder. "That s all right, Joey, they're friends of mine. You're in no danger in my establishment."

As Wells sat back down, Sheriff Monte Carson and his deputy, Jim, approached their table. "Everything all right here, Louis?" Monte asked, his thumb on the hammer of his Greener.

"Certainly, Monte. Why do you ask?"

"A couple of punchers came over to the jail and said Joey Wells was in town and drew down on 'em. They said it looked to them like he was loaded for bear and had some business with you."

Louis smiled reassuringly at Monte. "Unhand those scatterguns and you and Jim join us for some coffee. Mr. Wells here and I were just having a pleasant conversation about Louis Carbone and Al Martine."

"Carbone and Martine? Last I heard, those two reprobates were down in Mexico, tryin' to raise longhorns." He chuckled. "You got to be smart as a rock to try and herd longhorns."

"About all they seem to raising at the present time is hell, according to Mr. Wells," Louis said.

Monte fixed his gaze on Wells. "Mr. Wells, I'm Monte Carson, sheriff of Big Rock, and this is my deputy, Jim Morris." He gave a half smile. "I hope we're gonna be friends, and that you're not planning any . . . excitement here in my town."

Wells stared back at Monte, his gaze unflinching. "Sheriff, I been on horseback fer over a month now, an' the only excitement I plan is ta find a bed fer me an' a rubdown an' some grain fer my hoss."

"I hope you won't take offense at my nosiness, but just what brings you back to Big Rock?"

Wells hesitated. A private man, he wasn't used to discussing his affairs with strangers. After a moment he glanced at Louis and shrugged. "No offense taken, sir," he said to Monte. "I reckon it's yore job and ya got a right ta ask." He took a small drink of his whiskey and began to make a cigarette as he talked, his eyes on his hands as he folded the paper and sprinkled tobacco on it from a small cloth sack. "'Bout six weeks back a group of Mexican Rurales and half-breed Mescalero Apaches raided my ranch down in Mexico, jest 'cross the border from Del Rio." He screwed the butt in the corner of his mouth and lit it, then raised his eyes to Monte's. "They killed two of my hands an' wounded my wife and son an' stole twenty of my beeves."

Jim blurted out, eyes wide, "They shot yore wife and kid?" His surprise came from the fact that in the West, women were treated with respect and deference by most cowboys. Men had been known to be shot or hanged for merely treating a woman with disrespect, and the thought of involving wives and children in feuds between menfolk was unthinkable to most citizens.

"Yeah. Soon's the raiders was gone, I took Betty and little Tom 'crost the Rio Bravo into Del Rio and had the doc there patch 'em up." Wells looked down at his hands, clenched white-knuckled on the table before him. "Still don't know if'n my boy's gonna be able to walk. They shattered his leg bone with a rifle bullet."

"How many were there that attacked you?" asked Louis.

"Thirty, maybe thirty-five." Wells gave a tight smile. "I was a mite too busy to count 'em at the time. They left six fer the buzzards ta eat at my place."

When Wells paused, Monte asked, "That why you're up this way?"

"Yep. After I got my kin taken care of, I tracked the murderin' bastards ta a town called Bracketville, where they sold my cattle. One of 'em stayed behind to sample the nightlife, an' he tole me he an' the others had been hired by a man name of Murdock ta work at a ranch over at Pueblo, Colorado. Seems this Murdock won the ranch in a crooked poker game just 'fore he was run outta Texas by some Rangers who didn't like his back-shootin' ways."

Monte frowned. "I've heard of Jacob Murdock. The exsheriff of Pueblo is a friend of mine. He says Murdock is crooked as a snake's trail. According to my friend, Murdock's men threatened to kill the townspeople if they didn't vote for his kid brother, Sam Murdock, for sheriff." Monte waved at the waiter, held up two fingers, and pointed at the coffeepot.

Jim said, "That's be Ben Tolson?"

"Yeah. Ben tole me that ever since Murdock took over the ranch, the Lazy M he calls it, there's been complaints of cattle and calves missing and turning up on Murdock's spread."

Wells paid close attention as Monte spoke. One of the lessons he'd learned in his years as a hunted outlaw was to gather as much information about his opponents as he could. He had a term for it. He called it "having an edge." He knew he had beaten men as fast as, and maybe faster with a gun than he was. He did it by always making sure he had an edge; the sun at his back and in the other's eyes, an element of surprise, or just the simple fact he always made sure to have grain to feed his big roan stallion instead of hay. He had outrun and outlasted many a pursuer, because grain gives a horse more "bottom," the abilty to run longer, while hay-fed mounts give out.

"Didn't Tolson investigate the complaints?" Louis asked

"Sure," Monte answered. "But witnesses against Murdock had a nasty habit of gettin' themselves killed before they could testify against him, and 'fore long Ben was out of a job." Monte cut his eyes to Wells. "You got a tough row to hoe if you're plannin' to go up against Murdock, especially if he's got thirty new gun hawks on his payroll and his brother as sheriff."

Wells shrugged, patting his Colt Navy in his shoulder holster. "Don't matter none ta me. Better men than this Murdock been tryin' ta plant me fer years." His eyes grew hard and seemed to change color, causing the hair on the back of Monte's neck to stir. "I'm still forked end down an' all of them are food fer worms."

Wells looked up, eyes narrowed as the batwings opened and a man entered. Dressed in buckskin shirt and trousers, wearing a brace of Colt .44s tied down low, the left-hand gun butt forward, he stopped just inside the door and paused to let his eyes adjust to the semidarkness, just as Wells had done before. He was a few inches over six feet tall, with massive shoulders and arms straining his buckskin shirt. His eyes were blue as spring skies and cold as winter ice, and his hair was blond. Wells knew without asking he was looking at Smoke Jensen, a man as famous, and as deadly, as he was.

As Smoke approached their table, Louis smiled and gestured. "Howdy, Smoke. Come join us."

Smoke stood there, his eyes appraising Wells, while he waited to be introduced. He nodded greetings to Monte and Jim as Louis said, "Smoke Jensen, meet Mr. Joey Wells."

Wells stood, his head reaching only to the middle of

Smoke's chest. He stuck out his hand. "Pleased ta meet cha, Mr. Jensen."

Smoke's big hand swallowed Wells's. "Likewise, Mr. Wells." He hesitated, then said with a serious expression, "If only half of what I've heard about you is true, I hope your visit to Big Rock is a social one."

Wells nodded. "I've heard a mite about ya too." He picked up the Bowie knife from the table and handed it to Smoke. "Louis Carbone and Al Martine send their regards."

Smoke took the knife, turning it over in his hands, admiring its workmanship. "Carbone and Martine, huh?"

"Yeah. Said this was ta remind ya they still owe ya a debt, an' ta let 'em know if'n ya ever need 'em."

Smoke hooked another chair from a nearby table with his boot and pulled it over. The waiter appeared with a fresh pot of coffee and a handful of mugs. While they drank their coffee, Smoke and Wells talked cattle talk, discussing the difficulties of raising longhorns in Mexico and shorthorns in Colorado. From their conversation, one would never know they were two of the most feared gunfighters in the territory.

Wells managed a laugh or two when Smoke and Louis recounted some tales of Carbone's and Martine's exploits during the Lee Slater fracas of a few years back. Smoke got the feeling Wells hadn't had much to laugh about for sometime. He also found, to his surprise, he liked the man. Wells was straightforward, with none of the arrogance or swagger seen in most shootists Smoke had met.

After a while, saying they had rounds to make, Monte and Jim left. While Smoke ate his breakfast, Louis gave him a short version of why Wells came to Colorado.

Smoke glanced up from his bacon and eggs. "You figuring on going up against Murdock and his gang alone?"

Wells nodded. "Don't know no other way. One thing I learnt in the war, sometimes a lone man kin do more damage than an entire brigade."

Smoke considered what Wells said. "You're probably right. If this Murdock is as crooked as Monte says, he's most likely got his ranch set up like a fort. A frontal assault wouldn't stand a chance of succeeding. And his brother, the sheriff, would be sure to warn him if a group of strangers showed up."

"One man, though, slippin' in under cover o' darkness, could be in an' out 'fore they knew what hit 'em."

Louis tipped smoke from his nostrils and contemplated the plume as it rose toward the ceiling. "Getting in won't be the problem. Getting out is another matter."

Wells's face grew hard. "I figger ta take some lead all right, but if'n word gits around in Mexico that you kin shoot up Joey Wells and not pay the price, then I'm good as dead anyhow."

"There is that to consider," Smoke said as he finished his coffee and stood. "However, if you're not in too big a hurry to kill those *bandidos,* I'd be proud to have you spend a day or two out at Sugarloaf."

Wells hesitated. "Well . . ."

Smoke shrugged. "It's a long ride to Pueblo, and you don't want to take on that bunch until you're well rested."

"And you won't find a better cook or hostess in Colorado than Sally Jensen," Louis added.

"You gents talked me into it. I'll just feed and water my hoss and we kin be on our way."

"While you do that, I've got to go see Monte about some wanted posters on me that are still floating around New Mexico. It shouldn't take me more than a half hour or so."

Wells reached into his pocket, but Louis held up his hand. "There's no charge for the food. Consider yourself my guest as long as you're in town, Mr. Wells."

Wells stuck out his hand. "Like I said, my friends call me Joey."

He and Smoke walked through the batwings and Smoke

pointed out the livery stable before he turned to walk toward Monte's office.

Wells stepped into his saddle and began to walk his big roan stallion down the street, eyes searching rooftops and alleys out of lifelong habit As he passed the general store, he saw a figure step out of the shadows, a rifle to his shoulder pointing at Smoke's back. Wells drew and fired in one motion, his .44-caliber slug entering the ambusher's left eye, blowing out the back of his head.

When the Colt boomed, Smoke crouched, wheeling, his hands full of iron. He saw Wells's pistol leaking smoke, still aimed at the bushwhacker as he toppled backward. The streets filled with people, Monte and Jim coming on the run with Greeners leveled at Wells.

"Hold on, Monte!" Smoke yelled. "Joey saved my life!"

A crowd gathered around the body as Smoke bent to check him for life. He was dead as a stone. "This is one of the gang of bounty hunters that attacked me this morning."

"Bounty hunters? There's no bounty on you," Monte said.

Smoke pulled the folded poster from his shirt pocket and handed it to the sheriff. "It's a long story. Come on over to your office and I'll fill you in."

Before leaving, he stuck out his hand, staring into Wells's eyes. "Joey, I owe you."

In the West, this was more than a statement—it was a pledge. A promise that whenever or wherever Wells needed help, Smoke would be there for him.

Wells took Smoke's hand, shrugging. "I never could abide back shooters." He leaned over and spit in the corpse's face before leading his horse toward the livery.

Monte said in a low voice, "I guess this means you're gonna help him go up against Murdock."

Smoke grinned without answering, his face alive with savage anticipation.

5

Sally and Joey hit it off immediately. Perhaps she saw in the small proud man the same qualities that had attracted her to Smoke Jensen—his independence, his refusal to allow anyone to hurt his family or friends without paying the price, and his complete lack of pretension and arrogance For his part, Sally reminded Joey of his wife, Betty. Fiercely loyal to her man, she accepted without question any friend of Smoke s as a friend of hers and nothing was too good for the gentleman who had saved her lover's life.

Sally outdid herself with supper, stuffing the two men with beefsteak, homemade biscuits, and fresh vegetables from her garden until they couldn't eat another bite. After the meal she shooed them out to the porch with mugs of rich, dark coffee and cigars while she cleaned the kitchen.

Smoke called Cal and Pearlie from the bunkhouse to meet his guest, and the two young cowboys were thrilled to make the acquaintance of such a living legend. Cal even brought over a couple of dime novels written by Ned Buntline that had Joey's picture on the cover, blowing away a group of Kansas Redlegs.

Smoke laughed when Joey blushed, embarrassed by the teenager's obvious hero worship. The pistoleer finally got serious, looking directly into Cal's eyes as he said, "Cal boy, killin' a man ain't hardly never nothin' ta be proud of, no more'n killin' a rattler is. Truth is, ever one o' those Redlegs forfeited their right ta live by what they done in the war." He hesitated while he puffed on his cigar, watching smoke drift on the cool night breeze. "Killin' in a war, face-ta-face in battle, is one thing, an' I don't have no hard feelin's again any soldiers, blue or gray, who fought with honor. But the Redlegs turned their backs on honor an' gunned down unarmed men an' boys who'd given up their weapons an' surrendered."

Cal said, "Tell us what happened, Mr. Wells. How did you let them git the drop on you?"

Joey smiled sadly, his eyes far away. "It'd been a long, cold war, boy. My men and I had been livin' in our saddles for what seemed like months, with no word of back home or kinfolk nor nothin'. We'd been livin' like animals, hunted, runnin' when we had to, only ta stop and turn occasionally and attack back at 'em when they was least expectin' it."

Joey paused to build a cigarette, stick it in the corner of his mouth, and take a drink of coffee before he continued. "The Redlegs raided and burned Dayton, Missouri, an' we retaliated by doin' the same thing ta Aubry, Kansas. They dogged our tails all the way back ta the mountains on that little fracas."

He leaned back against a porch post and stared at the stars as he spoke. "We slept in our saddles, or in the timber under bushes an' leaves an' grass, shivering, never darin' ta unsaddle our hosses." He glanced at Cal. "Slept with the reins in our hands most o' the time. Covered our hosses' hooves with burlap or cloth to muffle the noise they made and tried to slip through the Indian Nations back to Texas. Had to take some time to heal our wounded and replace our grub an' ammunition."

"When you got safely back to Texas, why didn't you just stay there?" asked Cal, his eyes wide in the starlight.

Joey shook his head. "T'weren't the way of it, Cal boy.

The Missouri Feud don't say you fight till yore tired an' hungry an' then quit. Nope, the way o' the feud is ta fight till ya win or ya die."

Joey reached up a finger to flick the ash off his cigarette, then continued. "As the 'Federates began to lose more an' more o' their battles, an' the blue-bellies began to git thick as fleas on a hound dog along the border, we started to lose some o' the best we had. Bloody Bill died with his hands filled with iron, Bill Quantrill was kilt in a runnin' gunfight, and lots more whose names I cain't recollect just now was lost to the feud.

"When Lee surrendered at Appomattox, word started circulatin' that we'd git amnesty pardons if'n we surrendered." He nodded, looking down at his hands clasped around his mug of coffee. "Lots of the boys were gittin' homesick, wantin' ta see their mamas and papas and wives again.

"We sat 'round the campfire, talkin' it up an' down and all around. One of the fellahs said he'd been ta town and saw a poster that said if'n we'd raise our hands and promise not ta cause no more grief and be loyal ta the Union, an' turn in our guns, we'd be set free ta go on back home."

He looked at Smoke. "You fought in the war, Smoke. You must know how good that sounded ta boys who'd been in the bush fightin' fer nigh on three year or more."

Smoke nodded, staring at his cigar tip, watching the smoke curl and twist on the evening breeze. "Yes. After a while it seems you only dreamed about home, and many young men began to feel it wasn't real, only the fighting and dying were real."

Joey grinned, his scar making the smile into a sneer. "That's the way it was, all right. I sat there 'round that fire, my hat pulled down low, holdin' the reins of my hoss as I always did, and thought it over. By then I was might near the oldest and toughest of the bunch, an' I knew they was waitin' ta see which way I'd tilt.

"I didn't want no more friends ta die in my arms or 'cause o' me and my feud. I didn't say nothin' when ol' George Tilden tole 'em he was ridin' in. He got up and stepped into his saddle, and they all to a man follered him."

He grinned again. "Damn if they wasn't a ferocious lookin' bunch o' men. Most of us carried three or four pistols, a shotgun or two, and maybe a rifle in a saddle boot. Lot of knives too, but we didn't git ta use them overly much, most of our fightin' bein' from horseback.

"They stopped when they saw I was still squattin' by the fire. Davey Williams asked me if'n I was goin' in, an' I tole him I reckoned not.

"Tilden tipped his hat an' wished me luck, as did the others. They rode off toward the Union camp five miles to the south, ready to make their peace an' git on home."

Pearlie asked softly, "Why didn't you go, Joey?"

Joey flipped his cigarette out into the night, took a cigar when Smoke offered it, and thought silently for a moment. "It's a hard thing to explain, Pearlie. I guess I just didn't have no place to go home to. My cabin was burnt ta the ground an' my family all kilt." He shook his head, his eyes glittering in the light, as he struck a lucifer and held the burning flame to his stogie. "An' the mountain code I'd always been raised ta believe in said ya didn't quit a feud till yore enemies was all dead." He cut his eyes to Pearlie, and the fierce look in them made Pearlie sit back, as if he were afraid he might be attacked.

"My loyalty was ta my dead wife and baby, and my obligation was ta the feud." He shrugged. "It was as simple an' as complicated as that, I guess.

"One boy stayed with me, Collin Burrows. He'd been ridin' with me more'n two years an' he said he didn't have no place to go neither."

Cal said, "What happened when the others tried to turn themselves in?"

Joey's eyes took on a haunted look, as if the ghosts of his past were not far from his thoughts.

"Tilden led our boys right up to the Union camp, hands held high, white 'kerchiefs tied to rifle barrels."

Joey took the cigar out of his mouth, spit on the ground, then replaced it between his lips. "Colonel Waters an' his second in command, Johnny Sutter, welcomed 'em in with big grins on their faces, tellin' 'em they was doin' the smart thing."

He sighed. "Collin an' me watched from a ridge over-lookin' the camp. We stood there in mistin' rain with our hands over our mounts' noses so they wouldn't smell the other hosses and nicker. After Colonel Waters got all our boys gun an' such, he walked back to his tent and closed the flap."

Joey's eyes narrowed. "Guess he didn't have the stomach to watch what was gonna happen next. Sutter lined the boys up and tole 'em ta raise they right hands an' swear allegiance to the Union. While they was swearin', Sutter gave a signal an' some blue-bellies pulled up a tarp on a wagon containin' a Gatlin' gun."

Joey paused and Cal sucked in his breath, knowing what was coming.

"Their soldiers cranked the handle on that gun and mowed my boys down like they was cuttin' wheat in a harvest."

Pearlie said, "Oh, no! What'd you do?"

Joey pursed his lips. "Collin an' me swung into our saddles an' charged right into that camp, both our hands filled with iron. I put a ball into Sutter's arm, spinnin' him around, and then took out five or six others with my Colts. Collin did the same, an' we jest kept right on ridin' on through the camp, screamin' an' givin' our rebel yells."

Cal's eyes were big in the moonlight "And you both got away?"

Joey shook his head. "We got away, but Collin took a rifle bullet in his chest. Took 'im four days ta die, four days o' pain an' agony as we hid from the blue-bellies in swamps and creek bottoms while they searched fer us."

"Did you kill Sutter?" Smoke asked.

Joey's lips curled. "Not then. He survived that wound. Took me another year and a half 'fore I finally stood face-ta-face with him and blew him to hell for what he done that day."

He glanced at Smoke, his eyes cold and hard. "When those soldiers shot my friends down like that, they became no better'n animals an' deserved what they got."

Smoke nodded. "Kind of like those *bandidos* of Murdock's."

"Yep," Joey said, staring at the end of his cigar, glowing in the darkness.

"Bandidos?" asked Pearlie.

When Joey didn't answer, Smoke told Cal and Pearlie about how the Rurales and Apaches raided Joey's ranch and wounded his wife and son, and how Joey planned to make them pay for what they had done.

"But," Cal protested, "you can't go up against an entire gang of thirty or forty men by yourself."

Smoke spoke up beforeJoey had a chance to reply. "He isn't going to be alone—I intend to be there with him."

Joey looked up quickly. "That ain't my plan, Smoke!"

"I know, but seeing as how I'd be lying in Big Rock with my brains decorating the dirt if you hadn't taken a hand, I'm obligated to return the favor."

"But . . ."

"No buts, Joey. It's a matter of honor, and two men stand a better chance of coming out of this alive than only one."

Cal and Pearlie glanced at eather other, smiled, and nodded. Pearlie said, "An' four men stand a better chance than two. Cal and I'd be proud to ride with you and Smoke, Joey."

Joey looked from one to the other of his new friends gathered around him on the porch, his eyes soft. "Thank you, boys, but a man's got to kill his own snakes and saddle his own horse."

Cal snorted, smiling. "'Cept when a snake needs killin', it don't much matter who kills it, long as it gits kilt! Now"—he hitched up his belt and expanded his chest—"when do we ride?"

Joey laughed and looked at Smoke. "This boy's plumb full o' piss an' vinegar!" Joey hesitated a moment, then said, "Tell ya what. I'll mosey on over ta Peublo, an' if I see I can't get the job done alone, I'll send for you boys first thing."

Smoke shook his head, his eyes sad. "If that's your last word, we have to accept your wishes, but I still think you're making a mistake."

Joey shrugged. "Won't be the first I made."

Smoke nodded at Cal and Pearlie. "Now, you gwo rough-and-tumble pistoleers get on over to the bunkhouse and get some sleep. Daylight's going to come mighty early, and you still got some fences to mend before first snowfall."

The two young men took off toward the bunkhouse with disappointed glances back over their shoulders.

Joey shook his head, smiling. "You got a couple o' good boys there, Smoke. They kin o' your'n?"

"No. I just got lucky in the hiring, I guess," Smoke said, thinking of the different ways the two youngsters had come to work for him. Calvin Woods, going on seventeen now, had been just fourteen when Smoke and Sally had taken him in as a hired hand. It was during the spring branding, and Sally was on her way back from Big Rock to Sugarloaf. The buckboard was piled high with supplies, because branding hundreds of calves makes for hungry punchers . . . .

As Sally slowed the team to make a bend in the trail, a rail-thin young man stepped from the bushes at the side of the road with a pistol in his hand.

"Hold it right there, miss."

Applying the brake with her right foot, Sally slipped her hand under a pile of gingham cloth on the seat. She grasped the handle of her short-barreled Colt .44 and eared back the hammer, letting the sound of the horses' hooves and the squealing of the brake pad on the wheel mask the sound. "What can I do for you, young man?" she asked, her voice firm and without fear. She knew she could draw and drill the young highwayman before he could raise his pistol to fire.

"Well, uh, you can throw some of those beans and a cut of that fatback over here, and maybe a portion of that Arbuckle's coffee too."

Sally's eyebrows rose. "Don't you want my money?"

The boy frowned and shook his head. "Why, no, ma'am. I ain't no thief, I'm jest hungry."

"And if I don't give you my food, are you going to shoot me with that big Colt Navy?"

He hesitated a moment, then grinned ruefully. "No, ma'am, I guess not" He twirled the pistol around his finger and slipped it into his belt, turned, and began to walk down the road toward Big Rock.

Sally watched the youngster amble off, noting his tattered shirt, dirty pants with holes in the knees and torn pockets, and boots that looked as if they had been salvaged from a garbage dump. "Young man," she called, "come back here, please."

He turned, a smirk on his face, spreading his hands. "Look, lady, you don't have to worry. I don't even have any bullets." With a lightning-fast move he drew the gun from his pants, aimed away from Sally, and pulled the trigger. There was a click but no explosion as the hammer fell on an empty cylinder.

Sally smiled. "Oh, I'm not worried." In a movement every bit as fast as his, she whipped out her short-barreled .44 and fired, clipping a pine cone from a branch, causing it to fall and bounce off his head.

The boy's knees buckled and he ducked, saying, "Jiminy Christmas!"

Mimicking him, Sally twirled her Colt and stuck it in the waistband of her britches. "What's your name, boy?"

The boy blushed and looked down at his feet. "Calvin, ma'am, Calvin Woods."

She leaned forward, elbows on knees, and stared into the young man's eyes. "Calvin, no one has to go hungry in this country, not if they're willing to work."

He looked up at her through narrowed eyes, as if he found life a little different than she described it.

"If you're willing to put in an honest day's work, I'll see that you get an honest day's pay, and all the food you can eat."

Calvin stood a little straighter, shoulders back and head held high. "Ma'am, I've got to be straight with you. I ain't no experienced cowhand. I come from a hardscrabble farm and we only had us one milk cow and a couple of goats and chickens, and lots of dirt that weren't worth nothing for growin' things. My ma and pa and me never had nothin', but we never begged and we never stooped to takin' handouts."

Sally thought, *I like this boy. Proud, and not willing to take charity if he can help it.* "Calvin, if you're willing to work, and don't mind getting your hands dirty and your muscles sore, I've got some bands that'll have you punching beeves like you were born to it in no time at all."

A smile lit up his face, making him seem even younger than his years. "Even if I don't have no saddle, nor a horse to put it on?"

She laughed out loud. "Yes. We've got plenty of ponies and saddles." She glanced down at his raggedy boots. "We can probably even round up some boots and spurs that'll fit you."

He walked over and jumped in the back of the buckboard.

"Ma'am, I don't know who you are, but you just hired you the hardest-workin' hand you've ever seen."

Back at Sugarloaf, she sent him in to Cookie and told him to eat his fill. When Smoke and the other punchers rode into the cabin yard at the end of the day, she introduced Calvin around. As Cal was shaking hands with the men, Smoke looked over at her and winked. He knew she could never resist a stray dog or cat, and her heart was as large as the Big Lonesome itself.

Smoke walked up to Cal and cleared his throat "Son, I hear you drew down on my wife."

Cal gulped. "Yessir, Mr. Jensen. I did." He squared his shoulders and looked Smoke in the eye, not flinching though he was obviously frightened of the tall man with the incredibly wide shoulders standing before him.

Smoke smiled and clapped the boy on the back. "Just wanted you to know you stared death in the eye, boy. Not many galoots are still walking upright who ever pulled a gun on Sally. She's a better shot than any man I've ever seen except me, and sometimes I wonder about me."

The boy laughed with relief as Smoke turned and called out, "Pearlie, get your lazy butt over here."

A tall, lanky cowboy ambled over to Smoke and Cal, munching on a biscuit stuffed with roast beef. His face was lined with wrinkles and tanned a dark brown from hours under the sun, but his eyes were sky blue and twinkled with good-natured humor.

"Yessir, boss," he mumbled around a mouthful of food. Smoke put his hand on Pearlie's shoulder. "Cal, this here chowhound is Pearlie. He eats more than any two hands, and he's never been known to do a lick of work he could get out of, but he knows beeves and horses as well as any puncher I have. I want you to follow him around and let him teach you what you need to know."

Cal nodded, "Yessir, Mr. Smoke."

"Now, let me see that iron you have in your pants."

Cal pulled out the ancient Colt Navy and handed it to Smoke. When Smoke opened the loading gate, the rusted cylinder fell to the ground, causing Pearlie and Smoke to laugh and Cal's face to flame red. "This is the piece you pulled on Sally?"

The boy nodded, looking at the ground.

Pearlie shook his head. "Cal, you're one lucky pup. Hell, if'n you'd tried to fire that thing, it'd of blown your hand clean off."

Smoke inclined his head toward the bunkhouse. "Pearlie, take Cal over to the tack house and get him fixed up with what he needs including a gun belt and a Colt that won't fall apart the first time he pulls it. You might also help pick him out a shavetail to ride. I'll expect him to start earning his keep tomorrow."

"Yessir, Smoke." Pearlie put his arm around Cal's shoulders and led him off toward the bunkhouse. "Now, the first thing you gotta learn, Cal, is how to get on Cookie's good side. A puncher rides on his belly, and it 'pears to me that you need some fattin' up 'fore you can begin to punch cows."*

Pearlie had come to work for Smoke in as roundabout a way as Cal had. He was hiring his gun out to Tilden Franklin in Fontana when Franklin went crazy and tried to take over Sugarloaf, Smoke and Sally's spread. After Franklin's men raped and killed a young girl in the fracas, Pearlie sided with Smoke, and the aging gunfighters he had called in to help put an end to Franklin's reign of terror.**

*Vengeance of the Mountain Man
**Trail of the Mountain Man

* * *

Pearlie was now honorary foreman of Smoke's ranch, though he was only a shade over twenty years old himself.

Joey pitched his cigar out into the night air, watching sparks fly as it tumbled to the ground. "Awfully lucky, I'd say."

Later that night, as Smoke and Sally undressed for bed, she turned to him. "Smoke, I know you feel honor bound to offer to help Joey out against this Murdock gang . . . ."

He walked to her and wrapped his arms around her, pulling her head against his chest "Darling, it's something I have to do. That man doesn't stand a chance if he goes it alone."

She tilted her head back and kissed him lightly on his chin. "I know, sweetheart, and I'm not going to ask you not to go." She pushed him back and held him at arm's length, staring into his eyes. "I just want you to promise me that you'll be careful if he asks you to help. If you go and get yourself killed, I'll be really angry with you!"

He stuck out an index finger and made an X over his chest "Cross my heart, I'll be careful. I just hope he comes to his senses before it's too late." Then he smiled and leaned over to blow out the lantern. "Now I think it's about time I thanked you for that wonderful supper you cooked."

She laughed low in her throat as she pulled her night dress over her head. "Why, sir, whatever do you mean?"

6

Joey had Red and his packhorse loaded and ready for travel before dawn the next day. Sally fixed a breakfast of scrambled eggs and bacon and biscuits with mounds of grape jelly for their farewell meal. Cal and Pearlie were invited and pestered Joey for tales of his exploits chasing Redlegs, until Smoke finally said, "Boys, let the man eat and enjoy his food. He s got a long way to travel and, if he's like most cowboys, his camp meals aren't going to be near this good."

Joey nodded as he stuffed more eggs and bacon into his mouth. "That's right. My Betty is a fine woman, but I swear she could learn something about cookin' biscuits from Mrs. Jensen."

Sally handed him a sack. "I fixed you a batch of bear sign. I never met a man yet who didn't appreciate pastries."

Pearlie raised his eyebrows. "I hope you have some left over for the hands, Miss Sally. My stomach's been sorely missing your bear sign lately."

"Oh, there might be one or two still in the oven."

Cal snorted. "One or two? Heck, Pearlie's not happy 'less he's got seven or eight to himself."

Joey stood and wiped jelly from his lips with a napkin. "Smoke, boys, Mrs. Jensen, I 'preciate yore hospitality, but

I got to git goin'." He patted his stomach. "That is if I ain't gained so much weight with all this good cookin' that Red won't be able to carry me."

He mounted up, waved once more, and walked Red off down the trail toward, Big Rock without looking back.

Smoke stood with his arm around Sally, watching him ride off. "That man was born with the bark on, as Preacher would say."

Joey was at the last turn of the trail, where Smoke's property ended and the road turned toward Big Rock, when Red perked up his ears and shook his head, snorting.

Joey eased back on the reins, having learned to trust the big roan's instincts. "Somethin' up there, big fellow?" he whispered to the stallion. He peered through an early morning ground fog, but all he could see was a narrow path as it bent around a stand of pines about twenty yards ahead. He cocked his head, listening. There was something wrong; the bird sounds that had accompanied him all the way from Smoke's cabin were silent.

He eased his Greener short-barreled scattergun out of his saddle boot, released hammer thongs on his Colts, and stepped quietly from his saddle. He untied his dally rope to the packhorse and slapped it on its rump, sending it trotting down the path.

Watching where he stepped to avoid making any noise, he slipped off the trail into dense undergrowth of pines and scrub trees to his right and tiptoed through timber toward the bend ahead.

As he approached the spot, he smelled smoke. Someone was smoking a cigarette up ahead, someone who shouldn't be there. He eased up to an Indian hawthorn bush and peeked through the branches.

There were two Mexicans, and what appeared to be two

Mescalero Apaches squatted behind trees, all with guns drawn, all watching the trail. Joey waited until his pack-horse came into sight, and the men pointed their pistols at the animal, then he stepped from cover, earring back the hammers on his Greener.

At the harsh metallic click of the hammers being cocked, the men glanced back over their shoulders. "Mornin', gents. Lookin' fer me?" Joey growled.

As the men whirled, bringing up their guns, Joey let loose with both barrels of the express gun. The shotgun exploded and kicked back, shooting fire and heavy loads of buckshot into the two Apaches, almost blowing them in half, sending their bodies jerking and twisting to sprawl dead on the ground.

In the same motion, Joey dropped the Greener and slapped leather, drawing his Colts in a movement so fast, the Mexican bandits barely had time to cock and aim their pistols before he was spraying lead at them.

The first one took bullets in the chest and face, dying where he stood. The second got off one shot, which hit Joey in the side of his rib cage, tearing a chunk of meat out of his back as the bullet exited. The force of the bullet spun him around, saving his life as the ambusher's next slug went high and wide, pocking bark off a pine tree, where Joey had been standing.

Just before he hit the ground, Joey snap-fired another round, hitting the gunman in the forehead, exploding his head in a red mist and dropping him like a stone.

Joey lay there on a soft carpet of pine needles, fire burning in his chest, clutching his left arm tight against his body, trying to stop the bleeding. The small clearing was choked with gun smoke, and the heavy smell of cordite made Joey cough, groaning at the pain it caused him. He lay back against the pine tree, thinking of the time he had nursed Collin Burrows after his chest wound, wondering if he was going to end up the same way. . . .

* * *

Joey helped Collin from his horse, his arms around the boy's shoulders. He was so weak from loss of blood, he couldn't stand without help. Joey lowered him to the ground under thick branches of an oak tree, hoping it would keep some of the driving rain off him. He covered Collin with a saddle blanket and went to search for the roots, mosses, and bark his grandmother had used to make poultices to heal injuries when he was a boy.

He built a small fire and mashed the moss and leaves together in a tin cup, pouring in water. When the liquid boiled, he would add pieces of the bark to make a tea that might get Collin through the night. From the way the blood was dripping from his mouth, and the bright red bubbly nature of it, he was lung shot, hit hard and dying.

Joey watched the rain, cursing the war and all the men in it. He had seen too many young men, boys really, die for a cause they knew little about. As he sat in the rain, he whittled on the bark, stripping off small splinters to boil into tea.

After a moment, Collin groaned and began to talk to himself, delirious with fever and pain and infection. "Dad, where are ye? Mom's lookin' fer sis, an' ya gotta help me find her. . . ." His voice trailed off as he drifted into a fitful sleep. Joey smoothed the hair back out of his eyes, laying his hand for a moment against his cheek, as if it might soothe his pain a bit.

After dark fell, a group of Redlegs rode close by, and Joey lay over Collin, covering his mouth with his hand to keep him from crying out and giving away their position. When they had gone, Joey removed his hand, and noticed there was no breathing. He sighed, climbed stiffly to his feet, and walked to his horse to get his shovel. He would bury Collin in the mud of Missouri, dirt he had fought honorably to defend for reasons he probably never understood.

* * *

Joey felt lightheaded, but shook the feeling off, knowing he would die there if he passed out. Pushing thoughts of Collin from his mind and ignoring his discomfort, he crawled on hands and knees twenty yards to the middle of the trail and whistled for Red. The big horse trotted up moments later, bending its head to sniff and lick at Joey, nervously stamping its feet as it smelled blood and gun smoke in the air.

Joey pulled himself to his feet using his horse's reins and clung to the saddle. He opened his saddlebag and took out an extra shirt he carried there, stuffing it as hard as he could against his wound. Too weak to climb into the saddle, he lay across it and pulled Red's head back toward the Jensens' ranch house. "Come on, big fellah, git me back there," he groaned. Red began to walk back up the trail, turning his head to see why his master didn't get in the saddle as usual.

Joey had traveled less than a hundred yards before Smoke and Cal and Pearlie came galloping down the path to meet him, guns drawn, expressions grim.

Without pausing to ask questions, Smoke leaned sideways in his saddle and swung his big arm around Joey's waist and lifted him effortlessly onto his lap. "Cal, shag your mount into Big Rock and get Doc Spalding back here pronto! Pearlie, you scout around here and make sure there isn't anyone left alive, and bring Joey's horses back to Sugarloaf when you're done."

He jerked Horse's head around and took off back up the trail as fast as his Palouse could ride.

Dr. Cotton Spalding took a final stitch in a gaping hole in Joey's back and tied the silk in a surgeon's knot, bringing the edges of the wound neatly together. As he cut the strands, he looked over at Sally. "You did a good job stopping his bleeding, Sally. You probably saved this young man's life."

Sally gave a lopsided grin, glancing at Smoke. "I've had plenty of practice on my husband, doctor."

Joey sleeved sweat off his forehead and tried to look over his shoulder at his back. "How soon 'fore I can ride, doc?"

Cotton shook his head. "If the wound doesn't suppurate, and you get plenty of rest and nutritious food, about two weeks, I'd say. I'll take the stitches out in ten days, another couple of days to get the kinks and stiffness out, and you'll be good as new. Luckily, the bullet missed your lung and stayed in the meat of the latissimus dorsi muscle on your side. You'll be plenty sore, but from the looks of all these other scars on your body, you're used to being shot."

Joey nodded, a rueful grin on his pale face. "Yes, I've taken a little lead in my days."

Cotton snorted. "More than a little, I'd say." He washed blood off his hands in a basin next to the bed and stood up.

"Sally, make sure he eats lots of beef and stew and soup with meat in it. That'll help him replace the blood he's lost. Change his dressings twice a day, and call me if he starts to chill or have a fever."

"Thank you, Cotton," Smoke said.

"Yeah, thanks, doc," Joey added. "I owe you one."

The doctor looked down at Joey, "Pay me back by staying out of the path of any bullets in the near future."

"You kin bet on it," Joey replied.

After the doctor left, Smoke pulled up a chair and sat next to Joey's bed. "You know who those men were who ambushed you, Joey?"

He nodded. "Most likely part of the band of raiders that stole my cattle and shot up my ranch."

Smoke looked puzzled. "Any idea how they knew you were after them, or where you would be?"

Joey shrugged. "Only thing I can figger is that Mex I

questioned in Bracketville. I cold-cocked him right before Carbone and Martine stopped me in front of the saloon. He must've come to and heard them tellin' me ta stop by Big Rock an' look you up. I guess he sent Murdock a telegraph and Murdock sent those men to keep me from comin' after him and messin' up his plans."

Smoke nodded. "That makes sense. Maybe when we get to Pueblo, we can ask Murdock about it."

Joey's eyes narrowed. "Whatta ya mean, we, Smoke? I thought we settled all that."

Smoke shook his head. "That was before someone tried to kill a guest on my spread. Remember when you said if word got around that they could shoot up your ranch, you might as well pack it in?"

Joey nodded.

"Same thing goes here in Colorado. I am not without my enemies, and I cannot afford to let anyone think they can ride in here and try to kill someone on my place and get away with it." He spread his arms. "So I'm going to Pueblo to speak with Mr. Jacob Murdock, with or without you. You have a choice, to ride with me, or both of us can go our separate ways."

Joey smiled. "Well, when you put it that way, I can see that your honor demands you answer this assault." He arched an eyebrow. "You sure you wasn't born in Missouri, Smoke?"

Pueblo was like a town under siege. People walked around, heads down, avoiding Sam Murdock and his deputies whenever possible. It was as if criminals were running the city. He and his men walked the streets and boardwalks arrogantly, and the slightest sign of disrespect or questioning of their authority was liable to be met with a blow from the butt of a rifle, or worse.

Several businessmen who questioned the results of the recent sheriff's election had their businesses broken into and their stocks ruined. One of the town councilmen was found with his throat cut after publicly calling for a wire to be sent to the governor's office asking for help. That effectively ended any active resistance to Sam Murdock's reign of terror in Pueblo.

Ben Tolson moved out of town to a small cabin and bided his time. He knew sooner or later Murdock would make a mistake, and he planned to be there to help the town pick up the pieces.

Colonel Emilio Vasquez stood quietly just inside the tree line, staring at the pasture before him. A small herd of cattle moved slowly in the moonlight, munching grass while their calves bleated loudly, demanding milk. Vasquez earned his nickname, El Machete, by his habit of hacking *peóns* and *campesinos* to death with a long, razor-sharp, broad-bladed knife. Jacob Murdock's offer of triple wages for men who weren't afraid to do a little killing was tailor made for him and his group of twenty-five of some of the worst killers in Mexico.

When Vasquez and his men had reined up in front of Murdock's ranch house, he hired them on the spot. While in Texas, Murdock often heard tales of El Machete and knew he was just the kind of cold-blooded killer he needed to build his empire in Colorado.

Over tequila and cigars in his study, Murdock told Vasquez he would make him rich so long as he obeyed the rancher without question.

Vasquez's lips curled in an evil grin. "I love this country. Where else can *un hombre* get *mucho dinero* for doing what he love—killing gringos!"

Now Vasquez was about to earn his money. Jonah

Williams, the rancher who owned the cattle Vasquez was observing, had complained to Sheriff Ben Tolson before he lost the election that a number of his calves were missing, and he thought they were on Murdock's spread. When Jacob Murdock's brother was installed as sheriff, Williams let it be known he was going to ask for U.S. marshals to investigate his charges.

Murdock gave Vasquez the job of changing Williams's mind any way he could.

Vasquez squinted, seeing a lone rider approaching the herd from the direction of Williams's ranch house, barely visible in the distance. He knew Williams had a habit of checking his cattle every night before he went to bed. He walked back into the trees and grabbed his horse's reins from his second-in-command, Sergeant Juan Garcia. The sergeant was every bit as vicious and cruel as Vasquez, though not nearly as intelligent.

As he stepped into his saddle, Vasquez grunted, *"Listo?"*

"Sí mi capitan," Garcia replied with a grin. "The gringo will sleep well tonight, eh?"

Vasquez tilted his head back to gaze at the moon and stars shining brilliantly in a cold, clear sky. *"Sí* Juanito. It is *un grande noche* for dying, is it not?"

The two *bandidos* laughed as they walked their horses out of the trees and toward the beeves in the valley. When they were about fifty yards from the cattle, Vasquez and Garcia dismounted. Vasquez reached up and adjusted the scabbard he had slung across his shoulder with a rawhide strap. The scabbard was positioned so the handle of the machete it held was sticking up behind his neck, within easy reach.

Jonah Williams saw the two riders and veered his mount toward them, pulling his Winchester from its saddle boot and earing back its hammer. When he rode up, Garcia was bent over with his horse's leg pulled up, peering at its hoof.

"What're you two men doin' on my spread?" he called, leveling the rifle at them.

Vasquez grinned, his yellow-stained teeth gleaming in the moonlight as he spread his hands wide and shrugged. "*Buenos noches, señor.* My compadre's horse, she pulled up lame."

Williams walked his bronc closer until he was in front of Vasquez. "That don't answer my question, does it? Now, you gents keep them hands where I can see 'em and tell me what you're doin' out here in the middle of the night."

Vasquez raised his hands until they were next to his head. He continued to grin, watching Williams's eyes as Garcia straightened and began to turn. When Williams's eyes flicked to the side to watch Garcia and his rifle barrel turned toward him, Vasquez grabbed the handle of his machete and drew it in one lightning-quick movement. The three-foot-long blade sparkled and reflected the moon as it whistled down, severing Williams's right arm just below his elbow.

Williams screamed and dropped his rifle, grabbing at his bloody stump with his left hand. Vasquez swung backhanded, catching Williams on the side of his head with the blunt edge of the machete, knocking him sideways off his mount.

While Williams lay on the ground, semiconscious, blood pumping out of his ruined arm, Vasquez and Garcia jumped into their saddles and rode in a circle to a far side of the herd. Once there, they drew their pistols and began firing into the air and yelling, sending frightened animals stampeding over the dying rancher, trampling him to death.

The killers wheeled their horses and trotted off toward Murdock's ranch. Vasquez laughed. "Like I said, compadre, it's a good night for dying."

Murdock was in his study, smoking a cigar and sipping bourbon while going over his books, when the door opened and Vasquez swaggered in.

Murdock frowned as he looked up, his hand wrapped around the butt of a Colt in his desk drawer. "Don't you know to knock before entering a man's home, Vasquez?"

Vasquez grinned insolently and spread his hands wide as he gave a small bow. "Pardon, señor, I meant no offense."

Murdock's nose wrinkled. The man smelled as if he had drunk an entire bottle of tequila. "Well, what do you have to report?"

Vasquez plucked a cigar out of the humidor on Murdock's desk, bit an end off, and spit it on the floor before lighting it with a lucifer he struck on his front tooth. "Señor Williams will not be here to look for his calves. The poor hombre fell off his horse in front of his cattle and they ran over him. I think he be plenty dead."

Murdock nodded, a slow smile creasing his face. "Oh, I'm sorry to hear that." He puffed his cigar and watched smoke spiral toward the ceiling as he leaned back in his chair and put his boots on his desk. "I hope our new sheriff doesn't try to arrest you for this killing," Murdock said with a wide grin.

Vasquez chuckled. "Maybe you could put in word for me?"

"Oh, I think Sam has more important things on his mind than investigating the accidental death of a small rancher." He stroked his chin. "I wonder if the widow Williams will want to sell the ranch now that her husband's deceased?"

Vasquez's eyes narrowed. "You want to *buy* his cattle?"

Murdock shrugged. "At the right price, of course." He pointed his stogie at Vasquez. "I want you to ride into town and have Sam and his men spread the word that it would be . . . unhealthy for anyone else to make a bid on Williams's place."

Vasquez grinned as he picked up Murdock's bottle of bourbon and drank from it. "*Sí,* I tell Sam to make the other gringos understand."

7

Joey recuperated at Smoke's ranch for thirteen days. Dr. Spalding removed his stitches on the eleventh day, stating he had never seen a man heal so quickly.

Joey told him, "Doc, this ol' body's had plenty practice healin' itself from bullet holes. It ought ta know how by now."

The last two days, Smoke and Joey had been hunting turkey and pheasant and relaxing before taking off for Pueblo and Jacob Murdock. As they walked a field, carrying twenty-gauge American Arms shotguns loaded with bird shot over their shoulders, Smoke asked, "Tell me about how you finally got to Sutter, Joey. After almost two years of you killing every other Redleg in the country, he must have known you were coming after him."

Joey smiled. "Oh, that he did, Smoke. The coward never went anywhere without his squad of guards with him. He always rode with seven men, seasoned killers every one, when he was out huntin' me."

"Where did the final showdown take place?"

"Just south of San Antonio, Texas. I'd gone to Texas to let the heat die down, and to heal up some minor wounds I'd suffered in my last fracas. I spent a week in San Antone"— he cut his eyes at Smoke and smiled—"some mighty pretty señoritas, 'specially to a man who's been on the run fer almost two year."

Just then they flushed a covey of pheasant and both men leveled their shotguns and fired in the blink of an eye. Three birds fell to the ground, while one flew off in a circle, one leg hanging down.

"You got yours, I missed one of mine," Smoke said.

Joey shrugged. "It's a might easier when they don't shoot back, ain't it?"

As Smoke chuckled and nodded, Joey continued with his story. "I guess I must've pissed off someone in town, or they heard about the money on my head. Anyway, some lowlife wired Sutter an' his men I was in San Antonio and they came bustin' on down to do me in." He bent to pick up his birds and put them in the burlap sack he had tied to his belt. "I was sleepin' in the hotel when I heard boots on the stairs." He smiled at Smoke. "Them guards was mean, but they wasn't too bright. Didn't bother to take his shoes off to try an' sneak up on me. If'n he had, I'd be forked end up now."

He pulled a plug of Bull Durham out and sliced off a chunk, biting it off his knife as he cut it. After he chewed for a moment, he continued. "One thing ya learn on the owl hoot trail when yore bein' hunted is ta always sleep ready fer action. I had my boots an' guns on in about two seconds an' was halfway out the window when he kicked in my door. He wasted two bullets shootin' the señorita, who was screamin' an' hollerin' to beat the band, and I put a .44 slug in his left eye. I guess the sight o' blood an' brains blowing out the back of his head discouraged the two with him, fer they hightailed it back down the stairs."

He spit and sleeved a dribble off his chin with the back of his arm. "Sutter an' the others was waitin' fer me on the street below, an' there didn't appear to be a surplus o' options fer me at that point."

"What did you do?"

"I went right back in the window, lit a lantern, and set the hotel on fire, then I went out in the hall and started screamin' and hollerin' *fire* as loud as I could." He grinned as he spit again. "Hell, ya shoulda seen it, Smoke. Naked women an' gents dressed only in their boots an' hats all scramblin' down those stairs and climbin' out o' windows and such, it was a sight ta see. When the smoke got heavy enough, I just joined in the crowd o' people and slid out right under Sutter an' his men's noses, keepin' my head down an' my hands filled with iron just in case."

"Then what?"

"I got Red an' shagged on out of town fer a mile or two an' made a cold camp."

"Weren't you afraid they would try and follow you?"

He shook his head. "Naw. They'd had ta ride day an' night ta catch me in town, an' I knowed they was dead tired. 'Sides, they didn't have no idea which way I went when I left town."

"I see, so you knew you had some time before they would get on your trail."

"Yep, but the next thing is the best. What's the first thing a man's gonna do after weeks o' ridin' the trail when he gets to a decent-sized town?"

"Only three things I know of. Get some good food, get some whiskey or a woman, and take a bath."

Joey nodded. "An' if'n ya been ridin' hard fer three or four days, ya gonna want ta git the bath first, so ya can enjoy the other two later."

Smoke smiled. "You didn't . . ."

"Yeah, I did. I caught 'em in a bathhouse, with more than their pants down. I killed the first three with my Arkansas Toothpick there wouldn't be any noise ta alert the others. Slit their throats an' just let 'em sink down in the water." He grinned. "Probably set that bathhouse man's business back when word got around what had happened. Anyway, the other four guards was in the next room, all soakin' an' smokin' an' braggin' about how they was gonna git the prettiest woman. Sutter, being the leader, had gone first and was up in his room shaving by then.

"I stepped into the room, hands hangin' down, fingers flexin' like they do when ya know yore gonna have ta draw, an' them fellows' eyes just about popped outta their heads." He cut his eyes at Smoke again. "If'n they'd been anybody else 'sides Redlegs, I'd of given 'em a chance. As it was, while they was scramblin' to git outta the tubs and grab they guns, I just filled my hands and began to blast away. They was all dead, all seven of 'em without gittin' off a single shot.

"I punched out my empties, reloaded my Colts, an' went out in the street below Sutter's window. I knew he'd heard the shots and knew I was back, so I yelled up at him and told him ta come on out if'n he wasn't no coward."

"The sheriff or his deputies give you any problems?"

Joey's teeth gleamed in the Colorado sunshine. "Not when I tole 'em who I was and who I was fixin' ta kill. Them Texicans are good ol' boys, an' they had a soft spot in they hearts fer us gray-bellies."

"Did Sutter come out?"

"Not at first, but finally when he saw there wasn't no other way, he came on out in the street. We faced each other and I asked him where Colonel Waters was, him bein' the only other Redleg I hadn't already kilt. He said the dirty yellow coward had run off back East, said he was tired of war and fightin' an' such. I looked him in the eye an' tole him his commanding officer was a back-shootin' coward, just like Sutter and all his men were.

"Well, that did it. There were too many people standin' around watchin' fer him to take that and not respond. When his hand twitched toward his holster, I drew and shot him in the stomach, doubling him over and curlin' him up."

Smoke and Joey walked another twenty yards before Joey added, "I was sure sorry it took him only two days to die."

He looked at Smoke. "I wanted him to last at least four, like Collin did."

They flushed another two coveys of pheasant, and Smoke brought down a large tom turkey. Figuring they had plenty for dinner, they took their burlap sacks back to the ranch house. Joey and Smoke were out behind the bunkhouse, cleaning their birds, when Monte Carson rode up, his horse lathered as if he had galloped the entire way.

Smoke waved a bloody hand covered with feathers at the sheriff. "Hey, Monte. Park your horse and stay for dinner. Sally's going to fix fried turkey and pheasant."

Monte jumped to the ground, breathing hard. "I got some news you two might want to hear."

"Oh?" Smoke asked "Does it concern Jacob Murdock?"

"Yeah." Monte sleeved sweat off his forehead. "You think Sally might have some coffee made?" He reached back and rubbed his butt with both hands. "Either I been too long at a desk job, or they're making saddles harder than they used to!"

Smoke and Joey grinned as they washed their hands in a rain barrel. "Or maybe you're just getting old, Monte," Smoke said as he clapped the sheriff on the back and led the men toward his porch.

Sally came out and gave Monte a brief hug. "Good morning, Monte. We don't get to see you out here often enough. Would you like some breakfast or coffee?"

"Just coffee, please, Sally." He patted his ample paunch. "I've got to cut back on the vittles or get a bigger horse."

Sally smiled as she took the birds Smoke and Joey had cleaned and went into the cabin. A few minutes later she reappeared with three mugs and a steaming pot of coffee. After the men were settled in their chairs with mugs in their hands, she placed a platter covered with fresh biscuits next to them, along with jars of butter and jam. "I'll leave you men to your talk while I cook those birds for lunch." She looked inquiringly at Monte. "Will you be able to stay, Monte?"

He licked his lips. "For a taste of your fried pheasant and turkey? Of course!"

After she left, Smoke spoke around a mouthful of biscuit. "What have you heard about Murdock, Monte?"

Joey looked up from smearing butter on his biscuit, interested in what was coming.

"Well, I wired Ben Tolson a couple of days ago and asked him to keep me informed of any goings-on at the Lazy M."

"Ya tell him why ya wanted to know?" drawled Joey.

Monte grinned. "My mama raised only one fool, an' that was my brother Billy."

After Smoke and Joey chuckled, he continued. "I got a wire back from Tolson this morning, bright and early."

"What's the news, sheriff?" Smoke asked.

"Seems a week or so after the sheriff's election, a rancher named Williams said he was going to ask U.S. marshals to investigate Murdock's operation. He claimed Murdock was rustling his calves."

Joey nodded, eyes squinted in concentration as he listened. "That don't surprise me none. Any man who'd hire the likes o' Vasquez an' his gang wouldn't be above stealin' another man's beeves."

"Uh-huh," Smoke said. "And that's probably not all he's got in mind, or he wouldn't need that many gunnies on his payroll."

Monte added, "Williams's wife brought his body into town two days ago in a buckboard. Said he got killed the night before in a stampede out at his ranch."

Smoke frowned. "Well, that happens. Is there anything to tie Murdock or his men to the killing?"

"Yeah, his wife couldn't explain how her husband managed to get his right arm chopped off clean at the elbow."

Joey's face hardened as he whispered, "El Machete."

Smoke and Monte stared at him. "El Machete?" Monte asked. "What's that?"

Joey explained to them that the leader of the Rurales who rode against him, Vasquez, was known to use a machete, and that he was a vicious killer who enjoyed hacking men to death, especially gringos.

"What's the new sheriff going to do about it?" Smoke asked.

Monte shrugged. "What do you think? There weren't any witnesses, and Murdock has twenty men who'll swear he never left his ranch that night."

"That figgers," Joey said. "Murdock don't sound like a man who'd do his own dirty work."

"That's not all. Tolson says Williams's wife has put her spread up for sale. She's going to go back East as soon as the funeral's over."

"Oh?"

"Yeah. Tolson says it's a prime piece of land, lots of water and grass and a sizable herd of shorthorns." He began to build a cigarette as he talked. "Williams's place abuts the Lazy M, and the river that runs through it supplies all of Murdock's water. Tolson says whoever buys it will have control over the water Murdock needs to feed his stock."

Joey rubbed his chin. "That's right interestin'."

Monte lit his cigarette and took a deep puff. "Even more interesting is the fact that no one seems eager to buy the place. Two local ranchers who put in early bids on the place withdrew their money after having the shit kicked out of 'em by persons unknown."

Joey said, "Those persons unknown were probably wearin' badges when they did the kickin'."

Smoke nodded, a slow grin curling his lips. He looked at Joey. "Joey, I've got an idea. How about you and I investing in a ranch in Pueblo? Might be a way to cause Murdock a passel of trouble."

Joey shrugged. "I ain't exactly flush with cash right now, Smoke. 'Bout all my savin's are tied up down in Mexico."

Smoke smiled. "Oh, money's no problem. I think I can

convince the bank in Big Rock that investing in prime ranch property in Pueblo is a good idea . . . especially since Sally is president of the bank board and owns the building it's in."

"But, Smoke, I don't know nothin' 'bout ranchin' in Colorado."

"I'm not saying we have to run the ranch forever. But from what Monte's told us, Murdock is getting rich and powerful off the backs of poor people." He pulled a cigar out and lit it. "It's been my experience that the best way to hurt rich men is to take away all their money and power. That's a lesson Murdock won't soon forget!"

"When you put it that way, the idee does have some appeal to it."

Monte shook his head. "I hope you boys don't think Murdock is gonna just lie down and let you ruin him. He's sure to send his men against you, and with the sheriff being his kin, you don't stand much of a chance of a fair fight."

Joey looked at him, his eyes cold as glacier ice. "That's the part o' the plan I like best. When the law's crooked, an' people in town know it, it gives us an edge later if marshals are called in. If'n the Murdock brothers and their phony lawmen come after us, the real law cain't hardly take their part after this fracas is over."

Smoke smiled and spread his hands. "That's right. We'd just be innocent ranchers defending our property."

Monte snorted, still shaking his head. "You two are about as innocent as a fox in a henhouse with feathers all over his snout!"

Pueblo, Colorado, though not a large town when compared to Denver or Silver City, was considerably bigger than Big Rock and had both stagecoach and train service. Smoke and Joey took a Wells, Fargo and Company stage to get there as soon as possible. Cal and Pearlie followed by train so they could bring Smoke's Palouse stallion, Horse, and Joey's big roan stallion, Red, along with them.

Smoke decided not to bring any of his hands along, not wanting to tip their hand to Sam Murdock too early, and he figured they would be able to recruit plenty of help from ranchers who had been driven out of business by Murdock.

Their stage arrived at dusk, and ex-sheriff Ben Tolson was on hand to meet it, having been wired by Monte Carson to expect them. When they climbed down, Tolson walked up and stuck out his hand to Smoke. "Mr. Jensen, I'm honored to make your acquaintance. Any friend of Monte's is a friend of mine."

Smoke took his hand. "Howdy, Ben. Monte speaks very highly of you."

Tolson rubbed his chin, grinning. "Well, Monte and I go back a ways. We rode together a couple o' times when we were young pups, hiring out our guns in the range wars of a few years back."

Tolson was a large man with broad shoulders and thick, muscled arms, hands gnarled with early arthritis. He had a handlebar mustache and small goatee, neatly trimmed, under dark, bushy eyebrows. Smoke thought he didn't look like a man to trifle with.

"Like Monte, when I got married I figgered it was time to plant myself and quit galavantin' all over the country." He looked down at his hands, flexing them. "Plus, this rheumatiz makes using a short gun kind o' tricky."

"Ben, this is Mr. Joey Wells," Smoke said, inclining his head toward Joey.

Tolson's eyes narrowed for just a moment before he gave a lopsided grin and stuck out his hand. "I've heard a mite about you, Mr. Wells. You cast a long shadow fer such a young man."

Joey's lips curled up in what might have been a smile if his eyes hadn't remained as hard as stones. "In spite of what you've probably heard, Ben, I ain't never drawed on a man who didn't pull iron on me first, an' I ain't never kilt nobody that didn't deserve it."

"What do you plan to do now that Murdock's hijacked your town, Ben?" Smoke said to break the tension between the two men.

Tolson frowned. "Hell, I don't rightly know." He looked over his shoulder to see if anyone was listening. "Jacob Murdock and his worthless brother, Sam, have been ridin' roughshod over the smaller ranchers hereabouts and the businessmen in town who supported me during the election." He shook his head. "Most of those folks have been friends of mine for years . . . I don t want to let em down."

Smoke's expression grew serious. "Isn't there something you can do about it?"

"Not without proof that the election was rigged." Tolson patted his chest where his tin star used to lie. "When I put that badge on, I took an oath to uphold the law, and the law says the people have a right to elect whoever they want for sheriff, unless I can *prove* they stole the votes." He shook his head as he pulled a plug of tobacco out of his pocket and sliced a chunk off. He chewed a couple of times, then leaned to the side and spit a stream of brown juice into the dirt. "I can't prove anything against Murdock without havin' some witnesses who'll testify in court, and since the election, the only ones who tried to speak out have ended up deader than a stick. Now people who are willin' to talk are few and far between."

He spit again, showing Smoke and Joey what he thought of people too afraid to speak out against the Murdock brothers. "Things were simpler in the old days. Then, I would've had a . . . private talk with Murdock and tole him how much healthier it'd be if he and his no-good kin moved on down the line."

"Still sounds like a good idee to me," Joey drawled in his soft Southern accent.

Tolson cut his eyes to Joey. "Yeah, well, you don't have a governor who's tryin' to make Colorado Territory a state. One complaint from Murdock, who is still the duty-elected sheriff of Pueblo, and I'd have a passel of U.S. marshals down here chewin' on me like buzzards on a deer carcass." He shook his head and spit again. "No, much as I like Monte, and much as I respect your reputation, Smoke, I can't be a part of any vigilante justice here in Pueblo." He shook his head. "If I did that, I'd be no better than Murdock and his crew."

Smoke smiled and spread his hands, an innocent look on his face. "You don't have to worry about us, Ben. Mr. Wells and I are just honest ranchers come down here to inquire about buying a spread we hear is coming up for sale."

Ben chuckled. "Yeah, I bet. Anyway, I just wanted you gents to know where I stand. If we can get proof, or someone willing to testify, I'll stand with you against the Murdocks. Otherwise, I got to keep my head down until that time comes." Tolson glanced at the Colts hung low on their hips and Henry rifles slung over their shoulders. "I can see you men don't travel light."

Joey stuck a cigarette in the corner of his mouth and struck a lucifer on the hammer of his Colt. As the match flared, making his eyes glow with a feral glint, he growled, "Like you said, Ben, it's a dangerous country, an' the law cain't always protect a fellah."

Ben nodded, his own eyes hard in the flickering light. "You know, I almost hope Murdock does come after you boys, and I hope I'm there to see it. If anybody can take that man down a notch or two, you two can!"

He pointed over his shoulder. "Take your bags on over to Mrs. Pike's hotel. The food ain't great, but it's cheap and it's plentiful."

Joey wiped his mouth with his sleeve. "They serve

whiskey there? After twenty-four hours on that stage, my mouth's so dry, I could plant cotton in it."

Tolson chuckled. "After you fill your bellies, come on over to the Silver Dollar Saloon. Murdock's usually there playin' poker till about midnight in a high-stakes game." He grinned and winked. "I figure it's about time he sees what he's up against."

8

It was going on ten o'clock before Smoke and Joey had eaten their fill, washed the trail dust off, and changed into fresh clothes. On their way to the saloon, Smoke put his hand on Joey's shoulder. "Joey, we're liable to run into the men who attacked your ranch and shot up your family in the saloon. Do you think they'll recognize you?"

Joey gave a sardonic grin. "No. The onliest ones got close enough ta see my face didn't survive the sight. The ones that got away stayed well outta range."

Smoke's expression was solemn. "Do you think you can hold your temper and stick to our plan?"

Joey nodded. "Only by knowin' that's the only way we kin git *all* the bastards an' not jest one er two."

As they stepped up to the batwings, Smoke loosened the rawhide hammer thongs on his Colts and whispered, "Be sharp, Joey."

"Only way ta be, Smoke, an' live ta see my wife an' boy again."

The saloon was like hundreds of others in the gold rush and ranching towns of the West. A long wooden bar across one wall, a piano in a corner being tortured by a player with more enthusiasm than talent, and gaming tables scattered throughout the room. In spite of numerous kerosene lanterns, the room was gloomy and dark, the air suffused with a suffocating cloud of cigar and cigarette smoke combined with the pungent aroma of unwashed bodies and stale beer and whiskey.

Ben Tolson was at a table to one side of the room, sitting by himself with a mug of beer in front of him. He had his Greener across his lap.

As they entered, Tolson gave a small nod toward a table in the far corner of the room. A large, blustery man with carrot-red hair and muttonchop sideburns sat there, laughing too loudly and acting as if he owned the place. He wore a black coat and vest over a white shirt with a ruffled front and sported a large gold-nugget ring on the little finger of his left hand. Three other men, also wearing suits, were seated at the table. Two Anglos and two Mexicans were standing behind Murdock, eyes searching the room for any sign of danger to their boss, their hands resting on their pistol butts.

There was no sign of anyone who might be Sheriff Sam Murdock or any of his deputies in the saloon.

Joey stiffened, then spoke low out of the side of his mouth on the way to the bar. "El Machete."

He looked toward the tall, lean Mexican standing next to Murdock.

Smoke and Joey walked across the room and leaned on the counter, facing one another so they could each cover the other's back.

Joey flipped a gold double eagle toward the barman. "Bottle o' whiskey, an' I want one with a label on it."

"Yes, sir!" the bartender said as he pulled a bottle from beneath the bar and placed it and two glasses in front of them.

Joey poured drinks while Smoke observed El Machete out of the corner of his eye. The killer was staring at Joey, eyes squinted, a puzzled expression on his face as if he was trying to remember where he had seen him before.

Smoke lit a stogie while Joey made a cigarette and stuck it in the corner of his mouth. As smoke curled up around his face, Joey asked the barman in a loud voice, "I hear tell there's a ranch up fer sale hereabouts?"

The bartender stopped wiping the counter and cut his eyes toward Murdock before replying, "Oh? Where'd you hear that?"

"Around," answered Joey. He drained his glass without removing the cigarette from his mouth and poured another.

Smoke, peering over Joey's shoulder, noticed they had Murdock's full attention. He had stopped talking and was staring in their direction, as if trying to hear what Joey was saying over the noise of the cowboys in the saloon.

"I also hear it's a prime piece o' land with good water an' stock."

The barman began to sweat as he inched away from them. "I wouldn't know nothin' about that, mister. I just tend bar here." He busied himself with his rag, keeping his head down and his gaze averted as if he was afraid of being seen talking to them.

Murdock nodded over his shoulder at El Machete, who whispered something in Sergeant Garcia's ear, causing the big man to grin widely. He hitched up his belt and walked toward the bar.

Smoke leaned over and spoke low. "Uh-oh, trouble coming."

The fat Mexican stood behind Joey and placed a ham-sized hand on his shoulder. "Señor, I think you make a beeg mistake."

Joey winked at Smoke, then stared at Garcia. He looked like a child next to the huge man, his head barely reaching Garcia's chest. "You talkin' to me, mister?"

"*Sí.* The *ranchito* you askin' about, she is spoken for already."

Joey leaned his head back to glare up into Garcia's eyes, blowing smoke in his face. "Oh? That ain't what I heard."

The saloon became deathly quiet. The cowboys stopped their jawing, and sensing a confrontation watched to see what would happen. Even the piano player stopped beating the keys and spun on his stool to see what was going on. Smoke noticed out of the corner of his eye that Ben Tolson had put his beer down and placed his hand on the butt of his scattergun, ready for trouble. The ex-gunman had a slight smirk on his face, enjoying the action.

Garcia stuck out an index finger as big as a sausage and poked Joey s shoulder with it as he spoke. "Señor, I tole you, there is nothing in this place for you."

Joey stepped away from the bar and squared his shoulders, his eyes changing color as he stared at Garcia. "The last man touched me like that is eatin' with his left hand now." He glanced down at Garcia's ample paunch. "From the looks o' yore belly, ya need both hands to shovel in yore tortillas an' frijoles, so why don't ya back off an' I'll not hurt ya?"

Garcia threw back his head and laughed, then swung a fist at Joey's head. Quick as a snake, Joey reached up and grabbed the hand in midair with his left hand, squeezing. Knuckle bones cracked with a sound like dry twigs snapping.

Garcia screamed, "Aiyeee," and dropped to his knees. As the Mexican fumbled at his belt for his pistol with his left hand, Joey drew in one fluid motion and slammed the barrel of his Colt across the man's face, flaying his forehead open with the raised front sight and snapping his head back. Garcia's eyes crossed and glazed over. After a few seconds the outlaw fell facedown on the floor, his boots beating a tattoo on the boards as he flopped like a fish out of water, blood pumping from his wound to cover his face and chest and pool on the wooden floor.

El Machete took a step forward and Joey glared at him. Joey extended his arm, hammer back on his pistol, pointing it between Vasquez's eyes. "Hey, Mex, this trash a friend of your'n?"

Vasquez stopped, his hands out from his sides, his face burning red at the insult. He nodded slowly, hate filling his eyes. *"Sí."*

"Then why don't ya take his fat ass outta here 'fore I kill him?" Joey snorted in disgust, holstered his gun, and turned his back on the infuriated man as if he posed no threat.

Joey poured himself another drink and said in a loud voice so all could hear, "It's gittin' so a man cain't have a peaceable drink anymore without some greaser son of a bitch gittin' in his face!"

Vasquez slapped leather, but stopped when Smoke's pistol appeared in his hand as if by magic. The mountain man eared back the hammer on his Colt with a loud click and put the barrel against the side of Vasquez's head. "Your fat friend started it, Vasquez. Now, why don't you and your compadres take him out of here 'fore my friend puts a window in your skull?"

Murdock glared at Smoke and Joey, a speculative gleam in his eye. He growled from the corner, "Vasquez, take him back to the ranch, I'll handle this."

It took Vasquez and three other men to lift Garcia and carry him from the saloon, sweating and grunting under the load. Smoke and Joey glanced at Murdock, their lips curled in derisive smiles, then holstered their pistols. They took their whiskey and glasses and sat at a table to the far side of the saloon, where they had an unobstructed view of the room and a wall at their backs.

Murdock got up from his table and walked over to where Tolson sat, observing the action with a slight smile on his face. After talking with Tolson for a few minutes, beady pig-eyes watching Joey and Smoke, Murdock returned to his poker game. A half hour later the game broke up. Murdock pocketed his winnings and motioned for the bartender to bring him a bottle of whiskey. He spoke quietly to one of his two remaining bodyguards, who stared at Smoke and Joey as Murdock talked.

The cowboy, an Anglo with his pistol tied down low on his right hip in a fancy rig, sauntered toward Smoke and Joey's table, scowling and trying to look mean. He stopped in front of them, legs spread and hands on hips. "Mr. Murdock wants to talk with you," he snarled.

Smoke took the stogie out of his mouth and tapped an inch of ash on the man's boots. "Okay."

When Smoke and Joey remained seated, the gunny got a puzzled look on his face. "I tole you, Mr. Murdock wants to talk to you!" he repeated.

Joey shrugged, not looking up as he made another cigarette. "Yore boss has somethin' ta say, send him over. We'll listen."

Murdock's man stood there, chewing his lips, trying to decide what to do next. "You want Mr. Murdock to come to you?" he asked, not believing his ears.

Smoke shrugged as though he didn't particularly care one way or the other.

"He ain't gonna like that much."

Smoke looked at Joey. "You care what Mr. Murdock likes or don't like?"

Joey's lips curled in a half smile as he stuck the cigarette in the corner of his mouth and lit it. "Not enough so's ya can tell it."

The gun hawk's face blushed red, and his right hand dropped near the handle of his pistol, fingers flexing.

Joey's smile faded and his eyes narrowed, cold and intent as a rattler's about to strike. "Cowboy, ya wanna live ta see tomorrow, you trot over there like a good little dog an' tell yore boss what we said." His shoulders moved in a small shrug. "Otherwise, make yore play an' I'll kill ya where ya stand. Makes no difference ta me either way."

The man saw death in Joey's eyes, and sweat began to bead on his forehead. With a mumbled curse he spun on his heel abruptly and stalked back across the room toward Murdock. They talked for a moment before Murdock smiled, shaking his head. He picked up his whiskey and walked to their table, followed by his two guards.

"Mr. Jensen, Mr. Wells, I'm Jacob Murdock. I'd like to have a word with you."

Smoke nodded. "We know who you are, Murdock. You're welcome to sit and chat, but send your trained dogs there back to your table. We don't want them stinking up our end of the room."

One of the men stepped forward, but Murdock stopped him with an outstretched arm. "Well, I can see you are as tough as your reputation makes you out to be, Mr. Jensen."

Joey smiled insolently. "Yeah, he was born with the bark on, all right."

Murdock inclined his head at his men, sending them back to his table to wait for him. He took a seat and poured himself a glass of whiskey. "Mr. Wells, Mr. Jensen, I'd like to propose a toast. To . . . the possibility of a mutually profitable business venture." He held up his glass.

Smoke and Joey glanced at each other, then back at Murdock. Neither man picked up his glass. "Before we go to drinkin' together, Murdock, why don't ya git ta the meat of the thing? Say what ya came here to say, plain an' simple," Joey said.

Murdock looked unsure of himself, his eyes darting back and forth between Smoke and Joey, his fat fingers nervously twisting the hair of his sideburns.

He raised his glass to drink, and Smoke noticed his hand was trembling slightly. An expert at reading men, Smoke knew this to be a sure sign of a coward, nervous without his gun hands to back his play. Smoke glanced at Joey, knowing he realized it too.

"When Ben Tolson over there told me who you were, I got to wondering why two famous pistoleers had come to Pueblo, and why you are interested in buying a ranch out here in the middle of nowhere."

Smoke and Joey remained silent, leaning back in their chairs, sipping their whiskey and smoking, neither bothering to reply.

Murdock, confronted by silence, cleared his throat, dropping his eyes to stare at his drink. "If it's work you're looking for, I'm paying triple wages to men who know how to handle a gun." He raised his gaze, a hopeful expression on his face. "I'm planning on building the biggest spread in these parts, and I can make you rich." He hesitated, then added, "And if you're not partial to ranching, my brother is sheriff of Pueblo now, and I feel sure he can always use a couple of men who are good with their guns."

Joey snorted. "Smoke's already rich Murdock. He could buy and sell ya ten times over without breakin' a sweat." He shrugged. "As fer me workin' fer ya or yore worthless little shit of a brother, if I saw either one of ya on fire, I wouldn't piss on ya to put ya out!"

Murdock looked stunned. It was obvious few men had the courage to talk to him in this fashion. He scowled, glancing at Smoke "Them your feelings too, Jensen?"

Smoke dropped his cigar into Murdock's whiskey glass and leaned forward, speaking loud enough for everyone in the room to hear. "Let me be frank with you, Murdock. Joey and I don't have any use for men like you. To us, you're lower than pond scum. Not only do you rob and steal what other men have spent their entire lives building, but you're too cowardly to do it yourself. You hire stupid men who are as worthless as you to do your dirty work." He stuck a finger in Murdock's face. "Joey and I intend to put you out of business, Murdock.

We're going to take everything you've got and give it back to the people you stole it from."

Murdock's face reddened and his head snapped back as if he had been slapped. As he opened his mouth to reply, Joey interrupted to say in a loud voice, "An' ya kin tell those bastards that ride fer your brand that if'n they git in our way, we'll kill every mother's son of 'em."

Murdock's eyes narrowed. "You talk awfully big for just two men," he snarled.

Smoke smiled. "Oh, two men?" He stood and glanced around the saloon at the cowboys, who were silent, listening to what was being said. "People of Pueblo," he called in a loud voice, "I'm Smoke Jensen, and my partner here is Joey Wells." He smiled at the reaction on the punchers' faces when they recognized his and Joey's names. "We intend to buy the Williams spread when it comes up for auction and we're going to be hiring hands in the morning." He started to sit, then stood back up. "Oh, and incidentally, we also intend to shut Mr. Murdock's operation down and send his ass back where he came from, him and that sorry bastard of a brother of his. If you boys know anyone that kind of work would appeal to, send 'em over to the hotel at nine in the morning."

Before Smoke could sit down, Murdock's two bodyguards jumped up from their table and grabbed iron. Murdock dove out of his chair onto the floor as Smoke and Joey drew their Colts in the blink of an eye and fired.

Though spectators would argue for weeks over who fired first, the big .44s exploded as one, the slugs taking the two gunmen in their chests and blowing them backward to land spread-eagle on the table, their pistols still in holsters. The action was over so fast, Ben Tolson didn't have time to raise his shotgun before the echoing blasts died away.

Smoke looked down at Murdock sprawled cowering on the floor, his hands covering his head; Smoke nudged him none too gently with his boot. "I think it's time you went on home, Murdock, and tell your boys we'll be seeing them."

Murdock scrambled to his feet and took one look at the ruined bodies of his gunnies. "That was cold-blooded murder! I'll see that the sheriff hangs the both of you."

Smoke looked around at the crowded saloon. "Anybody here see us murder anyone, or was it self-defense?"

Several of the cowboys, evidently no friends of Murdock's, spoke up. "They drawed on you first, mister. We all seen it."

Another man, awe in his voice, said, "At least, they *tried* to draw first."

Murdock muttered a curse and stomped out of the saloon, his eyes glaring hate at the men in the room.

Smoke and Joey sauntered over to the two dead men. Smoke's bullet had taken his man square in the heart, while Joey's was a couple of inches to the center, having entered the man's breastbone and blown out his spine.

Smoke grinned as he punched out his brass and reloaded. "Looks like your aim was off a tad, Joey."

Joey made a disgusted face. "Yeah, 'course, I did git off the first shot."

Smoke laughed. "Oh, is that so?"

Tolson walked up, shaking his head. "Mary Mother of Christ, I never seen nothin' so fast in all my born days. You men are quick as greased lightnin'! Them boys didn't even clear leather 'fore they was dead."

Jacob Murdock was as mad as he could ever remember being. He was pacing his study, cursing under his breath, while Vasquez and one of his men who had some medical training were trying to put stitches in Garcia's face so he wouldn't bleed to death.

As Murdock reached for his decanter of bourbon, he heard the fat Mexican scream, *"Madre de Dios . . ."* Serves the fat bastard right, thought Murdock, letting a little sawed-off runt like that Joey Wells beat the shit out of him.

After a moment Vasquez sauntered into the room. "I think he will live, but it will be some time before he ride and shoot again."

Murdock whirled and pointed his finger at Vasquez. "Tell the stupid son of a bitch that he'll get no pay until he's fit to work again!"

Vasquez's eyes narrowed, but all he said was "As you wish, señor." After a moment he lowered his eyes, walked to Murdock's desk, took a fat cigar out of his humidor, and rolled it as he slid it under his nose. "Ah, *es muy bueno.*" He struck a lucifer on his pistol butt and lit the cigar, then poured some of Murdock's whiskey into a crystal goblet.

He dropped onto a couch, put his feet up on a small table in front of the sofa, and sat there, smoking and drinking and watching Murdock pace.

Murdock took a deep drink of his bourbon and said, "I thought you told me these men you hired are all tough hombres."

Vasquez shrugged. "They are plenty tough, señor. But that does not mean that there are not men who are tougher, or most fast with pistols." He narrowed his eyes. "I do not think I seen anyone faster than those two gringos tonight." He shrugged again and upended his glass, drinking it dry. "Of course, fast is no good against many guns at one time, or against guns one cannot see. I will take care of these mens, do not worry."

Murdock stubbed out his cigar in an ashtray on his desk. "Don't worry? How can I not worry? The auction of the Williams ranch is tomorrow morning. What if this crazy man does what he says and buys the ranch?"

Vasquez stood and stretched and yawned. "I said, do not worry, señor. Your brother and his men will be there, and I and my men will be there. This Smoke Jensen and Joey

Wells may be fast with *las pistolas,* but they are not loco enough to go up against all of us tomorrow. You will see."

Murdock finished his bourbon and turned red, fearful eyes on Vasquez. "You better be right, Emilio, you better be right."

9

By the time Joey and Smoke finished breakfast the next morning, there were over thirty cowboys lined up outside the hotel, looking for work. They hadn't seen anything of Sheriff Sam Murdock yet, and figured he and his men were waiting until they could make their play in a nonpublic place. There were just too many witnesses to the gunplay the night before for Sam Murdock to try and arrest them.

Smoke left Joey to do the hiring while he walked to the train depot to meet Cal and Pearlie. He hated to admit it, but only two days into their scheme to dethrone Murdock he was already sick of being in a city. Smoke had been a mountain man for about as long as he could remember, and more than two or three days without being on horseback up in his beloved high lonesome and he became homesick. He grunted, thinking to himself he also missed lying next to Sally at night in their own bed at Sugarloaf.

The train pulled into the station with squealing brakes and great hissing clouds of steam, its whistle echoing a mournful scream. Smoke walked back along the tracks until he came to the livestock car. It had two-by-four boards with spaces between and mounds of hay on the floor. Just as he got there, the big door was slid back and Cal and Pearlie jumped down, shouting, "Hey, boss, we made it!"

Sprigs of hay stuck out of their hair and they were dusty and covered with soot, their shirts showing many small holes where hot cinders from the engine had burned through, but they seemed very happy to have arrived. "Whoo-eee, Smoke," Cal shouted, "you should have seen us move! That engine was flying as fast as the wind on the down slopes." He shook his head and sleeved sweat and dust off his forehead. "I never traveled so fast in all my born days."

Smoke grinned and shook the boys' hands. "Glad you made it okay. How are the horses . . . any trouble?"

"Naw," Pearlie drawled, "not too much. Horse did okay, but that Red of Joey's is a snake-eyed bronc, all right."

"Oh?"

Cal snickered. "Seems as how Pearlie's got hisself a scar or two now."

Pearlie shoved Cal. "Listen, pup, I'm still ramrod of Sugarloaf, an' don't you forgit it an' let yore mouth overload yore butt."

"What happened?" asked Smoke, smiling at the young men's play.

Pearlie shrugged. "Nuthin'. I bought me a sack o' apples at the stop at Junction City an' gave one to each of our horses and kept a couple for me and Cal." He looked over his shoulder at the big red roan's nose, which was sticking through the spaces in the side of the boxcar, sniffing him. "Ol' Red there, he musta figgered since he was the biggest, he deserved more than just one apple."

Cal couldn't wait. "You should've seen it, Smoke. One minute Pearlie was liftin' that apple toward his mouth an' the next the apple and Pearlie's arm up to the elbow was in Red's mouth. If'n Pearlie'd been any slower, we'd be callin' him lefty now."

Smoke bit his lip to keep from laughing at the mental image of the young man trying to get the big red horse to let his arm go. "He hurt you any?"

Pearlie's face flamed as he gave Cal a look that would peel varnish off a table. "Naw, he wasn't tryin' to hurt me he was jest hungry."

Smoke whistled and Horse came to the open door of the car, snuffling and nickering at the sound of his master's call. "Get that ramp set up and let's get these mounts out and let them walk off their stiffness."

Soon the three men were leading their horses toward the livery stable, while Cal and Pearlie stared around at the town with wide, wondering eyes. "Smoke, I ain't never seen so many people in one place at one time," whispered Cal.

"Me neither," said Pearlie. "They's packed together like beeves in a corral at brandin' time. Seems to me they'd git on each other's nerves, livin' so close together all the time."

Smoke nodded. "Quite often they do, Pearlie. There aren't many days go by that several of them aren't killed by their neighbors." He glanced around at the teeming crowds of people, horses, wagons, and buckboards jostling along the streets and boardwalks. "That's why I like the high lonesome so much. If God wanted man to live like ants, all swarming over one another, He wouldn't have made so much space and so few people."

They arrived at the livery and made arrangements for their horses to be boarded, specifying a daily rubdown and grain to be available for them at all times.

On the way to the hotel, Pearlie asked Smoke if he thought the dining room might still be open. "I swear, Smoke, I must've lost four or five pounds on that train. I ain't eaten a decent meal since I left Sugarloaf."

"We'll see if the cook there can't scare you up a dozen eggs and some bacon and biscuits," Smoke answered.

Pearlie held up his hand with his thumb and index finger

two inches apart. "And maybe a small steak, an' some taters, fried like Louis Longmont's cook André does 'em?"

Smoke laughed. "Yeah, but remember, we're here to buy a ranch, and I can't have you eating up all our money before it goes up for sale."

In the hotel dining room, while Cal and Pearlie shoveled in groceries like they hadn't eaten in a week, Smoke filled them in on the events of the night before at the saloon.

"Jiminy," exclaimed Cal, eyes wide, "I'd give a month's wages to have seen that!"

Joey squinted at the young puncher through smoke trailing from the cigarette in his mouth. "If'n it's gunplay yore wantin' ta see Cal boy, you'll git yore fill of it 'fore this fracas is over. Jacob Murdock and his brother don't strike me as men ta take kindly ta our messin' up their plans."

Smoke nodded, his expression serious. "Joey's right. Murdock's a back-shooter if I've ever seen one." He glanced around the table at his friends. "From now on, we better all ride with our guns loose, loaded up six and six. I want us to travel in pairs, with one watching the other's back. I figure either Murdock's men or the sheriff and his deputies will make another play at us before the auction tomorrow, and I want us to be ready for it."

Joey motioned for the waiter to bring another round of coffee. "When do ya think it'll happen, Smoke?"

"My guess is he'll wait until it's dark, then send some men to call on us while we're asleep. He won't dare do anything in the open, not till his back's up against a wall." He leaned forward, speaking low. "Now, here's what we're going to do . . ."

At two o'clock in the morning, with heavy storm clouds scudding across the sky and obscuring the moon, the hotel was quiet. Two men walked their horses into the alley between the hotel and a dry goods store. Silent as ghosts, they climbed up to stand on their saddles and pulled themselves onto the balcony that circled the second story of the building. Tiptoeing quietly, they unlimbered shotguns from rawhide straps on their backs and eared back the hammers.

At the end of the balcony they peered into the open window of the room supposed to be occupied by Smoke and Joey. In the darkness they could just make out two forms lying covered on the beds in the room and could see gun belts and hats hung on bedposts and boots standing next to the beds.

Jesse Salazar looked at his friend and grinned widely, his gold tooth gleaming in the sparse moonlight reflected off the clouds. The other man nodded, and they aimed their scatterguns at the forms under the covers and fired four barrels of buckshot into the rooms, shredding sheets and mattresses and blowing bed frames into kindling wood.

Surrounded by billowing clouds of cordite gun smoke, they laughed and began to run back down the balcony to where they left their mounts.

The two assassins stopped abruptly when they saw four men standing side by side, watching them.

"Evenin', gents. You lookin' fer us?" drawled Joey Wells.

Salazar screamed, *"Madre de Dios"* as he dropped his shotgun and grabbed for his pistol.

Four Colts boomed, spitting flame and smoke and shattering the stillness of the night. Salazar took two bullets in the chest from Smoke and one in the throat from Cal. His accomplice was hit twice in the belly by Pearlie, and twice in the face by Joey, once between the eyes, and one bullet entered his open mouth and exited out the back of his head, taking most of his brains with it. Both Salazar and his partner were blown off the balcony to fall spinning to the ground, dead before they hit the dirt.

As hotel lights began to wink on and a crowd gathered, Joey took a cigarette out of his mouth and flipped it over the balcony rail to land smoldering on Salazar's shirt. He yawned. "Well, that takes care o' that. Me fer some shuteye, boys. It's been a long day."

Smoke punched out his empties and reloaded his Colt. "I'll explain what happened to the sheriff when he gets here. Hell"—he looked around at the gathering crowd—"he was probably watching it anyway."

"You think you'll need any help, Smoke?" Pearlie asked.

Smoke shook his head. "No. Too many people around to see what he does. Sam Murdock is a coward just like his brother. He won't do anything tonight. You boys better get some sleep . . . but keep your windows locked and the curtains drawn."

While Smoke talked to Sheriff Sam Murdock, who at first tried to arrest him, until the crowd shouted him down, Cal and Pearlie prepared their room for their night's sleep.

Pearlie took the mattresses off their two beds and propped one over the windows and the other over the door. He sat on the wooden bottom of the bed and began to take his boots off.

Cal stood with hands on hips, looking at what his partner had done. "Just how are we supposed to sleep, Pearlie? You done took all the mattresses and put 'em where we cain't git to 'em."

Pearlie shook his head. "Better that than to wake up dead, Cal boy. Now, git yore butt in bed and git some shuteye."

Cal stooped to remove his boots. "That's easy for you to say, Pearlie, you could sleep in a buckboard goin' down Rocky Road back home. I'm tired of sleepin' in places not fit fer man nor beast, like that cattle car on the way down here."

"Hell, what're you complainin' about? We had plenty of food and water and hay to lie down on. What more could a man want?"

Cal peered at him as he leaned over to blow out the

lantern. "Well, I don't call having to use horse apples as pillows livin' in the lap of luxury!"

It seemed as if everyone in town was gathered at the courthouse the next morning. Judge Cornelius Wyatt banged his gavel for silence and glared out at the crowd over wire-rimmed spectacles perched on the end of his nose. "Order in the court!" he shouted. After the townspeople got quiet, he continued in a normal tone of voice. "We're here this morning to settle a matter before this court concerning the sale of Mrs. Williams's ranch. Ora Mae Williams and some of her friends"—he looked directly at Ben Tolson, who was sitting in the back row—"have asked me to preside to make sure there are no . . . irregularities in the proceedings."

He glanced to his side, where Sheriff Sam Murdock and one of his deputies were standing with shotguns cradled in their arms, eyes scanning the crowd for trouble. Murdock's eyes lingered for a moment on Smoke and Joey, sitting in the rear, narrowing as if daring the two to bid on the property.

Judge Wyatt picked up a sheet of paper and began to read aloud from it. "The property consists of two sections, about thirteen hundred acres, ranch house, bunkhouse and out-buildings, three corrals, and two wells. There are roughly five hundred head of cattle that go with the ranch. The boundaries are, on the north a line from—" He hesitated, took his glasses off, and glared around the room. "Oh, hell, everyone here knows where the ranch is. I'll forgo reading the boundary lines and start the bids."

Jacob Murdock, sitting in the front row with five of his hired guns, raised his hand and called out, "I bid three thousand dollars."

"I have three thousand bid. Any other offers?"

A voice from the rear of the room spoke up. "Judge, I have in my hand a letter of credit drawn on the Bank of Big

Rock, Colorado. I ask that you determine how much cash Mr. Murdock has on hand before we proceed any further."

The judge squinted his eyes, peering nearsightedly toward the speaker. "With what purpose, Mr.—uh—just who am I speaking to?"

"Smoke Jensen, your honor. I plan to bid one thousand dollars more than whatever amount Murdock can come up with." Smoke smiled and spread his arms. "No need to prolong these proceedings any more than is necessary."

Murdock and Vasquez jumped to their feet, El Machete's hand close to his pistol. There was a loud murmur from the crowd of citizens, and Cal and Pearlie and several cowboys Joey had hired stood, staring at the Mexican, their hands near their guns. There was a loud double-click as Sam Murdock and his deputy eared back the hammers on their shotguns.

Jacob Murdock put his hand on Vasquez's arm and shook his head at his brother. He said to the judge, "Your honor, I must protest this most unusual statement by Mr. Jensen."

Wyatt peered down at Murdock, his lips pursed. "Well, Mr. Murdock, it is a bit unusual, but . . . in no way is it illegal." He smiled. "In fact, it seems very straightforward to me. Do you have a letter of credit from a bank indicating the amount of cash you have available for the purchase of this property?"

"Why, uh, no, your honor." Murdock frowned and glanced around at the people in the room. "But everyone here knows I'm good for whatever I bid."

The judge scowled. "That's not the question, Mr. Murdock." He waved the papers in his hand in the air. "Mrs. Williams has stipulated in her bill of sale that the purchase is to be cash only, no promissory notes." He looked out over the room. "Is anyone here from the bank?"

A short, fat man in a black suit stood, nodding nervously as he cut his eyes toward Murdock and his gunmen, then toward the sheriff in front of the room. "Yes, your honor. I'm

Thaddeus Gump, president of the board of directors of the bank here in Pueblo."

Judge Wyatt leaned back, crossing his arms. "Well, you heard what Mr. Jensen said. Just how much money does Mr. Murdock have on deposit with your bank?"

Gump licked his lips, his eyes flicking back and forth like a cornered rat. He took a handkerchief out of his pocket and blotted sweat from his forehead. "Uh, if I could have a moment to confer with Mr. Murdock, your honor?"

Wyatt banged his gavel. "I'll recess for five minutes for you and Mr. Murdock to come up with a bid, then I'm going to sell this parcel to the highest bidder."

Murdock and Gump walked to a corner of the room and talked for a moment, Murdock gesturing angrily and shaking his finger in Gump's face. Finally, a red-faced, sweating Gump approached the judge. "Your honor, with cash on hand and by virtue of a mortgage on the Lazy M ranch, the bank is prepared to offer up to nineteen thousand dollars for the Williams ranch."

Murdock smirked at Smoke, evidently thinking he had won. He knew the ranch wasn't worth more than eight or nine thousand dollars and seemed to feel sure an ex-gunfighter like Smoke Jensen wouldn't be able to cover that amount. The judge raised his eyebrows. He, too, knew that was an unheard-of amount of money for the property in question. He shook his head and looked at Smoke. "Mr. Jensen?"

Smoke walked to the front of the room. He wanted to see the look in Murdock's eyes when he answered. "Your honor, I bid twenty thousand dollars for the Williams ranch." He handed Wyatt his letter of credit and stood there as the judge read it. Wyatt's eyes widened and his mouth dropped open. He looked up. "This guarantee is for any amount up to one hundred thousand dollars!"

As everyone in the courtroom began to talk at one time, Murdock jumped to his feet, his face red with anger. "Your honor, I must again protest this proceeding! How are we to know this letter of credit, no doubt from some small town bank, is genuine?"

Judge Wyatt smiled and held out the paper for Murdock to read. "Oh, I'd say it's good. It's signed by Henry Wells, president of Wells, Fargo and Company." He banged his gavel. "Mr. Jensen, you've bought yourself a ranch!"

The people in the room, no friends of Murdock's and his men, crowded around Smoke and Joey, clapping them on the back and congratulating them.

Murdock threw the letter at the judge and stormed from the room, followed by El Machete and his other gunmen. Vasquez paused as he passed Smoke to growl, "You'll never live to work that ranch, gringo." He fingered the handle of his machete as he glared at Smoke.

Joey squeezed between them, looking up with his face just inches from the Mexican's. "I'm gonna enjoy makin' you eat that blade, *cabrón.*"

At the word *cabrón,* worst insult a Mexican could get, Vasquez's face blanched, his lips pulled back in a snarl, and his hand fell to his pistol. Before the gunny's gun was half out of its holster, Joey's Colt was drawn, cocked, and stuck against his stomach. "Go ahead, pepper-belly, an' I'll blow yore guts all over the floor!"

Sheriff Sam Murdock stepped up and put the barrel of his shotgun between the two men. "What's goin' on here? Wells threatenin' you, Vasquez?"

Tolson, accompanied by at least ten local businessmen and cowboys, said, "Hold on there, Sam." His voice dripped with scorn. "Everyone here saw what happened. Vasquez made his play first." He gave a snort of disgust. "Your boss is waiting for you outside." He inclined his head toward the door. "I'd suggest you get on out there 'fore someone has to carry you out on a board."

The sheriff's face blazed red and his eyes narrowed with

hate. The Mexican let his pistol slide back down into its holster and said to Joey, *"Cuidado, buscadero.* I see you later." He stalked out of the room, followed by Sam Murdock and his deputy.

As Smoke, Joey, Cal, and Pearlie walked to the hotel, Cal asked, "What did those Mexican words he said to you mean, Joey?"

Joey smirked. "Roughly translated, it meant watch yore ass, tough guy."

10

Smoke, Joey, Cal, and Pearlie were having lunch at the hotel, celebrating their victory over the Murdock brothers, when Ben Tolson walked up, a worried look on his face.

Smoke waved a hand. "Pull up a chair and join us, Ben."

Joey paused, his fork halfway to his mouth. "Hey, compadre, you look like someone shot yore hoss. Anything the matter?"

Tolson signaled their waiter for coffee and leaned forward, speaking low. "Yeah. Sam Murdock's over at the Silver Dollar, getting alkalied. He's shooting his mouth off about how he's gonna make sure none of you live to set foot on the Williams ranch."

Joey snorted. "That's just whiskey talk. He's too smart ta try somethin' like that."

Tolson shook his head. "No, you got it wrong, Joey. Jacob Murdock's the smart one, Sam's an idiot. He's just liable to try and make good on his threats."

Smoke shrugged. "Well, Ben, what do you suggest we do about it? I'm not about to give the ranch back."

Ben took his coffee from the waiter, added sugar, and blew on it to cool it. He sipped for a moment in silence, then looked at Smoke. "How about you and your men coming out to my cabin? You could stay out there until the papers for the ranch are ready. It'd at least get you out of town and out of Sam's sight."

Joey shook his head. "That wouldn't exactly be a good idee, Ben. Think on it a minute. Long as we're here in town, anything Sam an' his brother do will be seen by a lot of people."

Smoke interrupted. "Joey's right, Ben. If we go out to your place, either of the Murdocks could hit us and later claim it was done by someone else, or even that we started the trouble." He shook his head. "No, I think the best thing for us to do is stay right here in Pueblo."

Joey said, "I'll tell ya what, pardner, you could help us by spreadin' the word around ta your friends ta kinda hang around town the next day or so and observe what goes on. That way, if Murdock is dumb enough to call us out or try an' ambush us, there'll be plenty of your friends that kin vouch fer us."

Tolson nodded. "You're right, I just hadn't thought it through." He drained his coffee cup and stood. "I'll tell everyone I can count on to be honest to keep a sharp eye out, and I'll be around too, just in case you need an extra gun or two."

Smoke looked up. "We don't intend to get you involved in our troubles, Ben."

"I told you before, Smoke. I won't stand for vigilante justice, or for innocent people getting gunned down in my town." He grinned widely. "Even if they're not quite as innocent as they claim."

As the group finished lunch, Smoke said, "Cal, Pearlie, I want you to be extra careful. Keep your guns loose and loaded up six and six, and watch each other's back. Don't let Murdock or his men goad you into making the first move."

He spoke to Joey. "What about the men you hired for the ranch? Can we count on them if worse comes to worst?"

Joey shook his head. "I don't think so, Smoke. They're

ready to do whatever I ask 'em, but they're punchers, not shootists. I wouldn't want any of 'em ta git hurt on my account."

"Okay," Smoke said, "then that means it's just the four of us, five if we count Ben. I hear Murdock has at least ten deputies, though I don't know how many will follow his lead in this."

"Have you seen 'em, Smoke?" Cal piped up. "They look like he hired 'em outta a jail. They ain't one of 'em I'd trust to walk my dog."

Pearlie looked at him, eyebrows raised. "You ain't got a dog, Cal."

Joey chuckled. "He's right, Smoke. We gotta figger they all gonna be agin us if push comes ta shove."

Pearlie grinned, fearless as always. "If we git in a gun-fight, I don't want to stand next to Cal, the bullets just seem to seek him out!"

Smoke smiled. "You and Cal go up to our rooms and bring down Joey's Greener and my American Arms express guns and some shells. If we have to shoot into a crowd, there's less chance of some innocent bystander getting killed if we use the scatterguns."

After the two younger men left to fetch the shotguns, Smoke looked at Joey. "I hate it that I've gotten those two mixed up in this. It isn't their fight."

Joey smiled and put his hand on Smoke's arm. "Yes, it is, Smoke. They ride for you, and you're ridin' agin Murdock, so they's agin Murdock too. It's a matter of their honor, just as it is ours. When you ride for a brand, you also ride for the man behind the brand."

Smoke shook his head. "It's more than that with Cal and Pearlie. Since my children have been in Europe with Sally's family, those two have become like my own kin."

"I know," said Joey. "An' I know they look on you as they would their own paw. But when it comes time to stand up and be a man, you cain't hold 'em back."

Cal and Pearlie returned then, carrying the shotguns. Both were short-barreled, enabling them to be held and fired almost like pistols. Smoke and Joey took the guns, and each put a handful of shells in their pockets.

Smoke stood, looking at his partners. "Time we quit hiding in this hotel and step outside and see what Murdock has planned."

As he finished talking, Ben Tolson entered the room, carrying his own Greener. "Looks like bad news, boys. Sam Murdock and his men are all on the street, hanging around the boardwalk, waiting for you to come out."

"Oh?"

"Yeah, and he's told the townspeople to get off the streets, that he's gonna arrest you for murdering those two men in the saloon the other night."

"That'll never stand up in court," Smoke said.

Tolson shook his head. "Murdock don't plan to ever let it come to trial. If you let him take you to jail, you'll be dead before dawn."

Smoke flipped his American Arms shotgun open and checked the loads, then snapped it shut. "Okay, if that's the way he wants it, that's the way it'll be." He looked at the others. "Ready?"

All nodded, and the five men walked through the hotel door and out into the Colorado sunshine, side by side, pistols loose and shotguns cradled in their left arms so their right hands were free.

Smoke saw Murdock step out into the street to his left, three of his men with him. He glanced to the right, where another seven men were standing on the boardwalk, watching with hands near pistols.

Smoke spoke low, out of the side of his mouth. "Joey and I'll take Murdock and the men with him, you three take the gents to the right if they join in."

Murdock held up his left hand, his right held low by his

pistol. "Hold it right there, Jensen. I'm arrestin' you and Wells for the murder of two men in the saloon. Throw down your guns and come peacefully."

As the sheriff talked, Joey pulled a slab of Bull Durham from his shirt pocket and bit off a corner. He chewed for a moment, then leaned to the side and spit, his eyes never leaving Murdock.

Smoke glanced up and down the street. Though the townspeople had been warned, every window of every shop and storefront was crowded with onlookers. He said, "Murdock, you're a liar. You know that fight was in self-defense, and so do the people of this town."

Murdock shook his head. "Don't matter none what the people of the town think. I'm the sheriff and I say you're under arrest. You gonna throw down your guns, or am I gonna have to kill ya?"

Joey spoke to Smoke, but loud enough for everyone to hear. "If he grabs iron, Smoke, you put one in his heart, and I'll put one 'tween his eyes, then we'll kill everyone with him who tries to draw on us."

The color drained from Murdock's face, and he glanced nervously behind him at the three deputies standing there. "You men don't have a chance." He pointed down the street toward his other seven deputies. "I've got you outnumbered three to one."

Tolson stepped up next to Smoke and Joey. "Two to one, Murdock. I'm standing with them."

Joey spit again. "Two to one makes it about even, I'd say. 'Course, it don't matter what the odds are, 'cause yore gonna git the first two slugs, Murdock. You'll be dead before the smoke clears."

Murdock licked his lips and took a step backward. "Wait a minute . . ."

Joey called out loudly, "Either make yore play, you

sniveling coward, or throw down that badge and crawl on home to your big brother."

That was too much for Murdock, coward though he was. He growled and slapped leather.

Before his gun moved an inch, both Joey and Smoke had their Colts out and firing. One slug pierced the sheriff's badge on his left breast and another punched a hole at the top of his nose between his eyes, exploding his head and showering the men behind him with blood and brains.

The three deputies grabbed iron, a lifetime too late. Joey and Smoke both let go with both barrels of their scatterguns, firing left-handed, shooting fire and smoke and buckshot toward the men. Their bodies were shredded by the .38-caliber shot and thrown backward to land all tangled up, pieces of arms and legs and guts intermingled in one pile.

When Smoke and Joey fired on Murdock, the seven men to the right all grabbed for their guns. Tolson leveled his Greener and took out two of them with a double-barreled blast that rocked windows for a city block. Cal's and Pearlie's fists were full of iron in an instant, and the two young men cocked and fired so fast, it sounded to onlookers as if a Gatling gun were exploding in one long staccato blast. Of the five remaining men, three managed to clear leather and get off some shots, their bullets pocking dirt and wooden posts behind Cal and Pearlie.

Pearlie grunted once but kept firing. Cal emptied his right-hand Colt Navy and drew his other left-handed. He and the last standing deputy fired simultaneously. The deputy's head rocked back, the top of his scalp blown off. Cal bent and spun around, a short cry escaping his lips before he bit the dirt.

The street was heavy with the smell of gun smoke and blood and the excrement of dying men. Ears rang and gunshots still echoed between buildings for seconds after the last shot was fired.

Smoke and Joey, untouched, looked to see how their compatriots were doing, Smoke moaning low under his breath when he saw Pearlie's face covered with blood and Cal lying unmoving on the ground. Tolson was standing, eyes wide, breathing hard, not a mark on him.

The entire episode had taken less than two minutes from start to finish, and had cost the lives of seven men and wounded four more, two of whom would later die from their wounds.

Smoke bent over Cal while Joey turned Pearlie around to see where the blood was coming from. He removed Pearlie's hat, and saw a neat groove down the side of his head, just above his ear, where a bullet had gouged his scalp. Joey pursed his lips as he removed his bandanna and placed it against the laceration. "Looks like you stood too close to Cal, Pearlie."

Pearlie grinned. "Yeah, how is . . ." His face dropped and he quickly knelt next to Smoke and grabbed Cal by the cheeks. "Cal, you little shit, don't you die on me!"

Smoke slipped his Bowie knife out and slit Cal's shirt, peeling the blood-soaked fabric away from his chest. Just below his rib cage was a small, neat hole. Smoke rolled him over, and where the slug exited was a wound as big as a fist, oozing blood.

Joey pushed Pearlie out of the way and bent to examine the wound. "I don't see no guts nor smell any shit." He raised his eyes to look at Smoke, who had tears coursing down his cheeks. "If the slug missed his bowels, he's gonna be all right." He looked up at Pearlie. "Git the doc over here pronto, boy, an' maybe yore friend will live."

While the undertaker was still picking up bodies off the street, Ben Tolson called an emergency meeting of the town council. Pearlie told Smoke and Joey to go on and attend the meeting, he would stay by Cal's side while the doctor stitched up the hole in his back. When the doctor stuck the needle in, and Cal groaned in pain, Pearlie said, "It's your own damn fault, Cal. If you didn't have such an attraction for lead, you wouldn't be lying here, moanin' and groanin'."

Cal looked up through pain-clouded eyes and touched the bandage on Pearlie's head. "You okay, partner?" he croaked through dry lips.

Pearlie grinned. "Yeah 'ceptin I wish the doc would hurry up and get you back together. I'm getting hungrier by the minute."

Cal s lips curled in a small smile. "When he's done, I'll buy you some lunch, to make up fer bringing all those bullets our way."

Pearlie nodded. "You're on, partner."

At the council meeting Tolson stood before the mayor and businessmen. "Now that Sam Murdock and his men are dead, I've got evidence they threatened a number of people before the last election." He held up a stack of papers. "I have over a hundred signatures on this affidavit that men were told they'd be killed if they campaigned or voted for me."

The mayor banged his gavel, nodding his head. "I've heard the same thing," he said. "In light of this new evidence, I make a motion that pending a new election next month, we ask Ben Tolson to once again assume the duties of sheriff of Pueblo."

The council members all shouted out aye. The mayor banged his gavel again. "Motion passes unanimously. Mr. Tolson, you are now sheriff of this city."

"Before I take the job," Tolson said, "I want to make sure I have the complete support of the council and can do whatever I deem necessary to make this city safe for all citizens."

The mayor looked around, and the councilmen all nodded their heads. "That will not be a problem, sheriff," he said.

Ben stood and pinned on the star that Murdock had been

wearing, the one with a bullet hole through the center, still covered with the dead man's blood. "My first official act will be to appoint Smoke Jensen and Joey Wells as deputy sheriffs."

Smoke and Joey glanced at each other; this was news to them.

"Then I'm going to post the town as a gun-free zone, all weapons to be checked upon entering the city limits. Next, I'm posting the town off limits to any employees of the Lazy M ranch, including Jacob Murdock."

One of the councilmen raised his hand. "Can we do that?"

Tolson shrugged. "I'm the sheriff, I can do whatever I want."

Smoke stood up. "Ben, you're right. You and the town can do whatever you want, but I don't think Murdock is going to take this lying down." He looked around the room, his expression serious. "Murdock has over thirty hard cases working for him. Know this, if you try to shut him out of town, he's liable to fight. If the town isn't ready to back Ben's play, with your guns and perhaps your lives, you better let him know now."

Ben nodded. "Smoke's right. As soon as I post the town, it's gonna be like waving a red flag in front of a bull. We can expect trouble, and probably sooner rather than later."

The mayor stood. "I for one am tired of living under Murdock's thumb. This was a decent, law-abiding town before he moved here and took over the Lazy M. I would like for it to be that way once again, and if it takes the blood of good men for that to happen, then so be it."

All the councilmen stood and clapped and cheered. The mayor said to Ben, "There is your answer, sheriff. Go and do what you think is necessary."

"I'll post the town tonight, and I'd like you to call a town meeting first thing in the morning, Mr. Mayor. We'll need to get the people ready for what is almost sure to happen next."

11

That night, over supper in the hotel dining room, Tolson met with Smoke and Joey. Cal and Peàrlie were also present. Other than looking pale and drawn, and occasionally taking a nip from the bottle of laudanum the doctor had given him, Cal was doing okay.

Tolson, between bites of steak, said, "All of my previous deputies have agreed to come back to work, and I've hired another five, who I know are handy with long guns. All together, that gives me fifteen men, counting you four."

Smoke nodded. "What are your plans for sealing up the town?"

"I haven't had time to give it much thought."

Smoke looked over at Joey. "Joey, you've had some experience in getting in and out of garrisons in the past. Any suggestions?"

Joey nodded. "We need some warnin' when Murdock's men are comin'. I'd post a couple of sentries three or four miles out of town on the main roads from the Lazy M. I don't think Murdock will be expectin' much resistance, so I doubt if he'll go to the trouble of circling around and comin' in on our back side."

Tolson nodded, and began to make some notes on a scratch pad with a pencil.

"Second, I'd post a man at every entrance to the city, with a big fire bell, in case Murdock's men git by the sentries for one reason or another."

"What about placement of men in the town?"

"No question about it, the best place for your men with long guns and scatterguns is on the roofs. I'd have most of your men on both sides of the street, about every two or three buildings. They'd have a clear field of fire and they'd be hard to hit from horseback with pistols."

Tolson looked up from his pad. "Anything else?"

"Yeah, at the meeting in the mornin' I'd tell all the women-folk and kids to stay off the streets for the next couple of days. The way you're puttin' the pressure on and screwin' it down tight, I don t 'spect it'll take Murdock long to make his play."

Smoke nodded. "That's right. Without being able to buy supplies, he can't afford to wait too long."

"One other thing. I'd hold off posting the town against firearms until this is over. I'd warn every citizen to carry a shotgun or a pistol, even those that don't knew how to use 'em. If there's enough lead flying around, some of it's bound to hit somebody, hopefully Murdock and his men."

Tolson looked up, his eyes worried. "This could turn out to be a bloodbath, couldn't it?"

Joey shrugged. "It's your town, you got to decide if it's worth fightin' for or not."

One of Tolson's deputies came running in the hotel dining room. "Hey, boss. Jacob Murdock and some of his men are riding into town."

Tolson stood, put his hat on, and pulled it down tight. He grinned. "Time to let Murdock know who's running the show now."

The group went outside to stand in the twilight in front of

the hotel. Murdock reined in his horse and sat looking down at Tolson and the men behind him.

"I hear Jensen and Wells gunned down my brother in cold blood." His eyes flicked over Smoke and Joey, who stared back at him. Then he noticed the star on Tolson's chest. "You the sheriff now Tolson?"

"Yes."

"Well, what are you going to do about it?"

Tolson shrugged. "Nothing. It was a fair fight, and your brother drew first."

"I just saw his body. His pistol was still in leather."

"I said he drew first, I didn't say he drew fastest. He made his play and got killed for it. That's all there is to say on the matter."

"That's not all I got to say on it!"

Joey stepped forward, his hands hanging near his pistols. "I shot your cowardly brother right between the eyes, Murdock. If you"—he cut his eyes to Vasquez and Garcia, whose face was still heavily bandaged, sitting on their horses behind Murdock—"or anyone else has anything to say about it, I'm ready."

Vasquez muttered, "Let me kill this *gabacho,* Mr. Murdock."

Murdock held up his hand. "Not now, Emilio. They got us outnumbered." He tipped his hat at Tolson. "You win for now, Tolson. I'm going to pick up my brother's body and take it out to the ranch, but I'll be back tomorrow with more men."

"You better come prepared to fight, Murdock. I'm posting Pueblo off limits to you and your men. The only way you'll get into town is to blast your way in."

"That the way you want it, Tolson?"

He shrugged. "That's the way it is, Murdock. Now, get your brother and get your trash out of my town."

Before he rode off, Murdock growled, "I'm gonna tree this town, Tolson, and you with it."

* * *

The town meeting the next morning went as expected. Smoke stood up to address the citizens. "People of Pueblo, it is time for you to take a stand against the tyranny of Jacob Murdock. He and his men are planning to try and take your town away from you, and force you to live under his thumb. Let me say this, nobody has ever treed a western town, nobody. Nearly every man in this town is a combat veteran of some war, whether it was against Indians, outlaws, the Union Blue or the Rebel Gray. Back in September of seventy-six, Jesse James and his outlaw gang tried to collar Northfield, Minnesota. They were shot to rags by the townspeople." He looked out over the crowd. "Your sheriff and I expect no less of you."

The crowd cheered and waved shotguns and rifles in the air, and showed they were solidly behind Tolson and his plan to rid the area of Murdock and his gang. Sentries were posted on roads leading to town and at each entrance to the city, with fire bells nearby, as Joey had suggested. Men with rifles and shotguns were on roofs, ready for whatever Murdock had planned.

At the same time as the town meeting was going on, Jacob Murdock was standing on his porch, over forty hard-case gunnies on their mounts in front of him.

"Men, I intend to tree Pueblo and kill those bastards Wells, Jensen, and Tolson. If you men do that for me, there'll be an extra month's pay in your packet."

As the men cheered and waved their guns in the air, he held up his hand for silence. "And to the man who puts a bullet in any of the three I mentioned, it's an extra thousand dollars."

The gun hawks cheered and yelled again. Murdock shouted, "Now, are we ready to ride?"

"Yes," they shouted.

"Then shag your mounts, boys, 'cause there's money to be made in Pueblo today!"

The crowd of gunmen whirled their horses and galloped off toward Pueblo in a cloud of dust, not one of them thinking for a minute that most of them wouldn't be coming back.

By noon the city resembled a ghost town, with no one on the streets other than Tolson and his men. Businesses were locked and barricaded, owners sitting vigil with weapons ready.

At each entrance to the city limits, two wagons were lashed together with ropes, ready to be pulled across to block the streets after the outlaws were within the town. The killers would be able to ride in, but getting out alive was going to be next to impossible.

It was one-thirty in the afternoon when a sentry from the north side of town came galloping down the street in a cloud of dust, firing his pistol. He shouted, "They're comin', they're comin'!"

Smoke, Joey, Cal, and Pearlie joined Tolson on the street. "How many?" Tolson yelled.

"Looks like over thirty men, all wearing bandannas over their faces, and they're all carryin' rifles and shotguns, loaded for bear!"

"Get to your places, men," Tolson shouted, earing back the hammers on his Greener and taking his place in a doorway.

Smoke and Joey went to the opposite side of the street and crouched down behind water barrels stacked there for that purpose. Cal and Pearlie jumped into the back of a buckboard and lay flat, peeking over the sides.

Cal said, "You sure you want in this wagon with me?" He fingered the large bandage on his side. "You know how I attract bullets."

Pearlie snorted, "Somebody's got to be here to plug the holes in your hide so you won't bleed to death. Might as well be me." When Cal grinned, Pearlie added, "Besides, if I let you get kilt, Miss Sally'd probably never make me bear sign again."

Within five minutes the bandits arrived, shooting wildly in every direction, yelling and screaming in Spanish and Apache dialects as they rode down the main street, sending dust and gun smoke billowing around them.

As soon as they were inside the city limits, wagons at either end were pulled across streets behind and before them, trapping the killers between them.

Smoke and Joey stood, ignoring the buzzing and whining of slugs passing all around them, and began to fire into the crowd of riders with deadly accuracy. Smoke's first bullet took a man in the face, blowing half his head away, catapulting him beneath the hooves of his fellow riders.

Joey's first shot took a man's hat off; his second punched a hole in his chest and blew out his spine, killing him instantly.

Tolson stepped out of his doorway and let loose with both barrels, knocking two men from their saddles and spewing blood and guts into the air. In the next instant, a slug slapped into his left shoulder, spinning him around and back through the door.

Cal and Pearlie were firing rapidly, gun barrels glowing a dull red, spitting gun smoke and flames. A huge man, his bandanna barely covering the bandages on his face, rode at the wagon containing Cal and Pearlie, screaming and firing his pistol into the wood of the buckboard.

One of his slugs ricocheted off the wood and sliced through Cal's left earlobe, taking it off clean. As Cal ducked and grabbed at his head, Pearlie cursed and rose up, taking careful aim as the *bandido* charged. He squeezed his trigger and put a bullet in the man's throat, snapping his head back and knocking him from his horse to bounce and roll in the dirt.

Men on the rooftops stood and began to pour a withering blanket of fire into the raiders, decimating their ranks.

Michael Thomas, manager of a general store, aimed over the balustrade and fired twice, knocking two outlaws from their saddles before a slug blew his jaw away, killing him instantly.

Jesse Monroe, gun shop owner, stood calmly, firing from his shop's door, his wife and teenage son reloading for him He took out six men, then a chest wound drove him to the ground. Two bandits jumped from their horses and ran into the door, to be blown to hell by Mrs. Monroe with her husband's Greener. She screamed furiously, stepped outside, and began to fire a pistol, hitting nothing but scaring the hell out of several riders.

Sammy Layton, a pimply-faced sixteen-year-old livery boy fired a Winchester .22 pop gun from the hayloft of his father's establishment, stinging and wounding several men, until a bullet tore a chunk out of his side. He was thrown back into the hay, where he vomited once, then rolled back over, picked up his rifle, and continued to fire, blood streaming from his wound.

Twin teenagers, Missy and Bobby Johanson, fired pistols from the open window of their mother's dress shop. A Mescalero Apache jumped from his horse and ran screaming into the room. Mrs. Johanson, her own pistol empty, grabbed a nearby parasol and stabbed the Indian in the gut, running the pointed end of the umbrella through the savage to protrude from his back. He stood there, a look of complete surprise on his face, until he died.

Donovan James, a seventy-year-old veteran of the Indian Wars, fired a .50-caliber Civil War musket until he ran out of gunpowder, then pulled ancient matching army cap-and-ball pistols from his double-rigged holsters and stood in an alleyway, firing and cocking, his frail arms bucking with each shot. When a wounded Mexican wearing a Rurale uniform pitched off his horse in front of James, he aimed and pulled triggers, both guns empty.

The Mexican struggled to his feet, a grin on his face. "Now you die, gringo."

"Not yet, slimeball," the old man growled. He pulled a twelve-inch-long Bowie knife from his belt and stuck it in the Mexican's belly, then shoved the dying man off his knife and began to reload his pistols.

A rider came thundering at Smoke and Joey out of the dust, an Apache tomahawk raised high like a sword, ready to swing. Smoke and Joey both pulled triggers, hammers falling on empty chambers. As the Indian neared, Smoke hurriedly punched out his empties, but knew he didn't have time to reload before the man would be upon them.

Joey didn't hesitate. He threw down his pistol and ran toward the rider. He took a giant leap up onto a hitching rail as he ran and catapulted himself forward into the rider's body, knocking him to the ground. As bullets whined around him, he and the rider came to their feet at the same time. Smoke had his pistol reloaded but couldn't get a clear shot. Joey was in the way, so he gave covering fire to protect him from other riders, killing two and wounding one.

The Apache pulled his mask down and grinned as he raised his tomahawk for a fatal blow. He was one of the group that had attacked Joey's ranch. *"Chinga tú, gringo!"* he shouted.

Joey crouched and pulled his Arkansas Toothpick from its scabbard on the back of his belt. As the tomahawk whistled down, he parried the blow with his knife, sending sparks flying. He screamed a rebel yell and stepped into the Indian's body, burying his blade to the hilt in his stomach.

The Apache's eyes widened in pain and shock, and Joey twisted the blade and jerked it upward, ripping his chest open and tearing his heart out. As the man fell before him,

Joey leaned over and spit tobacco juice into his staring, dead eyes as he holstered his knife,

Billy Bob Boudreaux, one of the men on the rooftops, was shot in the neck and fell tumbling to crash through a roof over the boardwalk. Another businessman, Darren Jones, shot in the stomach, fell forward through his window, sending glass shards sparkling in the sunlight.

Smoke saw three of the raiders jump from their horses and run bent over, dodging bullets, into an alley on his side of the street. Smoke began reloading his Colts as he jogged back down an alley next to where he was.

Just before he reached the end of the passageway, he put his back against a wall and eased to a corner of the building, peering around it carefully. The three bandits were walking slowly along the back street, pistols in hands as they looked for a way out of the trap they were in.

Smoke pulled his hat down tight, squared his shoulders, and stepped out into the street, Colts hanging in his hands at his sides. "You boys lost?" he called.

The men whirled and pointed pistols his way, shouting in Spanish as they began to fire wildly. Smoke raised both hands and fired from the hip without taking time to aim. His Colts boomed and bucked in his hands, spitting death and destruction into the killers. One of their bullets nicked Smoke's neck, and another took his hat off, but he kept firing.

Two of the men went down, bleeding from chest and stomach, writhing in their blood in the dirt of the street.

The third spun, hit in his arm by Smoke's last shot. He straightened as Smoke's hammers fell on empty chambers. With an evil grin he raised his pistol and took aim at Smoke's face. *"Adiós, pendejo,"* he spat out as he eared back his hammer.

From behind Smoke came an explosion and the whine of a bullet passing close by his ear. He ducked instinctively as the man facing him doubled over, clutching his stomach before he toppled to the ground, dead.

Smoke said without looking behind him, "Nice shooting, Joey. Thanks."

Joey didn't answer, he was busy ejecting brass casings from his Colt and reloading.

By the time Smoke and Joey ran back down the alley to the main street, the gunfire had begun to die down as most of the raiders were killed or blown wounded out of their saddles. Three men managed to squeeze their mounts around the wagons at the end of town, shooting sentry Jerry Wilson dead as they made their escape, riding low over their saddle horns back toward the north. One had a machete hanging from his belt, bobbing up and down with the motion of his bronc.

Men gathered riderless, milling horses and began to line bodies along the boardwalk, shoveling dirt over blood pools in the street. The raiders were laid in one section, fallen townspeople in another. The doctor was busily attending to wounded citizens, ignoring wounded bandits. Smoke and Joey walked over to the buckboard where Cal and Pearlie were still lying.

Smoke shook his head at the sight of Cal with blood streaming down his neck from his partially shot-off ear.

Joey laughed out loud. "Damn, Pearlie, you were right. This boy is plumb lead-hungry."

"Come on, Joey, don't you start on me too," Cal complained, one hand to his torn ear.

Smoke saw Pearlie on hands and knees, crawling in the wagon. "Pearlie, what the hell are you doing?"

Pearlie looked up and winked. "I'm lookin' for Cal's ear. Maybe the doc can sew it back on."

Smoke saw two men carrying Tolson out of a building on

a makeshift stretcher. He and Joey rushed over to him, calling out, "Hey, Ben, how're you doing?"

He shook his head, grimacing. "Hell, it's the same damn shoulder I been hit in three times already. This makes four bullets in the same place."

Joey smiled. "That much lead in ya, it's a wonder ya don't lean to the side when ya walk."

"Seriously, Ben, you did a good job. Murdock's gang must be pretty well shut down now," Smoke said.

Tolson waved the men carrying his stretcher to stop. He leaned up on one elbow. "I don't know, Smoke. All the men who got away were wearing masks. We all know it was Murdock, but I don't know as I can prove it."

Joey said, "I don't need no proof, sheriff. I saw the machete hangin' on the belt of one that got away, so my business here isn't finished yet."

"Give it a few days, Joey, just till I get on my feet again, and we'll ride out to Murdock's together and see what he has to say for himself . . . all right?"

Joey scratched his chin. "I guess I can wait a couple o' more days." He looked at Smoke. "Maybe we can spend the time lookin' over the ranch you bought."

Smoke slapped his forehead. "Damn, I clean forgot about the Williams place in all the excitement. We'll go out tomorrow and take a look at it, though I doubt we'll be needing it now that Murdock is finished."

Joey shook his head. "Don't go countin' him out just yet, Smoke. Cuttin' the tail off a snake don't always kill it. You got to git the head to make sure."

A sweating Jacob Murdock twirled the dial of his office safe as fast as he could. Vasquez stood behind him, pulling a cork from Murdock's bourbon.

Murdock took a handful of cash from his safe, counted

out twenty-five bills, and put the rest back in the drawer. He slammed the heavy iron door shut and spun the dial again to lock it.

He rose and took a glass full of whiskey from Vasquez, who merely upended the bottle and gulped his straight.

"Here is twenty-five hundred dollars, Emilio. Five hundred is for you, the other two thousand is for the men I want you to hire."

Vasquez spread his hands. "Señor, *es finito,* give it up, Jensen and Wells beat us. Is time to go to greener pastures."

Murdock took a long, slow drink of the bourbon and sleeved sweat off his forehead. "You don't know who we're dealing with here, do you?"

Vasquez shrugged. "A couple of gringo gunfighters. So? In a few weeks they will move on and forget Emilio and Jacob."

Murdock shook his head. "No, I don't think so. That small one, the one with the Southern drawl, that's Joey Wells."

"Again I say, so?"

"During the Civil War a group of over a hundred and fifty men, called Kansas Redlegs, betrayed and killed Joey's friends. It took him two and a half years, but he tracked every Kansas Redleg in that group, all one hundred and fifty of them, and shot them dead . . . sometimes taking on three or four at a time."

Vasquez narrowed his eyes. "Emilio *es no* Redleg."

Murdock refilled his glass and sat behind his desk, taking out a long, thick cigar and lighting it. As smoke curled around his head, he pointed the cigar at Vasquez. "Tolson told me that a group of Mexican and Indian *bandidos* raided Joey's ranch, stole his cattle, and shot his wife and son. You wouldn't know anything about that, would you, Emilio?"

The Mexican's eyes gave him away, first narrowing, then opening wide as he spread his hands. "Me, señor?"

"Don't bother denying it, Emilio. Why do you think Wells and Jensen showed up here? They certainly weren't after me."

The Mexican nodded. "Señor, one question. What makes you trust Emilio with your money? What if I take money and don't come back?"

Murdock smiled. "Remember the Redlegs, Vasquez? Joey Wells will hunt you down and kill you unless you come back here with the meanest guns you can buy. It's your only chance of living long enough to get gray hair."

"You are correct, Señor Murdock." Vasquez took the stack of one-hundred-dollar bills and stuffed them in his coat. "Where will I find these men?"

Murdock pursed his lips. "Colorado Springs, I think, is the best bet. It is right on the edge of a mountain range, where men on the run from the law go to hide out, and it's only about forty miles from here. From there you can wire other nearby towns and have the word put out I'm hiring, and paying top wages, for men not afraid of Smoke Jensen or Joey Wells. With their reputations, there ought to be plenty of men willing to make their name by taking them down. Tell them they have one week to get here, then we'll make our move."

Vasquez nodded. "*Sí* señor."

"And, Emilio, unless you want to spend the rest of your life looking over your shoulder every time you enter a town, you'd better get some good men."

12

It was three days before the doctor gave the okay for Tolson to ride out to the Lazy M and confront Murdock. Smoke, Joey, Cal, and Pearlie rode along in case some of Murdock's regular ranch hands tried to stop the sheriff.

On the way to the ranch house, the group could see several herds of beeves in the distance, being tended to by punchers on horseback.

Smoke pointed out the activity to Tolson. "Doesn't look much like Murdock has packed up and left, does it?"

The sheriff looked over his shoulder at Smoke. "You didn't expect it to be that easy, did you?"

Murdock was waiting for them on his front porch as they approached. "Howdy, gents. What can I do for you?"

Tolson said, "We come to talk to you about the raid on Pueblo a few days ago."

Murdock took the cigar out of his mouth and examined its tip. "Yeah, I heard about that. Seems some of those Mexican workers I hired went crazy and attacked the town." He looked back up at Tolson. "I certainly hope you killed or captured all of them."

Tolson pursed his lips, his eyes narrow. "And you didn't know anything about all this?"

Murdock spread his arms. "Of course not, sheriff. I'm a law-abiding rancher. One day last week the men just up and left the ranch without a word to me about where they were going." He shrugged. "I thought maybe they just quit and were going looking elsewhere for work, you know how Mexes and half-breeds are."

"What about Vasquez? He leave with the others?" Joey asked, staring intently at Murdock.

Murdock shook his head. "No, Mr. Vasquez is on an errand for me." He glared back at Joey, his gaze flicking to Smoke for a moment. "I sent him over to . . . to another town to hire some men to replace the Mexicans that left."

"You know when he'll be back?"

"I think he'll be here within the next couple of days. Why do you ask?"

Joey smiled with his lips but not with his eyes. "Oh, I got a few things I wanna discuss with him."

Now it was Murdock who smiled just as evilly as Joey. "Well, I'll be sure and tell him to look you up when he gets back, Wells. Now, if there's nothing further, gentlemen?"

Tolson snorted. "We'll be seeing you, Murdock."

Murdock nodded. "Yes, yes, I think you will, sheriff."

As they walked their horses toward town, Joey said, "Sheriff, I know Vasquez was in that raid. I recognized him."

Tolson glanced to the side, then shook his head. "Not good enough, Joey. With those masks on, we'd never prove it was him. Hell, half the Mexes I know carry those machete things when they work."

"So, what next, Ben?" Smoke asked.

"Damned if I know," Tolson answered. "Guess we'll just have to wait and see what Murdock's got up his sleeve." He glanced at Smoke. "But I can tell you one thing, I'll bet we won't like it one bit."

After a few minutes be asked, "What do you gents plan to do?"

Joey said, "I'm waitin' fer Vasquez ta git back ta town. Once I'm done with him, I guess I'll head back ta Texas."

Smoke spoke up. "Joey, let's cut to the north on the way back to town and take a look at the ranch I bought."

"Okay with me. See ya later, Ben."

The Williams spread was only a matter of an hour's ride north of Murdock's place. As the four men crested a ridge, they could look down over sprawling hills and meadows of lush green mountain grass.

"What do you think?" Smoke asked Joey as they sat looking at fields filled with cattle.

"Right purty, Smoke." He grinned. "Mite greener than my place in Mexico." He pulled a plug of Bull Durham out of his shirt and took a bite. "Hell, those ol' longhorns on my ranch had to walk for miles ta find a clump o' grass worth the effort it took ta eat it."

"Let's go check out the ranch house, Smoke. We can see what supplies we need to buy when we get back to town," said Pearlie.

Cal chimed in. "Always thinkin' 'bout your stomach, Pearlie."

Pearlie looked hurt. "If don't, who will?"

They rode down the hill toward a log ranch house on the horizon. It was a sprawling place, with two large corrals and an open-sided barn nearby.

They opened the door and entered. "Open some windows, boys. It's a little musty in here," Smoke said.

Joey stared at the floor. It was made of split hardwood beams, and Mrs. Williams had scrubbed and polished it until it shined. "Who-eee, Smoke. This sure beats hell out of my dirt floor back home," said Joey.

Smoke nodded, looking at the window curtains and many small things the Williamses had done to make this cabin a home. "It's a shame someone killed him. From the looks of this place, they must've been a happy couple."

Joey walked around the room, running his hands over the handmade furniture and tables. "Yeah, it looks real home-like, don't it?"

Pearlie emerged from the kitchen with a wide grin on his face. "Pantry's full. We won't have to buy hardly any food-stuffs nor cookin' supplies. The owner just packed up and left everything like it was, I guess."

Smoke looked at Joey. "Probably couldn't wait to get shut of this place and the memories of her dead husband."

Smoke said, "Come on, boys, let's get back to town. We better get those hands Joey hired out here working the cattle before they all wander off."

"Or before someone takes them off," Joey added, glancing out the window to the south, toward Murdock's spread.

As the four men rode into Pueblo, one of Tolson's deputies stepped off the boardwalk and waved them down. "Smoke, Sheriff Tolson wants to see you at his office as soon as you can get there."

"Something wrong?"

The man shook his head. "I'll let him tell you."

They spurred their mounts into a trot toward Tolson's office. As they dismounted, he stepped through the door to meet them. "More bad news."

Smoke and Joey looked at each other, wondering what was going on. Smoke asked, "What is it, Ben?"

"It seems Vasquez has been successful in his search for more hired hands for Murdock. A few of 'em just rode into town on the way to his place." He inclined his head at the saloon down the street. "Wanna go meet them?"

Smoke shrugged. "Sure."

Tolson stepped back into his office, grabbed his Greener, and joined them as they walked down the boardwalk. "These are some of the worst specimens of humanity I've ever seen.

Evidently Vasquez went over to Colorado Springs, 'bout forty miles north of here, and spread the word Murdock was hiring gun hands."

Joey smiled. "Good. That's one more reason to kill him."

They stepped into the saloon and took a table over to one side. Across the room was a table with five men seated at it, still covered with trail dust, passing around a whiskey bottle. The gunnies were too intent on their booze to notice Smoke's group enter the saloon.

Smoke's eyes narrowed, then he grinned. "Well, I'll be damned."

Tolson looked at him. "You know these galoots, Smoke?"

Smoke chuckled. "Yeah, you could say that, Ben."

Joey watched the men for a moment, shaking his head. "Jesus, but they look like they been rode hard and put up wet. That one on the end there has had a horse stomp on his face for sure, an' the one in the middle cain't hardly walk, looks more like a duck waddlin'."

Smoke nodded. "And you notice how that other one kind of sits on the edge of his chair, like his butt's not all there?"

Pearlie said, "I recognize the one dressed all in black with the big silver belt buckle. I knew him a bit back when I was sellin' my guns, that's Ace Reilly." He glanced at Smoke. "You said he went back East with Nap Jacobs."

"He did. Matter of fact, I told him if I ever saw him again, I was going to kill him."

Joey leaned back and waved to the barman for a whiskey. He pulled a cigar out of his pocket and lit it with a lucifer. "That sounds like there's a story behind you knowing these fellahs, Smoke. How 'bout tellin' it?"

Smoke shrugged, his eyes boring holes in Ace's back. "It all started a while back, after a federal judge named Richards issued a phony warrant on me for killing his brother. I had holed up in the high lonesome and a passel of bounty hunters and outlaws came up after me. Man name of

Slater put up thirty thousand dollars for anyone who could drill me. . . ."

Smoke hiked what he figured was about three miles through wild and rugged country, then stopped and built a small, nearly smokeless fire for his coffee and bacon and beans. While his meal was cooking and the coffee boiling, he whittled on some short stakes, sharpening one end to a needle point. After eating, he cleaned the plate and skillet and spoon and packed them away. Then he went to work making the campsite look semipermanent and laying out some rather nasty pitfalls for the bounty hunters and outlaws.

Curly Rogers and his pack of hyenas were first to arrive. Smoke was back in the timber with a .44-.40 long gun, waiting and watching.

The outlaws didn't come busting in. They laid back and looked the situation over for a time. They saw a lean-to Smoke had built, and what appeared to be a man sleeping under a blanket, protected by overlaid boughs.

"It might not be Jensen," Taylor said.

"So what?" Thumbs Morton said. "It wouldn't be the first time someone got shot by accident."

"I don't like it," Curly said. "It just looks too damn pat to suit me."

"Maybe Slim got lead into him?" Bell suggested. "He may be hard hit and holed up."

Curly thought about that for a moment. "Maybe. Yeah. That must be it. Lake, you think you can injun up yonder for a closer look?"

"Shore. But why don't we just shoot him from here?"

"A shot'd bring everybody foggin'. Then we'd probably have to fight some of the others over Jensen's carcass. A knife don't make no noise."

Lake grinned and pulled out a long-bladed knife. "I'll just slip this 'tween his ribs."

As Lake stepped out with the knife in his hand, Smoke tugged on a rope he'd attached to the sticks under the blankets. What the outlaws thought to be a sleeping or wounded Smoke Jensen moved, and Lake froze, then jumped back into the timber.

"This ain't gonna work," Curly said. "We got to shoot him, I reckon. One shot might not attract no attention. Bud, use your rifle and put one shot in him. This close, one round'll kill him sure."

Bud lined up the form in his sights and squeezed the trigger. Smoke tugged on the rope, and the stick man rose off the ground a few inches, then fell back.

"We got him!" Bell yelled, jumping up. "We kilt Smoke Jensen. The money's our'n!"

The men raced toward the small clearing, guns drawn and hollering.

Taylor yelled as the ground seemed to open up under his boots. He fell about eighteen inches into a pit, two sharpened stakes tearing into the calves of his legs. He screamed in pain, unable to free himself from the sharpened stakes.

Bell tripped a piece of rawhide two inches off the ground and a tied-back, fresh, and springy limb sprang forward. The limb whacked the man on the side of his head, tearing off one ear and knocking him unconscious.

"What the hell!" Curly yelled.

Smoke fired from concealment, the .44-.40 slug taking Lake in the right side and exiting out his left side. He was dying as he hit the ground.

"It's a trap!" Curly screamed, and ran for the timber. He ran right over Bell in his haste to get the hell into cover.

Smoke lined up Bud and fired just as the man turned, the slug hitting the man in the ass, the lead punching into his left buttock and blowing out his right, taking a sizeable chunk of meat with it.

Bud fell screaming and rolled on the ground, throwing himself into cover.

Thumbs Morton jerked up Bell just as the man was crawling to his knees, blood pouring from where his ear had once been, and dragged him into cover just as Smoke fired again, the slug hitting a tree and blowing splinters in Thumbs's face, stinging and bringing blood.

"Let's get gone from here!" Curly yelled.

"What about Taylor?" Thumbs asked, pulling splinters and wiping blood from his face.

"Hell with him."

With Curly supporting the ass-shot Bud, and Thumbs helping Bell, the outlaws made it back to their horses and took off at a gallop, Bud shrieking in pain as the saddle abused his shot-up butt.

Smoke lay in the timber and listened to the outlaws beat their retreat, then stepped out into his camp. He looked at Lake. The outlaw was dead. Smoke took his ammo belt and tossed his guns into the brush. He walked over to Taylor, who had passed out from the pain in his ruined legs. He took his ammunition, tossed his guns into the brush, and then jerked the stakes out of the man's legs. The man moaned in unconsciousness.

Smoke found the men's horses, took the food from the saddlebags, and led one animal back to the campsite. He poured a canteen full of water on Taylor. The man moaned and opened his eyes.

"Ride," Smoke told him. "If I ever see you again, I'll kill you."

"I cain't get up on no horse," Taylor sobbed. "My legs is ruint."

Smoke jacked back the hammer on his .44. "Then I guess I'd better put you out of your misery."

Taylor screamed in fear and crawled to his horse, pulling himself up by clinging to the stirrup and the fender of the saddle. He managed to get in the saddle after several tries. His face was white with pain. He looked down at Smoke.

"You ain't no decent human bein'. What you're doin' to me ain't right. I need a doctor. You a devil, Jensen!"

"Then you pass that word, pusbag. You make damn sure all your scummy buddies know I don't play by the rules. Now ride, you bastard, before I change my mind and kill you!"

Taylor was gone in a gallop.

Later, another bunch tried to sneak up on Smoke. Smoke released his hold, and the thick springy branch struck its target with several hundred pounds of driving force. The outlaw was knocked from the saddle, his nose flattened, and his jaw busted. He hit the ground and did not move. Smoke led the horse into the timber, took the food packets from the saddlebags, and then stripped saddle and bridle from the animal and turned it loose.

Smoke faded back into the heavy timber at the sounds of approaching horses.

"Good God!" a man's voice drifted through the brush and timber. "Look at Dewey, would you."

"What the hell hit him?" another asked. "His entire face is smashed in."

"Where's his horse?" another asked. "We got to get him to a doctor."

"Doctor?" yet another questioned. "Hell, there ain't a doctor within fifty miles of here. See if you can get him awake and find out what happened. Damn, his face is ruint!"

"I bet it was that damn Jensen," an unshaven and smelly outlaw said. "We get our hands on him, let's see how long we can keep him alive."

"Yeah," another agreed. "We'll skin him alive."

Smoke shot the one who favored skinning slap out of his saddle, putting a .44-.40 slug into his chest, and twisting him around. The man fell and the frightened horse took off, dragging the dying outlaw along the rocks in the game trail.

"Get into cover!" Horton yelled just as Smoke fired again.

Horton was turning in the saddle, and the bullet missed him, striking a horse in the head and killing it instantly. The animal dropped, pinning its rider.

"My leg!" the rider screamed "It's busted. Oh, God, somebody help me."

Gooden ran to help his buddy, and Smoke drilled him, the slug smashing into the man's side and turning him around like a spinning top. Gooden fell on top of the dead horse, and Cates screamed as the added weight shot pain through his shattered leg.

Horton and Max put the spurs to their horses and got the hell out of there, leaving their dead and wounded behind. Smoke slipped back into the timber.

"He's up there," Ace Reilly said, his eyes looking at the timber line in the morning light. The air was almost cold this high up.

Big Bob Masters shifted his chew from one side of his mouth to the other and spit. "Solid rock to his back," he observed. "And two hundred yards of open country ever'where else. It'd be suicide gettin' up there."

Ace lifted his canteen to take a drink, and the canteen exploded in his hand, showering him with water, bits of metal, and numbing his hand. The second shot nicked Big Bob's horse on the rump, and the animal went pitching and snorting and screaming down the slope, Big Bob yelling and hanging on and flopping in the saddle. The third shot took off part of Causey's ear, and he left the saddle, crawling behind some rocks.

"Jesus Christ!" Ace hollered, leaving the saddle and finding cover. "Where the hell is that comin' from?"

Big Bob's horse had come to a very sudden and unexpected halt, and Big Bob went flying out of the saddle to land against a tree. He staggered to his feet, looking wildly around him, and took a .44 slug in the belly. He sank to his knees, both hands holding his punctured belly, bellowing in pain.

"He's right on top of us," Ace called to Nap. "Over there at the base of that rock face."

Smoke was hundreds of yards up the mountain, just at the timber line, looking and wondering who his new ally might be. He got his field glasses and began sweeping the area. A slow smile curved his lips.

"I married a Valkyrie, for sure," he muttered as the long lenses made out Sally's face.

He saw riders coming hard, a lot of riders. Smoke grabbed up his .44-.40 and began running down the mountain, keeping to the timber. The firing had increased as the riders dismounted and sought cover. Smoke stayed a good hundred yards above them, and so far he had not been spotted.

"Causey!" Woody yelled. "Over yonder!" He pointed. "Get on his right flank—that's exposed."

Causey jumped up and Smoke drilled him through and through. Causey died sprawled on the still-damp rocks from the misty morning in the high lonesome.

"He's up above us!" Ray yelled.

"Who the hell is that over yonder?" Noah hollered just as Sally fired. The slug sent bits and pieces of rock into Noah's face, and he screamed as he was momentarily blinded. He stood up, and Smoke nailed him through the neck. Smoke had been aiming for his chest, but shooting downhill is tricky, even for a marksman.

Big Bob Masters was hollering and screaming, afraid to move, afraid his guts would fall out.

Smoke plugged Yancey in the shoulder, knocking the man down and putting him out of the fight. Yancey began crawling downhill toward the horses, staying in cover. He had but two thoughts in mind: getting in the saddle and getting the hell gone from this place.

"It's no good!" Ace yelled. "They'll pick us all off if we stay here. We got to get down the slope."

The outlaws crawled back downhill, staying in cover as much as they could. Haynes, Dale, and Yancey were the first to reach their horses, well out of range of Smoke's and Sally's guns.

Haynes looked up, horror in his eyes. A man dressed all in black was standing by a tree, his hands filled with Colts.

"Hello, punk!" Louis Longmont said, and opened fire.

The last memory Haynes had, and it would have to last him an eternity, was the guns of Louis Longmont belching fire and smoke. He died sitting on his butt, his back to a boulder. Yancey tried to lift his rifle, and Louis shot him twice in the belly. Dale turned to run, and Louis offered him no quarter. The first slug cut his spine; the second slug caught him falling and took off part of his head.

"We yield!" Nap Jacobs yelled.

"Not in this game," Louis called.

The pinned-down gunmen looked at each other. There were four of them left. Nap Jacobs, Ace Reilly, and two of Slater's boys, Kenny and Summers.

"I ain't done you no hurt, Longmont!" Ace yelled. "You got no call to horn in on this play."

"But here I am," Louis said. "Make your peace with God."

The silent dead littered the mountain battlefield. Below them, an outlaw's horse pawed the ground, the steel hoof striking rock.

"And I don't know who you is over yonder in the rock," Nap yelled. "But I wish you'd bow out."

"I'm Mrs. Smoke Jensen!" Sally called.

"Dear God in heaven," Ace said. "We been took down by a damn skirt!"

"Disgustin'!" Nap said.

Kenny looked wild-eyed. "I'm gone," he said, and jumped up. Three rifles barked at once, all the slugs striking true.

Kenny was slammed backward, two holes in his chest and one hole in the center of his forehead.

Nap looked over at Ace. "This ain't no cakewalk, Ace. We forgot about Smoke's reputation once the battle starts."

"Yeah," Ace said, his voice low. "Once folks come after him, he don't leave nobody standin'."

"I got an idea. Listen." Nap tied a dirty bandanna around the barrel of his rifle and waved it. "I'm standin' up, people!" he shouted, taking his guns from leather and dropping them on the ground. "I walk out of here, and I'm gone from this country, and I don't come back." He looked at Ace. "You with me?"

"All the way—if they'll let us leave."

"I ain't playin', Ace. If they let us go, I'm gone far and long."

"My word on it."

"How about it, Jensen?" Nap shouted.

"It's all right with me," Smoke returned the shout. "But if I see you again, anyplace, anytime, and you're wearing a gun, I'll kill the both of you. That's a promise."

"Let's go," Nap said. "I always did want to see what's east of the Mississippi."*

Joey nodded at the end of Smoke's tale. "And which of them do we have here?"

"Curly Rogers is the one in the brown vest, Taylor's the one with the gimpy legs who can't walk right, Bud's the one sitting on the side of his chair 'cause I shot his butt off, and Dewey's the one with the ruined face."

"And that leaves the one in black, Ace Reilly," added Pearlie.

Smoke got up out of his chair, saying, "Excuse me, men, I got some business to attend to."

*Code of the Mountain Man

Tolson put his hand on Smoke's arm. "Smoke, what are you gonna do?"

Smoke inclined his head toward the table across the room. "I told Taylor and Reilly if I ever saw them again, I was going to kill them. That's what I intend to do."

Tolson frowned. "You can't just walk over there and shoot down two men like they was animals."

Smoke grinned. "I gave my word, Ben. Besides, those two *are* animals, and they're wanted in more states than you can count."

Joey cleared his throat. "Ben, stay out of it. Smoke is right, he warned 'em and they decided to try his hand, or they wouldn't be here."

Ben reluctantly let go of Smoke's arm, and the mountain man walked across the room toward the table, hands hanging loose.

13

Curly Rogers looked up and saw Smoke Jensen walking toward their table. He nudged Taylor with his elbow, interrupting some story he was telling Bud about the good old days before law came to the West.

"What?" Taylor said irritably, turning to Rogers. He saw him staring and followed his gaze, blanching and turning pale when he saw Smoke standing in front of him, feet apart, hands hanging next to his Colts.

As the men at the table became aware of Smoke, all talking and joking stopped and they turned in their chairs to face the mountain man.

"Afternoon, gents," Smoke said, his voice low and without welcome.

Curly Rogers half stood in his chair. "You got no call to roust us, Jensen. We ain't breakin' no laws or nothin.'"

Smoke's eyes flicked around the table, pausing at each man for just a moment, causing each to lower their eyes. "Oh, I'm not rousting you, Rogers." His eyes lit on Reilly and Taylor and his hand came up to point at them. "But I do have some unfinished business with these two."

"Whatta ya mean?" asked Taylor, sweat beginning to form on his forehead.

"Remember the last time we met?" Smoke asked.

"Yeah," answered Taylor, trying to put some bluster in his voice. "You put some wooden stakes through my legs and ruint 'em. I cain't hardly even walk on 'em now," he said, his voice turning from bluster to whine.

"That's not what I meant. Do you remember what I told you as I let you ride off that day?"

"Uh . . . no, I don't believe I do."

Smoke glanced to Ace Reilly. "How about you, Ace? You remember?"

The gunman tried a laugh that didn't come off. "Yeah, you said you was gonna kill me if you ever saw me again."

He looked around at his friends. "But you cain't do that. I'm just sittin' here, peaceably drinkin' with my partners, not causing nobody no trouble."

He glared defiantly at Smoke, then glanced over at the table where Tolson sat, his badge on his chest.

"You, mister, are you the sheriff of this town?"

Tolson nodded once, his lips tight.

"Are you gonna sit there and let this . . . this gunfighter threaten honest citizens for no reason?"

Tolson smirked. "I'll tell ya what I'll do, mister. I'll stop this right here and now and we can mosey on over to my office and go through my wanted posters. If I don't find any mention of you or your friend, I'll let you ride on out of town."

Reilly's face slowly turned red. "And if there is somethin' there? You'll put us in jail?"

Tolson shook his head. "No. If you're wanted for anything more than spitting on the street, then I'll just step aside and let my deputy there, Smoke Jensen, do his duty."

Taylor whined. "But, sheriff, that's not fair."

Curly Rogers spoke up. "Don't worry, men, there's five of us and only one of him. He won't dare start anything with those odds."

Chairs scraped back and four men from Smoke's table

stood and spread out—Joey, Cal, Pearlie, and Ben. "I'm Joey Wells," Joey said, "and normally I don't interfere in another man's business." He leaned over and aimed a stream of brown tobacco juice at a spittoon. "And if Smoke wants to call them two out, that's his business. However, if any o' the rest o' ya want to enter the dance, I guess I'll just strike up the band and dance along."

The other three with him nodded, grim smiles on their faces.

Curly held up his hands. "Now, wait a minute. I want no part of this. We just answered a call for work out at the Murdock place. There's a whole lot of us goin' out there."

"Oh, and who might they be?" Smoke asked.

"Uh, why, there's Horton, Max, Cates, and Boots, and maybe Gooden."

Smoke shook his head. "Same sorry bunch of no-account losers who are too lazy to work and too cowardly to face a man. Back-shooters every one."

"If you'll back off, we'll just be headin' on out of town, Jensen," Curly said, preparing to stand up.

"Keep your seat until this is over. Then you can leave, but if you head out to Murdock's, I can promise you the same treatment."

He inclined his head toward Taylor and Reilly. "One at a time, or both together. Guns, boots, fists, or knives make no nevermind to me, boys, but today you die. Pick your poison."

Taylor said, "I cain't fight, I'm a cripple. Look at what you done to my legs."

"Your hand is okay, and you're wearing a pistol. Use it, or die where you sit."

Taylor started to get up, then tried to draw before Smoke was ready. His gun was half out of his holster when twin explosions shattered the quiet of the room and he was hit twice in the chest, blown backward over his chair to land sprawled on his back with a look of surprise on his face.

Curly's face fell and he murmured, "Jesus, I never even saw him draw, it was like the guns just appeared in his hands."

Reilly held up both hands, a look of terror on his face. He got up and began backing out of the saloon. "I cain't match that, Jensen. I'm gettin'on my hoss and hightailin' it outta here."

Smoke holstered his guns. He reached into the back of his belt and withdrew a pair of black gloves with pads over the knuckles. As he put them on, he grinned savagely. "No need to leave Pueblo so soon, Ace. You knew I was here when you came, so you must have wanted to dance. Well, let's do it."

Smoke's right hand lashed out and caught Ace flush on the nose, splattering it across his face and sending blood spurting. His head snapped back, and he screamed. "No, leave me alone, you devil!" he said, backpedaling as fast as he could.

Smoke kept walking toward him, keeping time with him. With every step, Smoke whipped a short jab to Ace's body. First his chest, then his ribs, then his stomach. After a few steps, Ace tried to block the blows, which then fell on his arms, bruising them and making them knot up.

As Smoke punched, he breathed out through his nose in short, explosive grunts, to be answered by Ace's bellows of pain as the blows landed. Ace finally saw he wasn't going to get away and tried to make a fight of it. He braced his feet and began to windmill his arms, shouting and yelling as if he could scare the mountain man away.

Smoke leaned right and left, letting Ace's wild blows barely miss his face, answering each swing of Ace's with a punch or jab of his own. In a very few minutes Ace's face began to look like ground-up meat. His nose was broken and spread all over his face, his teeth were broken-off stubs protruding through lacerated, bleeding lips, and his eyebrows were split, pouring blood down his cheeks to drip onto his shirt.

Finally, Smoke, tired of torturing the man, set his feet and swung a right cross with all his might. The blow lifted Ace off his feet and dislocated his jaw with a loud crack He fell backward to lie unmoving, moaning in the dirt.

Smoke turned his back and began walking to the saloon, when suddenly a warning shout rang out from Cal. "Smoke, watch out!"

Smoke crouched and whirled, drawing his Bowie knife in one smooth motion. Ace was rushing toward him, blood streaming from his ruined face, hand holding a knife above him, ready to strike at Smoke's back.

With a motion quick as a striking rattler, Smoke flicked his Bowie knife underhanded. It spun the regulation three times and impaled itself to the hilt in Ace's chest, stopping his rush instantly.

Ace stood there for a moment, looking at the knife handle protruding from his chest as if he couldn't believe it, then he groaned and fell dead to the ground.

Smoke stepped to him, put his boot on his chest, and yanked his knife out. He paused to wipe the blade on Ace's fancy black silk shirt, then put it in its scabbard.

Rogers, Bud, and Dewey were watching silently from the boardwalk. Smoke glared at them through narrowed eyes. "You men are free to leave, but remember what I said. If you go to work for Murdock, spend your money fast. You won't live to enjoy it."

Curly said, "You cain't tell us who to work for, Jensen. It's a free country."

"You're right, Curly. It is a free country, and you're free to choose to live or to die. I say this to each of you. If I ever see you again and you're wearing guns, I will shoot you down on sight. Do I make myself clear?"

The men nodded and climbed on their mounts. After a brief consultation, Bud rode south out of town, and Curly and Dewey rode north, toward Murdock's ranch.

Joey spit brown juice into the dirt next to Ace's body. "I guess we'll be seein' them again."

Smoke nodded, eyes squinted against the sun as he watched Curly and Dewey ride toward the Lazy M. "I wonder how many of my old enemies Murdock's hired."

Joey chuckled. "If he's managed to find some o' mine too, there ought ta be a passel of folks out there plannin' how ta take us down." He spit again. "That's the price o' leadin' an interesting' life, pardner."

Tolson stepped up and stood over Ace's corpse with his hands on his hips. He said, "If Murdock's put the word out that he'll pay whoever puts lead in you two, we may be seein' a lot of this sort of varmint comin' to town." He removed his hat and scratched his head. "Wonder if I might not oughta start watching the train and stage arrivals?"

"Wouldn't hurt to put a couple of men on that, Ben. At least then we'd have some idea of what we're going to be up against in the next few weeks," Smoke said. He shook his head. "I sure wish he would have given up his idea of treeing this town and starting his own empire here in Colorado. This area's getting too civilized for that sort of thinking nowadays."

"Not all that civilized when you stop to think I'm the only law up against him now. The U.S. marshals won't come unless I ask for 'em, and if I do, why then he'd just lay low and wait for 'em to leave again. This country is just to blamed big to police on a day-to-day basis from the territorial capital."

Joey put his hand on Ben's shoulder. "You haven't done so bad, Ben. I think the people o' Pueblo oughta be proud of how you've stood up to that snake. That took a lotta courage."

Tolson snorted. "I got no shortage of courage, but we may have a shortage of gun hands if Murdock lures a bunch of hard cases up here to do his dirty work for him." He looked at Cal and Pearlie, then back to Smoke and Joey. "You men are 'bout the best with short guns I ever seen, but all told, we're only ten to fifteen men. I don't relish goin' up against thirty or forty gun hawks by ourselves."

Smoke said, "Can't be helped, Ben. We can't ask the

townspeople to take a hand in this, unless they ride on the town itself again, and I don't think Murdock is dumb enough to try that again."

Joey looked north toward the Lazy M. "No, I figger he and his men'll try ta hit us out at the ranch, where we won't have no backup. He'll either try an' pick us off one by one, or he'll just come at us one night with lots of guns blazing, hoping to get us pinned down in the ranch house."

Tolson nodded. "Joey's right, Smoke. You ain't got a lot of cover out there, you're gonna be sitting ducks for Murdock's men."

Smoke scratched his chin. "Well, I have a few ideas about how to fix that." He turned to the others. "Come on, boys, let's go out to our spread and see what we can do to even up the odds a little bit."

14

Low, dark snow clouds covered the sun, accentuating the chill in the north wind blowing down from mountain peaks surrounding Pueblo. Smoke, Joey, Cal, and Pearlie were riding the pastures and fields of the Williams ranch, now known in town as the Jensen spread.

Joey shook his head, a wry smile on his face. "Smoke, even though this is mighty purty land, lots of graze, and a good-lookin' herd o' beeves, I think you paid a mite too much fer it."

Smoke nodded, looking at rolling hills and cattle milling in fields, munching thick, green mountain grass. "Yeah, I guess you're right. But over the years since I've settled down with Sally, a lot of gun hawks have tried my hand looking to make a quick reputation. It turns out a goodly number of those were wanted men with prices on their heads. Every time we planted one of those pistoleers, Monte Carson would wire the governor's office and the money just sorta poured in." He stopped his horse and bent his head, using his hat to shield the wind while he lit a cigar. Exhaling a cloud of smoke into the rushing north wind, he said, "Though I never killed a man for the reward, it seems kind of fitting to use that money for something worthwhile, and right now I can't think of anything more worthwhile than to put a crimp in Murdock's plan of building an empire in Colorado."

"I cain't hardly argue with that." Joey gazed at the surrounding mountains, already topped with snow. "I like it up here, Smoke. The view sometimes gits kinda boring in Texas, an' those longhorns will surely try a man's soul."

Smoke glanced at Joey, knowing what he was feeling. Smoke fell in love with the high country the first time he saw it too. "Thinking about maybe staying up here when this is all over?"

Joey shrugged. "This is a good and decent country, an' most o' the people that come out here are good folks, like you and Sally and Cal and Pearlie." He pulled the brim of his hat down against the wind. "Once we've rid this territory of that skunk Murdock, I may jest bring the wife an' boy up here and see what they think."

Smoke smiled. "Oh, I think they'll feel about like you do. This land needs people like you and your family, Joey, and I hope they get to see it with you."

Their conversation was cut short when Cal and Pearlie, who had ridden on ahead, came galloping back to them. "Smoke," Pearlie yelled, pointing over his shoulder, "I think we found what yore lookin' for!"

Smoke and Joey followed the two younger men as they rode over a nearby hillock into a valley. The river running through the ranch had eroded down into the dirt to create a small canyon carved out of underlying sandstone. The canyon walls were about twenty feet deep and made a sharp bend around a series of boulders left by an ancient glacier.

Smoke rode Horse to a ledge overlooking the course of the river, noticing how it emerged from a wide, flat valley before it entered the canyon.

"You're right, Pearlie. This is perfect. "He pointed at the boulders near the bend in the river. "If we dynamite those rocks there into the canyon, they'll block the water and back it up into the valley over there."

Joey pursed his lips and nodded. "An' from the lay o' the land, by the time the river fills the valley and starts ta overflow, it looks like it'll run on down that slope over yonder and miss Murdock's ranch off to the west." He grinned. "When we cut his water off, his beeves are gonna git mighty thirsty."

Smoke smiled. "If anything will force his hand, that will. I don't want him to be able to sit around and wait for his men to pick us off little by little. Stopping the river means every day he waits, he loses more cattle."

Cal said, "We better make sure we're good and ready for him before we do it, then."

Smoke took Pearlie by the arm. "Pearlie, I want you and Cal to ride over to the west and check out the ranches downstream from us. Talk to the owners and see if they mind if we divert the river to run through their land, but tell them to keep it under their hats. No need giving Murdock any advance warning of what we're up to."

"Yes, sir."

Smoke pulled a burlap sack out of his saddlebags and handed it to Pearlie. He leaned in close and in a low voice said, "There's something else I want you to do for me while you're riding around . . ."

When Smoke finished telling Pearlie what he wanted, Pearlie and Cal wheeled their mounts to leave, and Joey said, "Remember what Vasquez said to me the other day? *Cuidado* partners, *cuidado!*"

As they rode off, Pearlie noticed Cal had a wide grin on his face. "What're you smilin' at, boy?"

"Joey called us *partners!*" He stuck out his chest and sat straighter in his saddle. "Pearlie, we're partners with two of the toughest men on the face of this earth."

Pearlie nodded, replying, "You got that right, Cal."

* * *

After they finished inspecting the herd, Joey and Smoke headed for the ranch house. There were twenty cowboys seated on the porch and in the front yard waiting for them.

After Joey fixed several pots of coffee and passed out mugs to the punchers, Smoke stood on the porch in front of the group. "Men, I know some of you owned your own spreads and some of you rode for other brands that were taken over by Jacob Murdock. I suspect that all of you know Murdock and his gunnies aren't happy about me buying the Williams ranch."

One of the cowboys, an older man with salt and pepper hair, called out, "Yore right, Mr. Jensen. You sure put a burr under that bastard's saddle, an' that's fer sure."

As the men laughed, Smoke nodded, his face grim. "Yeah, I did. What that means, though, is that Murdock isn't going to take this lying down. He's hired more hard cases to replace those we killed in town, and I expect him to send his gun hawks around to try and run us off this spread. That means gunplay is more than likely, it's inevitable."

"Let 'em come," a younger puncher called, waving his pistol in the air. "We'll be ready!"

Smoke held up his hands to stop the cheering that followed this remark. "I know you men are game, or you wouldn't be here, but Murdock's *bandidos* and new hires are experienced gunmen and outlaws—murderers all, and most of you have never shot at another man in anger."

The group sobered, some looking at the ground and shuffling their feet as they recognized the truth of Smoke's statement. "Now, here's my plan. My partner, Joey Wells, is going to work with each and every one of you to determine who is good enough with a gun to stand against Murdock's killers. Those who are experienced with short guns and rifles will undergo further training by Joey and myself and will be used as perimeter guards and sentries." Smoke smiled. "As most of you know, Joey has had a little experience fighting against and defeating forces far superior in numbers and in firepower."

As the men nodded, some winking at Joey, Smoke continued. "The other men will be given shotguns to carry for protection, but will be used primarily to run the ranch and take care of the herd." Smoke paused a moment to light a cigar and finish his cup of coffee. "Make no mistake about it, boys, this is a dangerous business. Some of us are going to take lead, and some of us are going to die."

He looked around at the men, liking what he saw. None appeared daunted by the prospect of giving their lives to rid Colorado of Jacob Murdock and his henchmen.

"For that reason, I've decided that every man who signs to ride for my brand will be made a partner, be given an equal share in the ranch, and will draw double wages until the operation shows a profit."

As the men cheered at this surprising news, Joey stepped forward. "You men with wives and young'uns don't need to worry neither. If worse comes ta worse and ya don't make it through this dust-up, yore families will be taken care of an' will git yore share of the ranch."

Smoke held up a paper. "Now, if you men will step up here and sign or make your mark, you'll all be full partners in the Rocking C ranch, named in honor of Mr. Colt, who's going to help us make Murdock wish he'd stayed in Texas and never set foot in Colorado!"

Two days passed without Smoke and his friends hearing or seeing anything of Murdock or his new hands. Joey had been working from dawn to dusk with Smoke's new hired hands to see if any showed an aptitude for using gunplay.

Joey shook his head. "Smoke, we may 'o bitten off more'n we kin chew."

Smoke refilled Joey's cup of coffee and sat at the kitchen table with him. As Joey built a cigarette, Smoke lit a stogie. "That bad, huh?"

Joey stuck the cigarette in the corner of his mouth. "Ya know, partner, I been livin' with these Colts strapped on so long, they're like a part o' me. Shootin' an' killin' jest seemed ta come naturally ta me, like it was born in me to be what I am."

Smoke smiled. "I know the feeling, Joey. I started young too." Smoke's eyes glazed as he stared out the window at mountain peaks visible in the distance, thinking back to when he came to the mountains with his dad and met Preacher. . . .

Emmett Jensen returned from the war to Missouri to pick up his son, Kirby. He sold their farm for gold and he took Kirby and headed west on two horses, all they owned trailing behind on two pack mules.

The elder Jensen was heavily armed: a Sharps .52-caliber rifle in a saddle boot, two Remington Army revolvers in holsters around his waist, two more pistols in saddle holsters, left and right of the horn. And he carried a gambler's gun behind his belt buckle, a .44-caliber, two-shot derringer. His knife was a wicked-looking, razor-sharp Arkansas Toothpick in a leather sheath on his left side.

Young Kirby carried a Colt Navy, .36 caliber, with an extra cylinder that a man named Jesse James had given him when Kirby let Bloody Bill Anderson and his men water their horses at his farm in Missouri.

The Jensens were someplace west of Missouri and east of the Pacific Ocean when they met up with the dirtiest, smelliest man young Kirby had ever seen. The man was dressed entirely in buckskin, from the moccasins on his feet to his wide-brimmed leather hat. A white, tobacco-stained beard covered his face. His nose was red and his eyes twinkled with mischief. He reminded Kirby of a skinny, dirty version of Santa Claus. He sat on a funny-spotted pony, two pack animals with him. He said he was called Preacher. It wasn't his real name, but he'd been called Preacher so long, he near about forgot his Christian name.

Shortly after parting ways, Preacher galloped up to the pair, his rifle in his hand. "Don't get nervous," he told them. "It ain't me you got to fear. We fixin' to get ambushed . . . shortly. This here country is famous for that."

"Ambushed by who?" Emmett asked, not trusting the old man.

"Kiowa, I think. But they could be Pawnee. My eyes ain't as sharp as they used to be. I seen one of 'em stick a head up out of a wash over yonder while I was jawin' with you. He's young, or he wouldn't have done that. But that don't mean the others with him is young."

"How many?"

"Don't know. In this country, one's too many. Do know this: We better light a shuck out of here. If memory serves me correct, right over yonder, over that ridge, they's little crick behind a stand of cottonwoods, old buffalo wallow in front of it." He looked up, stood up in his stirrups, and cocked his shaggy head. "Here they come, boys . . . rake them cayuses!"

Before Kirby could ask what a cayuse was, or what good a rake was in an Indian attack, the old man had slapped his bay on the rump and they were galloping off. With the mountain man in the lead, the three of them rode for the crest of the ridge. The packhorses seemed to sense the urgency, for they followed with no pullback on the ropes. Cresting the ridge, the riders slid down the incline and galloped into the timber, down into the wallow, the whoops and cries of the Indians close behind them.

Preacher might well have been past his so-called good years, but the mountain man had leaped off his spotted pony, rifle in hand, and was in position and firing before Emmett or Kirby had dismounted. Preacher, like Emmett, carried a Sharps .52, firing a paper cartridge, deadly up to seven hundred yards or more.

Kirby looked up in time to see a brave fly off his pony, a crimson slash on his naked chest. The Indian hit the ground and did not move.

"Get me that Spencer out of the pack, boy," Kirby's father yelled.

"The what?" Kirby had no idea what a Spencer might be.

"The rifle. It's in the pack. A tin box wrapped up with it. Bring both of 'em. Cut the ropes, boy."

Slashing the ropes with his long-bladed knife, Kirby grabbed the long, canvas-wrapped rifle and the tin box. He ran to his father's side. He stood and watched as his father got a buck in the sights of his Sharps, led him on his fast-running pony, then fired. The buck slammed off his pony, bounced off the ground, then leaped to his feet, one arm hanging bloody and broken. The Indian dodged for cover. He didn't make it. Preacher shot him in the side and lifted him off his feet, dropping him dead.

Emmett laid the Sharps aside and hurriedly unwrapped the canvas, exposing an ugly weapon with a pot-bellied, slab-slided receiver. Emmett glanced up at Preacher, who was grinning at him.

"What the hell you grinnin' about, man?"

"Just wanted to see what you had all wrapped up, partner. Figured I had you beat with what's in my pack."

"We'll see," Emmett muttered. He pulled out a thin tube from the tin box and inserted it in the butt plate, chambering a round. In the tin box were a dozen or more tubes, each containing seven rounds, .52 caliber. Emmett leveled the rifle, sighted it, and fired all seven rounds in a thunderous barrage of black smoke. The Indians whooped and yelled. Emmett's firing had not dropped a single brave, but the Indians scattered for cover, disappearing, horses and all, behind a ridge.

"Scared 'em," Preacher opined. "They ain't used to repeaters; all they know is single shots. Let me get something outta my pack. I'll show you a thing or two."

Preacher went to one of his pack animals, untied one of the side packs, and let it fall to the ground. He pulled out the most beautiful rifle Kirby had ever seen.

"Damn!" Emmett softly swore. "The blue-bellies had some of those toward the end of the war. But I never could get my hands on one."

Preacher smiled and pulled another Henry repeating rifle from his pack. Unpredictable as mountain men were, he tossed the second Henry to Emmett, along with a sack of cartridges.

"Now we be friends," Preacher said. He laughed, exposing tobacco-stained stubs of teeth.

"I'll pay you for this," Emmett said, running his hands over the sleek barrel.

"Ain't necessary," Preacher replied. "I won both of 'em in a contest outside Westport Landing. Kansas City to you. 'Sides, somebody's got to look out for the two of you. Ya'll liable to wander 'round out here and get hurt. 'Pears to me don't neither of you know tit from tat 'bout stayin' alive in injun country."

"You may be right," Emmett admitted. He loaded the Henry. "So thank you kindly."

Preacher looked at Kirby. "Boy, you heeled—so you gonna get in this fight, or not?"

"Sir?"

"Heeled. Means you carryin' a gun, so that makes you a man. Ain't you got no rifle 'cept that muzzle loader?"

"No, sir."

"Take your daddy's Sharps, then. You seen him load it, you know how. Take that tin box of tubes too. You watch out for our backs. Them Pawnees—and they is Pawnees—likely to come 'crost that crick. You in wild country, boy . . . you may as well get bloodied."

"Do it, Kirby," his father said, "And watch yourself. Don't hesitate a second to shoot. Those savages won't show you any mercy, so you do the same to them."

Kirby, a little pale around the mouth, took up the heavy Sharps and the box of tubes, reloaded the rifle, and made himself as comfortable as possible on the rear slope of the slight incline, overlooking the creek.

"Not there, boy." Preacher corrected Kirby's position. "Your back is open to the front line of fire. Get behind that tree 'twixt us and you. That way, you won't catch no lead or arrow in the back."

The boy did as he was told, feeling a bit foolish that he had not thought about his back. Hadn't he read enough dime novels to know that? he chastised himself. Nervous sweat dripped from his forehead as he waited.

He had to go to the bathroom something awful.

A half hour passed, the only action the always-moving Kansas winds chasing tumbleweeds, the southward-moving waters of the creek, and an occasional slap of a fish.

"What are they waiting for?" Emmett asked the question without taking his eyes from the ridge.

"For us to get careless," Preacher said. "Don't you fret none . . . they still out there. I been livin' in and 'round injuns the better part of fifty year. I know 'em better—or at least as good—as any livin' white man. They'll try to wait us out. They got nothing but time, boys."

"No way we can talk to them?" Emmett asked, and immediately regretted saying it as Preacher laughed.

"Why, shore, Emmett," the mountain man said. "You just stand up, put your hands in the air, and tell 'em you want to palaver some. They'll probably let you walk right up to 'em. Odds are, they'll even let you speak your piece; they polite like that. A white man can ride into nearabouts any injun village. They'll feed you, sign-talk to you, and give you a place to sleep. 'Course . . . gettin' *out* is the problem.

"They ain't like us, Emmett. They don't come close to thinkin' like us. What is fun to them is torture to us. They call it testin' a man's bravery. If'n a man dies good—that is, don't holler a lot—they make it last as long as possible. Then they'll sing songs about you, praise you for dyin' good. Lots of white folks condemn 'em for that, but it's just they way of life.

"They got all sorts of ways to test a man's bravery and strength. They might—depending on the tribe—strip you, stake you out over a big anthill, then pour honey over you. Then they'll squat back and watch, see how well you die."

Kirby felt sick to his stomach.

"Or they might bury you up to your neck in the ground, slit your eyelids so you can't close 'em, and let the sun blind you. Then, after your eyes is burnt blind, they'll dig you up and turn you loose naked out in the wild . . . trail you for days, seein' how well you die."

Kirby positioned himself better behind the tree and quietly went to the bathroom. If a bean is a bean, the boy thought, what's a pea? A relief.

Preacher just wouldn't shut up about it. "Out in the deserts, now, them injuns get downright mean with they fun. They'll cut your eyes, cut off your privates, then slit the tendons in your ankles so's you can't do nothin' but flop around on the sand. They get a big laugh out of that. Or they might hang you upside down over a little fire. The 'Paches like to see hair burn. They a little strange 'bout that.

"Or, if they like you, they might put you through what they call the run of the arrow. I lived through that . . . once. But I was some younger. Damned if'n I want to do it again at my age. Want me to tell you 'bout that little game?"

"No!" Emmett said quickly. "I get your point."

"Figured you would. Point is, don't let 'em ever take you alive. Kirby, now, they'd probably keep for work or trade. But that's chancy, he being nearabout a man growed." The mountain man tensed a bit, then said, "Look alive, boy, and stay that way. Here they come." He winked at Kirby.

"How do you know that, Preacher? Kirby asked "I don't see anything."

"Wind just shifted. Smelled 'em. They close, been easin' up through the grass. Get ready."

Kirby wondered how the old man could smell anything over the fumes from his own body.

Emmett, a veteran of four years of continuous war, could not believe an enemy could slip up on him in open daylight. At the sound of Preacher jacking back the hammer of his Henry .44, Emmett shifted his eyes from his perimeter for just a second. When he again looked back at his field of fire, a big, painted-up buck was almost on top of him. Then the open meadow was filled with screaming, charging Indians.

Emmett brought the buck down with a .44 slug through the chest, flinging the Indian backward, the yelling abruptly cut off in his throat.

The air had changed from the peacefulness of summer quiet to a screaming, gun smoke-filled hell. Preacher looked at Kirby, who was looking at him, his mouth hanging open in shock, fear, and confusion. "Don't look at me, boy!" he yelled. "Keep them eyes in front of you."

Kirby jerked his gaze to the small creek and the stand of

timber that lay behind it. His eyes were beginning to smart from the pounding of the Henry .44 and the screaming and yelling. The Spencer that Kirby held at the ready was a heavy weapon, and his arms were beginning to ache from the strain.

His head suddenly came up, eyes alert. He had seen movement on the far side of the creek. Right there! Yes, someone or something was over there.

I don't want to shoot anyone, the boy thought. *Why can't we be friends with these people?* And that thought was still throbbing in his brain when a young Indian suddenly sprang from the willows by the creek and lunged into the water, a rifle in his hand.

For what seemed like an eternity, Kirby watched the young brave, a boy about his own age, leap and thrash through the water. Kirby jacked back the hammer of the Spencer, sighted in the brave, and pulled the trigger. The .52-caliber pounded his shoulder, bruising it, for there wasn't much spare meat on Kirby. When the smoke blew away, the young Indian was facedown in the water, his blood staining the stream.

Kirby stared at what he'd done, then fought back waves of sickness that threatened to spill from his stomach.

The boy heard a wild screaming and spun around. His father was locked in hand-to-hand combat with two knife-wielding braves. Too close for the rifle, Kirby clawed his Colt Navy from leather, vowing he would cut that stupid flap from his holster after this was over. He shot one brave through the head just as his father buried his Arkansas Toothpick to the hilt in the chest of the other.

And as abruptly as they came, the Indians were gone, dragging as many of their dead and wounded with them as they could. Two braves lay dead in front of Preacher; two braves lay dead in the shallow ravine with the three men; the boy

Kirby had shot lay in the creek, arms out-stretched, the waters a deep crimson. The body slowly floated downstream.

Preacher looked at the dead buck in the creek, then at the brave in the wallow with them, the one Kirby had shot. He lifted his eyes to the boy.

"Got your baptism this day, boy. Did right well, you did."

"Saved my life, son," Emmett said, dumping the bodies of the Indians out of the wallow. "Can't call you boy no more, I reckon. You be a man. now."

A thin finger of smoke lifted from the barrel of the Navy .36 Kirby held in his hand. Preacher smiled and spit tobacco juice.

He looked at Kirby's ash-blond hair. "Yep," he said. "Smoke'll suit you just fine. So Smoke it'll be."

"Sir?" Kirby finally found his voice.

"Smoke. That's what I'll call you now on. Smoke."*

Smoke forced his mind back to the present as Joey continued talking. "I been workin' with these cowboys fer two days now, an' I'm not too hopeful they'll be of much use to us when the goin' gits rough." He took a drink of coffee and flicked ash off his cigarette with his finger. "Don't git me wrong, they's all game as banty roosters, and they ain't afeared o' nothin', but I'm afraid these boys are gonna git theyselves kilt. They's good punchers an' kin all sit a hoss and wrangle beeves like they was born to it, but cain't but one or two hit a target with a shotgun from more'n twenty feet away. Another two or three are all right with a long gun as long as they got time ta git set an' take aim." He smirked. "'Course, that's when they ain't got hot lead buzzin' over they heads. In a pitched battle . . ." He shrugged his shoulders and stared down into his cup.

* *The Last Mountain Man*

Smoke frowned. "Maybe this wasn't such a good idea I had. I sure don't want the blood of these boys on my hands."

Cal came bursting in the door, pistol in his hand. "Smoke, Joey, we got riders comin'!"

Smoke and Joey grabbed iron and ran out the door.

15

In the distance, four riders rode at a leisurely pace toward the ranch house. As they approached, Joey, with both hands full of iron, said, "Murdock must not think too much of us ta send jest four hombres ta call."

Smoke frowned. "That doesn't seem likely." He reached inside the door and grabbed his binoculars and raised them to his eyes. After staring at the riders for a moment, he chuckled. "Well, I'll be damned." He handed the glasses to Joey. "Like the preacher always says, the good Lord will provide." He holstered his Colt and stepped out into the yard to greet their visitors.

When the men rode up, Pearlie slapped Cal on the shoulder. "Ol' Murdock better watch his ass now. We got reinforcements!"

Louis Longmont and his cook, André, were accompanied by Sheriff Monte Carson and the old mountain man, Puma Buck. André was leading a packhorse with two huge boxes strapped to its side.

The men dismounted and shook hands all around. Louis said, "Puma here came to town for supplies and I told him what you were doing. He said he had too many years invested in teaching you how to be a mountain man to let you come up here and be killed by flatlanders."

Puma leaned to the side and spit brown tobacco juice into the dirt. "That's right, boy," he said to Smoke, his faded blue eyes sparkling. "I promised Preacher I'd watch yer topknot, an' I intend to keep my word."

Louis added, "When he said he planned to come up here and assist you in your endeavor, I decided it was time I took a vacation." He patted the Colt tied down low on his thigh. "Besides, I've been neglecting my firearm practice, and a man in my profession cannot afford to get rusty."

Smoke smiled. "And André?"

The French cook gave a short bow. "Monsieur, food poisoning and malnutrition will kill as surely as a bullet. I am here to make sure that you are fed properly." He pointed at the boxes on the packhorse. "I purchased ample supplies in town so we may eat as God intended man to." Without another word he went into the house to inspect the kitchen facilities. He emerged a moment later, a look of disgust on his face as he emptied a pot of thick black coffee into the dirt. *"Merde,* it is worse than I suspected. You gentlemen will soon have coffee fit to drink." He motioned for Cal and Pearlie to bring in his supplies and turned back into the kitchen, mumbling to himself in French.

Smoke looked at Monte Carson. "What about you, Monte? Who's minding the town?"

Monte shrugged. "I figured it was time for Jim to take on some additional responsibility." He grinned. "When Ben Tolson wired me about your plans and about how you were outnumbered three to one and how Murdock was sending all over the country for hard men to come try your hand, I thought it was time I paid my old ridin' partner a visit. It may have been a few years, but I ain't forgotten how you helped me out when I needed it."

"How'd you all get here so soon?"

Puma Buck glared at Smoke. "We rode on that infernal Iron Horse goin' quicker than God ever intended man to go!" He sniffed and spit again. "I'll tell you what, son, that's the first time this old beaver's been scairt in twenty years."

Joey laughed. "When was the last time ya was scairt, Mr. Puma?"

Puma glanced at Joey and winked. "Back in the winter o' fifty-three, when an injun squaw tole me she was gonna move into my lean-to, permanent!"

André stuck his head out of the door. "Gentlemen, coffee is served."

The group sat around a large dining room table and helped themselves to mugs of André's dark, rich coffee. Puma Buck took a tentative sip and made a face.

André glared at the old mountain man. "You do not approve of my coffee, monsieur?"

Puma took another drink and swished it around in his mouth. "Oh, it tastes jest fine, Mr. André. Right flavorful."

Smoke grinned. "The coffee is excellent, André, it's just that Puma is used to mountain-man coffee. It's a mite . . . thicker."

Puma nodded. "Like my old friend Preacher used to say, the secret to good *cafecito* is it don't take near as much water as you think it do."

As the men laughed, Smoke said, "When a mountain man's through drinking his coffee, he uses what's left over to paint the side of his lean-to. It fills the chinks and keeps wind from whistling through the cracks."

Puma nodded, pursing his lips. "It does git a mite chill up in the high lonesome, boys." His faded blue eyes twinkled and Smoke knew a tall tale was about to follow.

"Why, jest last winter, another ol' mountain man, Dupree, and I was sittin' 'round the fire after a blizzard blew through, an' it was so cold, we had to thaw our words out in a skIllet 'fore we could hear what we was sayin'."

Cal's eyes grew wide, "Jimmy," he said in an awed voice.

Puma glanced at him and smiled. "Yeah, it was so cold that winter, our piss froze 'fore it hit the ground." He took a half-smoked cigar out of his pocket and lit the stub. "We had yeller icicles all 'round camp till the spring thaw."

After a few more stories of mountain lore, the men got serious. Smoke stood and said, "Thanks to our friends from Big Rock, the odds against us are a little better, but we're still sitting ducks out here in the open. Now"—he leaned forward, both hands on the table—"here's what I plan to do to even the odds a little more . . ."

After he finished outlining his plans, Smoke took his visiting friends on a short tour of the ranch. He especially wanted them to become familiar with the terrain surrounding and near the ranch house itself. He led them through a small copse of trees off to the right, a pile of boulders less than a hundred yards from the house, and along a dry creek bed that ran from the left of the house out toward the barns and corrals.

Puma looked around at what Smoke had shown them, then nodded as he recalled Smoke's plan of defense for the ranch. "You got a tricky mind fer a young beaver, Smoke." He lit a cigar and smiled through the smoke. "Ol' Preacher'd be right proud of his young'un if'n he were here."

"Thanks, Puma." Smoke rode back to the ranch house but stayed on his horse as the others dismounted. "Joey, hold on a minute. Let's you and me head on into Pueblo and have a talk with Ben to see what the latest is on Murdock's men coming into town."

Louis said, "You want some company, Smoke?"

"No, Louis. I'd just as soon not have anyone else in town see you. No need for Murdock to know we have help."

"Well, you ride with your guns loose, compadre. Murdock may have some men staked out in town just waiting for a chance at your back."

Smoke inclined his head at the short cowboy riding next to him. "Why do you think I asked Joey to ride along? Because of his good looks?"

Joey grinned, rubbing the deep scar on his face. "Must be that, 'cause I cain't cook worth a damn."

"If you all can get some of those traps and deadfalls and such ready, I'd appreciate it. There's no telling how much time we have before Murdock gets tired of waiting."

Louis tipped his hat. "You got it, boss. We'll stay out here miles from civilization and women and whiskey and cards and do all the dirty work while you go into town and have some fun."

Smoke just shook his head, chuckling as he and Joey rode off toward Pueblo.

When they reached the city limits, Smoke and Joey both reached down and loosed the rawhide thongs on their hammers. They knew they were riding into danger, for there were always cowards and back-shooters who wanted to earn reward money the easy way. Smoke intended to show them it wasn't going to be as easy as they counted on.

As they progressed down Main Street, both pair of eyes were constantly searching for the furtive move, the too-quickly averted face, the downcast eyes. Both also kept their eyes peeled for movement on rooftops and in darkened alleyways, favorite spots for ambushes.

They reached Tolson's office without incident and went inside. He was at his desk, poring over a stack of wanted posters and telegraph wires from other sheriffs in the surrounding states. He looked up quickly when they opened the door, his hand going automatically toward the short-barreled Greener on his desk.

"Whoa there, Ben. It's just us," Smoke said with a smile. "Getting kinda jumpy?"

Tolson grinned, sitting in his chair and putting his feet up on his desk. "Grab a sit-down, boys. There's coffee in the pot, but it might be a bit thick by now. It's been cookin' since noon."

Smoke said no thanks while Joey poured himself a cup. "Any news from our friend?" Smoke asked, sitting across from Ben in one of two straight-back chairs in front of his desk.

Tolson nodded. "There's been a steady stream of newcomers to town, some of 'em pretty rough-lookin' characters. A couple, with faces I recognized on the posters here, I either sent away or run out of town. But it's gettin' honest folks won't hardly go into the saloon at all, and I stay away unless I got at least two deputies with me."

Joey frowned. "It gettin' that bad, Ben?"

The sheriff shrugged. "Oh, it's okay, I guess. The obvious gun hawks, the real ones with some experience, know not to make trouble in town. It's the others that are gettin' out of hand."

Smoke smiled, looking at Joey, who nodded. "You mean the young punks with the ivory-handled pistols with notches cut in the handles and an attitude like a dog with a sore paw?" Smoke asked.

"Or the ones who walk around town pickin' fights with store clerks and farmers, acting mean and nasty so everybody will know they're tough?"

Ben grinned. "I can see you have both had some experience with these idiots. Half the time I don't know whether to laugh or to beat the shit out of the little snots."

Joey's face grew serious. "You cain't afford to take them too lightly, Ben. 'Member, a slug from an idiot will make you just as dead as one from an expert." He shook his head. "Over the years, my . . . notoriety has caused me to have to face down dozens of these young punks. I have tried my best not ta kill them, but they are usually too stupid to take a chance ta live if you give it to 'em."

Smoke looked out the window at the setting sun. "Ben,

you have been working too hard. How about if Joey and I take you to the saloon for a couple of drinks, then over to the hotel for a steak about two inches thick?"

Tolson arched an eyebrow. "You want to check out the saloon and see what riffraff is there now, don't you?"

"Sure," Smoke answered. "Sometimes a little show of force will save lives in the long run."

Tolson got his hat and Greener and walked with Smoke and Joey down the street to the saloon. As they approached, two men with unshaven faces and wrinkled, dirty clothes threw their cigarettes down and stepped into the saloon ahead of them.

Joey said, "Uh-oh. We may have trouble."

Tolson asked, "Why?"

Smoke answered, having noticed the two men just as Joey had. "Those two men ducked into the saloon when they saw us coming. Now, they may just want a front seat for the action, or they may be getting set to hit us as we come through the front door, 'fore out eyes adjust to the lights inside."

Joey touched Tolson on the shoulder. "Ben, why don't you and your Greener hurry up on ahead of us and slip in the back door to the place. Give a whistle if we need to come in with our hands full of iron."

He nodded and jogged on ahead of the pair of gunfighters, who continued to saunter down the street as if they hadn't a care in the world.

At the batwings they paused, then, hearing no whistle, pushed through and in.

The saloon was crowded, men standing elbow to elbow at the bar, and almost every seat at every table taken. The piano player was plunking his keys, looking nervously over his shoulder, sweat pouring off his forehead and staining his shirt.

Smoke saw Tolson in the rear of the room, next to a post. He spread his arms and shrugged; he hadn't seen anything suspicious.

Smoke glanced at the second-story balcony, but there was no one there and all the doors he could see were shut. They would have ample warning if someone tried to step out of a door and shoot them from above.

Joey looked around the room, his eyes passing over, then stopping and returning to the piano player, whose face looked like that of a man about to faint.

Joey stepped a couple of feet to the side and said quietly, "Smoke," and inclined his head to the piano man.

Smoke nodded. "It doesn't seem that hot in here to me, does it to you, Joey?"

Joey shook his head. He pointed at the piano player and said, "Move aside, please."

The man dove off his bench just as two men rose up from behind the piano with guns in their hands. Before the two could pull triggers, both Joey's and Smoke's hands were full of iron and their Colts were exploding, spitting flame, smoke, and lead.

The two men were both hit in the face and neck and chest, being thrown backward and up against a wall, where they slid to the floor, leaving trails of blood on the wall. Before the echoes of the shots had stopped, Smoke and Joey had holstered their guns and were taking seats at a table in a corner. The two men who were already seated at the table got hastily to their feet and walked to the bar, squeezing in among the men gathered there.

Ben Tolson pushed through the crowd and took one of the empty seats next to Smoke. "How'd you men know they was there?" he asked.

Smoke shrugged. "Instinct, I guess. The place was too quiet. Other than the piano playing, there wasn't the usual talking and yelling you see when there's a group of men getting seriously drunk."

Joey nodded. "They was all standing, staring, as if they was waitin' fer somethin' ta happen. When I saw the piano player was the only man in the place makin' a racket, an' he was sweatin' to beat the band"—Joey shrugged too—"I figgered somethin' behind the piano must be makin' him powerful nervous."

Tolson shook his head. "Boys, I spent half my life on the owl hoot trail, and you two make me feel like I didn't learn nothin'."

Smoke smiled a sad smile. "Well, it's not exactly the kind of knowledge one is proud to have acquired."

Joey looked around at the other men in the saloon, then nudged Smoke with his elbow. "Would ya look at that, Smoke?"

Smoke followed his gaze to a group of men at a table across the room. They were all wearing what they evidently thought rough and tough gunfighters ought to wear: fancy silk shirts in black and red, shiny boots with elaborate engraved designs in the leather, and double-holster rigs with pearl-handled or fancy carved butts on their pistols. A couple even had silver belt buckles and conchos on their hatbands.

Smoke laughed out loud, turning to say to Joey, "They look more like San Francisco pimps than gunmen."

Joey cut a plug of Bull Durham and stuck it in his mouth. As he chewed, he smiled back. "You know, Smoke, over the years I met quite a few o' the best shootists in the country." He shook his head. "An' ain't one of 'em ever dressed like thet."

One of the men across the way, so young the mustache he was trying to grow looked like it had been chewed on by a rat, called out, "You gents see somethin' you think is funny?"

The saloon got suddenly quiet as everyone waited to see what would happen.

Smoke said, "And who might you be, young man?"

The skinny youth, acne still on his face, sat up straight and tugged at his vest. "I'm the San Francisco Kid."

This caused both Smoke and Joey to throw back their heads and guffaw uncontrollably.

The San Francisco Kid stood up, hands next to nickel-plated Peacemakers in a double rig. "I don't let nobody laugh at me, mister, especially not some old has-been gunslingers."

An older man sitting next to him stood up too. "And I think you owe this man an apology."

"And you are?" Joey asked, trying to control his grin.

"Turkey Creek Bob Jackson."

Smoke sobered. He had heard of Jackson. He had a reputation as a man who enjoyed killing, especially when he could do it from behind. He was a bounty hunter, and always brought his men in across their saddles, usually shot in the back.

Smoke and Joey got to their feet while Ben scooted his chair back out of the way. Smoke said, "I hear you should change your name to Back-shooting instead of Turkey Creek."

"Go for your guns, you old farts," the Kid called, hunching his shoulders and spreading his fingers out, getting ready.

Joey asked, "How much money ya' got, Kid?"

A puzzled expression came on his face. "Why?"

Joey shrugged. "Just wanted to, know if ya got enough on ya to pay the undertaker fer buryin' ya."

The Kid looked around, eyes flicking over the crowd. "I ain't gonna need buryin', you are."

"How about you, Bob?" Smoke asked. "You earned any money by shooting someone in the back this week?"

Bob began to sweat, realizing he had backed himself into a corner. "Wait . . . wait a minute." He held out his hands, palms out. "This ain't no affair of mine."

Smoke said, "Then you shouldn't have bought chips if you didn't want dealt into this hand. Now, slap leather, or drop your guns and crawl out of here on your yellow belly."

That was too much even for the coward named Bob. Both he and the Kid grabbed iron. Smoke and Joey fired their Colts at almost the same time, Joey's shot hitting the Kid in the stomach and doubling him over, to sprawl facedown on the table. Smoke's bullet hit Bob in the base of his throat, punching through and blowing out his spine, almost decapitating him. Neither of the men had cleared leather. Both their pistols were still in their holsters.

Joey walked over and gently lowered the Kid to the floor. "What's yore real name, Kid?" Joey asked as his eyes fluttered open.

"Jesus, it hurts . . . it hurts so bad."

"Not for long, Kid, it'll be over soon," Joey whispered.

"My name's Sammy, Sammy Beaufort." He reached up and grabbed Joey's shirt. "Will you have someone wire my ma? She lives in Denver. Let her know . . . tell her . . ." The Kid's eyes glazed over, staring at eternity.

"Damn that Murdock," Joey growled. He looked up at Smoke and Ben and his eyes were wet. "I thought when I settled with Vasquez, it'd be enough." He shook his head. "Now he's done made me kill this boy, all 'cause o' that reward he put on our heads."

Joey stood and faced the crowd. "I tell all of ya, git the word ta Murdock. The next time I see him, I'm gonna dust him through and through, whether he's heeled or not. There won't be any talkin' or jawin', but the lead is damn shore gonna fly. Let him know!"

16

On the way back to the Rocking C ranch, Joey and Smoke rode with their guns loose. They knew it was even money whether Murdock would have men posted on the trail back to Smoke's ranch. Ben had offered to send some men with them, but they declined.

"No need of putting your men in danger, Ben. We're in this until it's over and we can't hide behind your deputies all the time."

"'Sides," Joey said, sticking a plug of tobacco in his mouth, "Smoke and me can take care o' ourselves pretty good."

Tolson grinned. "Damned if you can't." He stuck out his hand. "Ride easy, men, and watch your rear."

"Onliest way ta ride nowadays," Joey answered.

They stepped into their saddles and rode out of town at an easy canter, in no great hurry.

As they rode, Smoke cut his eyes over at Red, Joey's big roan stallion. "That Red is some animal, Joey."

Joey reached up and patted his mount's neck. "Yeah, he is. He ain't never let me down, an' we been in some pretty tough spots together. He's outrun an' outlasted ever kinda animal from Indian ponies to Thoroughbred Morgans from England." He grinned at Smoke, his teeth white under a full moon. "Long as he gits his grain, he'll run till I tell 'im ta stop or his heart bursts, whichever comes first."

Smoke nodded. "Same with Horse here. He's bred out of an old Palouse Preacher gave me name of Seven, but he's got more bottom than most Palouse ponies and an easier gait for long riding."

Joey glanced at Horse. "Yeah, he looks ta be a mighty fine piece o' horseflesh."

"When this is over, if we're still upright, how about you letting me breed a couple of Palouse mares I've got back at Sugarloaf to Red? Might make some interesting colts."

"Only if you let me take one or two back to Texas with me."

"Deal," Smoke said, "if you go back to Texas."

Joey's eyes narrowed. "What's that supposed ta mean?"

"Well, I thought when Betty and Tom are healed enough to travel, we might just bring them on up here and let them take a look at Colorado." Smoke shrugged. "After all, I already have one ranch, and someone's going to have to run the Rocking C after I leave." He looked at Joey. "I figure you'd be the logical one for that job, if you're interested."

Joey stared at Smoke for a moment. "This wouldn't be in the way o' charity, would it?"

"Hell no. Remember, we're all part owners of the ranch, in it together. I'm going to expect a good return on my money, and you'll earn everything you make, believe me."

Joey nodded. "I'll think on it, Smoke, I surely will." He glanced up at the sky, shining golden in moonlight, snow-covered peaks glistening and sparkling like they were sprinkled with diamond dust. "It is a mighty purty country, one God has smiled on, I think."

They were about halfway to the Rocking C, with heavy timber on either side of the trail, when Joey whistled softly to himself. "Smoke, look up yonder, 'bout a hundred yards or so, on top o' that small hillock. There's some boulders and such, an' I just caught a glimpse of somethin' shiny up there, like moonlight reflectin' off a gun barrel."

Smoke cut his eyes northward but couldn't see anything amiss. "Tell you what, Joey"—he glanced at scudding clouds in the sky—"those clouds are going to cover the moon in a minute. When it gets dark, turn Red into the timber. I'll follow, and then we can injun up on whoever is up there waiting on us."

"You got it, partner."

Five minutes later the moon disappeared behind the clouds and the two men pulled their mounts into the forest on the left side of the trail. They stepped out of their saddles and crouched behind a large stand of pines. Without a word both men knelt in the sandy loam and smeared the dark dirt over their faces and hands to hide their white skin. Then, simultaneously, they pulled their knives from scabbards and took off at a trot through the woods toward a small rise ahead.

At the foot of the hill Smoke waved Joey to the left and he slipped to the right, neither making a sound on the soft carpet of pine needles underfoot.

Slowing to a careful walk, Smoke inched up the rising ground, shuffling his feet so as not to break a branch and give their enemies any warning.

He crouched at the base of a series of boulders and listened. He heard a slight cough and the creaking of leather as someone shifted position above.

Smoke put his back to the rock and eased around it, to find four men kneeling with rifles aimed at the trail below.

One of the men whispered to another, "They oughta be outta those trees by now. What the hell are they doin' takin' so long?"

"You think they saw us, Jesse?" the man answered.

"Naw, they couldn't see this far at night, even with the moon."

"I don't like this, Dave," another said, his voice hoarse. "I'm shaggin' outta here, boys."

Smoke saw Joey's face appear at the other side of the small clearing, and he nodded at him.

As the man stood and turned to leave, he found himself face-to-face with a huge shape with a blackened face. Smoke growled, "Too late, partner," and stuck his knife to the hilt in the startled man's chest just below the rib cage, angling the blade upward to pierce his heart.

With a short, sobbing gasp, the man looked at the hilt of the blade, then up at Smoke. His eyes clouded and he fell facedown with a soft thump.

Jesse looked back over his shoulder, "Willie, what's . . ."

Smoke stepped toward him, holding his blood-smeared knife in front of him. "Willie's dead, and you're next," he said.

Jesse yelled, "You!"

Smoke said, "Yeah, howdy," and slashed backhanded across Jesse's throat, nearly severing his head from his body. Jesse croaked and gurgled, strangling on his own blood and fell, clutching his bloody neck in both hands.

"Son of a bitch," one of the others yelled, and pointed his rifle at Smoke.

To Smoke, in the moonlight, the hole in the end of the Winchester's barrel looked big enough to fall into.

As the man sighted along the rifle barrel, his eyes suddenly opened wide and he screamed a blood-curdling scream into the night. "Aiyee . . ." and pitched forward onto his rifle with Joey's Arkansas Toothpick protruding from his spine.

The final man aimed his rifle and pulled repeatedly on the trigger, getting nothing but metallic clicks for his troubles. Joey stepped to him and hit him flush in the mouth with a balled-up fist, flattening his nose and sending blood spraying into the air.

The assassin's eyes crossed, and he fell as if he had been poleaxed, unconscious before he hit the ground.

"Ya gotta cock it first, dummy," Joey said to the fallen man.

Smoke dipped his head. "Thanks, Joey."

Joey shrugged, "Better late than never, I guess."

"I'd say you were right on time, partner."

Smoke bent and effortlessly picked the unconscious man off the ground and slung him over his shoulder. "Let's find their horses and we'll take them and this hombre back with us to the ranch," Smoke said.

"Okay," Joey answered as he bent to pull his knife from the back of the dead bushwhacker.

Joey and Smoke passed two sentries at the edge of his property and waved as they rode on by. "Good to see the boys are taking this seriously," Joey observed.

Smoke nodded. "Yes. Wouldn't do for us to be caught napping when Murdock sends his men to call."

As they approached the ranch house, Smoke and Joey saw a large campfire built about twenty yards from the house.

"What the hell?" Joey said.

Smoke grinned. "That's probably Puma. He never could abide sleeping indoors unless there was a blizzard howlin', and then he'd bitch about feeling closed in."

Sure enough, Puma was sitting cross-legged in front of the fire, Cal and Pearlie sprawled on the ground in front of him, listening raptly to his tall tales of the good old days.

Louis Longmont and Monte Carson had carried chairs from inside the house and were sitting there, listening and drinking coffee. When Louis saw Smoke and Joey arrive, he inclined his head toward Puma and rolled his eyes, grinning.

Puma was telling the boys about the time Smoke had called twenty old mountain men in from the high lonesome to help him deal with Tilden Franklin and his bunch of hired killers.

"You shoulda seen it, boys, some of those coots were pushin' eighty and more. They was spoilin' fer one more fight, didn't none of 'em wanna die in bed." He lit a stubby cigar off a burning twig from the fire and stared at the two young boys in front of him. "The only fittin' way fer a mountain man to die is with his guns blazin' in a hail of lead."

He took a sip of his coffee and made a face. "Anyway, there was at least twenty of the wildest, rootin'est, tootin'est old beavers that ever forded a mountain stream all gathered together to give Preacher's boy a hand. There was Charlie Starr, Luke Nations, Pistol Le Roux, Bill Foley, Dan Greentree, Leo Wood, Cary Webb, Sunset Hatfield, Crooked John Simmons, Bull Flagler, Toot Tooner, Sutter Cordova, Red Shingletown"—he paused—"give me some time and I'll name some more."

Pearlie glanced at Cal. "He's tellin' the truth, Cal. I was there fer that fracas."

Puma continued. "Old Tilden Franklin and his gunnies was holed up in a town he'd founded named Fontana. Well, there wasn't no other way so the mountain men headed on into the jaws of hell. . . ."

Hardrock, Moody, and Sunset were sent around to the far end of town, stationed there with rifles to pick off any TF gun hand who might try to slip out, either to run off or try and angle around behind Smoke and his party for a box-in.

The others split up into groups of twos and threes and rode bunched over, low in the saddle, to present a smaller target for the riflemen they had spotted lying in wait on the rooftops in Fontana. And they rode in a zigzagging fashion, making themselves or their horses even harder to hit. But even with that precaution, two men were hit before they reached the town limits. Beaconfield was knocked from the saddle by rifle fire. The one-time Tilden Franklin supporter wrapped a bandanna around a bloody arm, climbed back in the saddle, and, cursing, continued onward. Hurt, but a hell of a long way from being out.

The old gunfighter, Linch, was hit just as he reached the town. A rifle bullet hit him in the stomach and slapped him out of the saddle. The aging gun hand, pistols in his hands, crawled to the edge of a building and began laying down a withering line of fire, directed at the rooftops. He managed to knock out three snipers before a second bullet ended his life.

Leo Wood, seeing his long-time buddy die, screamed his outrage and stepped into what had once been a dress shop, pulling out both Remington Frontier .44s, and letting 'em bang.

Leo cleared the dress shop and all TF riders before a single shot from a Peacemaker .45 ended his long and violent life.

Pearlie settled down by the corner of a building and with his Winchester .44-.40 began picking his shots. At ranges up to two hundred yards, the .44-.40 could punch right through the walls of the deserted buildings of Fontana. Pearlie killed half a dozen TF gun hawks without even seeing his targets.

A few of Tilden's hired guns, less hardy than they thought, tried to slip out the rear of the town. They went down under the rifle fire of Moody, Hardrock, and Sunset. Bill Foley, throwing caution to the wind, like most of his friends having absolutely no desire to spend his twilight years in any old folks home, stepped into an alley where he knew half a dozen TF gunnies were waiting and opened fire. Laughing, the old gunfighter took his time and picked his shots while his body was soaking up lead from the badly shaken TF men. Foley's old body had soaked up a lot of lead in its time, and he knew he could take three or four shots and still stay upright in his boots. Foley, who had helped tame more towns than most people had ever been in, died with his boots on, his back to a wall, and his guns spitting out death. He killed all six of the TF gunslicks.

Toot Tooner, his hands full of Colts, calmly walked into what was left of the Blue Dog Saloon, through the back door, and said, "I declare this here game of poker open. Call or fold, boys"

Then he opened fire.

His first shots ended the brief but bloody careers of two cattle rustlers from New Mexico who had signed on with the TF spread in search of what Tilden had promised would be easy money. They died without having the opportunity to fire a shot.

Toot took a .45 slug in the side and it spun him around. Lifting his pistol, he shot the man who had shot him between the eyes just as he felt a hammer blow in his back, left side. The gunshot knocked him to his knees and he tasted blood in his mouth.

Toot dropped his empty Colts and pulled out two Remington .44s from behind his gun belt. Hard hit, dying, Toot laughed at death and began cocking and firing as the light before his eyes began to fade.

"Somebody kill the old son of a bitch!" a TF gunhand shouted.

Toot laughed at the dim figure and swung his guns. A slug took him in the gut and set him back on his butt. But Toot's last shots cleared the Blue Dog of hired guns. He died with a very faint smile on his face.

Louis Longmont met several TF gun hands in an alley. The gambler never stopped walking as his Colts spat and sang a death song. Reloading, he stepped over the sprawled bloody bodies and walked on up the alley. A bullet tugged at the sleeve of his coat and the gambler dropped to one knee, raised both guns, and shot the rifleman off the roof of the bank building. A bullet knocked Louis to one side and his left arm grew numb. Hooking the thumb of his left hand behind his gun belt, the gambler rose and triggered off a round, sending another one of Tilden Franklin's gun slicks to hell.

Louis then removed a white linen handkerchief from an inside breast pocket of his tailored jacket. He plugged the hole in his shoulder and continued on his hunt.

The Reverend Ralph Morrow stepped into what had been the saloon of Big Mama and the bidding place of her soiled doves and began working the lever on his Henry .44. The boxer-turned-preacher-turned-farmer-turned-gunfighter muttered a short prayer for God to forgive him and began blasting hell out of any TF gun hawks he could find.

His Henry empty, Ralph jerked out a pair of .45s and began smoking. A lousy pistol shot, and that is being kind, Ralph succeeded in filling the beery air with a lot of hot lead. He didn't hit a damn thing with the pistols, but he did manage to scare the hell out of those gun hands left standing after his good shooting with the rifle. They ran out the front of the saloon and directly into the guns of Pistol Le Roux and Dan Greentree.

Ralph reloaded his rifle and stepped to the front of the building. "Exhilarating!" he exclaimed. Then he hit the floor as a hard burst of gunfire from a rooftop across the street tore through the canvas and wood of the deserted whorehouse.

"Shithead!" Ralph muttered, lifting his rifle and sighting the gunman in. Ralph pulled the trigger and knocked the TF gunman off the roof.

Steve Matlock, Ray Johnson, Nolan, Mike Garrett, and Beaconfield were keeping a dozen or more TF gun slicks pinned down in Beeker's general store.

Charlie Starr had cleared a small saloon of half a dozen hired guns and now sat at a table, having a bottle of sweetened soda water. He would have much preferred a glass of beer, but the sweet water beat nothing. Seeing a flash of movement across the street, Charlie put down the bottle and picked up a cocked .45 from the table. He sighted the TF gun hand in and pulled the trigger. The slug struck the man in the shoulder and spun him around. Charlie shot him again in the belly, and that ended it.

"Now leave me alone and let me finish my sodie water," Charlie muttered.

The Silver Dollar Kid came face-to-face with Silver Jim. The old gunfighter grinned at the punk. Both men had their guns in leather.

"All right, Kid," Silver Jim said. "You been lookin' for a rep. Here's your chance."

The Silver Dollar Kid grabbed for his guns.

He never cleared leather. Silver Jim's guns roared and bucked in his callused hands. The Kid felt twin hammer blows in his stomach. He sat down in the alley and began hollering for his mother.

Silver Jim stepped around the punk and continued his prowling. The Kid's hollering faded as life ebbed from him.

Smoke met Luis Chamba behind the stable. The Mexican gunfighter grinned at him. "Now, Smoke, we see just how good you really are."

Smoke lifted his sawed-off shotgun and almost blew the gunfighter in two. "I already know how good I am," Smoke said. "I don't give a damn how good you . . . were."

Smoke reloaded the ten-gauge sawed-off and stepped into a stable. He heard a rustling above him and lifted the twin muzzles. Pulling the triggers, blowing a hole the size of a bucket in the boards, Smoke watched as a man, or what was left of a man, hurled out the loft door to come splatting onto the shit-littered ground.

Smoke let the shotgun fall to the straw as the gunfighter Valentine faced him.

"I'm better," Valentine said, his hands over the butts of his guns.

"I doubt it," Smoke said, then shot the famed gunfighter twice in the belly and chest.

With blood streaking his mouth, Valentine looked up from the floor at Smoke. "I . . . didn't even clear leather."

"You sure didn't," the young man said. "We all got to meet him, Valentine, and you just did."

"I reckon." Then he died.

Listening, Smoke cocked his head. Something was very wrong. Then it came to him. No gunfire. It was over.*

"Jiminy," Cal whispered as Puma finished his story. Then Cal punched Pearlie in the shoulder, giving him a hard look. "Why didn't you tell me about that, you skunk?"

Pearlie blushed. "Shucks, Cal. I didn't do much, Smoke and the mountain men did most of the fightin'."

Louis Longmont stood and stretched. "Puma, you oughta write penny dreadfuls, the way you embellish a story so."

Puma looked up through slitted eyes. "I don't know what that word means, but I hope fer yore sake it don't mean what I think it do!"

Monte laughed. "No, Puma, he just means you tell a hell of a fine tale."

Smoke stepped out of his saddle and pulled on his dally rope, bringing the horse with the unconscious ambusher forward. They had slung him over the saddle and tied his hands to his feet under the bronc's belly.

When Joey cut him down and rolled him over onto his back in the dirt, Pearlie said, "Jesus, what happened to his face? A mule kick him?"

Smoke grinned. "No, it was just Joey's fist."

Louis called out to the ranch house, "André, some coffee for Smoke and Joey, please."

He looked at the blood-splattered shirts and dirt-covered faces of his two friends.

* Trail of the Mountain Man

"You two look like you've had an eventful ride back from town."

Smoke nodded. "Monte, would you see if you can wake up that galoot while Joey and I wash up? Then we'll see if he can give us any useful information about the size of Murdock's new gang."

17

Smoke's friends were arranged around the campfire when he and Joey finished washing the outlaws' blood off their faces and hands and changed clothes.

Smoke walked outside to stand over the man whose face Joey had smashed. He was conscious, tied hand and foot, and squirming on the ground, looking around at the unfriendly faces surrounding him.

"What's your name, cowboy?" Smoke asked, his tone neutral, neither friendly nor angry.

"Moses, Moses Jackson," the gunny answered, blood still trickling from his bent, shattered nose.

"Want to tell me why you and your friends were out there waiting to bushwhack Joey and me?"

"We weren't gonna kill you, we was just gonna—" He stopped, evidently in too much pain to think up a good lie.

"Uh-huh,"Joey growled, "you was jest sittin' there, guns cocked and aimed, waitin' to blow us to hell."

Moses lowered his eyes, moaning softly when movement caused his pain to flare.

"Did Murdock send you out to do us in?"

"I ain't sayin' anything else. Go on and get the sheriff and have him take me to jail."

"So that bastard Ben Tolson can let you escape? I don't think we'll send for him just yet," Smoke said, his tone becoming harder.

Puma Buck, his eyes feral in reflected firelight, stepped up to stand practically on top of the young man. "If he's not gonna talk, Smoke, let me skin 'im." He cast cold, furious eyes down at the gunman. "I ain't skinned nobody fer two, maybe three years now, but I'm damned if'n I've forgotten how to git the job done."

Moses' eyes widened at the sight of the old mountain man holding his sharp blade before him. Moses twisted his head around to look up at Smoke. "You can't let that old coot near me. I know my rights."

Joey squatted on his heels next to Moses' head. "You gotta right ta die, boy, that's all. The manner o' yore death is all we gotta decide now." He raised his eyes to stare at Puma's big buffalo-skinning knife. "Personally, as the galoot ya was fixin' ta back-shoot, I kinda like the idee of lettin' old Puma have his way with ya, 'specially since ya don't seem inclined ta tell us nothin' anyhow."

Monte leaned over the wounded man, eyes squinted and mean. "Skinnin's too good for him. Let's just scalp him, cut off his ears and dick, and send him back to Murdock." He grinned. "I'm sure they'll welcome him back with open arms, since he failed in his mission."

"You can't do that!" Moses hollered, twisting against his ropes. "Vasquez'll chop me to bits if you send me back." He looked from man to man, his eyes hopeful. "Just let me go and I'll ride out of Colorado and you'll never see me again."

Smoke chuckled low in his throat. "Cowboy, you're a confessed killer and back-shooter. Why would we let you ride off to hire out your gun and murder somebody else?"

"I swear, I'll put my guns up and never ever shoot anybody again."

At this, everyone around the fire laughed. The man obviously would say anything to save his worthless hide. They had all seen Sunday-morning drunks hung over after getting alkalied on Saturday night swear off booze. This was no different.

Puma placed his knife against Moses' chest and cut his shirt buttons off with a gentle movement. "Hmmm, looks like my old blade is a mite rusty and dull. That'll make skinnin' him awful tough. I might even have to take a rest in the middle o' the job 'fore I'm done and git back to it later."

"No, no, please . . ."

Smoke leaned over, his hands on his knees, staring down at Moses. "Then tell us what you know about Murdock's plans. How many men he has, when he plans to hit us, and who he's got riding with him."

Moses licked blood-caked lips, his eyes flicking from Puma's knife to Smoke and back again. "If I tell you what I know, will ya let me go?"

Smoke pursed his lips, appearing to consider the offer. "If what you have to say helps us, then I'll promise you we won't kill you. But"—he pointed his finger at the man—"if I let you ride out of here in one piece and I ever see you wearing a gun again, I swear I'll shoot you down without a second thought. Deal?"

Moses nodded vigorously. "Murdock's got at least forty or fifty men out at his ranch now, and more may be on the way." He glanced at Joey and Smoke. "I guess the chance to make a name by killin' you and Mr. Wells has attracted a whole bunch of hard men."

Joey smirked. "Havin' a chance to do it don't always git it done, son. Go on."

"Well, Murdock don't let the hired hands in on his plans, but I figger from the way he's talking, he is going to send his men out here to the ranch if he can't get you any other way. He's mighty pissed about you gunning down his brother."

Smoke nodded. "Any idea of when he plans to call the raid?"

Moses shook his head. "Like I said, I'm way down on the

totem pole, and he don't confide in me. But he did mention he was afraid if he waited overly long, the U.S. marshals would be called in, and he sure don't want that to happen."

Louis spoke up from the edge of the firelight. "You know any names of the gents riding with him?"

"Lord, you want me to name 'em all?"

"As many as you can remember," Smoke answered, and nodded at Louis, who took a small tablet from his coat pocket and a silver-encased pencil with which to write the names down.

"Well, there's a group of about eight or ten who said they owed you from when they went up in the mountains after you a couple o' years ago. They kinda hang together, always talking about how badly you treated 'em. Couple of 'em have some awful scars on their faces where they said you beat the shit out of 'em."

Smoke nodded. "That'd be the men riding with Curly Rogers. Dewey and Boots are the ones wearing scars on their faces from the last time I . . . had a talk with them. Horton, Max, Cates, Gooden, and Art South are the others I suspect have come to get their revenge after they failed to get the bounty on me during the Lee Slater mixup. Continue, Moses."

"There's a handful of half-breeds, Jake Sixkiller, Sam Silverwolf, and Jed Beartooth. They hang with a couple of Mexes name of Felix Salazar and Juan Jimenez, who said you boys killed some kin of theirs at the hotel in town the other night."

"Uh-huh, go on."

"Then there's some real bad hombres, those with a reputation already who aim to make their place in history, so they say. The Silverado Kid, Black Jack Morton, Bill Denver, One-Eye Jackson, and Slim Watkins." He paused and licked his lips again. "I think even Murdock and Vasquez are afraid of those gunmen."

Monte raised his eyebrows and looked at Joey, who was

frowning. They had all heard of these men, murderers, rapists, robbers, and killers every one. Men who enjoyed killing and maiming, whether for profit or just for the fun of it.

Moses inclined his head toward Puma. "There's even one like him, an old . . . an elderly man dressed all in buckskins and fur who looks older than dirt, with long, shaggy gray hair and beard. He says he's a mountain man named Beaver-pelt Solomon, and he wants a chance to kill some other man's kid, man name of Preacher."

Smoke glanced at Puma, whose face was red with anger. "That old bastard!" he exclaimed. "He once stole some beaver pelts from Preacher. Preacher beat the shit out of him and hung that moniker on 'im to let everyone know he was a thieving son of a bitch." He smiled savagely. "It worked, too, wouldn't nobody have nothin' to do with him after that." He looked off toward the mountain peaks in the distance. "The high lonesome can git mighty lonesome if'n even yore so-called friends won't palaver with ya once in a while, an' Beaverpelt wasn't welcome at anybody else's camps after Preacher put the word out on 'im."

"Any others?" Smoke asked Moses.

"Just Shotgun Sam Willowby and Gimpy Monroe. They're kinda old too, but they still know how to draw and fire. To hear them tell it, they was killin' people back in the gold rush days of forty-eight. The other day, a couple of the younger ones made the mistake of calling them old farts, and they blowed them to hell without even breaking a sweat." Moses' eyes were wide. "Then they put ropes on the bodies and dragged 'em out in the pasture for coyotes and wolves to eat!"

Smoke shook his head at the number of guns Murdock had been able to hire and the speed with which they'd all come to Colorado. "That about it?"

"Oh, there's a passel more, but not any other big names, just a bunch of men like me, trying to make a living the only way they know, from hiring out their guns. A group of men who fought down in New Mexico and Arizona during the time of the Lincoln County war. Pretty hard old boys, I suspect, but they keep to themselves and aren't much for bragging or fighting with the others." He hesitated, then said, "Oh there's one other man. Wears an old Union Army uniform coat and carries a sword on his belt. Says his name's Colonel Waters and he has a debt to pay to Joey Wells."

Joey smiled, but there was no warmth in it. "He was with the Redlegs who killed my men. He's the only one I couldn't track down. I was told he changed his name and moved back East to get away from me." His grin faded and his eyes turned snake hard. "Guess he got tired of runnin' and is ready to face his maker, and I intend to oblige him."

Smoke said, "That all you can tell us, Moses?"

"That's all I know, Mr. Jensen, honest."

"Put him on his horse, boys, but keep his guns and ammunition."

As Cal untied Moses, Smoke put his hand on his shoulder and stared into his eyes. "Just making sure I remember your face, son, 'cause if I ever see it again, you're a dead man. Now, get out of my sight."

"Thank you, Mr. Jensen, thank you," Moses said as he stepped into his saddle.

Puma waved his knife at the man. "Smoke's a generous man, Moses, don't you ever forget how close you came to tastin' my steel."

After Moses rode off at full gallop in case they changed their minds, Smoke poured himself a cup of coffee from a pot Puma had sitting on the campfire embers. He took a drink and looked around at his men, his expression grim.

"Boys, this doesn't sound at all good."

Monte nodded. "Murdock's sure got himself some prize shooters, that's for sure."

Louis said, "I've heard of some of them, of course, the

Silverado Kid and Black Jack Morton got run out of Tombstone a year or so ago. Evidently they were too mean for even that hellhole."

Monte added, "Yeah, it's said they killed women and kids, anybody who angered 'em, and they was easy to anger, so I've heard."

Smoke lit a cigar and puffed as he talked, the smoke whisked away on a cold wind blowing from the mountains. "The bunch riding with Curly Rogers are mean and won't hesitate to back-shoot a man, but they're not overly endowed with either courage or intelligence. Bill Denver and Slim Watkins made their name in the mining country of northern Colorado and New Mexico. There's paper out on them for robbing stages, trains, and miners. They killed without warning and without provocation, according to the newspaper accounts. They have ropes waiting for them in more than twenty towns I know of."

Monte said, "I ain't heard of but two of the half-breeds, Sam Silverwolf and Jed Beartooth, and they're both wanted in Arizona. Seems they like to rape women to death, mostly Indian women, or they wouldn't be alive to give us grief. I never read nor heard anything of Jake Sixkiller."

Cal said, "I have. Ned Buntline wrote a piece about him a few months ago in one of my dime novels. Sixkiller likes to use a shotgun loaded with nails and rocks and stuff, and then, if anybody's still alive, he scalps 'em." He frowned. "Buntline said he stayed mostly in California, but I guess he came east to get away from his reputation out there."

"What about Beaverpelt, Puma? He anything special to worry about?" Smoke asked.

"Not if you're armed and facin' him," the mountain man said with a look of disgust and loathing on his face. "He's a sneak and a coward. But he's supposed to be pretty good with an old Sharps .52 he carries. He's the only one we have to worry about doin' us any damage from a distance." He looked down at his knife and wiped it on his pants. "Let me take care of that ol' buzzard. It'd be my pleasure to finish what Preacher started years ago."

Smoke drained the last of his coffee from his mug. "I got an idea."

Louis smiled. "About time, boss. What is on your mind?"

Smoke glanced at Joey. "Joey, what is the last thing a commander with an overwhelming superiority in numbers and firepower expects the opposing army to do?"

Joey grinned and nodded. "Attack."

"How about we even up our odds a little?"

Monte's brow furrowed. "You can't mean we're gonna ride against Murdock and fifty men? That'd be suicide! They'd cut us down like autumn wheat."

"A frontal assault's not exactly what I had in mind. Sally brought some books back from her last trip out east to visit her parents. They were about some Japanese fighters called ninjas."

"What are ninjas?" Pearlie asked.

Louis answered in a thoughtful tone, his eyes on Smoke. "Individuals who swore allegiance to the warlords of feudal Japan, the shōgun. Ninja were called 'invisible killers' because they dressed all in black, attacked at night, and killed without being seen or heard, using their hands and short swords called *katana* on their victims."

Smoke grinned. "Exactly. We're about to become American ninjas."

18

Smoke said to his friends gathered around the campfire, "Here's what we're going to do. Joey, Puma, and me will infiltrate Murdock's compound. Louis, you and Monte and Cal and Pearlie are going to stay back a couple of miles from Murdock's ranch house to hold our horses and give us cover in case we have to make tracks out of there in a hurry. If they come chasing us, they'll ride right into your bullets without expecting an ambush."

Louis frowned. "How come you and Joey and Puma get to have all the fun while the rest of us stay on the outskirts of the action?"

"Because, you young pup," Puma said, "Joey learned how to sneak around enemy camps in the war, and Smoke and I learned how to injun up on people from the best teachers they is, mountain men."

Smoke put his hand on Louis's shoulder and said, "Puma's right, Louis. I know you're not afraid of the devil himself, and you're a hell of a shootist in a gunfight. In fact, there isn't a man I'd rather have on my right hand in a fracas than you. But this is different. One mistake, one inadvertent noise, one slipup, and you not only get *yourself* killed, but all of us. That's why I'm leaving you to the job you can do best, protecting our backs with your guns."

Louis held up his hands, smiling. "Okay, okay, you don't have to shine me on. I agree I haven't your experience in sneaking around at night and being quiet like a ninja, but at the first sound of gunfire, I'm not waiting to see if you come out of there, I'm coming in after you!"

"Me too," chimed in Monte.

Smoke nodded. "Fair enough. That okay with the rest of you—Cal, Pearlie?"

Pearlie nodded and Cal said, "Yes, sir, but I feel like Mr. Longmont. I'd rather be with you when you go in."

Pearlie jabbed him with an elbow, frowning.

"Well, I would," Cal said, rubbing his arm.

"I know you would, Cal, but this doesn't mean you're going to miss out on the action. Believe me, after we stir up this hornet's nest, there'll be enough fighting for all of us."

When he finished talking, Smoke went into the cabin and came out with a can of bootblack. "Here, all of you smear this over any skin showing. Also, I want you to take off anything that sparkles or makes noise, don't wear any spurs or metal that will clank or make a sound. Joey, I've got an extra pair of moccasins you can wear when we sneak into their camp."

"What about us?" Monte asked. "Why do we have to blacken our faces if we're not gonna be near the ranch house?"

Smoke said, "All of us need to do this. When there's a potential for a night fight, it never hurts to be prepared. Remember, they can't hit what they can't see, and remember how sound carries over open ground."

He looked at Pearlie. "You have that burlap sack I asked you to get for me?"

The young man nodded.

"Did you do what I asked you to do?"

"Yeah, I did it, but, boss, I gotta tell ya, I thought you was crazy."

Smoke grinned. "You see why, now?"

"I think so, an' I'm sure glad I'm on your side." He went over to the barn and returned a moment later with a large burlap sack with a cord tying off its opening. The bag had a lump in the bottom that writhed and moved on its own.

Joey's eyes lit up. "That what I think it is?"

"Yeah," Smoke answered.

"Whoo-eee, there's gonna be dancin' at Murdock's place tonight."

As they mounted up, Smoke said, "Remember, the object tonight isn't a high body count, the object is to spread fear. A scared man will frighten others, his fear spreading like a plague. A dead man is just dead."

Joey snorted. "'Course, a dead man cain't shoot ya neither."

On the way to Murdock's, Smoke stopped his group at the edge of his property and alerted the three men serving as sentries that they might be riding hard when they returned and not to fire on them inadvertently.

Smoke signaled his riders to a halt on a crest of a small rise, about two miles from Murdock's ranch house. It was a measure of Murdock's overconfidence in his superior numbers that he hadn't bothered to post guards.

Smoke put his field glasses to his eyes and swept the area for a moment. "I don't see anything between us and the ranch house. There's no sign of dogs or sentries."

Joey shook his head. "The man is dumb beyond belief."

"I guess he figures those desperadoes will protect him from harm," Louis said.

Smoke grinned in the darkness. "Well, we'll see about that shortly."

Smoke, Joey, and Puma dismounted, handing their reins to Louis and Monte, while Cal and Pearlie found some low rocks on the hillock to get behind. Louis made the mistake of asking Puma if he was going to be okay to walk the distance to the house.

Puma glared at him for a moment, then just smiled. "Yeah, an' I kin do it with ya on my back if'n I need to, young'un."

The trio took off toward Murdock's at a fast walk, estimating it would take them about twenty minutes to cover the two miles, being careful not to make any noise. Luckily, the fall skies were full of low-hanging storm clouds and the moon was already set for the night, so there was no light to give them away.

Murdock had two large corrals on the far side of his house, and both were full of mounts. Joey whispered he estimated there to be least fifty horses, maybe more.

The area around the house was quiet, and the bunkhouse was off on the other side of the corrals, almost two hundred yards from the ranch house. Smoke pointed to an area nearer the house, where there were several groups of widely spaced campfires burned down to glowing embers. He cupped his hands around his mouth and whispered, "The regular punchers are probably in the bunkhouse. I think the gun hawks are around the fires, sleeping outside."

The American ninjas noted there were five or six blanket-covered forms around each of the dying fires. Puma whispered, "I count twelve camps. There must be over sixty men down there."

Joey answered in a low voice. "That means either Moses was lyin' or more men have joined up in the last day or so."

Smoke nodded at Joey and motioned to the group of camps on the left with an outstretched ann. He touched Puma and pointed to the right, then, as they eased off, Smoke took the middle collection of sleepers.

Smoke walked slowly, shuffling his feet in the dirt so he

would not step on a twig or stick, and walked crouched over so as not to highlight himself against the horizon.

When he came to the closest of the sleeping outlaws, he put his sack down, placed his hand over the man's mouth, and sliced the blade of his Bowie knife quickly across his throat. The outlaw bucked and struggled for a moment, Smoke holding him down until he quieted, drowned in his own blood.

Smoke then made an incision around his head and pulled the killer's scalp free from his skull. He and Puma and Joey had agreed to kill only one man in each small camp, showing the others it could just have easily been them. He flipped the scalp onto the embers of the fire, where it began to slowly sizzle and burn. He then stepped to the next man and gently wrapped a rawhide thong around his boots, tying them together. A few feet farther on, he slipped a man's gun out of his holster, flipped open the loading gate, and emptied his shells in the dirt next to the fire, close to red-hot coals. Crawling to the next slumbering form, Smoke slit his belt and pants button with his Bowie knife. At the end of this group of men, Smoke opened the end of his sack and shook out one of its inhabitants, then quickly walked to the next camp, fifteen yards away, to repeat his actions.

Puma was overjoyed to find in his second group the mountain man known as Beaverpelt Solomon. He didn't want the thief and killer to die without knowing who did it, so Puma grabbed his mouth and pricked him lightly under the chin with the point of his skinning knife.

Beaverpelt's eyes started to open, then widened in surprise as he recognized Puma's blackened face leaning close to his in the darkness, the old man's eyes glittering white with hate. Puma held his knife where Beaverpelt could see it, whispering low in his ear, "Preacher and Smoke send their regards." As Beaverpelt reached up to grab Puma's hand, Puma sliced quickly across the mountain man's throat.

He held on tight, staring into Beaverpelt's face until both light and life died in his eyes.

Not content with merely scalping the traitor to the mountain men, Puma also slit his pants open and cut off his genitals, sticking them in his mouth to protrude obscenely from his beard.

Puma, like Smoke, unloaded many of the sleeping men's weapons and sprinkled bullets near the red-hot embers, knowing it wouldn't be long before they heated up enough to explode, sending slugs of lead flying everywhere.

Joey didn't scalp his last victim. After he was dead, he put his Arkansas Toothpick behind the man's neck and jerked quickly upward. The razor-sharp blade sliced through skin, vertebrae, and windpipe, severing the head from its body. Joey found a long stick next to the fire and impaled the head on it, its lifeless eyes looking nowhere. He stuck the other end in the dirt, to stand like a sentinel next to the man's headless body.

When Joey and Puma were through, Smoke went silently among all the camps, depositing some of his burlap sack cargo in each one.

He trotted back to them, in a hurry now because the burning scalps were beginning to make a terrible stench. The trio quickly walked for fifty yards, then stopped. They turned their backs to the camps so their lights wouldn't be seen, and Joey and Puma struck lucifers and lit cigars. Holding out the red-hot tips, they all lit fuses to bundles of dynamite and lobbed them into the camps, using the ones with longer fuses first and the shorter fuses last.

After they had thrown all they had, the three men began to jog away at a ground-eating pace toward the rise where their friends waited. About halfway there, they were met by Louis, leading their horses. As they climbed into their saddles, the bundles of dynamite began to explode, and men began to scream and shout. Guns were fired at shadows and at comrades, thought to be enemies in the darkness.

In one of the camps, Charlie Jacobson rolled over and stretched, yawning. His outstretched hand encountered something wet and sticky next to him. He leaned over toward Billy Preston, his riding partner, and gagged at what he saw. He opened his mouth to scream just as all hell broke loose around him.

A packet of two sticks of dynamite tied together exploded fifteen feet away, tearing bark off a nearby pine tree and sending razor-sharp shards of wood spinning through the night to impale Charlie's face and chest. Now he screamed as if his lungs would rupture.

Johnny Blackman jumped to his feet and started to run as dynamite went off behind him. He took one step, and his tied-together feet locked, sending him sprawling facefirst into the campfire embers. As he rolled away, red-hot bullet casings near the fire exploded, sending molten chunks of lead into Johnny's body in three places, killing him where he lay. His clothes, covered with embers, caught fire, and his flesh began to char and roast, adding to the horrible stink of burning scalps.

Willie Clayton rolled over at the first blast of dynamite and covered his head with his hands. As the echoes of the blast died down, he looked up, straight into the dead eyes of a head on a stick, staring sightless down at him. His mind snapped and he jumped to his feet, drew his pistol, and began to fire indiscriminately around at anything he saw moving. After he shot two of his camp mates, the third put a bullet into Willie to save his own life.

Felix Salazar jumped to his feet, his pistol in his hand. As he tried to run, his pants fell down and tripped him, to land squirming on his friend Juan Jimenez. Jimenez, frightened out of his wits, slashed his long stiletto blade into Salazar, ripping his abdomen open and spilling his guts in the dirt.

Jake Sixkiller's life ended when a packet of dynamite thrown by Joey landed two feet from his sleeping form. He rose when he heard the sputtering fuse and reached to grab it as it went off. It blew his right arm off at the shoulder, and the force of the explosion made pulp of his eyes and mincemeat of his face. The killer of women and children rolled in the dirt in blind agony, screaming for the mercy of a God he had always denied existed, until he bled to death.

Dewey, the man whose face Smoke had caved in and ruined, scrabbled on his hands and knees until he was up against a tree, which he hugged for dear life. As he sat there, something crawled across his leg. Terrified, Dewey brushed it away with his hand. He felt a sharp stinging in his palm, and jerked it back. The rattler whose fangs were embedded in his hand came with it, flying through the air to wrap around Dewey's neck, where it again sank its fangs directly into his jugular vein. When the poison hit Dewey's brain, he began to jerk and dance in a seizure, biting his tongue completely in two, drooling and snapping his jaws until his teeth broke off. He died within three minutes of the first bite.

By now, fire-heated bullets were exploding like strings of firecrackers, drilling men in arms, stomachs, legs, and heads. Over ten men were killed and another fifteen wounded by the dynamite and bullets, either from the fire or from their compatriots, who were shooting in terror at anything that moved.

Smoke and his men sat on the rise, watching the chaos they had caused, laughing at the antics of the screaming, hollering men below when they discovered the Colorado diamondback rattlers Smoke had unleashed in their midst. More than one man shot his foot off that night trying to kill the vicious reptiles, and two actually died from snakebite and fear.

Finally, as dawn approached, Smoke and his friends rode back to the Rocking C ranch, satisfied with a good night's work.

Vasquez and Murdock finally got their men to calm down and stop shooting each other. Torches and lanterns were lit, and they began to try to make sense of what had happened.

Murdock stood with his hands on his hips, looking around at the mess, and at the dead, dying, and wounded desperadoes he had hired.

"Goddamn that Jensen and Wells!" He grabbed Vasquez by the arm. "Just look at what they've done!"

"Señor, try to calm yourself," Vasquez said, peeling Murdock's grasping fingers from his arm. "It is over for now."

"But, how . . . when . . ."

"I tole you we should have guards posted," the Mexican said, shaking his head. "Those hombres are loco, they do not know fear."

"But I've got sixty men here. Who would try and attack when they're so outnumbered?"

"You no have sixty men anymore, señor. Maybe half . . ."

"Fuck the men! There's another fifteen coming in the next few days, we'll just wait for them to get here, then I'm gonna make those bastards pay for this."

"I wonder why they didn't kill more men?"

"What do you call that?" Murdock fairly screamed, pointing at the number of men lying dead or wounded.

Vasquez shook his head. "They were here among us, they could kill many more if they wanted."

Murdock just shook his head. "They killed enough, and wounded plenty more. Now I'm gonna have to put off killin' 'em until I get some reinforcements, and some of these men need time to heal."

Only when the sun came up did Murdock realize how badly his men had been demoralized. After the wounded

were carried inside and attended to, and the dead stacked
in a row behind the house, another seven men packed up
their gear and prepared to ride off.

Murdock and Vasquez stood before the men as they sat on
their horses. "Why are you men leaving? We'll have plenty
more gun hands in a couple of days and then we'll take out
Jensen and Wells and their entire force."

Black Jack Morton said, "Mr. Murdock, you don't understand what happened last night. The man lying next to me
was gutted and scalped, and my gun was emptied and put
back in my holster." He shook his head. "They coulda just
slit all our throats and we'd never have known what hit us."

The man sitting next to him, famous as a fearless fighter
in the New Mexico range wars, said, "They was sendin' us a
message. They was tellin' us they're not afraid of us, an' they
kin kill us anytime they want to." He jerked his horse's reins
around. "An' I fer one believe 'em. Yore money's no good to
a dead man, Mr. Murdock. I'll see ya around, maybe." With
that final word, the seven men galloped off, straight west, to
avoid both Pueblo and Smoke Jensen's ranch.

19

Murdock paced angrily around his study, scowling and cursing as he sipped his bourbon. "Goddammit, I want to kill that Smoke Jensen and Joey Wells so bad, I can taste it. I knew they were gonna be trouble the minute I laid eyes on them!"

Vasquez was sitting on a couch against a far wall, leaned back with his feet crossed on a small table, smoking a cigar and watching smoke curl toward the ceiling. "You know, Señor Murdock, I think you were right what you tole Emilio. That Wells will never rest until he kill me. I think I plenty glad we have more men coming soon."

Murdock shook his head. "I wish they were already here. If they don't get here in the next day or two, I'm afraid more of our men will leave. That raid last night really spooked them."

Murdock stopped pacing long enough to bend over his desk and pluck a cigar out of his humidor. He ran it under his nose, inhaling its rich aroma, then lit it with a lucifer, rotating it so it would burn evenly. As smoke billowed around his head, he pointed the stogie at Vasquez like a pistol. "Emilio, I want you to watch the men real close. If any of 'em start talkin' about leaving, you got to stop 'em quick, make an example of 'em." He raised his eyebrows. "You understand what I'm saying?"

"*Sí, señor.* We must make them understand they are to be more afraid of me than of the gringos, Wells, or Jensen."

Murdock, braver now that he had some bourbon under his belt, sat one hip on the edge of his desk. "You put a bridle on your men for a week or two, let the dust settle a bit, then we'll deal with Mr. Jensen and Mr. Wells once and for all!"

Over the next few days Joey drilled the punchers they had hired unmercifully, trying to teach them in a short while what it had taken him years to learn about guerrilla warfare. Soon he began to seem less grim and even smiled occasionally. "Smoke, I never woulda believed it, but them boys are makin' real progress." He grinned. "They ain't ever gonna be pistoleers, but at least they ain't gonna shoot themselves in the foot if'n somebody draws down on 'em."

Smoke gripped his shoulder. "That's because they have a good teacher, Joey. You're the best man with a short gun I've ever seen!"

"Well," Joey said, blushing, "I don't know 'bout that, but ever one o' these boys have got some hair. I wished I'd o' had 'em ridin' with me agin those Kansas Redlegs."

Smoke smiled. "Oh? I heard you did all right all by yourself, Joey."

Joey shrugged, smiled, and went out to drill the hands some more. After he left, Smoke and his friends got busy setting up the defenses around the ranch house he had planned against the raid they all knew was coming. Puma Buck, not one to sit around and wait for trouble, took off alone to roam the hills and woods surrounding Murdock's ranch. He would alert Smoke to any movements there signaling preparations for an attack.

When all preparations were made, Smoke dynamited the

rocks above the river running through his ranch, blocking its flow down to Murdock's spread. Within two days Murdock and Ben Tolson rode out to the ranch house.

Smoke told Louis and Monte Carson to stay out of sight and walked out to meet the two riders. "Howdy, Ben. What can I do for you?"

Tolson, a half smile on his face, pointed to Murdock. "Mr. Murdock here has lodged a complaint against you, Smoke. He says you've blocked off the water to his ranch."

Murdock's face purpled in rage. He pointed his finger at Smoke. "Jensen, you son of a bitch, I know my rights! That riverbed runs through my place, and I got the right to use any water in it to feed my herd!"

Smoke shrugged. "Why, I reckon you're correct, Mr. Murdock, and you're certainly welcome to use any water that comes onto your property." He smiled. "Trouble is, the river must have eroded the walls of a canyon where it comes through my spread. Seems some boulders fell and dammed up the river." He glanced at Tolson and winked. "I don't see how I can be held accountable for forces of nature."

Murdock looked at Tolson. "Sheriff," he almost shouted, "that ain't all. The other night Jensen and Wells rode onto my place and killed and wounded a bunch of my hands. I want him arrested for murder!"

Tolson glanced at Smoke. "Well, what do you say, Smoke?"

Smoke considered the two men, his face serious. "I sure hate to hear that your cowhands got shot up, Murdock." He raised his eyebrows. "Did anyone see who did it?"

Murdock glared hate at Smoke. "You know we didn't, Jensen. The murdering bastards attacked us at night, while we were sleeping."

Smoke spread his hands and shrugged. "If you didn't see the men who attacked you, I don't see how you can blame it on me." He smirked. "Maybe it was some of those Mexican and Indian gunslingers who rode on the town last week coming back to haunt you."

"Bullshit! I know it was you. You've shot up my men and now you're trying to kill my cattle by cutting off my water."

Smoke stared at the rancher, his eyes cold and hard. "Your cattle? Way I hear it, Murdock, there's some doubt about just whose cattle those are on your spread." He smiled, but there was no friendliness in his face. "Maybe we could have the sheriff and some of the other ranchers around here ride on over and take a close look at your brands, just to make sure none of them have been altered. While we're at it, we could also take a look at those cowboys that got killed and see if they're really punchers . . . or gun hawks who got only what they deserved."

"Why, you . . ." Murdock's hand fell toward his pistol, but Tolson laid a hand on his arm.

"I don't think you want to do that, Mr. Murdock." Tolson shook his head. "I don't fancy hauling your body all the way back into Pueblo draped across your horse."

Murdock took a deep breath and settled back in his saddle. Venom dripped from his voice as he said, "You haven't seen the last of me, Jensen."

Smoke's lips curled in a smirk. "No, I reckon not. But I am looking forward to the next time you come calling, Mr. Murdock. And you be sure to bring your friend Vasquez with you. Joey Wells wants to have a little . . . chat with him."

As Murdock jerked his reins and whirled his mount around to leave, Smoke said, "Ben, why don't you come in for a cup of coffee before you head back to town? There's an old friend of yours wants to say hello."

Tolson watched Murdock ride off in a cloud of dust. He shook his head and climbed out of his saddle. "I wouldn't underestimate that man, Smoke. He may be full of hot air, but he's had some mean ol' boys come ridin' through Pueblo headin' for his ranch the last couple of days."

Smoke walked him to the house. "I've got some hard men with me too, Ben."

When he entered the room, Ben's eyes lit up and he broke into a wide grin. "Monte Carson, you ol' son of a gun!"

The two men shook hands, clapping each other on the shoulder. "What are you doing up here?" Ben asked.

"Hell, I figured it'd been way too long since I had a palaver with my old sidekick, and when I heard my friend Smoke might be in need of help, I thought I could stand a little time off from sheriffing."

"It's surely good to see you, partner. Been a long time since I had anybody interesting to swap lies with."

André appeared in the door to the kitchen. "Monsieur Tolson, would you care to join the other gentlemen for breakfast?"

Tolson glanced at the Frenchman and raised his eyebrows. "Why, sure, long as Carson here didn't do none of the cooking. As I recollect, his biscuits an' fatback weren't fit for man nor beast."

As they walked into the dining room, Monte introduced Louis and André to Tolson. Ben said. "Longmont? I seem to remember a Longmont ran a saloon in Silver City a while back. That you?"

Louis smiled. "Yes, sir. I had a small establishment there for a while, until the mines began to play out."

André spooned heaping helpings of scrambled eggs mixed with chopped onions and hot peppers into their plates, and placed a platter of pancakes and blueberries in the middle of the table.

Tolson speared two flapjacks onto his plate and began to eat. Between bites he said, "Back then I was riding with Curly Bill Bodacious, and he told me you pulled up stakes after . . . a fracas involving one of the city officials."

Longmont nodded. "The mayor's son, actually. He was a headstrong, spoiled young man with an excess of money and a paucity of brains. He fancied the favors of a young lady named Lilly Montez." Louis smiled in remembrance. "She was a beauty. Long, shiny black hair, pretty face and complexion, and legs that went from here to there. Evidently, she and young Boyd had a lovers' quarrel and she decided to make him jealous. She began to hang around my place, trying to interest me in her more obvious charms. About the only ladies I was interested in then were the four that reside in a deck of cards, so I declined her offer of companionship."

Smoke snorted. "That's the first time I've ever heard of you turning a lady down."

Louis shrugged. "I was younger then and intent on making my fortune Anyway, Lilly complained to Boyd I had 'insulted her honor' and he felt compelled to call me out. . . ."

Louis picked up two gold double-eagles and flipped them nonchalantly into a pile of money in the middle of the poker table. "I'll see your bet, Clyde, and raise you a couple of eagles."

The batwings flew open and Boyd McAlister stormed into the saloon. He stood just inside the door for a moment, breathing hard. His wild eyes searched the room, lighting on Louis at his usual corner table. Hitching up his gun belt, he stomped over to stand across from Louis. "Longmont, I'm callin' you out!"

Louis glanced over the cards in his hand at the young firebrand. "I'm in the middle of a game here, Boyd. Why don't you go to the bar and have a beer. I'll be with you in a few minutes, and we can discuss whatever it is you have on your mind."

Boyd's face turned red. "There ain't nothin' to discuss, Longmont. You insulted Lilly, an' I'm gonna make you pay!"

Louis shrugged. "What's your hurry, boy? If you insist on this foolishness, you're going to be a long time dead. Another few minutes of life shouldn't matter one way or another." Louis looked away and said, "Now, Clyde. I've called and raised. You in or out?"

Beads of sweat formed on Clyde's face as he glanced nervously over his shoulder at Boyd. "Jesus, Louis," he whispered hoarsely, "don't you think . . . ?"

Louis removed his cigar from his mouth and studied its glowing tip. "I think, Clyde, that your two pair won't stand up against my hand. The question before us at the moment is, what do you think?"

Clyde carefully peeked at his hole card again. He had a pair of queens, an ace, and a ten showing faceup, and an ace in the hole. Louis had four hearts showing faceup. If he had a heart in the hole, his flush would beat Clyde's two pair and take the pot, over six hundred dollars.

Finally, Clyde flipped his cards over. "No, I think you got that flush, Louis. No need throwing good money after bad."

Louis raked in the pot with both hands, a wide grin on his face. "Good call, Clyde. You know I never bluff." He stacked coins and folded bills and stuffed them all in his pockets.

Across the room Boyd gulped his beer and yelled, "I'll be waitin' outside for you, Longmont."

Louis flipped a rawhide thong off the hammer of his Colt, tied down low on his right leg, saying, "I've never seen anyone so eager to die." He walked toward the batwings. He glanced over his shoulder in time to see Clyde turn over Louis's hole card. It was the deuce of clubs.

Clyde snorted. "A busted flush. Your hand was worthless."

"Like I said, Clyde, I *never* bluff . . . well, hardly ever." Louis straightened his hat and squared his shoulders, mumbling "No guts, no glory" to himself as he stepped through the door into bright Colorado sunshine.

Boyd, with two of his friends flanking him, was standing in the middle of the dirt street.

Louis stepped off the boardwalk and faced the men. "Three against one. That makes the odds about even," he called. He nodded at the two cowboys with Boyd. "You boys ready to die for your friend?"

Boyd glanced from side to side. "We ain't gonna die, Longmont. We're gonna dust you through and through."

Louis shrugged and fastened his coat into the back of his belt, out of the way of his draw. "You called this dance, Boyd. Time someone has to pay the band. Make your play."

Four hands slapped leather simultaneously, and Colts exploded, sending clouds of cordite gun smoke to blot out the sun. Louis's first shot took Boyd in the chest, punching out his back and throwing him backward. His gun was still in its leather. Louis crouched a little and spun to the right, cocking and firing in one lightning-fast move. His second shot took the man on Boyd's left full in his face, blowing teeth and blood into the air. He'd gotten his gun out, but it was still pointed down. As the dying man's finger twitched, his gun went off, blowing a hole in his foot. The third cowboy got off a round that tore through Louis's coat but missed flesh. Louis swung his gun and cocked and fired a third time in less than three seconds, hitting the puncher high in his chest, spinning him around and dropping him facedown in the dirt.

Louis took a deep breath and holstered his Colt. He walked to his horse, tied to a rail post nearby, and stepped into the saddle. Louis rode slowly out of town, never looking back.

As Louis finished his tale of the gunfight in Silver City, Cal, with eyes wide, said, "Gosh, Mr. Longmont, that must've been something to see!"

Louis stubbed out his cigar with a wry grin. "Well, Cal, gunfights are always more fun to watch than to participate in."

Joey nodded. "That's for damn sure."

20

Puma Buck walked his horse slowly through underbrush and light forest timber in the foothills surrounding Murdock's spread. His mount was one they'd hired in Pueblo on arriving, and it wasn't as surefooted on the steep slopes as his paint pony back home was, so he was taking it easy and getting the feel of his new ride.

He kept a sharp lookout toward Murdock's ranch house almost a quarter of a mile below. He was going to make damned sure none of those *buscaderos* managed to get to drop on Smoke and his other new friends. He rode with his Sharps .52-caliber laid across his saddle horn, loaded and ready for immediate action.

Several times Puma had seen men ride up to the ranch house and enter, only to leave after a while, riding off toward herds of cattle, which could be seen on the horizon. Puma figured they were most likely the legitimate punchers Murdock had working his cattle, and not gun hawks he'd hired to take down Smoke and Joey. A shootist would rather take lead poisoning than lower himself to herd beeves.

Off to the side, Puma could barely make out the riverbed, dry now, that ran through Murdock's place. He could see on the other side of Murdock's ranch house a row of freshly dug graves. He grinned to himself, appreciating the graves, some of them his doing, and the way Smoke had deprived the man of water for his cattle and horses.

Puma knew that alone would prompt Murdock to make his move soon; he couldn't afford to wait and let his stock die of thirst.

As Puma pulled his canteen out and uncorked the top, ready to take a swig, he saw a band of fifteen or more riders burning dust toward the ranch house from the direction of Pueblo. Evidently they were additional men Murdock had hired to replace those he and Smoke and Joey had slain in their midnight raid.

"Uh-huh," he muttered. "I'll bet those *bandidos* are fixin' to put on the war paint and make a run over to Smoke s place."

He swung out of his saddle and crouched down behind a fallen tree, propping the big, heavy Sharps across the rough bark. He licked his finger and wiped the front sight with it, to make it stand out more when he needed it. He got himself into a comfortable position and laid out a box full of extra shells next to the gun on the tree within easy reach. He figured he might need to do some quick reloading when the time came.

After about ten minutes the gang of men Puma was observing arrived at the front of the ranch house, and two figures Puma took to be Murdock and Vasquez came out of the door to address them. He couldn't make out their faces at the distance, but they had an unmistakable air of authority about them.

As the rancher began to talk, waving his hands toward Smoke's ranch, Puma took careful aim, remembering he was shooting downhill and needed to lower his sights a bit, the natural tendency being to overshoot a target lower than you are.

He took a deep breath and held it, slowly increasing pressure on the trigger, so when the explosion came it would be a surprise and he wouldn't have time to flinch and throw his aim off.

The big gun boomed and shot a sheet of fire two feet out of the barrel, slamming back into Puma's shoulder and almost knocking over his skinny frame. Damn, he had almost forgotten how the big Sharps kicked when it delivered its deadly cargo.

The targets were a little over fifteen hundred yards from Puma, a long range even for the remarkable Sharps. It seemed a long time but was only a little over five seconds before one of the men on horseback was thrown from his mount to lie sprawled in the dirt. The sound was several seconds slower reaching the men, and by then Puma had jacked another round in the chamber and fired again. By the time the group knew they were being fired upon, two of their number were dead on the ground. Just as they ducked and whirled, looking for the location of their attacker, another was knocked off his bronc, his arm almost blown off by the big .52-caliber slug traveling at over two thousand feet per second.

The outlaws began to scatter, some jumping from their horses and running into the house, while others just bent over their saddle horns and burned trail dust away from the area. A couple of brave souls aimed rifles up the hill and fired, but the range was so far for ordinary rifles that Puma never even saw where the bullets landed.

Another couple of rounds fired into the house, one of which penetrated wooden walls, striking a man inside in the thigh, and Puma figured he had done enough for the time being. Now he had to get back to Smoke and tell him Murdock was ready to make his play, or would be as soon as he rounded up the men Puma had scattered all over the countryside.

Several of the riders had ridden toward Smoke's ranch and were now between Puma and home. "Well, shit, old beaver. Ya knew it was about time for ya ta taste some lead," he mumbled to himself. He packed his Sharps in his saddle boot and opened his saddlebags. He withdrew two Colt Army .44s to match the one in his holster and made sure they were all loaded up six and six, then stuffed the two extras in his belt. He tugged his hat down tight and eased up into the saddle, grunting with the effort.

Riding slow and careful, he kept to heavy timber until he came to a group of six men standing next to a drying riverbed, watering their horses in one of the small pools remaining.

There was no way to avoid them, so he put his reins in his teeth and filled both hands with iron. It was time to dance with the devil, and Puma was going to strike up the band. He kicked his mount's flanks and bent low over his saddle horn as he galloped out of the forest toward the gunnies below.

One of the men, wearing an eye patch, looked up in astonishment at the apparition wearing buckskins and war paint charging them, yelling and whooping and hollering as he rode like the wind.

"Goddamn, boys, it's that old mountain man!" One-Eye Jackson yelled as he drew his pistol.

All six men crouched and began firing wildly, frightened by the sheer gall of a lone horseman to charge right at them.

Puma's pistols exploded, spitting fire, smoke, and death ahead of him. Two of the gun slicks went down immediately, .44 slugs in their chests.

Another jumped into the saddle, turned tail, and rode like hell to get away from this madman who was bent on killing all of them.

One-Eye took careful aim and fired, his bullet tearing through Puma's left shoulder muscle, twisting his body and almost unseating him.

Puma straightened, gritting his teeth on the leather reins while he continued firing with his right-hand gun, his left arm hanging useless at his side. His next two shots hit their targets, taking one gunny in the face and the other in the stomach, doubling him over to leak guts and shit and blood in the dirt as he fell.

One-Eye's sixth and final bullet in his pistol entered Puma's horse's forehead and exited out the back of its skull to plow into Puma's chest. The horse swallowed its head and somersaulted as it died, throwing Puma spinning to the ground. He rolled three times, tried to push himself to his knees, then fell facedown in the dirt, his blood pooling around him.

One-Eye Jackson looked around at the three dead men lying next to him and muttered a curse under his breath. "Jesus, that old fool had a lotta hair to charge us like that." He shook his head as he walked over to Puma's body and aimed his pistol at the back of the mountain man's head. He eared back the hammer and let it drop. His gun clicked . . . all chambers empty.

One-Eye leaned down and rolled Puma over to make sure he was dead. Puma's left shoulder was canted at an angle where the bullet had broken it, and on the right side of his chest was a spreading scarlet stain.

Puma moaned and rolled to the side. One-Eye Jackson chuckled. "You're a tough old bird, but soon's I reload, I'll put one in your eye."

Puma's eyes flicked open and he grinned, exposing blood-stained teeth. "Not in this lifetime, sonny," and he swung his right arm out from beneath his body. In it was his buffalo-skinning knife.

One-Eye grunted in shock and surprise as he looked down at the hilt of Puma's long knife sticking out of his chest "Son of a . . ." he rasped, then he died.

Puma lay there for a moment, then with great effort he pushed himself over so he faced his beloved mountains. "Boys," he whispered to all the mountain men who had gone before him, "git the *cafecito* hot, I'm comin' to meet ya."

Smoke was sitting with his friends around the dining room table as dusk approached.

He looked at Cal and said, "Where's Puma got to? He knows to be back here before dark."

Cal shrugged. "I dunno, Mr. Smoke. He sat up most of last night, starin' at the fire and singing some old Indian song. Then this mornin' he put some red and yeller and blue paint on his face and took off toward the mountains with that big old Sharps of his acrost his saddle."

Smoke jumped to his feet. "Damn, Cal, why didn't you tell me this sooner?"

"Why?" the boy asked, a frightened, puzzled look on his face.

"'Cause that was his death song he was singing, and that paint on his face meant he was going on the warpath, probably intended to do as much damage to Murdock as he could before they killed him!"

"Jiminy, Smoke, I'm sorry . . . I didn't know."

Smoke grabbed his hat and Henry rifle and ran out the door, everyone in the cabin following him. They all loved the old man and weren't about to let Murdock and his men kill him, that is if they weren't too late.

Smoke and his five friends rode hard toward Murdock's ranch, leaning over their saddle horns, grim, determined looks on their faces.

It was almost an hour before they galloped up to the scene of Puma's charge. Dead bodies lay everywhere, and horses milled, grazing on the green grass near the old riverbed.

Smoke jumped out of his saddle before Horse came to a stop and ran to where Puma lay, still staring at the mountains.

Smoke knelt and cradled the old man's head in his lap. Puma gazed up at him through watery, faded blue eyes. "Hey, pardner, I kicked some ass today," he whispered through dry, cracked lips.

Smoke, tears in his eyes, nodded. "You sure did, Puma."

Puma reached up and put his palm against Smoke's cheek.

"Don't fret, young beaver. There's been somethin' goin' wrong inside me the last coupla months, an' I didn't hanker to die in no bed. The only fittin' way fer a mountain man to die is with his hands full of iron, spittin' lead and laughin' at death."

"Puma, I'll make sure the other mountain men know of this day and sing about it around their campfires until there are none of us left."

"Say good-bye to the fellahs fer me, Smoke. An' if Preacher's waitin' fer me on the other side, I'll tell him what a good job we did raisin' our boy."

Smoke started to reply, but then noticed it wasn't necessary. Puma was with his friends, and he had all eternity to hunt, where streams never dried up and the beaver and fox were plentiful, and where there was always someone to listen to his tall tales of the ways of the mountain men.

Smoke stood, cradling Puma in his arms like a baby. He faced the others with tears running down his cheeks. "I'm going to take him home, up into the high lonesome, and bury him. I'll be back at the ranch tomorrow."

Louis put his hand on Smoke's shoulder. "Smoke, if it's all right with you, I'd be honored to go with you and see Puma off." The gambler and gunfighter who had killed dozens of men in his life choked back a sob, his eyes filling. "I've ridden with many men in my years out west, but none of them could hold a candle to Puma Buck."

Joey, Cal, Pearlie, Monte, and Ben Tolson all stepped forward, nodding their heads, wanting to go too.

Smoke said, "I think Puma would consider it an honor if all of you came along to wish him well on his last journey."

He climbed up on Horse and began to ride up the hill toward distant mountain peaks, Puma's friends following.

They buried Puma that night next to a high mountain stream, near a beaver dam. As Smoke prepared to place the body in the grave, Cal stepped up and handed Smoke Puma's buffalo-skinning knife. "I took this out of the last man Puma killed."

Smoke glanced down at the long, sharp knife, then back up into Cal's eyes. "I think he would want you to have it, Cal. And, Pearlie, you take his pistols."

Smoke looked down at the small figure in his arms. "He always thought of you boys as his grandkids, and I know he'd be proud if you'd honor his memory by taking the things that he always kept by his side."

After the grave was filled, Smoke built a campfire and the men sat up until dawn listening to Smoke tell them about the life of one of the greatest mountain men who ever lived. "Singing his song," as Smoke called it, paying tribute to a man he held as close in memory as his own father.

The next afternoon Smoke and his friends were gathered around the dining room table. "Joey, when I came up here with you, it was because of a debt I owed you for saving my life." He drained his coffee cup, reddened eyes hard. "Now it's gotten real personal. I don't intend for Murdock or any of his hired thugs to live through the next few days."

Joey spoke up. "Smoke, because of Puma's sacrifice, we've got time ta get ready."

Smoke asked, "When do you think they'll hit, Joey?"

The ex-soldier pursed his lips, humming tunelessly for a moment. He narrowed his eyes. "If'n they're smart, which I'm not sayin' they are, there's only two good times ta attack a fortified position. Once is right at dusk. Man can't hardly see well enough ta shoot anything then, eyes plays tricks on 'im. The other time is round about two, three in the mornin', when a body's deepest asleep."

"You're right," Smoke said. He pulled a cigar out of his pocket and lit it. "However, I'm like you. I don't think Murdock is smart enough to wait for the right time. He's so pissed off now after our two attacks on his home, I think he'll send those hired guns and outlaws of his here as soon as they can get ready."

Joey squinted out the window at shadows along the fence. "Well, it looks ta be 'bout three, three-thirty now, an' it's a good two-hour ride from Murdock's place." He built a cig-arette and stuck it in the corner of his mouth, striking a lucifer on his pistol handle. As he puffed, he nodded. "I 'spect they'll be here just 'fore dark, 'bout five or so."

Smoke stepped to the door and surveyed the land between his and Murdock's ranch. "If they come straight here, they'll be coming from the south, and the setting sun will be off to their left, our right. I'll station a group of hands with long guns in that copse of cottonwoods over there, and another with shotguns in that group of boulders about fifty yards south of it. They can dig in and use the trees and rocks for cover, and they'll be firing on Murdock's men from out of the sun as they ride past."

Louis rubbed his cheeks, he hadn't shaved for two days and had an unaccustomed growth of whiskers on his usually clean-shaven face. "What about those other little surprises you have planned for those miscreants? Are they all pre-pared and ready to go?"

Smoke glanced at Cal and Pearlie, whose job it had been to get the traps and deadfalls ready. "How about it, men?"

Pearlie and Cal both nodded. "We're primed and loaded for bear, Smoke."

21

Murdock stood on his porch with his hands on his hips, Vasquez standing next to him, looking at the group of men gathered in front of him.

Curly Rogers had just come back from finding One-Eye Jackson and his men's dead bodies by the riverbed. Sandy Billings, the member of the group who had run away, told him where the fracas took place. Rogers said, "They're all dead, Mr. Murdock. Weren't no other bodies around, though there was some blood might've been from that old mountain man who attacked 'em."

Murdock said to Billings, "You say this old codger rode right down on your group of six men by himself?"

"Yes, sir. His face was all painted with Indian war paint, and he was yellin' and screamin' and firin' them big old Colt Armies like some demon outta hell!"

Vasquez's lip curled in a sneer. "And you, señor, you rode away without fighting?"

Billings dropped his eyes, his face flushing. "Yeah, I did." He looked up defiantly. "And I'd do it again. That old bastard was crazy or something, 'cause he sure wasn't afraid of dyin'."

Vasquez nodded. "But you were, *cabrón*." He stepped

down off the porch and walked to stand face-to-face with Billings. "We all ride for Señor Murdock," he said, glancing around at the group of gunfighters gathered there. "He pay us money to fight, not to run away like small children."

He looked back at Billings and slapped him hard across the face, driving the man to his knees. "This is what happens to cowards," Vasquez said, and drew his machete and slashed down at Billings, catching him between his shoulder and neck, almost decapitating him.

Billings flopped to the ground, thrashing and screaming as his blood pumped out to spray several men nearby. After a moment the gunman lay still, his blood soaking into the dry earth around him.

Vasquez held his blood-covered machete above his head. "Remember, vaqueros, is better to stay and die like men than to taste my blade."

Murdock's eyes were squinted, looking hard at his hired guns. "We have Jensen and his men outnumbered three or four to one. Any man who's afraid to ride against those odds, I have no use for." He inclined his head toward Vasquez. "If you want to quit, turn in your resignation to Vasquez right now."

He paused for a moment, but no one moved to take advantage of his offer. "Okay, then. Load up your weapons and feed and water your horses. We ride against Jensen in an hour."

As the men dispersed, the Silverado Kid stepped over to Vasquez. "Emilio, I can see you think you and your knife are big shit." He took the cigarette out of his mouth and flicked it at the Mexican. "Billings was a friend of mine. When this is over, if you're still alive, I'm gonna dust you for what you just did."

Vasquez smiled, his eyebrow arched. "Why for you defend coward?"

"He was married to my cousin, an' he wasn't no coward. That old man took down five hombres, none of 'em slouches with guns." He pointed his finger at Vasquez. "Sometimes it makes more sense to run than to fight, an' that's somethin' you oughta think about after this little fracas, Mex."

The Kid walked off toward the corral to get his horse without looking back at Vasquez.

Shotgun Sam Willowby leaned across his saddle and spoke in a low voice to Gimpy Monroe. "Gimpy, I don't know about you, but these wages ain't looking as good right now as they did in Pueblo."

Gimpy straightened from adjusting his stirrups. "Yore right, Shotgun." He looked around to make sure no one could hear. "I'm thinkin' o' kinda gittin' lost on the way to this little shindig and makin' my way back to New Mexico."

Shotgun Sam nodded. "Yeah, sounds good to me. We'll just hold back on the reins a mite and ride to the rear till we cross that riverbed, then make a sharp turn and shag our mounts toward home."

Curly Rogers and his group of men stood next to the corral, tightening cinch belts and straightening saddles and blankets on their mounts. "Well, boys, it's about time we paid that bastard Jensen back for what he did to us up on that mountain," Rogers said, looking over his bronc at the others.

Boots fingered his facial scars and bent and misshapen nose. "Yeah, that son of a bitch is goin' to be sorry he marked me up like this. I'm gonna put one 'tween his eyes for leavin' me lookin' like a hoss stomped me."

"You're gonna have to stand in line," Cates said, limping around his horse's rear end to pick up his saddlebags. "I cain't hardly walk on the leg he shattered, an' in the winter it pains me so, I cain't get no sleep at all." He stuck his thumb in his chest. "I'm gonna be the one that curls him up!"

Gooden, another member of the group, shook his head. "You boys don't have nothin' to gripe about. That bullet Jensen put in my side messed up my bowels somethin' fierce. I hadn't had a normal shit in two years, and I can't eat nothin' heavier than oatmeal or I git the runs." He stared at the others. "If anybody has a reason to blow Jensen to hell, it's me."

Twenty feet away, Sam Silverwolf and Jed Beartooth were discussing the upcoming battle. "Jed," Sam said as he flipped open his loading gate and checked the rounds in his pistol. "After we kill the gringos, I want to go back to Pueblo." He raised his eyebrows and grinned. "The women are very pretty there, no?"

Jed Beartooth grinned back and grabbed his crotch with his hand. *"Sí,* I too am ready for another kind of riding, amigo."

Bill Denver said to his partner, Slim Watkins, "Slim, you hear what the Kid said to Vasquez over there?"

Watkins nodded, not being much for talking.

Bill asked, "Who do you think'll win in that little dust-up? The Kid or Vasquez?"

Watkins spit a brown stream over his horse's back, shifted his tobacco wad to his other cheek, and replied, "I'll give you two-to-one odds and bet twenty dollars on the Kid if'n it's with guns. I'll give you even money if'n it's with knives."

Bill said, "You're on, cowboy."

The man named Colonel Waters rode up to where Murdock and Vasquez sat their horses. "Murdock, Vasquez," he said, "I intend to kill Joey Wells personally. He was responsible for the death of over a hundred and fifty of my men after the war."

Vasquez stuck one of Murdock's cigars in his mouth and lit it. "So, señor, what you tell us this for?"

Waters shrugged. "Just to let you know what I intend to do. I don't care overly much about the others you're fighting. My attention is going to be on killing Joey Wells."

Murdock grinned. "That's fine with me, colonel. But you're going to have to get through the others to get to Wells, so take your best shot."

The man in the Union coat tipped his officer's hat and

rode off to join the rest of the gun hawks as they gathered in front of the corral.

Vasquez glanced at Murdock and tapped his head. *"Es muy loco."*

Murdock laughed. "I don't care if he's crazy, long as he can fire a pistol and don't turn tail and run when the fighting starts."

He spurred his horse to the front of his group of men. "Let's ride, men. *Vamanos!* " he called, and wheeled his mount and rode off toward the Rocking C, over fifty of the toughest, meanest gunnies from several states following.

Smoke stepped out the door of the cabin to talk to the men they had hired in Pueblo, who were waiting outside for instructions.

"Boys, there's trouble riding our way. Unless I'm mistaken, Jacob Murdock has hired a bunch of professional gunfighters and outlaws to ride for his brand. They're on their way here to kill us so Murdock can have this land and set up his empire in Colorado. If that happens, he'll next take over the town of Pueblo and will again install his own man as sheriff."

He pulled a cigar from his pocket and lit it as he talked. "Do you want that to happen?"

His men all raised their voices to shout *no,* and a few held up rifles and shotguns and waved them in the air.

"Okay, but are you willing to die to keep Murdock from having his way?"

The men didn't yell this time, but everyone stared back at Smoke without flinching, nodding their heads, their eyes filled with determination.

"Thank you, men. Your sheriff, Ben Tolson, along with Joey Wells and Monte Carson and Cal and Pearlie and me are not going to let that happen either. We intend to stand alongside you and fight until Murdock and his men are all dead—or we are."

Louis and the others on the porch with Smoke stepped forward to stand next to him. Smoke said, "I'm going to let Joey Wells, who's been working with you men for the past few days, assign you your places in the upcoming battle. He knows your strengths and your weaknesses, and he's going to put you where you can do the most good."

Joey cut a chunk of tobacco off his plug of Bull Durham, stuck it in his mouth, and chewed as he talked. He pointed to one side of the crowd. "You Sammy, Joel, Tuck, and Benny. You an' your men who have been punchin' the cattle, I want you in the cabin here. Get your shotguns and rifles and get upstairs an' on the roof. I want ev'ry window and door double covered. Ya got a clear field o' fire for a hundred and fifty yards, so open them windows and git yourselves comfy, ya may be there awhile." He leaned over the hitching rail in front of the house and spit a brown stream into the dirt. "'Member what I tole ya 'bout them guns. Take your time and aim, fire only when ya have a good shot, we don't have a surplus o' ammunition, so use what ya have to good advantage."

He looked to the left side of the crowd. "Mike, Jimmy, Todd, and Josh, I want you to set up in that copse of trees over yonder to the right. We already got you some holes dug there and there's a couple o' fallen logs ta git behind. You are the men who are best with rifles, so you're gonna be a bit farther from the action. I want you all ta wait until Murdock and his gang are even with or maybe a bit past ya 'fore ya start to fire on 'em. Let 'em git good and close, then they'll be trapped 'twixt you and the men in the house."

Joey waved his arm toward the center group of men. "Tyler, you and Billy Joe and Tommy are my shotgun brigade. I want ya each carryin' a sack or two of shells and I want ya to git out there in that mess o' boulders yonder. We done got ya some logs and brush and such around some natural holes and caves in the rocks to git in and git outta the way if'n the lead gits too thick. You men are ta stay hidden until Murdock's riders git by ya. Then we'll have 'em boxed in between the house, the trees, an' the boulders."

As the men started to disperse, Joey shouted, "Now, remember what I said about our little surprises for the gunnies, and don't none of you fall into any of those traps, ya hear?"

Joey looked at Tolson. "Ben, with yore experience with that Greener, I'd like ya to stay on the first floor of the cabin, ta make sure none of the gunnies git close enough to set fire to it or to git inside. Okay?"

Tolson nodded and grinned. "Sure, Joey. I'll guarantee won't none of those bastards get through the door, unless it's over my dead body."

"Good. Now, Monte, I need you to get to the upper story of the cabin and keep those punchers calm up there. Ain't none of 'em able to hit nothin' with a gun, so I need someone to show 'em how to do it and to protect them if worse comes to worst."

Monte nodded, his eyes hard as flint. He glanced at Smoke. "These men are going to do you proud, Smoke, I'll see to it."

After everyone else had gone to their assigned positions, Joey looked at Cal and Pearlie and Louis and Smoke. "Thet just leaves us, men. What'll it be?"

Smoke said, "I think we get to be the cavalry, boys. If we get on our mounts and wait just over that rise over there until we hear gunfire, then we can swoop down in among the gun hawks and do a powerful lot of damage at close range."

Louis nodded, as did Cal and Pearlie.

Joey said, "I been fightin' on hossback fer so many years, I don't rightly know no other way. I'll be ridin' with the Jensen cavalry if'n you boys don't mind a rebel yell now and again."

Smoke laughed. "I rode with the Gray during the war too, Joey, and I may just join you in the yelling."

Joey smiled. "I knew ya was a man after my own heart, Smoke." He looked at Cal and Pearlie. "If you boys want to help, you can go out there and pour a little kerosene on our piles of wood. If they come at us after dark, we'll light the woodpiles so we can see where our surprises are buried."

Pearlie chuckled as he grabbed a can of kerosene from the kitchen and stepped off the porch. "I cain't hardly wait to see them boys' eyes when they come bustin' in here loaded for bear. Yes, sir, that's gonna be a sight to see."

Joey walked over and put his arm around Pearlie's shoulder, speaking low so only he and Cal could hear. "Boys," he said, "I've grown right fond o' the two o' you." He frowned and stared into Pearlie's eyes. "If either one o' ya git yore-selves kilt tonight, I'm gonna be right pissed off, ya hear?"

Pearlie grinned. "Yes, sir. I'll keep that in mind, and I want you to know, I'll watch after Cal and make him keep his fool head down."

Smoke, who had come up in time to hear what was said, nodded. "You do that, Pearlie, and don't you forget to keep yours down too."

Pearlie said, "Yes, sir, Smoke," and left to attend to pouring the kerosene and checking the other deadfalls and traps he and Cal had prepared.

André was in the kitchen, boiling large kettles of water for treatment of the inevitable wounds that were to occur, and making huge pots of coffee in case the battle lasted well into the night.

Smoke was left alone on the porch with Louis Longmont, Monte Carson, and Joey Wells. He pulled his Colts out and checked his loads as he spoke. "Well, gentlemen . . . friends. I guess it's about time we find out what we're made of."

Joey squinted through narrowed eyes. "Those boys we hired'll stand firm, Smoke, I kin tell ya that."

"I know, Joey. They're a fine bunch of men." He holstered his pistols and looked at his friends.

Louis smiled. "I'm going to enjoy riding with you and Joey. Hell, I may have kids someday and I'll not miss a chance to tell them I once rode and did battle with the famous Smoke Jensen and the infamous Joey Wells."

Smoke and Joey laughed, and Smoke said, "Then let's shag our mounts, boys. I want to get a little ways away from the ranch house so we can ride and attack without getting shot by our own men."

They waited while Cal and Pearlie mounted up and then rode toward Murdock's ranch at an easy trot. Smoke had Colts on both legs, a Henry repeating rifle in one saddle boot, and a Greener ten-gauge scattergun in the other.

Louis rode with one pistol in a holster on his right leg and had two sawed-off American Arms twelve-gauges in saddle boots on either side of his saddle horn. The two-shot derringer behind his belt would be useful only in very close quarters.

Joey had his Colt in his right-hand holster, his 36-caliber in his shoulder holster, and two short-barreled Winchester rifles, one in a saddle boot and one he carried across his saddle horn.

Cal had the twin Colt Navy .36-caliber pistols Smoke had given him that he used while riding with Preacher. He also carried a Henry repeating rifle slung over his shoulder on a rawhide strap.

Pearlie had double-rigged Colt Army .44s and a Greener twelve-gauge shotgun with a cut-down barrel for close-in work.

Joey glanced around at his compatriots and laughed. "Hell, boys, if Lee'd had this much firepower at Appomattox, he wouldn't have had to surrender."

22

The riders from the Lazy M came galloping toward Smoke's spread like an invading horde of wild men. They started shouting and hollering and firing their weapons toward the cabin while still well out of range.

Smoke, Joey, Louis, Cal, and Pearlie were bent low over their saddle horns behind a small rise in a group of pine trees, waiting for them to pass.

As they rode by, Joey cut a chunk of Bull Durham and stuck it in his mouth. He chewed a moment, then spit, a disgusted look on his face. "Guess those assholes are tryin' to scare us to death with all that yelping like injuns."

Cal, whose heart had hammered when he saw the number of men who rode by, took a deep breath, praying he wouldn't disgrace himself or Smoke in the upcoming battle.

Pearlie glanced at him and saw the sweat beginning to bead his forehead in spite of the chilliness of the early evening air. He reached over and punched Cal in the shoulder. "Don't worry none, partner, we're gonna teach these galoots a lesson they'll never forget."

Cal nodded, relaxing a little bit, knowing he was among friends who would fight with him, side by side, against the devil himself if necessary.

When Smoke heard gunfire being returned from the area of the cabin, he put his reins in his teeth, took his Greener ten-gauge in his left hand and his Colt .44 in his right, and spurred Horse forward, guiding the big Palouse with his knees.

Joey looped his reins over his neck, took his short-barreled Winchester rifle in his hands, jacked the lever down to feed a shell into the chamber, and rode after Smoke.

Louis filled both his hands with his American Arms express guns, eared back the hammers on all four barrels, and leaned forward, urging his mount over the hill.

Pearlie winked at Cal as he grabbed his Greener cut-down shotgun in his left hand and drew his Colt with his right. Before he put the reins between his teeth, he said, "Come on, cowboy, it's time to make some history of our own!"

Cal drew both his Navy .36s and took off after the others, teeth bared in a grin of both exhilaration and fear.

Murdock's men were in the trap Smoke had devised for them, caught with the shotgun brigade hidden among boulders at their rear, and off to their left, hidden in the setting sun, the men with rifles, and to the front, the cabin with its contingent of men who, though not accurate with their weapons, were pouring lead into the outlaws at a furious rate, hitting some by mere chance.

Cal and Pearlie had scattered a series of twenty small piles of kerosene-soaked wood across the clearing where Murdock's men were trapped, and those were now lighted, making the area look like an army camp with its campfires.

Just before Smoke and his band arrived from the bandits' right side, completing their boxing-in maneuver, Monte Carson, leaning out of an upstairs window, did as he had been instructed.

He began to fire his Henry repeating rifle, fitted with a four-powder scope, at the base of the small fires. The wood had been piled by Cal and Pearlie over cans of black powder, put in burlap sacks with horseshoe nails packed around them.

When Monte's molten lead entered the cans of powder, they exploded, sending hundreds of projectile-like nails in all directions and spreading smoke and cordite in a dense cloud to blind and confuse the enemy.

Men and horses went down by the dozen. Those not killed outright were severely wounded by both explosions and nails.

Other traps began to become effective. Several trenches had been dug, with sharpened spikes stuck in the bottoms. As first horses, then men on foot, began to step into the trenches, and horrible screams of pain from both men and animals began to ring out in the gathering darkness.

Curly Rogers and his group of bounty hunters were directly behind Vasquez and Murdock as they approached the cabin. Rogers was firing his Colts at the ranch house as he and his men passed the pile of boulders. A sudden explosion came from between two of the rocks, and Rogers felt as if someone had kicked him in the side. He was blown out of his saddle, three buckshot pellets in his side. He bounced and quickly scrambled to his feet, barely managing to avoid being trampled by his fellow outlaws.

Rogers clamped his left arm to his side, pulled out another gun, and ran toward the cabin, hoping to find another horse to get on. His feet went right through one of the deadfalls and his legs fell onto two sharpened spikes, sending agony racing through his body like a fire. He screamed, "Help me . . . oh, dear God, somebody help me!" As he flopped on the ground, wooden stakes impaled in his legs, and a bullet from the cabin aimed at another rider missed its intended target but didn't miss him. It severed his spine, ending his pain and leaving him lying paralyzed on the ground.

Cates, seeing the amount of resistance at the ranch, tried to veer his horse off to the left and escape. As he passed between two pine trees, the baling wire Cal had strung nine feet off the ground caught him just under the chin. Horse and rider rode on, but Cates's head stayed behind to fall bouncing on the ground like overripe fruit.

The half-breeds, Sam Silverwolf and Jed Beartooth, trying to escape the fire from the cabin and the trees, whirled their horses and headed for the boulders, intending to take cover there among the rocks.

Tyler and Billy Joe, leaders of the shotgun brigade, saw them coming and stepped into the open, guns leveled. Silverwolf got off two shots with his pistol, taking Tyler in the chest and gut, doubling him over. Billy Joe, twenty-two years old and never having fired a gun in anger before, stood his ground as slugs from the two half-breed killers and rapists pocked stone and ricocheted around him. He sighted down the barrel, waited until they were in range, and pulled both triggers at the same time. The double blast from the shotgun exploded and kicked back, knocking Billy Joe on his butt.

When he scrambled to his feet, breaking the barrel open to shove two more shells in, he saw the breeds' riderless horses run past. He squinted and looked up ahead of him on the ground. What he saw made him turn his head and puke. Silverwolf and Beartooth had been literally shredded by the twin loads of buckshot. There wasn't much left of the two murderers that would even be identified as human, just piles of blood and guts and limbs and brains lying in the dirt.

Juan Jimenez was jumping his horse over one of the small fires when Monte fired into it. Horse and rider were blown twenty feet into the air. Protected from most of the nails by his mount's body, Jimenez survived the blast, but both his legs were blown off below the knees, the stumps cauterized by the heat of the explosion. He landed hard, breaking his left arm in two places, white bone protruding from flesh.

When Jimenez looked down and saw both his legs gone, he screeched and yelled and began to tear at his hair, his mind gone. His agony ended moments later when Ben Tolson took pity on him and shot him from the doorway to the cabin.

The Silverado Kid, Blackie Bensen, and Jerry Lindy were riding next to each other. When the Kid realized the trap they were in, he yelled at his men to pull their mounts to the left. "Rush the trees over yonder, it's our only chance to get away," he hollered.

The three men rode hard at the trees, guns blazing, lying low over saddle horns. Mike and Jimmy were lying behind a log, their Henrys resting on it as they fired. Jimmy drew a bead on Blackie Bensen and fired. His first shot took Blackie in the left shoulder, spinning him sideways in the saddle. This caused Jimmy's next shot to pierce Blackie's right shoulder blade, entering his back and boring through into his right lung. The ruptured artery there poured blood into Blackie's chest, causing him to drown before he had time to die from loss of blood.

The Silverado Kid fired his Colts over his horse's head, two shots hitting home, one in Mike's chest, killing him instantly, the second careening off a tree to embed itself in Josh's thigh, throwing him to the ground.

Todd raised his Winchester '73 and pumped two slugs into Jerry Lindy, flinging the outlaw's arms wide before the twin hammer-blows catapulted him out of his saddle to fall under the driving hooves of the Kid's mount, shattering his skull and putting out his lights forever.

Jimmy's next shot grooved the Kid's chest on the left, causing him to rethink his objective. The Kid jerked his reins to the side and pulled his horse's head around to head back into the melee around the cabin. He'd had enough of the rifle brigade.

Explosions were coming one on top of another, billowing clouds of gunpowder and cordite hung over the area like ground fog on a winter morning, the screams of men hit hard and dying and those just wounded mingled to create a symphony of agony and despair.

Into this hell rode Smoke and his friends. Joey screamed his rebel yell at the top of his lungs—"Yee-haw"—striking fear into the hearts of men who knew it to be a call for a fight to the death.

Smoke answered with a yell of his own, and soon all five men charging the murderers and bandits were screaming, firing shotguns and pistols and rifles into the crowd as they closed ranks with them.

The mass of men broke and splintered as Smoke and Joey and Louis and Cal and Pearlie cut a swath of death through it with their blazing firepower and raw courage.

Smoke saw Horton and Max shooting at the cabin from horseback, while Gooden, Boots, and Art South were nearby on foot, their broncs lying dead at their feet, pierced by hundreds of horseshoe nails.

Smoke glanced at Louis and yelled, "Remember them?" and pointed at the group of men. Louis nodded, his eyes flashing. "Damn right," he said. Louis had been one of the men who rode up into the mountains to stand with Smoke against the bounty hunters in the Lee Slater fracas.

Louis bared his teeth in a wide grin. "Let's do it!" he yelled, and rode hard and fast at the killers with Smoke at his side.

Horton and Max saw the two men coming, Colts blazing, and screamed in fear. "Oh, Jesus," Horton shouted, "it's Jensen and that devil Longmont." He whirled his horse and tried to run. A slug from Louis's Colt hit him between the shoulder blades, throwing him off his horse. It took him ten minutes to die, ten minutes of blazing pain.

Max, less a coward than Horton, turned his mount toward Smoke and Louis and charged them, firing his pistols with both hands. Smoke fired twice with the Colt in his right hand, missing both times. Then he triggered the ten-gauge Greener he held in his left hand. It slammed back, throwing

Smoke's arm in the air, making him wonder momentarily if his wrist was broken.

The load of buckshot and nail heads met Max head-on. The lead exploded his body into dozens of pieces, scattering blood and meat over a ten-square-yard area.

Smoke stuck the Greener in his saddle boot and pulled his left-hand Colt. He began to alternate, firing right, then left, then right again as he continued his charge over Max's body toward Gooden, Boots, and Art South.

Gooden snap-shot at Louis and hit home, the slug tearing into the gambler's left thigh but missing the big artery there.

Louis returned the favor, punching a slug into Gooden's gut, doubling him over and knocking him to the ground. "Oh, no," he screamed, "not the stomach again!" He lay there, trying to keep his intestines in his abdomen, but they kept spilling out. Finally, Gooden gave up and lay back and died.

Art South fired at Louis and missed, but nailed his horse in the right shoulder, knocking Louis to the ground. He rolled and sprang to his feet, left hand pushing his wounded left leg to keep him upright.

Art South stepped closer to Louis and extended his hand, pointing his Colt between Louis's eyes. "Any last words, Longmont?" South asked, grinning.

"No," Louis said, and he pulled his derringer out from behind his belt and shot both .44 barrels into South's chest, blowing him backward to land at Boots's feet.

Boots swung his pistol toward the now-unarmed and defenseless Louis, who merely stared unflinchingly back at the outlaw.

Boots's lips curled up in a snarl until they disappeared into the hole Smoke blew in his face with his .44s. The bullets entered on either side of Boots's nose, blowing his cheekbones out the back of his head.

Smoke grabbed the reins of a riderless horse while Louis bent and picked up the Colt he had dropped. Smoke reached down and picked Louis up with one arm and swung him into the saddle.

"Thanks, partner," Louis shouted.

Smoke just smiled and rode off, looking for other prey. Cal and Pearlie had emptied their guns and were reloading, trying to keep their mounts from shying while they punched out empty brass casing and stuffed in new ones.

The Silverado Kid galloped over to where Bill Denver and Slim Watkins were riding, firing up into the cabin. Bill Denver shot into the second-story window, his slug taking Monte Carson in the side of the head and taking out a chunk of his scalp as it knocked him unconscious and blew him back out of sight. Two of the punchers in the room rolled Monte over and began dressing his wound, while a third picked up his rifle and took his place at the window.

The Kid shouted, "Look, Denver, Watkins, over there."

He pointed toward Cal and Pearlie, off to the side of the fracas, surrounded by the gunnies they had killed. "There's only those two young'uns between us and freedom. Let's dust the trail on outta here, boys," he cried.

Denver and Watkins nodded and wheeled their mounts to follow the Kid's lead. The three desperadoes spurred their broncs into a gallop, right at Cal and Pearlie.

Cal shouted, "Look out, Pearlie, here they come!"

With no time to reload his pistols, Cal dropped them and swung the Henry repeating rifle off his back and jerked the lever, firing from the hip without bothering to aim.

Pearlie holstered his still-empty pistols and shucked his Greener twelve-gauge with the cut-down barrel from his saddle boot. He eared back the hammers and let 'em down as Cal began to fire.

The Silverado Kid, scourge and killer of women and children, the man too tough for Tombstone, took three .44-caliber slugs from Cal's rifle, two in the chest and one in the left eye. His entire left side disappeared as he backflipped over his horse's rump to land spread-eagle and dead in the dust.

Denver and Watkins got off four shots with their pistols. The first shot took Cal in the right hip, above the joint, and punched out his right flank, blowing him out of the saddle.

The next shot missed, but the third and fourth both hit Pearlie, one burning a groove along his neck, and the other skimming his belly, tearing a chuck of fat off but not hitting meat.

Pearlie gave a grunt and doubled over, then straightened up and let both his hammers down, one after the other. Denver took a full load of 00 buckshot in the face, losing his head in the bargain, and Watkins's right arm and chest were disintegrated in a hail of hot lead from Pearlie's express gun.

Both men were dead before they hit the ground.

Pearlie jumped out of his saddle and sat cradling Cal's unconscious body in his arms while he reloaded his pistols. No one else was going to hurt his friend as long as he was alive to prevent it.

Jerry Jackson, train robber from Kansas, screaming curse words at the top of his lungs, rode his horse at the cabin, blazing torch in one hand and Colt in the other.

Ben Tolson stepped out of his doorway and onto the porch, his shotgun blasting back at Jackson.

Jackson was blown off his mount at the same time his .44 slug tore into Tolson's chest on the right side, spinning him around and back through the door he gave his life to defend.

Joey, his pistols and both Winchester rifles empty, stood up in his stirrups, looking for Cal and Pearlie. He wanted to make sure they were all right.

He heard a yell from behind him and looked over his shoulder to see Colonel Waters riding at him, his sword held high above his head, blood streaming from a wound in his left shoulder.

"Wells, prepare to die, you bastard," Waters screamed as he bore down on the ex-rebel.

Joey bared his teeth, let out his rebel yell again, and pulled his Arkansas Toothpick from its scabbard. He wheeled Red around and dug his spurs in, causing the big roan to rear and charge toward the Union man.

They passed, the sword flashing toward Joey's head. He ducked and parried with his long knife, deflecting Waters's blade, sending sparks flying in the darkness. Both horses were turned, and again raced toward each other. At the last minute Joey nudged Red with his legs, and the huge animal veered directly into Waters's smaller one, knocking both horse and rider to the ground.

Joey swung his leg over the saddle horn and bounded out of the saddle. He crouched, Arkansas Toothpick held waist-high in front of him, and waited for Waters to get to his feet.

The colonel stood, sleeving blood and sweat off his face. "You killed my men, every one, Wells, and now you are going to die."

Joey spit tobacco juice at Waters's feet. "Yore men, like you, Waters, were cowards who killed defenseless boys who'd given up their guns. They didn't deserve ta live, an' neither do you."

Joey waved the blade back and forth. "Come an' taste my steel, coward!"

Waters lunged, his sword outstretched. Joey leaned to his right, taking the point of the sword in his left shoulder while striking underhanded at Waters.

Joey's blade drove into Waters's gut just under his ribs and angled upward to pierce the officer's heart. The two men, gladiators from a war long past, stood there, chest to chest for a moment, until light and hatred faded from Waters's eyes, and he fell dead before the last of the Missouri Volunteers.

Murdock saw they were losing the battle and shouted at Vasquez, "Emilio, let's get out of here!"

The two men, who had managed to stay on the periphery of the gunfight, wheeled their horses and galloped back toward the Lazy M. They were able to escape Smoke's trap only because of the heavy layer of smoke and dust in the air. By the time the men in the boulders saw them coming, they were out of range of their shotguns.

The fracas lasted another twenty minutes before all the gunnies were either dead or wounded badly enough to be out of commission.

It was full dark by now, and the punchers in the cabin lighted torches, joined with men from the trees and boulders, and began to gather their wounded and dead. The injured who worked for Smoke were brought into the cabin and were attended to by André and the others. Their gunshot wounds were cleaned and dressed and they were given hot soup and coffee, and for those in pain, whiskey.

Smoke bent over Monte Carson, checking his bandages to make sure they were tight. Carson drifted in and out of consciousness, but Smoke was sure he would survive.

André fussed over Louis's leg wound, cleaning and recleaning it until finally Louis said, "Just put a dressing on it, André, there's others here who need you more than I do."

Smoke glanced at Louis, a worried look on his face. "Have you seen Cal or Pearlie or Joey, Louis?"

Louis looked up quickly. "Aren't they here?"

Smoke shook his head. "No."

Louis struggled to his feet, using a rifle as a cane. "Let's go, they may be lying out there wounded"—he glanced at Smoke, naked fear in his eyes—"or worse."

The two men walked among the dead and dying outlaws, ignoring cries for help and mercy as they looked for their friends. The outlaws deserved no mercy. They had taken money to kill others and would now have to face the consequences of their actions. A harsh judgment, but a just one.

Finally, Smoke spied the horse Pearlie had been riding,

standing over near a small creek that ran off to the side of
the cabin. "Over here," he called to Louis, and ran toward
the animal, praying he would find the young men alive.

He stopped short at what he saw. Joey, his left shoulder
wrapped in his bloodstained shirt, was trying to dress
Pearlie's neck and stomach wounds, but Pearlie wouldn't let
go of Cal to give him access. The young cowboy had one
hand holding his wadded-up shirt against a hole in Cal's
flank to stop the bleeding, while he held his Colt in the other,
hammer back, protecting his young friend from anyone else
who might try to harm him.

Smoke heard Joey say, "Come on, Pearlie, the fight's over.
Let me take care of where ya got shot, then we kin git Cal
over to the cabin fer treatment."

Pearlie shook his head. "I'm not movin' from here till I
see Smoke. I promised him I was gonna watch over Cal, and
I aim to do just that!"

Smoke chuckled as Louis hobbled up beside him. "Would
you look at that, Louis. Like a mother hen with her chick."

Louis grinned. "If I ever find a woman who'll take care of
me like that, I'll give up gambling and settle down."

"Pearlie, you've done a good job," Smoke said as he knelt
by Cal. "Now let Joey fix you up while I take Cal to the
cabin so André can patch his wounds."

Pearlie lifted fatigue-ridden eyes to stare at Smoke.
"Smoke, you got him?"

Smoke lifted Cal in his arms. "Yes, Pearlie, I've got him."

Pearlie mumbled, "Good," then let his pistol fall to the
dirt and passed out.

The next morning, after the doctor from Pueblo had been
summoned and he had come to the cabin to do what he
could, Smoke and his friends sat around a campfire outside,
the cabin being used to house the wounded.

"Well, we didn't do near as bad as I feared," Joey said. "We lost seven good men, and another eight will be a long time recovering."

He took his fixin's out and built himself a cigarette, sticking it in the side of his mouth and lighting it. He upended his coffee cup and drained it without removing the butt. "I'm damned sorry to lose Ben Tolson." He raised his head and looked at Smoke. "He was a fine man, one any man would be proud to call partner!"

"He'd do to ride the river with," Smoke said. These were two of the best compliments a westerner could give another cowboy.

Joey said, "If'n it's all right with you and the others, I'd like ta give his widow a share of the Rocking C. He earned it."

Smoke nodded. "He damn sure did. From what I'm told, if he hadn't stopped that last rider, he would've burned the entire cabin down and all the men with it."

Cal was lying on a makeshift cot before the fire, spooning down some of André's beef stew as fast as he could. He cut his eyes over to look at the bandage around Pearlie's gut. Though thin as a rail, Pearlie was a famous chowhound, being known to eat everything that wasn't tied down.

"Pearlie," Cal said with an innocent look in his eyes, "did I hear the doctor correct when he said if you didn't have that layer of fat around yore middle, you would've had a serious wound?"

"Yeah," Pearlie said, a suspicious tone to his voice. "So?"

Cal grinned. "So, I guess you can thank Miss Sally for savin' yore life, what with all the bear sign she makes that you scarf down." He winked at Smoke. "I guess no one will kid you anymore 'bout that gut around yore middle."

Pearlie looked down. "What gut? I don't have no gut!" He glanced back over at Cal, trying to look mean. "And if you didn't have this unnatural affection for lead, neither one of us would've gotten shot!"

After a few minutes Joey said, "Smoke, I've checked all the bodies, an' I don't see no sign of Murdock nor of Vasquez."

"I know. One of the boys you assigned to the boulders, Billy Joe I think it was, said right at the end a couple of riders got past them, headed back toward Murdock's place."

Joey struggled to his feet, unable to use his left arm because of the sling the doctor had put on it. "Well, no need to waste any time. I'm goin' after 'em 'fore they have time to split."

Smoke got up and brushed dirt off the seat of his pants. "I'm coming too. I got a score to settle for Puma Buck."

As the others started to rise, Smoke held out his hand. "No, boys. Joey and I started this alone, and we're going finish it alone." He smiled at his wounded friends. "Thanks for the offer, but this trail is ours and we have to ride it all the way to the end."

23

Smoke walked over to talk to Louis while one of the uninjured hands threw a saddle on Red and Horse.

"Louis, there's something I want you to do for me while we're over at Murdock's, settling things."

Louis looked up. "Anything, Smoke, as long as it doesn't include dancing." He tapped the large bandage André had wrapped around his leg. "I'm not too spry on my feet just yet."

"Oh, I think you will enjoy this little errand. You can even take the buckboard, with a pillow for your leg if need be."

"Oh?"

"Yes, I'd like you to ride into Pueblo and pick something up for me. I had Ben send a wire to Big Rock last time we were in town, and the . . . package ought to have arrived on today's train."

A slow smile curled Louis's lips. "I hope this package is what I think it is."

Smoke grinned. "Here's what I want you to do . . ."

Shotgun Sam Willowby and Gimpy Monroe were stuffing their faces and filling their guts at the hotel dining room in Pueblo with their horses packed and loaded outside for the long ride back to New Mexico.

Two pretty, young blond women accompanied by a small

boy walked into the hotel. As they sat down at a table across the room and ordered lunch, Shotgun Sam glanced around. They were the only patrons, since the dining hour had passed already.

He nudged Gimpy with his elbow. "Hey, Gimpy. What say we stroll on over there and say howdy?" The killer raised his eyebrows in a lewd grin. "We might git lucky an' knock off a piece or two of that fine-lookin' woman flesh."

Gimpy scowled. "You a randy old coot, Shotgun. Man o' yore age ought not be thinkin' with his dick all the time."

Shotgun spread his arms "What've we got to lose? The sheriff's out there shootin' it up with Murdock and his gang." His grin turned even more evil "Who's to stop us from whatever we want to do?"

Gimpy cut his eyes toward the women. He nodded as he chewed his steak. "You're right, an' they is right purty at that."

Shotgun added, "An' we gonna be a long time on the trail 'fore we git another chance like this. Let's do it."

Shotgun Sam picked up the Greener he was never without, hitched his belt over his fat gut, and swaggered over to the table where the ladies sat.

The pair of outlaws stood a few feet in front of their table, hands on hips.

"Howdy, ladies," Shotgun said. "My pardner and me was wonderin' if'n maybe you'd like to come up to our room an' have a little drink of whiskey with us." He tried a smile, revealing dirty yellow teeth.

Sally Jensen glanced up, then smiled, her beauty striking in the afternoon sunlight from the window. "I don't think so, cowboy. We're married ladies in town to meet our husbands."

Gimpy looked around at the empty room and shrugged. "I don't see no menfolk here. Seems a man shouldn't oughta neglect pretty girls like you two."

Betty Wells, who had grown up around men like these, was less refined and gracious than Sally. She gave the pair a scornful look and said, "Get lost, white trash, 'fore my husband comes in here and makes you wish you'd never been born."

Sally raised her napkin to her face to hide her smile at Betty's earthy way of talking.

Shotgun's face flamed red and he snorted through his nose. "Don't try an' git uppity with me, you bitch!" He eared back the hammers on his Greener with a loud double-click. "I asked ya nice, now I'm tellin' ya, git yore butt up and come with me or I'll have to scatter ya all over the room!"

Sally leaned back in her chair, a small smile curling the corners of her lips. She looked at Betty and winked where the men couldn't see it. "Sure, mister. Is it okay if we powder our noses first?"

Gimpy laughed a nasty laugh. "You can powder anything you want long as you hurry it up."

Sally nodded at Betty and glanced at their purses sitting on the floor. "Why don't you get your powder out, Betty, for these nice gentlemen?"

Betty grinned. "That's a right good idea, Sally."

The ladies picked up their purses and laid them on the table in front of them, snapped open the clasps, and put their hands inside at the same time.

With beautiful, sexy smiles, both Betty and Sally looked up at Shotgun and Gimpy and pulled the triggers on the short-barreled pistols both of them carried.

Their guns exploded, blowing out the bottoms of the purses, then blowing Shotgun and Gimpy back across the room, smoking holes in the middle of their chests.

The outlaws kicked and thrashed for a moment, then lay still.

The manager of the hotel came running into the room, a Colt in his hand. "You ladies all right?" he yelled.

Sally put her purse back on the floor, wiped her lips daintily with her napkin, and said, "Yes, sir, but could I have another cup of coffee, please?"

Betty looked over at him, smiling. "And could I see the dessert menu? Little Tom has been waiting all day for some cake, if you have any."

Smoke put a hand on Joey's arm and helped him climb up on Red, then he stepped into the saddle on Horse. They rode off toward the Lazy M and Murdock and Vasquez at an easy canter.

After a few miles Smoke noticed fresh blood on Joey's shoulder and a tight grimace of pain on his lips.

"This ride too much for you your wound, Joey? If it is, we can go back and wait a few days for the wound the doc stitched to knit together."

Joey shook his head, looking straight ahead. "I want to end this business, Smoke. All my life it seems I've been livin' with hate, first during the war, then after, when I was chasin' Redlegs." He took a deep breath. "The only time I've been at peace was with Betty, and then when little Tom came I thought my life was complete and all that anger was behind me."

He pulled a plug of Bull Durham out and bit off the end. As he chewed, he talked. "Since Vasquez and his men rode into my life, I've found all that hate and more back in my heart." He looked over at Smoke. "At first I thought I'd missed all the excitement of the chase, an' the killin'. But I've found that the hate festers inside of ya, an' I'm afraid if I don't git shut of it soon, I won't be fit ta go back to Betty. She's just too fine a woman ta have ta live with a man all eat up inside with hate an' bitterness."

Smoke smiled gently. "I don't think you, or Betty and Tom, have to worry about that, Joey. You've just been doing what any man would do, fighting to protect your family and your home." He slowed Horse and bent his head to light a cigar. When he had it going good, he caught up with Joey. "When you see the end of Vasquez, and Murdock, things'll go back like they were. The only hate I can see inside you is anger at the men who hurt your loved ones, and that's a good thing. A man who won't stand up for his family is no good."

Joey gave a tight grin. "You ought to be a preachin' man, Smoke. You sure know the right things ta say."

Smoke laughed until he choked on his cigar smoke. After he finished coughing, he said, "Now, that's a picture to think on, Smoke Jensen, holding Sunday revivals."

They stopped at the riverbed and watered their mounts in one of the small pools. "What are you going to do about the river once this is over?" Joey asked.

Smoke gave him a look he didn't quite understand, and said, "Oh, I think I'll leave that to the new ramrod of the Rocking C. It'll be his decision to make."

Another hour of easy riding brought them to the outskirts of the Lazy M. In the distance they could see two horses tied up to a hitching rail near the corral, away from the house. Smoke pulled Puma Buck's Sharps .52 from his saddle boot and began to walk toward a group of trees about a hundred yards from the house, keeping the trees between him and the house so Murdock and Vasquez wouldn't be able to see him coming.

Joey walked alongside, carrying a Henry repeating rifle in his right hand, hammer thong loose on his Colt.

Murdock was in his study, down on hands and knees in front of his safe, shoveling wads of currency into a large leather valise.

He and Vasquez had arrived back at his ranch at three in the morning and had taken a short nap, planning to leave the territory early the next morning. They slept longer than intended and were now hurrying to make up for lost time.

Vasquez was sitting at Murdock's desk, his feet up on the leather surface, a bottle of Murdock's bourbon in one hand and one of his hand-rolled cigars in the other.

"What you do now, Señor Murdock? Where you go?"

Murdock looked back over his shoulder, his hands full of cash. "I plan to head up into Montana. There's still plenty of wild country up there, a place where a man with plenty of money, and the right help, can still carve out a good ranch."

"What about Emilio?" Vasquez asked, his right hand inching toward his machete. He was looking at the amount of cash in the safe, thinking it would last a long time in Mexico. He could change his name, maybe grow a beard, and live like a king for the rest of his life.

Murdock noticed the way Vasquez was eyeing his money so he pulled a Colt out of the safe and pointed it at the Mexican. "Just keep your hands where I can see 'em, Emilio. I was planning on taking you with me, I can always use a man like you." He raised his eyebrows. "But now I m not so sure that's a good idea. I don't want to have to sleep with one eye open all the way to Montana to keep you from killing me and taking my money."

Vasquez smiled, showing all his teeth. "But, señor, you have nothing to fear from Einilio. I work for you always."

Murdock opened his mouth to answer, when he heard a booming explosion from in front of his house and a .52-caliber slug plowed through his front wall, tore through a chest of drawers, and continued on to embed itself in a rear wall.

Murdock and Vasquez threw themselves on the floor behind his desk, Vasquez spilling bourbon all over both of them in the process.

"Chinga . . ." Vasquez grunted.

"Jesus!" said Murdock.

Smoke hollered to the house, "Murdock, Vasquez. Come out with your hands up and you can go on living . . . at least until the people of Pueblo hang you."

The two outlaws looked at each other under the desk. "What do you think?" Murdock asked.

Vasquez shrugged. "Not much choice, is it? I think I rather get shot than hang. You?"

Murdock nodded. "Maybe I can buy our way out."

Vasquez gave a short laugh. "Señor, you not know man very well. Jensen and Wells not want money, they want our blood."

Murdock didn't believe him. Everyone wanted money. It was what made the world go round. "Jensen, Wells. I've got twenty thousand in here, in cash. It's yours if you turn your backs and let us ride out of here!" Murdock called.

His answer was another .52-caliber bullet tearing through the walls of his ranch house. It seemed nothing would stop the big Sharps slugs.

Murdock said, "I guess you're right."

Vasquez answered, "Besides, after they kill us, they take money anyway."

Murdock scrabbled on hands and knees to the wall, where he took his Winchester '73 rifle down off a rack. He grabbed a Henry and pitched it across the room to Vasquez. "Here, let's start firing back. Maybe we'll get lucky."

Vasquez chuckled to hide the fear gnawing at his guts like a dog worrying a bone. "And maybe horse learn to talk, but I do not think so."

They crawled across the floor and peeked out the window. They could see nothing, until a sheet of flame shot out of a small group of trees in front of the house and another bullet shattered the door frame, knocking the door half open and leaving it hanging on one hinge.

"Goddamn," Murdock yelped. He rose and began to fire the Winchester as fast as he could work the lever and pull the trigger. He didn't bother to aim, just poured a lot of lead out at the attackers.

"Vasquez," he whispered, "see if you can sneak out the back and circle around 'em. Maybe you can get them from behind."

"Hokay, señor," the Mexican answered. He crawled through the house, praying to a God he had almost forgotten existed that he make it to his horse. He wasn't about to risk trying to sneak up on Jensen and Wells. If he got to his horse, he was going to be long gone before they knew it.

He eased the back door open and stuck his head out. Good, there was no one in sight and no place to hide behind the cabin.

Crouching low, he ran in a wide circle to where he and Murdock had left their horses. He slipped between the rails on the far side of the corral and crawled on his belly across thirty yards of horse shit to get to his mount's reins. He reached up and untied the reins and stood up next to his bronc, his hand on the saddle horn, ready to leap into the saddle and be off.

"Howdy, El Machete," he heard from behind him.

He stiffened, then relaxed. It was time to make his play. Maybe, like Murdock said, he would get lucky.

He grabbed iron and whirled. Before his pistol was out of its holster, Joey had drawn and fired, his bullet taking the Mexican in the right shoulder. The force of the slug spun Vasquez around, threw him back against his horse, then to the ground. He fumbled for his gun with his left hand, but couldn't get it out before Joey was standing over him.

"Okay, Señor Wells. I surrender."

Joey's eyes were terrible for the Mexican to behold, They were black as the pits of hell and cold as those of a rattler ready to strike.

Joey leaned down and pulled Vasquez's machete from its scabbard on his back. "I don't think so, Vasquez."

He held the blade up and twisted it so it gleamed and reflected sunlight on its razor-sharp edge. Joey looked at him and smiled. "Guess what, El Machete?"

Suddenly Vasquez knew what the cowboy had in mind. "No . . . no . . . *por favor,* do not do this, señor!"

Joey pursed his lips. "Try as I might, Vasquez, I cain't think of a single reason I shouldn't."

With a move like a rattler's strike, Joey slashed with the machete, severing Vasquez's right arm at the elbow. The Mexican screamed and grabbed at his stump with his left hand.

"Remember Mr. Williams, El Machete?"

As Vasquez looked up through pain-clouded, terror-filled eyes, the machete flashed again, severing his left arm at the elbow.

Vasquez screamed again and thrashed around on the ground, trying to stanch the blood as it spurted from his ruined arms by sticking the stumps in the dirt. It didn't work.

Joey stood and watched as Vasquez bled to death, remembering his wife and son lying in their own blood because of this man.

Smoke continued peppering the house with the Sharps, until one of the slugs tore open the potbelly stove, setting the house on fire.

As flames consumed the wooden structure, Murdock began to scream. Just before the roof caved in, he came running out of the door, his clothes smoldering and smoking, holding a leather valise in one hand and a Colt in the other. He was cocking and firing wildly at Smoke, who stood calmly, ignoring the whine of the slugs around his head.

"This is for Puma Buck," he whispered, and put a slug between Murdock's eyes. His head exploded and he dropped where he stood, dead and in hell before he hit the ground.

Smoke walked over and picked up the valise, looked in it, smiled, and hooked the handles on his saddle horn.

He helped Joey up on Red, he climbed on Horse, and they headed home.

24

On the way back to the Rocking C, Smoke had to stop and reapply the dressings on Joey's shoulder. All the activity had reopened his wound and started it bleeding again.

"What's in the valise?" he asked.

Smoke smiled. "I'll show you when we get back to the ranch."

They got back up on their broncs and continued to ride, slower this time to make it easier on Joey's shoulder.

As they approached the cabin, Smoke glanced at the corral to see if his package had arrived. It had. There were four Palouse mares prancing in there, running and kicking up their heels, glad to be off that train and out in the open air again. There was also a small paint pony. Ready to be ridden.

Joey, tired and weak from loss of blood, rode with his head down and didn't notice the new arrivals.

Smoke helped Joey off Red and called, "Hello, the cabin. We got two hungry cowpokes here."

A petite blond woman walked out on the porch. She had her arm around a boy, about three or four years old, who walked next to her, a wooden brace on his right leg.

"Hungry cowpokes, are ye'?" she said, her hands on her

hips. "And how about your wives, who are starved for a little affection from their men?"

Joey's head jerked up, and his eyes lit up with happiness. "Betty. . . Tom . . ." He ran up the steps to the porch, all fatigue vanished, grinning like a madman. He threw his right arm around Betty and hugged her until she cried, "Stop that, you big galoot, you're going to break my neck." But her eyes were full of laughter. Joey then knelt and hugged, more gently this time, little Tom. "Yore leg . . . you're walkin'?"

Betty stood next to him, running her hands through her man's hair as he knelt next to their son. "The doctor says the brace can come off in two weeks. He thinks the leg will be good as new by then."

Joey looked up, tears in his eyes. "And you?"

"I'm fine, dear. The wound healed without complications." She frowned, looking at his bloody shoulder. "But I don't know about you. It looks like you've been up to your old tricks again."

He stood and laid his head on her shoulder, breathing deep, smelling her hair. "It's over, Betty. The feud is over and done with."

She said, "And you're home for good," mock anger in her voice. "No more galavantin' around doing your man things?"

Joey, famed killer of over two hundred men, looked sheepish. "No, dear. I'm home for good."

From inside the cabin a voice called, "Hey, cowboy, are you going to tell me hello or just stand there with your mouth open?"

Smoke jumped like he'd been shot. He had been so happy to see the Wellses reunited, he'd plumb forgot that Sally had come to Pueblo with them. He ran up the stairs and swept her up in his arms, whirling her around, kissing her, and whispering in her ear that he loved her.

* * *

Later, around the dinner table, Smoke explained to Joey what he had done. "I had Ben Tolson send a wire to Sally to see if she could arrange for Betty and Tom to ride the train up here. I knew you wanted them to see the country and see what they thought of it."

Sally patted Betty on the arm. "You have a wonderful wife and son, Joey. We've become fast friends already."

"I also had Sally bring up those Palouse mares we talked about for Red. It's time you carried on his bloodline, and I think they'd make a good cross."

"But what about that little paint pony out there? Surely you can't want to breed it to Red?"

Smoke shook his head. "No, that's for Tom. Soon's that splint comes off, it'll be time to put him on horseback and teach him to ride. That Indian paint will be perfect to learn on, small and gentle until he's ready for more."

"Smoke," Joey said, "I don't know what to say. You've done so much . . ."

Smoke put his hand on Joey's shoulder. "Don't say anything just yet. Take some time, show your family the country. If they, and you, like it up here like I think you will, then I want you to take over the Rocking C ranch."

"But, I cain't . . ."

"Yes, you can, Joey. Remember, you've got lots of partners and we're all counting on you to make this the best ranch in central Colorado." Smoke snapped his fingers. "Oh, I almost forgot."

He reached behind him and placed the leather valise Murdock had been carrying on the table in front of Joey. "Here's a little something from Murdock, to pay you back for all the pain and trouble he's caused you and your family."

Joey opened the valise, and he and Betty glanced in. She sucked in her breath and covered her mouth. "There must be a million dollars in there," she said.

Smoke smiled. "More like twenty thousand. It should be

enough to buy the Lazy M and its stock from the bank and combine the two ranches into one big enough to make some real money for all the men and the families of the men who helped us defeat Murdock."

Louis interrupted. "Unless, of course, you'd rather play a little poker with those greenbacks." He cracked his knuckles and smiled. "I'm a little rusty, but if you'll remind me how to play, we could start a game."

Betty reached over and grabbed the valise. "Oh, no, you don't, Mr. Longmont. This money's going straight to the bank, and then it's going to be put to use to help all our new friends at our Colorado home."

Joey raised his eyebrows and grinned.

Sally put her hand in Smoke's. "Looks like we have some new neighbors, Smoke."

THE FIRST
MOUNTAIN MAN:
PREACHER'S
FORTUNE

1

As with life itself, beauty and ugliness existed side by side in the country through which the lone man traveled. Stretches of barren desert alternated with bands of rich green vegetation that bordered the occasional stream. Ranges of pine-covered mountains shouldered up out of the arid landscape surrounding them. Some of the mountains were capped with snow that sparkled a brilliant white in the sun, a tantalizing reminder of coolness while down below the heat had set in, despite the fact that it was still early in the summer.

From time to time the traveler reined in his horse and sat there staring at the mountains. His only other companion, a massive, shaggy creature that appeared to be as much wolf as dog, sat down and waited patiently, tongue lolling from his mouth. The big cur was happy as long as he accompanied this particular human.

With their typical sanguinity, the Spanish explorers who had first come to this land more than a hundred years earlier had dubbed the mountains the Sangre de Cristos—the Blood of Christ. The man called Preacher could see how the mountains got the name. When the sun hit them just right, they did have a certain reddish hue to them that might remind somebody of blood. To Preacher, though, they were just mountains. One more obstacle to cross.

He had come up out of Texas after wintering there and was anxious to get back to his beloved Rocky Mountains, where he had spent so much of his life after running away from home as a boy. Texas had been all right. . . . A mite too humid for his tastes, maybe, especially over east in those thick, piney woods. But the American settlers who were moving in, such as that big strapping McCallister boy and his pretty, yellow-haired wife, seemed to be fine, feisty folks. If the Mexican authorities who ran the place didn't trod careful, they would have some real trouble on their hands in a few years. Americans wouldn't stand for being mistreated for too long. They were a peaceful people at heart, but they loved freedom and would fight for it if they had to, by God! Preacher expected those Texicans wouldn't be any different. He wouldn't have minded being around to watch the fun when they finally got tired of ol' Santa Anna's high-handed arrogance.

By that time, though, he would probably be back up in the mountains, trapping beaver. That was his true calling.

Well, that . . . and getting into trouble, seemed like.

"Come on, Horse," Preacher said as he heeled his mount into motion. "There's bound to be a pass up there some-wheres, and I reckon we better start lookin' for it." He rode toward the mountains at an easy lope, with the big wolflike dog bounding along ahead of him and the horse.

This Nuevo Mexico was part of Mexico, too, but the government didn't have the same problems here that it did over in Texas. There weren't nearly as many Americans around, although more traders and trappers from the States were drifting in all the time. Many of them had come to stay, too, unlike Preacher, who was just passing through. Charles Bent and Ceran St. Vrain had established a regular trade route between Santa Fe and St. Louis, and over the past few years, hundreds of wagons had gone back and forth over what folks had started to call the Santa Fe Trail. Preacher thought it a certainty that there would be trouble sooner or later between the American settlers and the Mexican government in Texas. Over here in New Mexico, it was just a likelihood.

But again, the possibility didn't worry Preacher overmuch. He liked a good scrap as well as the next man—well, better than some, to tell the truth—but he didn't go out of his way to look for a fight. It would be fine and dandy with him if nothing happened to delay his return to the Rockies and those clear, cold, high-country streams where there were scads of beaver just waitin' for him to take their pelts.

First, though, he had to get through the Sangre de Cristos, and before that he figured to stop for the night at a trading post he had heard about in Taos. It was supposed to be located at the foot of the mountains and was the last stop for travelers on their way north, the last outpost of any sort of civilization in that direction.

As a rule, Preacher wasn't that all-fired fond of civilization, but as he rode toward the mountains, he had to admit to himself that a drink of whiskey, a hot meal, and a soft place to lay his head for the night might not be such bad things.

There might even be a pretty woman at that trading post. He purely did love the sight of a pretty woman.

"Bring out the whores, old man!" Cobey Larson bellowed as he slammed a knobby fist on the bar. The rough planks that had been laid down between two whiskey barrels to form the bar jumped a little under the impact.

"I have told you, Señor," said the stocky Mexican man behind the planks. A worried frown creased his sweating forehead. "There are no women like that here, only my wife and daughter."

One of the other Americans, the barrel-shaped Arnie

Ross, laughed and said, "That sounds all right to me. I don't care who the hell they're related to, as long as they's soft and bouncy in bed."

The proprietor of the trading post, whose name was Vincente Ojeida, struggled to keep his composure in the face of these vulgar, insistent *americanos*. Their words were offensive to him and inflamed his blood with their insult to his honor, but he maintained a tight rein on his temper as he said, "If you wish supplies or whiskey, I can help you, but otherwise I cannot."

Larson leaned closer, a scowl on his whiskery face. "Are you tellin' me there ain't even any squaws around here we can lay with?"

Vincente shrugged eloquently. "I am sorry, Señor. Such is the way of things."

"Well, that may be all right for you. . . ." Larson reached to his waist and pulled a pistol that had been tucked behind his belt. It was already loaded and primed, and as he raised it he drew back the hammer. "But I ain't so philosophical. I been on the trail a damn long time, and I want a woman." He pointed the barrel of the pistol at Vincente's nose. "You get my drift, pepperbelly?"

Larson's companions laughed as they enjoyed the show their leader was putting on. There were four of them: the rotund Ross, Bert McDermott, Hank Sewell, and Wick Jimpson. McDermott and Sewell were cut from the same cloth as Larson, lean, buckskin-clad men with hawklike faces. Jimpson was bigger, towering over the others. His shoulders had filled the doorway of the trading post from side to side when he came through it. His brainpower didn't match his size, though. He was little better than a halfwit, devoted to Cobey Larson and willing to do anything Larson told him to.

Vincente had sensed that the five gringos were trouble as soon as he saw them saunter into the trading post. They arrived on horseback, with no wagons, so he knew they weren't traders. They could have been fur trappers or even prospectors—some people believed there was gold to be found in the mountains, and there would always be men who searched for precious metals—but they did not have the look of men accustomed to such hard labor.

That left only one real possibility as far as Vincente could see: The men had to be *bandidos,* robbers who preyed on the trade caravans.

There were no other customers in the trading post at the moment, which emboldened the Americans even more. They crowded up to the bar, and Larson repeated his demand. "Bring out your wife and daughter! I want to see 'em!"

Elgera and Lupita were in the storage room at the back of the trading post. It was mere luck that they had not been in the big front room when the Americans entered. But Vincente knew the door behind him was open a crack, and Elgera would have heard the loud voices of the visitors and realized that the best thing for her and her pretty fourteen-year-old daughter to do was to stay out of sight. She was smart as well as beautiful, and that was one more reason Vincente considered himself a very lucky man to have married her. He himself was not so intelligent, else he never would have mentioned the very existence of a wife and daughter to these beasts who walked like men. The words had slipped out before he could recall them. Now he had to try to repair the damage.

"They are not here, Señor," he said, trying to make his voice sound forceful. That wasn't easy when he was staring down the barrel of a pistol.

"You just said they were!"

"They live here with me, of course, but they are not here *now.*"

"Well, where the hell are they?"

Vincente wished he was better at thinking up lies. "They have gone to the mission," he said.

"Mission? What mission?"

"In the mountains," Vincente said, gesturing vaguely in the direction of the peaks that loomed over the trading post. "They have gone to pray in the church. A . . . a pilgrimage."

Larson brought the pistol closer to Vincente's face and prodded the tip of his nose with it. With an ugly grin on his face, Larson said, "I think you're lyin'. I think them women are here, and you just figure they're too good for the likes of us. Well, that's where you're wrong, pepperbelly. Trot 'em out here, or I'll blow your damn head off."

Vincente's heart slugged heavily in his chest. Elgera must have heard that threat, and he knew his wife well enough to know what she would do next. Unwilling to stand by and let her husband be murdered, she would rush out and take her chance with the *americanos*. He just hoped she would have the sense to hide Lupita somewhere in the storeroom first.

But it didn't come to that because, at that moment, another man said from the open front door of the trading post, "I wouldn't do that, friend. You shoot him and I'll have to pour my own drink, and I ain't in much of a mood to play bartender."

All five of the men swung around to look at Preacher. That meant the one who had the gun in his hand was sort of pointing it toward him, and Preacher didn't like that. Generally, whenever a fella pointed a gun at him, Preacher shot the son of a bitch before the son of a bitch could shoot him. It seemed only reasonable.

This time, however, he restrained the impulse to draw one of the pistols at his waist. He had been in the saddle all day, and he was tired. Killin' meant buryin', and digging graves was hard work.

"Who the hell are you?" the man with the drawn gun demanded.

To a bunch of hard cases like these, he probably didn't look like much. He was tall and lean—enough so that some folks might call him skinny—and dressed in buckskins that had seen better days. He hadn't trimmed his dark hair and beard in a while, so he supposed he looked a mite shaggy. A felt hat with a big, floppy brim was cocked back on his head. He looked almost sleepy as he leaned a shoulder against the doorjamb, but anybody who took the time to look close at the deep-set, piercing eyes under bushy brows would see that they told a different story.

"Who, me?" Preacher said mildly. "I'm just a pilgrim passin' through these parts, friend. Not lookin' for any trouble. Thought maybe I'd rest myself and my horse here for the night before we start over the pass in the mornin'."

"This ain't any of your business, so you'd be wise to keep your nose out of it."

"I expect you're right." Preacher brought his left hand up and laid a finger alongside his nose. "But this here proboscis of mine is too big to keep out of things sometimes. You like that word? Means long nose. I heard it once from a fella who had a lot of book learnin'."

"Ah, hell, Cobey," the short, round man said. "He's just a half-wit of some sort. Probably dumber than Wick." He jerked a thumb at the biggest member of the group, a huge young man with a dull expression on his face.

The one with the gun grunted and said, "Yeah." Addressing himself to Preacher, he went on. "Turn around and ride out of here, mister, if you're smart enough to know what's good for you."

Preacher chuckled. "You've sure got me figured out, friend. I'm nosy and I'm dumb."

"I ain't your friend, damn it! Quit callin' me that!" The man turned back to the stocky Mexican, who Preacher assumed was the proprietor of the trading post. "Now, are you gonna bring them women out here, or do I have to shoot you?"

"Women?" Preacher called. "What women? There's women here?"

Cobey looked back over his shoulder and said through gritted teeth, "Are you still here? This greaser's got a wife and daughter stashed somewhere, and we aim to have 'em!"

Preacher's left hand rubbed his bearded jaw. "I sure am glad you told me we ain't friends."

"What?" The gunman half-turned toward Preacher again, his annoyance showing plainly on his face.

"If we ain't friends," Preacher said, "then I don't have to feel bad about doin' this."

He drew his pistol and shot the man called Cobey.

2

The bullet ripped through Cobey's arm, missing the bone but gouging out a considerable hunk of flesh and splattering blood. It was his gun arm, which meant that the pistol in his hand flew across the room. It hit the wall and went off, but the heavy ball buried itself harmlessly in a barrel of flour.

Preacher hadn't been expecting trouble, so his pistol wasn't double-shotted. If it had been, Cobey probably would have been dead by now, but the fella was lucky. He got to live, as long as he didn't do anything else stupid.

The same went for his companions, so to keep them from getting frisky, Preacher pulled his second pistol and leveled it at them. He did it fast, while they were still gaping in surprise.

"You boys stand still," Preacher told them. "Fat boy, see to your friend. The rest of you, don't move."

Cobey had slumped to his knees in front of the makeshift bar and clutched his wounded right arm with his left hand. His face had gone gray under its tan, but Preacher had to give him credit for toughness. He hadn't yelled in pain, hadn't made a sound, in fact, other than breathing hard.

His round friend hurried over to him and knelt beside him. He pulled a dirty bandanna from a pocket in his buckskins and tied it tightly around the wound, trying to staunch the flow of blood.

The air in the trading post smelled like burned powder. Preacher looked at the proprietor and said, "Sorry about the mess, amigo. I know blood can be mighty hard to get up out of floorboards."

"That . . . that is all right, Señor."

The door behind the man swung open far enough for a woman to peer out into the front room. Preacher saw dark eyes and a mass of thick raven hair. When the woman rushed out and threw her arms around the proprietor, she revealed just how pretty she was. She was followed by a younger, smaller version of herself. The wife and daughter he had heard mentioned, Preacher decided. Nobody else they could be.

It would have been better if the two of them had stayed in the back room, out of sight. Preacher could understand, though, why the woman had wanted to rush out and make sure her husband was all right. She would have heard that shot and not been sure exactly what had happened.

But as it was, her presence, and especially that of her daughter, immediately made things worse. Because the biggest of the hard cases, who was built sort of like a mountain, stared at the girl for a couple of seconds and then said, "I want her." He took a lumbering step toward the bar.

"Hold it!" Preacher snapped. "Unless you boys want me to shoot him, you better grab your pard."

One of the men took hold of the giant's arm, but the big man shook off the grip like it was nothing. He took another step toward the girl, who shrank back with a look of horror on her face.

"Come here," the giant said to her. "I want to kiss on you."

The proprietor pushed his wife aside and moved quickly between his daughter and the big man. He reached onto a shelf and plucked a knife from it. The blade shone red, as if already drenched in blood, in the late afternoon sunlight that slanted through a window.

"Get back, Señor!" the proprietor said. "Get back, I tell you!"

Without waiting, he slashed at one of the giant's outstretched hands. The knife ripped a gash across the back of it. Blood welled from the wound as the giant snatched his hand back and howled in pain. "You hurt me!" he roared. Furious, he lunged forward, crashing into the bar and swinging his malletlike fists at the proprietor.

Preacher didn't have any choice then. The Mexican was half the size of the giant. He would wind up being beaten to death if Preacher didn't stop it.

The pistol in Preacher's left hand blasted. The ball hit the giant in the back of the leg, knocking it out from under him. He reeled and went down, finishing the job of demolishing the bar. Planks scattered around him and one of the whiskey barrels overturned. The bung popped out and the Who-Hit-John began to leak, glugging onto the floor and forming a puddle. The sharp reek of the stuff mixed with the tang of the gunpowder.

The other three men, knowing that both of Preacher's guns were now empty, rushed him.

Preacher was expecting that. He flung the left-hand gun as hard as he could, and in these close quarters, when the gun hit one of the men in the face, it pulped his nose and sent him staggering backward, blood gushing down over his mouth and chin. Preacher ducked under a roundhouse punch thrown by one of the other men and grabbed the front of the hombre's homespun shirt. A heave and an outthrust leg to knock his feet out from under him, and the man found himself sailing through the air to crash heavily to the puncheon floor.

That left Preacher only the short, round man to deal with, but to his surprise he quickly discovered that it was a little like fighting a buzz saw. The fella was a lot faster than he looked, and a flurry of hard punches seemed to come from every direction when he closed in. A couple of them landed solidly, knocking Preacher back a step. He caught his balance, set his feet, and swung a blow of his own, driving a fist into the man's belly. That was another surprise. The man was built like a barrel, and punching him in the stomach was about like hitting a barrel, one made of thick, stout oak. He didn't even grunt.

The fella with the broken nose was back in the fight, too. His bloody face was contorted in a snarl as he circled and grabbed Preacher from behind, pinning his arms to his sides. "Get him, Arnie!" he yelled thickly at the fat man. "Beat the hell out of him!"

Preacher figured he ought to consider himself lucky that they were all mad enough to fight with their fists, rather than pulling their guns. Dealing with three-to-one odds in a gunfight, and him with a couple of empty pistols at that, would have been a mite tricky. He was confident that he would have figured out a way to do it, but hell, a brawl like this was more fun, anyway.

He stomped back on the instep of the man holding him and then jerked his head back, too, snapping it into the man's face. More cartilage crunched in the already injured nose. The man screamed and let go just as the fat man charged Preacher again. Preacher dropped to the floor and went forward into the fat man's legs in a rolling dive. The fat man's momentum carried him over Preacher and into his howling friend. Both of them went down in a tangle of arms and legs.

Preacher rolled on over and came up on hands and knees in time to see that the man he had shot had gotten back on his feet. He had grabbed up an ax from a table where several of them lay, and now he swung the double-bitted tool at Preacher's head. Preacher dived aside at the last second. The ax head bit deeply into the wooden floor and lodged there.

Preacher came up from the floor, uncoiling like a snake as he threw an uppercut that landed on the wounded man's jaw. The impact of the blow shivered all the way up Preacher's arm, and he hoped he hadn't busted a knuckle or two. The punch lifted the wounded man off his feet and sent him slamming down onto his back. Preacher didn't think he would be getting up any time soon.

But that still left three men—well, two, since the one with the broken nose was lying huddled on the floor, his hands pressed to his face, whimpering—but those two might want to tussle some more. Preacher clenched his fists and waited to see if they were going to attack again.

He heard a familiar, ominous, metallic clicking sound from behind him. "Step aside, Señor!" the proprietor cried. "Step aside, and I will deal with these animals as they deserve!"

Preacher threw a look over his shoulder and saw the owner of the trading post standing there with a double-barreled shotgun in his hands. The man's face was dark with outrage, and Preacher could tell that he wanted to pull the triggers and blast all five of the hard cases into bloody shreds.

That didn't sound like such a bad idea, but Preacher knew it wasn't the right thing to do. He said softly, "Hold on there, amigo. I don't reckon you want to kill these men."

"Oh, but I do, Señor, I do!"

Preacher shook his head. "Right now you do, but I can tell by lookin' at you that you ain't the type to kill a man in cold blood. If you do, it'll eat on you from now on, and you wouldn't never know a minute's peace."

"The law would not blame me! I am defending my home and my family and my honor!"

"I ain't talkin' about the law. I'm talkin' about what's in your own heart."

The man hesitated. Preacher knew he had read him right. The barrels of the shotgun lowered slightly.

"That's right," Preacher said. "What you need to do is give me the shotgun. *I'll* kill 'em, and I won't never lose a second's sleep over it."

The man seized the opportunity and pressed the shotgun into Preacher's hands. He leveled it at the five men. From the terror-stricken looks on the faces of four of them—the giant with the wounded leg lay there sobbing in pain, not really knowing what was going on—they thought they were about to die.

"I will kill you," Preacher went on, "unless you pick yourselves up, get the hell out of here, and never come back. If you do, if you cause these good folks even one second of trouble or grief, I'll hear about it, and I'll hunt you down and kill you slow. I've lived with the Injuns, boys, and they taught me all their tricks. I can keep a fella alive for days, sufferin' more pain than you ever dreamed a man could suffer. It's up to you. Die now, die later . . . or be smart and live."

Cobey, the one Preacher had shot in the arm, looked at him and grated, "Who the hell are you?"

A grin stretched across the mountain man's lean face. "They call me Preacher."

The name meant something to a couple of the men, including the short, fat one. He said, "Damn it, Cobey, I've heard of Preacher. The Injuns call him Bear Killer. He fought a grizzly with just a knife."

The other one who recognized Preacher's name added, "We better do what he says. I ain't hankerin' to die today."

Cobey didn't look happy about it, but he couldn't ignore what his companions had told him. He struggled to his feet, clutching his wounded arm again, and said, "Get Wick, and let's get out of here."

It took all three of the other men, including the one who was still blubbering about his nose being busted, to lift the giant off the floor. All three of them supported him as he limped toward the door. As he went out, he twisted his head around to look one last time at the girl. "Pretty," he muttered. "Mighty pretty."

From the corner of his eye, Preacher saw a shiver go through the girl's slender form.

Cobey was the last one to back through the door onto the trading post's porch. "I ain't gonna forget you, Preacher," he said. "Our trails will cross again one of these days."

"You'd best hope not," Preacher said. "Next time, I might just shoot you on sight."

"Not if I shoot you first."

With that threat, Cobey turned away and stumbled after his friends, who were struggling to get the giant mounted on a rangy mule tied up outside along with the horses belonging to the rest of them.

Preacher stepped into the doorway and kept an eye on them as they mounted up. The shotgun was tucked under his arm now, but he could bring it into play in an instant if he needed to, and they knew it. He stood there, tall and vigilant, and watched as they rode away. He didn't go back inside until the five men were out of sight.

The proprietor and his wife and daughter had already started trying to clean up the mess that the brawl had made. Preacher set the shotgun on a counter at the side of the room and moved to help them.

"No, Señor," the proprietor said. "You have done enough already." He pulled a chair over. "Please, sit. Would you like something to eat or drink?"

"Maybe later," Preacher said as he nudged the chair aside. "Right now I'd like to help you straighten up. I'm partly to blame for that ruckus, I reckon."

"Not at all," the Mexican insisted. "Those gringo dogs deserve all the blame. No offense," he added quickly.

Preacher flashed a grin. "None taken. I can't speak for my dog, though. He might be insulted by the comparison."

That made him look around. Dog had trotted off into a nearby stand of pines as they rode up, probably sniffing out a rabbit or something, so he hadn't been around to take part in the fracas. Having the big cur at his side would have evened the odds considerably, but Preacher figured he had done all right on his own. He didn't see Dog, but he knew the animal would be back later.

Together, he and the Mexican righted the whiskey barrel before all of the fiery stuff could leak out. The fumes were still potent. Preacher waved a hand in front of his face and said, "A fella could get drunk just takin' a few deep breaths."

"Lupita, open all the windows," the proprietor said. "We must let more air in."

"Si, Papá," the girl said as she hurried to carry out his command.

The Mexican turned back to Preacher and extended his hand. "I am Vincente Ojeida. That is my wife Elgera and my daughter Lupita."

Preacher shook hands with the man and said, "Glad to meet you, Vincente. I reckon you heard my name."

"Sí. The fame of the mountain man called Preacher has reached even here."

Preacher waved a hand. "Fame's just a matter of luck, usually bad. You run into enough trouble and live through it, folks start to talk about you."

"Like killing a grizzly bear with only a knife."

"What folks don't mention," Preacher said dryly, "is that that ol' griz came might dang close to killin' me, too."

"And yet you live."

"I got an advantage some folks don't," Preacher said. "I'm just too blasted stubborn to die."

3

Preacher and Vincente put the planks on the barrels to form a bar again while Elgera and Lupita mopped up the spilled whiskey as best they could and straightened the chairs and tables that had been knocked over. Both of the females fussed over Preacher, sitting him down at one of the tables and hurrying off to the kitchen in the rear of the building to prepare a meal for him. Vincente poured a couple of drinks, brought them over to the table, and sat down with Preacher. He sipped the whiskey, licked his lips, and said in satisfaction, "Ah."

"I thought you fellas drank tequila, mescal, things like that," Preacher commented.

"As a young man I ate many worms from the bottom of a bottle," Vincente said, "but as I grew older and began to trade with Señors Bent and St. Vrain, I have learned to appreciate a good Scotch whiskey."

Preacher laughed. "I don't reckon I can argue with that."

Vincente grew more serious. "I cannot thank you enough for what you did, Señor Preacher. I knew those men were trouble as soon as they came in, but I could not reach my shotgun in time. They were between me and it."

"I'm a little surprised you don't carry a pistol."

"I am not a good shot," Vincente said with a shrug. "The fact of the matter is, I am a man of peace, more suited to running a trading post than I am to fighting. I need a shotgun if I want to hit anything." He drank a little more of the whiskey. "But you are right, Señor. From now on, I will always have a pistol close at hand."

"That's a good idea, out in the middle of nowhere like this. You never know when Injuns might come raidin'."

"The Indians in the area are peaceful, for the most part. It is the white men I worry about. Again, I mean no offense."

Preacher leaned back in his chair and cocked an ankle on the other knee. "I imagine there are a whole heap more gringos around here than there were before the Santa Fe Trail opened up."

Vincente nodded. *"Sí.* The wagon trains pass through here every few weeks. Also, trappers who run their lines in the Sangre de Cristos come here for supplies. This is the closest place they can trade their pelts."

Preacher's interest perked up at the mention of trapping. "Many beaver to be found up in them mountains?"

"Some. Not the same as farther north. But there are fewer men trapping this far south, so it evens out, so to speak."

"I was on my way back up to the Tetons, but I might tarry for a spell in the Sangre de Cristos, sort of check out the streams."

Vincente beamed at him. "You will always be welcome here, Señor Preacher."

"Make it just Preacher. Señor means mister, and I ain't never been too comfortable with that."

"Very well, Preacher. My house is your house."

Elgera and Lupita came in then with platters of tortillas and bowls of beans and a pot of stew that smelled enticingly of chilies. Preacher and Vincente dug in, and although the stew was so hot it bid fair to blister his innards, it went down well and Preacher thoroughly enjoyed it. He had such a good time eating and visiting with the Ojeida family, in fact, that he almost forgot about the violence that had taken place earlier in the trading post. He was mighty glad he had decided to stop here for the night.

Later, he tended to Horse and left the big stallion in a shed behind the main building. Dog came dragging in, licking his chops, so Preacher knew he had filled up on rabbit and prairie dog, more than likely. Vincente had offered to let Preacher have the trading post's one bedroom, saying that he and his family could make pallets for themselves in the main room, but Preacher wouldn't hear of it. The weather was warm, although at this elevation the temperature would cool off considerably by morning, and he had a good bedroll that would suit him just fine. He told Vincente that he would spread his robes under the nearby trees.

"That'll let me keep an eye on the place, too," Preacher added in a low voice as he and Vincente stood on the porch after supper. Night had fallen, and the heavens were ablaze with a canopy of bright, twinkling stars. "Just in case that bunch decides to come back."

"You do not think they would, do you?" Vincente asked with a worried frown on his face.

"No, I don't," Preacher answered honestly. "Shot up and beat up like they are, I reckon they went off somewheres to lick their wounds for a while. I don't think they'll bother you again. But you can't never tell for sure what two-legged skunks will do. They're worser than the four-legged kind."

"*Gracias,* Preacher. Sleep well."

"I always do. That's the sign of a clear conscience, I reckon."

Vincente hesitated. "I have heard it said that you have killed many men. . . ."

"Only them that needed killin'," Preacher said.

* * *

The five men sat huddled around a small campfire, not far from the foot of the pass. They passed around a whiskey bottle. Most of the time, the only sounds were the crackling of flames and an occasional muttered curse.

Cobey's arm hurt like blazes. Once they had made camp, he had ordered Arnie to clean out the wound with some of their whiskey. Arnie had been reluctant to use good liquor for that purpose, but Cobey had insisted. He'd told Arnie to clean the wound in Wick's leg the same way. Wick had whimpered and mewled like a hurt kitten the whole time.

There wasn't much they could do for Hank's busted nose. Arnie had tried for a while to push everything back into place, but he had given up because Hank was howling so much and thrashing around. "Let it heal crooked, for all I care," Arnie had said in disgust.

Bert McDermott, who had been lucky enough to come through the brawl with only a few bruises, had laughed and said, "Yeah, Hank, it ain't like you're so handsome the gals are linin' up for you. The rest of you is so ugly, chances are they'll never notice a little thing like a crooked nose."

Hank had taken offense at that, of course, and there might have been a fight if Cobey hadn't growled at them to put a cork in it and settle down. They did what he said. None of the others really wanted to cross Cobey Larson, especially when he was mad to start with.

Now, as they sat around the fire, being careful not to stare into the flames and ruin their night vision, Cobey took a nip from the bottle and said, "That bastard's gonna be sorry he ever crossed our trail."

"I'm already sorry he crossed our trail," Arnie said. "I was lookin' forward to some beans an' tortillas."

"I wanted some tequila," Bert said. "I can't stand greasers, but they make some fine booze."

Wick said, "That little girl sure was pretty. I wanted to comb my fingers through that long black hair of hers."

"That ain't all you wanted to do to her," Bert gibed.

Wick looked down at the ground and flushed in embarrassment, although it was hard to tell that in the ruddy glow of the campfire. "I wouldn't'a hurt her," he said. "I'd'a been real careful with her, like she was a little doll or somethin'."

Cobey wanted to tell them all to shut up their yammering. He was in no mood for it. But he suppressed his anger. These men were his partners, after all, and it wasn't their fault that they had run up against the man called Preacher.

As if reading Cobey's mind, Arnie asked, "You reckon it was really him?"

"Preacher, you mean?" Bert asked.

"Yeah. I've heard about him, but I never saw him before."

"I did," Hank Sewell put in, his voice sounding odd because his nose had swelled up and was closed off completely. "Saw him at a Rendezvous a few years ago, not long after he picked up the name Preacher. It was him, all right."

"How come you didn't know him right off?" Cobey asked.

Hank shrugged. "Well, it's been a while. And it ain't like him and me was ever friends. I just saw him once at a Rendezvous, that's all."

"Is he a bad man?" Wick asked. "He must be, because he hurt me."

"He's a dangerous man," Arnie said. "That's for damned sure."

Cobey snapped, "He's just a man. He can be killed like anybody else. And I intend to do it."

Arnie leaned forward and said anxiously, "We got a job to do, Cobey. We can't meet that fella at the tradin' post like we was supposed to. How're we gonna handle it now?"

"We're going to wait here," Cobey answered without hesitation. "The main trail passes right by here. If everything's goin' accordin' to plan, he ought to pass by in a few days, and we'll meet him then. No reason we can't go right ahead with the thing and get it done."

"And when it's done?"

The bottle had made its way back around the circle to Cobey. He lifted it to his lips and took a healthy slug. When he lowered it, he said, "By then we'll all be healed up, so we'll find Mr. High-and-Mighty Preacher and make him rue the day."

"Rue the day," Wick repeated. "It sounds nice."

Preacher meant to leave the trading post early the next morning, but after a peaceful night's sleep, Vincente Ojeida asked him for some tips on handling a pistol, and Preacher was in such a good mood that he agreed to spend the morning there.

Followed by Dog, Preacher and Vincente walked out to a large open space behind the trading post, where Preacher placed several fist-sized chunks of rock on the trunk of a fallen tree Vincente had been meaning to split up for firewood. Then he moved back about twenty paces and drew both pistols. While Vincente watched, Preacher lifted both weapons and fired them without even seeming to aim. Two of the rocks on the log blew apart.

"Dios mio!"

Preacher lowered the pistols and smiled. "Don't go gettin' the idea that I can do that ever' time," he cautioned. "Along about ever' seven or eight shots, I'm liable to miss one, 'specially if somebody's shootin' back at me."

"You can teach me how to do this?" Vincente asked enthusiastically.

"I seriously doubt it. Some hombres, and I happen to be one of 'em, are what you might call freaks o' nature. The Good Lord blessed us with the speed to get a gun into action in a hurry, and the steady hand and eye so that most of the time all we have to do to hit somethin' is to look at it. It's a God-given talent . . . although sometimes when there's so much killin' goin' on, it seems to me almost like the Devil might've had a hand in it, too. There's times, though, when it comes in mighty handy."

Vincente looked disappointed. "But you cannot teach me?"

"Not to do what I just done. With practice, though, you can be as good a shot, or better, than most folks you'll ever run into. Let me see your pistol."

Vincente held out the gun he had brought from the trading post. Preacher looked it over, nodded in satisfaction, and handed it back to him.

"That's a fine weapon, and it's been taken care of. It'll shoot true. Now load 'er up and let 'er rip."

"You want me to shoot at the rocks?" Vincente asked as he loaded and primed the pistol. His movements were fairly slow, but he didn't fumble with what he was doing. That was a good sign.

"Just pick one of them and aim at it," Preacher told him. "Don't get in a hurry, but don't waste a lot of time, either. The longer you stand there holding your arm outstretched with a gun in your hand, the heavier it's gonna get."

Instinctively, Vincente took a deep breath without Preacher having to tell him to do so. He aimed for a couple of seconds and then pressed the trigger. The pistol boomed and bucked upward in his hand. He lowered it, squinted through the cloud of powder smoke that floated in front of him, and said, "I missed!"

"The rock's still there, all right. Look right underneath it, though." Preacher pointed at a scar in the wood.

"Is that where the shot hit?"

"Sure is. You didn't miss but by a few inches. Try again."

Vincente began reloading. The look of disappointment that had been on his face a moment earlier had vanished swiftly. When he was ready, he took aim and fired again. This time one of the rocks shattered, the pieces flying apart as the heavy lead ball struck it. Vincente let out an excited whoop.

"There you go," Preacher said. "You got a good eye. I can tell that about you. All you need is practice, and you'll be a lot better shot than you ever thought you could be."

"I cannot thank you enough, Señor Preacher—I mean, Preacher. Can I shoot again?"

Preacher waved a hand. "It's your powder and lead. Have at it."

For the next half hour, Vincente practiced, with Preacher setting up more rocks on the log for him to use as targets. He still missed about as many shots as he made, but Preacher thought that was pretty good and said as much. When Vincente was ready to call a halt to the practice, he said, "You will stay and eat with us, and then this afternoon, after siesta, we will shoot again, no?"

Preacher rubbed his jaw. He'd been planning to ride out, but Vincente was good company and his womenfolks were good cooks, there was no doubt about that. And Preacher figured there were still more tips he could give Vincente that would make him an even better shot. For one thing, Vincente needed to understand that shooting at rocks on a log and shooting at a man who was trying to kill you as hard as you were trying to kill him were two entirely different things. Preacher figured that a good grasp of that truth was at least as important as knowing how to stand and hold the gun and aim.

"Sure," he told the eager Vincente. "I reckon I can tarry a while longer. That's one good thing about livin' wild and free—nobody's waitin' for you."

But even as the words came out of his mouth, a memory flashed through his mind, a memory of a girl with long dark hair and a gentle touch and a sweet smile . . . a girl long gone, who probably never would have been his, even if she had lived. Yes, living wild and free had its blessings. . . .

But it had its little curses, too.

4

What with one thing and another, three days went by and Preacher was still at the trading post. There were things around the place, like repairing the roof and the corral fence, that Vincente could use the help of another man for, and their shooting practice continued, too. Lupita had made friends with Dog, and the big brute was acting almost like a pup again. Preacher had ridden fairly hard from Texas, and Horse could use the rest. Preacher's only real worry was that if he stayed here too long, he might get fat from Elgera's cooking. He couldn't hardly empty his plate at mealtime before she had it filled up again.

Every day when he rolled out of his robes, he told himself that he'd be moving on. But good intentions, and all that . . .

He and Vincente were behind the trading post on the third afternoon. Vincente was practicing firing two pistols at the same time and not getting the hang of it. He had just lowered the empty weapons when Lupita came running around the building, calling, *"Papá, Papá!* Wagons coming!" Dog trailed behind her, barking excitedly.

Preacher and Vincente turned to face the girl. "One of the wagon trains of Señor Bent and Señor St. Vrain?" Vincente asked.

Lupita shook her head. "No, there are only two wagons. They come from the south."

"Travelers," Vincente said. "But where are they going?"

"Only one way to find out," Preacher said.

The four of them walked back around the trading post. Preacher saw the wagons trundling toward them along the trail, drawn by teams of mules. They were squarish vehicles with canvas covers over the backs. As they came closer, Preacher saw that a well-dressed man and woman sat on the driver's seat of the first wagon. They appeared to be in their twenties. The young man handled the reins and was doing a decent job of it. The second wagon was being driven by a stolid-faced Indian in white tunic and pants. A blue sash was around his waist, and a matching strip of cloth was tied around his head, holding back his thick, square-cut black hair. Next to him on the seat of the second wagon was a priest in a brown, hooded robe. Three Indians who resembled the one driving the wagon followed on horseback.

"Ricos," Vincente said quietly. "Rich ones, from Taos or Santa Fe, or perhaps even Mexico City. Why are they here?"

Preacher agreed with Vincente's assessment. The young couple's fancy clothes were indicators of their wealth, as were the sturdy wagons and the fine mule teams. The Indians were probably their servants. But Preacher didn't know why they had come to the edge of the Sangre de Cristos, or what the priest was doing with them.

Elgera came out on the porch, too, and watched with the others as the wagons pulled up to the trading post and stopped. The young man climbed down easily from the lead wagon's high seat and then turned to help the young woman descend to the ground. Together, they came to the bottom of the steps leading to the log building's porch.

They made a fine-looking pair. The boy was handsome and the gal was beautiful. Preacher couldn't decide if they

were married, or brother and sister. He thought he detected
a family resemblance that made him lean toward the latter
choice.

That was confirmed a moment later when the young man
said, *"Hola, señores y señora."* He took off his flat-crowned
hat, revealing thick, glossy black hair, and swept low in a
bow to Lupita. *"Y muy bonita señorita."*

Lupita blushed at the compliment, making her even
prettier.

The young man straightened and replaced his hat on his
head. "I am Esteban Felipe Alvarez, and this is my sister
Juanita Olivera Alvarez."

"Welcome to my trading post, Señor and Señorita," Vincente said. "I am Vincente Ojeida. This is my wife and daughter, and our amigo, Señor Preacher."

"Preacher?" The sharply spoken word came from the
priest, who had climbed down from the second wagon and
now came forward. The four Indians stayed deferentially in
the background. "You are a man of God?" The priest's expression as he looked up at Preacher made it clear that he
found that idea hard to believe.

"Not like you, Padre," Preacher replied, "although I
reckon I'm on good enough speakin' terms with the fella
you call El Señor Dios."

"If you are not a preacher, is it not presumptuous of you
to call yourself one?"

Most of the time, Preacher got along all right with men of
God, but he felt an instinctive dislike for this little priest.
The padre had thrown back the hood of his robe, revealing
that he was bald except for a fringe of hair around his ears
and the back of his head. He wasn't all that old, though,
probably no more than thirty.

Keeping his temper in check, Preacher said, "The Injuns
tagged that moniker on me. I got captured by a bunch of
Blackfoot who figured on torturin' me to death. I couldn't get

away from 'em, so I done the only thing I could. I started talkin'. I'd seen a street preacher one time, back in St. Louis, so I done like him and spouted the Gospel for ten or twelve hours straight. By that time, the Injuns decided that I was touched by the spirits—"

"The Holy Spirit?" the priest interrupted.

"Spirits that they found holy, anyway." Preacher shrugged. "They let me go, and that was all I cared about. The story got around, and I been knowed as Preacher ever since."

Vincente looked up from beside him and said, "You never told me that story, amigo."

"Well, I've only knowed you a few days, and you ain't asked about it yet."

"This is true."

The priest said, "I still think it is improper for a sinner to bear such a name."

"Last time I checked," Preacher drawled, "we was *all* sinners, old son."

The priest glared and might have continued the argument, but Esteban Alvarez said smoothly, "You must forgive Father Hortensio. He takes his calling very seriously."

The priest sniffed. "How else should I take it? What else in life could be more important than doing the work of our Holy Mother Church?"

As if he hadn't been interrupted, Esteban continued. "We have journeyed far, all the way from Mexico City, and would like to buy some supplies before we continue on our way. Can you accommodate us, Señor Ojeida?"

"Of course, Señor. Please, you and your sister come in."

So far, Juanita Alvarez had not spoken. But as she and her brother stepped onto the porch, Lupita came up to her and said, "Señorita, your dress is so . . . so beautiful! I have never seen anything like it!"

Juanita smiled at the girl and said, "*Gracias.* I have others in the wagon. Perhaps you would like to try one of them on before we leave?"

Lupita turned her excited gaze toward her mother. "Did you hear that? Can I try on one of the señorita's dresses, *Mamá?*"

"Perhaps," Elgera said. "We will see." She was frowning slightly, as if she didn't totally approve of the visitors. Preacher could understand that. Elgera probably didn't want her daughter's head getting filled with notions. Life out here on the Santa Fe Trail was hard, and there wasn't much time for extravagances.

Everyone went inside the trading post except Preacher and the Indians. Father Hortensio gave the mountain man an unfriendly look out of the corner of his eye as he went past, but Preacher ignored him. He didn't give a hoot whether or not some priest approved of him.

Preacher lingered on the porch instead and kept an eye on the Indians. He wondered what tribe they belonged to. Down in Texas, there were Comanches and Apaches, but these Indians didn't belong to either of those tribes. Navajo, maybe, he decided, although that didn't seem exactly right, either. He wasn't going to ask them. He didn't know if they even spoke English, and his Spanish, while good enough for him to get by, wasn't fluent by any means. They paid no attention to him. The three on horseback had dismounted, and now all four of them squatted on their haunches next to the second wagon and talked among themselves in guttural voices too low for Preacher to make out the words. He probably wouldn't have been able to understand their lingo, even if he knew what they were saying.

Vincente came back out onto the porch a few minutes later. "Señor Alvarez is picking out his supplies," he said. "I think he must be the richest man who ever stopped here."

"Did he say where they're bound?"

Vincente shook his head. "Up over the pass, that is all I know."

Preacher rubbed at his jaw as he frowned in thought. "Sort of out of place up here, ain't they?"

"It is true," Vincente said with a shrug. "The señorita, I can tell she is tired. The journey has been hard on her."

"They must have some mighty important reason to come all the way from Mexico City and go on up into the mountains like they're plannin'."

"*Sí*, but it is no business of mine."

"Mine, neither," Preacher said.

But he had a nagging feeling in the back of his mind that it might not stay that way.

Since it was already fairly late in the day, it came as no surprise when Esteban Alvarez decided that he and his sister and their companions would camp there at the trading post that night before moving on to the pass the next day. Vincente explained apologetically that he had no rooms to rent to the travelers, but Esteban told him not to worry.

"My sister sleeps in our wagon, and I have a tent for myself and Father Hortensio," he explained. "The Yaquis sleep under the wagons."

"Yaquis, eh?" Preacher said. "I wondered what tribe they belonged to."

"They come from the mountains of Mexico," Esteban said, "and are fierce fighters. But once they have declared their allegiance, there are no more loyal servants to be found anywhere."

Preacher hoped the young man was right about that. He had kept a close eye on the Yaquis, and they didn't look all that trustworthy to him. They had a sort of mean look in their eyes, like they would have enjoyed staking him out on an anthill and carving his eyelids off with their knives. The feeling was enough to make Preacher's hand itch to close around the butt of a pistol.

He kept his suspicions to himself, though, not wanting to alarm Vincente and Elgera without any reason. And he had to admit that the Yaquis had been on their best behavior so far. After dinner that night, everybody bedded down just like Esteban had said they would.

Preacher was restless and kept waking up during the night to check on the group camped near the trading post. As far as he could tell, everything was quiet and peaceful. The travelers rose early the next morning. While the Yaquis prepared the teams for leaving, Esteban, Juanita, and Father Hortensio went into the trading post for breakfast. Juanita carried one of her dresses, which she gave to Lupita. "It will be a little large on you, *chiquita*, but your *mamá* can take it up," she said with a smile.

Lupita clutched the dress to her and asked excitedly, "Can I keep it, *Mamá?*"

A little reluctantly, Elgera said, "That will be fine. *Muchas gracias, señorita.*"

"De nada," Juanita said casually.

Father Hortensio watched the exchange with a frown of disapproval on his face. "Vanity is a sin," he proclaimed to no one in particular.

Preacher was leaning against a pickle barrel beside the priest. In a quiet voice, he said, "So's bein' a sour-faced jackass who acts like he's got a corncob stuck up his butt."

The priest turned sharply toward him and hissed, "You dare—"

"These are good folks," Preacher cut in. "I don't mean to be disrespectful, Padre, but I won't stand by while they're bad-mouthed, neither."

"You do mean to be disrespectful," Father Hortensio sneered at him. "You are a heathen, Señor!"

Preacher shrugged. "I disagree, but even if you're right, I been called worse in my time."

The priest just scowled, shook his bald head, and turned

away. Preacher let him go. He sort of liked Esteban and Juanita, who didn't seem quite as spoiled as they might have been, given their wealth, but he was more than ready for the unpleasant little priest to move on.

After breakfast, that was what happened. The Indians had the wagons ready, so the Alvarez siblings climbed on board, as did Father Hortensio, and the little caravan moved out with waves and shouts of farewell from the Ojeida family. Preacher stood off to the side with Dog and watched the wagons roll toward the mountains. It took them a while, but eventually they were out of sight.

Vincente came over to Preacher. "You will stay again?" he asked.

"Sure. I wouldn't mind givin' those folks a good head start before I leave. I'm headin' the same direction, and I don't want to ride up on 'em and wind up havin' to travel with them. I've had enough of that priest."

Vincente crossed himself. "Father Hortensio is a man of God. He should be respected."

"Fella's got to earn my respect," Preacher said. "He don't get it just because he wears a padre's robes."

Vincente changed the subject, clearly not wanting to argue with this tall, lanky mountain man who had become his friend. They walked around behind the trading post and Vincente resumed his target practice, with Preacher making a suggestion from time to time that might improve his marksmanship.

More than an hour had passed fairly pleasantly in that manner when Preacher suddenly stood up from the tree stump where he had been sitting and cocked his head. Vincente noticed his reaction and asked, "What is it, Preacher?"

"I thought I heard somethin'. . . . There it is again!" Distant popping sounds came to his ears.

Vincente frowned. "I hear it, too. What is that?"

A grim look settled over Preacher's rugged face. "Those

are gunshots, Vincente," he said, "and it sounds like they're comin' from the pass."

Vincente's eyes widened. *"Caramba!* Señor Esteban and Señorita Juanita . . ."

Preacher nodded and said, "Yeah. It sounds like those young folks are in trouble. Bad trouble."

5

After the first flurry of gunshots, the sounds settled down to more regularly spaced intervals. Preacher heard them plainly enough as he was getting Horse ready to ride. It sounded to him like somebody had bushwhacked the Alvarez wagons and now had their occupants pinned down.

Of course, it was possible the shots had nothing to do with Esteban and Juanita and their companions. Preacher figured that was pretty unlikely, though.

Vincente came up to him as he finished tightening the saddle cinch. "I will go with you, Preacher," he declared. He had put on a sombrero and had two pistols tucked behind his belt.

Preacher shook his head. "No, I reckon that ain't a good idea. You've got a family and a business to look after, Vincente. Handlin' gun trouble is more in my line."

"But I can help you," Vincente protested. "I am a much better shot now. You have said so yourself."

"Maybe so, but there's things you don't know yet, and I ain't got time right now to teach you." Preacher saw hurt feelings flare in Vincente's eyes at that blunt statement. He reached out and squeezed the man's shoulder. "You're a damn fine fella, Vincente, but there's liable to be killin' work up there in the mountains, and you just don't know how to do that yet."

If you're lucky, Preacher added to himself, *you never will*.

He swung up into the saddle while Vincente stood there frowning. From atop Horse's back, Preacher said, "If I don't come back, you might ought to get word to Santa Fe about those young folks. The army might want to come up here and have a look around for 'em."

Vincente nodded. *"Sí.* I will do this."

Preacher returned the nod and heeled Horse into a fast trot. Dog bounded along beside them. Without looking back, he rode toward the Sangre de Cristos and the high pass that led through the mountains.

It wasn't hard to follow the wagon tracks leading to the pass. The Alvarez wagons were far from the first ones to use this trail. Over the past few years, hundreds of vehicles belonging to Bent and St. Vrain had traversed this path, carrying heavy loads of goods both ways between St. Louis and Santa Fe. The wheels of those wagons had etched ruts in the softer ground and had even left marks on the rockier stretches. Preacher still heard the faint popping of gunshots as he reached the base of the mountains and started up the trail to the pass.

At first the route swung back and forth and the slope was fairly gentle. The trail reached a point, however, where the climb was sharper. Horse managed it without much trouble, but Preacher sensed that even the valiant animal underneath him was laboring a bit more than usual. For mules or oxen pulling wagons, it would be a long, slow climb. It probably took most of a day for a wagon train to reach the top.

Preacher wondered how far Esteban and Juanita had made it before they were ambushed.

Again he cautioned himself not to jump to conclusions. Maybe it was one of the trade caravans that had been attacked. He figured they must be tempting targets for *bandidos* or renegade Indians, what with all the supplies they carried. Vincente hadn't said anything about expecting a caravan to come through today, but that didn't mean it was impossible.

He would find out soon enough, Preacher told himself grimly. The shots were louder now. He would be coming to the site of the trouble before too much longer.

About forty-five minutes had passed since he left the Ojeida trading post when he spotted a puff of smoke from a rocky bluff that shouldered out from the side of the mountain and overlooked the trail. The smoke was followed an instant later by the crack of a rifle, the sound traveling clearly through the thin air. Preacher reined Horse to a halt and studied the face of that bluff. Several more puffs of smoke spurted out from different points. There must be a ledge running across there, Preacher decided, and half-a-dozen or so gunmen were hidden up there, firing down at the trail. From where he was, a hump of ground shielded the trail itself from his sight. Preacher dismounted and, taking his rifle with him, strode up the rise so that he could see the trail.

His mouth tightened into a thin line at the sight of the two wagons stopped on a fairly level stretch about two hundred yards ahead of him. They were the Alvarez wagons, all right; he had no trouble recognizing them. One of the lead mules on each team had been shot and collapsed in its traces, bringing both vehicles to a halt. Preacher didn't see anyone on or around the wagons, but as he watched, a shot came from underneath one of them. The members of the party must have taken cover underneath the wagons when the shooting started.

Preacher wondered if any of them had been hit. There were no bodies lying around, at least not that he could see, and he told himself that was a good sign. Those pilgrims were in a bad fix, though. At the point where the wagons were stopped, the trail was about twenty feet wide. To the right, the bluff where the bushwhackers were hidden rose sharply. To the left of the wagons was a steep drop-off that fell several hundred feet to a canyon. There was no cover around the wagons themselves. The people hiding underneath them were pinned down, good and proper.

They weren't putting up much of a fight, either. An occasional shot came from under the wagons, but each time it drew heavy fire in return. The thick planks of the wagon bodies would probably stop most bullets, but the lead balls might ricochet from the stony surface of the trail and bounce around under the wagons, wreaking havoc.

Somehow, Preacher had to figure out a way to stop those ambushers, or the people with the wagons were doomed.

His brain, trained by years of living in dangerous situations despite his relative youth, swiftly considered and discarded several options. Riding down to the wagons wouldn't do any good; if he did that, then he'd just be trapped, too. He might have been able to climb above the ledge where the riflemen were concealed and fire down into their midst, but that would take too long. He was looking at a climb of an hour or more that way. And taking potshots at them from down here might annoy them, but he doubted if he could do any serious damage that way. The angle was such that the ledge shielded them.

Preacher lifted his gaze higher on the bluff. He saw several outcroppings of rock that were littered with boulders. He frowned as he studied the angles and did some rough figuring in his head. He thought that if he could get some of those rocks to moving, they might just roll down onto that ledge and cause some real problems for the bushwhackers. Of course, that would put the people even lower down with the wagons at some risk, too, but Preacher thought the slope was such that any falling rocks would fly out beyond the ledge and plummet on into the canyon far below. And there weren't enough boulders up there to cause a full-fledged avalanche.

It was worth a try, he decided. He couldn't see any other way to help the pilgrims trapped under those wagons.

He moved to the side of the trail and rested the barrel of his rifle on a rock, steadying it as he drew a bead on a likely boulder. His shot had to hit right under it, where the rock rested on the ground. If his aim was too high, the ball from his rifle would just splatter against the face of the boulder itself. He pulled back the hammer, sighted in as best he could, and pressed the trigger. The flintlock snapped, the priming powder went off with a hiss, and then the main charge exploded with a loud roar. The stock kicked hard against Preacher's shoulder.

The distance was too great. He couldn't tell where his shot had hit, or if it had done any good. But he knew it might take several more tries to dislodge the boulder. With quick, practiced movements, he reloaded the rifle, rested it on the rock again, and fired a second time.

By now the men on the ledge must have heard his shots and figured out that somebody else was taking cards in this game. Preacher wasn't surprised when a ball struck the rock wall above his head, causing a little shower of dust and rock splinters. The shot had missed him by several yards, so he didn't worry overmuch about it. He just finished reloading, brought the rifle to his shoulder, and let off another round.

This time he saw the boulder lurch forward a few inches before it came to a stop.

Something whined past his ear like a big insect. The ball kicked up dust in the trail behind him. He finished reloading and lifted the rifle again, nestling his beard-stubbled cheek against the smooth wood of the stock as he drew a bead. He pressed the trigger, and once again the rifle roared and kicked.

The boulder was poised on the bluff in a delicate balance. The men who had hidden themselves on the ledge to ambush the wagons had seen that it was a good place for a trap, but they had neglected to notice that they were placing themselves in harm's way as well. Now, as the boulder lurched forward again and began to roll, Preacher thought he heard faint shouts of alarm from the bushwhackers.

The boulder toppled headlong, bounced off a couple of other rocks, and started them rolling, too. With a rumble like distant thunder, the rockslide grew in breadth and power.

Preacher saw men leap to their feet and race for the far end of the ledge, where it curved back out of sight. Smaller rocks smashed down around them as they fled. Preacher finished reloading the rifle yet again and snapped it to his shoulder. Aiming quickly, he fired. He thought one of the bushwhackers staggered as if hit, but he couldn't be sure about that. Dust was beginning to rise, obscuring his view of the ledge.

He saw one of the men struck by a falling boulder, though. It swept the luckless victim right off the ledge and out into empty space. Screaming, the man plummeted toward the trail some fifty feet below. He fell past it, though, along with the rock that had knocked him from the ledge, and disappeared into the canyon. His scream faded away.

Preacher reloaded the rifle yet again and ran back to Horse, where he hung the weapon on its sling attached to the saddle. He swung up onto Horse's back, called, "Come on, Dog!" and rode hard for the wagons.

Clouds of dust hung in the air around the ledge. It wouldn't take long for them to blow away. But for the moment, even if the bushwhackers dared to venture back out onto the ledge, they wouldn't be able to see to shoot down at the trail. They would have to fire blind, if at all. Preacher wanted to take advantage of that momentary respite and get the wagons moving again.

The Yaquis must have heard the pounding of Horse's hooves on the trail, because they scrambled out from under the wagons, rifles in their hands. Before they could blaze away at Preacher, Esteban Alvarez followed them out and called, "No! Hold your fire!"

Preacher reached the wagons a moment later and didn't bother to dismount. He swept an arm toward a bend in the trail about a hundred yards ahead of them and shouted, "Let's go! Cut them dead mules loose and get the hell out of here! Once you're around that bend, maybe they won't be able to fire down on you!"

Esteban caught at his stirrup. "Señor Preacher!" he said. "We were attacked—"

"I know that, and them buzzards are liable to come back and make a second try at you if you just sit here waitin' for 'em!" He called out to the Yaquis in his rough Spanish, hoping they understood as he repeated his orders to cut the dead mules loose from the rest of the animals and move the wagons around the bend.

The Yaquis got to work while Esteban helped his sister and Father Hortensio crawl out from under the lead wagon. Preacher didn't think any of them had been wounded, which was mighty lucky. The bushwhackers had killed the mules first to stop the wagons, and that had given the travelers just enough time to scurry to safety underneath the heavy vehicles.

Preacher rode ahead, scouting around the bend. As he had hoped, there was enough of an overhang shielding the trail so that another ambush would be impossible right here. He wheeled Horse around and trotted back, glad to see that the Yaquis had gotten the dead mules cut loose from their harness. Two of the Indians had taken the reins and began pulling the wagons around the slaughtered animals. "Climb on!" Preacher urged Esteban, Juanita, and Father Hortensio. "We can't afford to slow down!"

Esteban had to help Juanita and Father Hortensio clamber up onto the wagons. The priest was clumsier and needed more assistance than the young woman. They managed, though, and the wagons rolled on toward the bend in the trail. The Yaquis who were driving had to saw on the reins and tug hard to make the mules cooperate. It wasn't easy with unbalanced teams. The other two Indians rode behind the wagons, leading the extra saddle horse. Preacher rode in front, his rifle now in his hands again in case he had to make a quick shot at the first sign of another attack.

There was no ambush, however, and slowly the crippled wagons made their way around the bend and into the shelter of the overhang. Preacher waved for the Yaquis to stop and called, *"Alto!"* The Indians hauled back on the reins.

Preacher rode over to the lead wagon. Esteban and Father Hortensio peered out the back of it, their faces pale and drawn. "Anybody hurt?" Preacher asked.

Esteban shook his head. "Only the two mules who were killed. When we heard the shots and saw the mules stumble, we knew we were under attack and got under the wagons. Luck was with us."

"God was with us," Father Hortensio corrected.

"You better hope he still is," Preacher said, "if you ever want to make it to the top of this pass alive."

6

Juanita Alvarez climbed out of the wagon, following her brother and Father Hortensio. She was as pale and frightened as they were, but she kept her back straight and her head up. Preacher saw that and admired her grit.

"Señor Preacher," she said. "You saved our lives. How did you manage to make the mountain fall on our attackers?"

"Well, it weren't hardly a whole mountain, just a few rocks," Preacher explained. "That slide probably looked and sounded worse'n it really was. But it spooked those old boys enough to make 'em turn tail and run, and that's all that matters."

"It did more than that to one of them," Esteban said. "I saw him knocked over the edge. He fell past us, all the way down into that canyon." A shudder ran through the young man's frame, and Father Hortensio made the sign of the cross and muttered a prayer.

"You're wastin' your breath, Padre," Preacher told the priest.

"Does not any man deserve to have his soul commended to God upon his death?" Father Hortensio challenged.

"If that bushwhacker shows up at the Pearly Gates, I expect St. Peter'll tell him to skedaddle, that there ain't no place for him. More than likely he's toastin' himself on the fires o' hell right about now."

"You cannot presume such a thing."

Preacher bit back the retort that almost came to his lips. He had bigger problems on his plate than arguing theology with a stiff-necked priest. "You folks fort up here for a while," he told them. "I'm gonna do a little scoutin' on ahead."

"You wish to join our party?" Esteban asked with a frown.

"I didn't say that. I reckon for the time bein', though, we're in this mess together, at least until we all get to the top of the pass."

With a warning for them to keep their eyes open and stay ready for trouble, he rode on up the trail, which soon resumed its steep climb.

Preacher didn't see any sign of the bushwhackers, and wondered if they could have given up. That ledge must have led to another trail that they had followed out of these rugged peaks and valleys. It didn't take long for his experienced eyes to see that the spot where the wagon had been attacked was the best place for an ambush in the pass. Anywhere else, the bushwhackers would have been exposed to any return fire.

That increased the likelihood that the wagons might be able to make it to the top without running into another assault. Preacher turned, rode back down to where the party of travelers waited, and urged them to get moving.

"Esteban, can you shoot a rifle?" he asked the young man.

"Sí, señor."

"Let that Yaqui handle the team. You take a rifle and mount up on that extra horse. You'll ride up front with me. The other two Injuns can bring up the rear. Tell 'em to be ready to fire."

Esteban nodded and passed along the orders.

Preacher turned to Father Hortensio. "How about you, Padre? Ever shot a rifle?"

The priest drew himself up and glared. "Of course not. As a man of God, I am also a man of peace."

Juanita spoke up. "I can use a rifle, Señor Preacher."

"Give your sister a gun," Preacher said to Esteban. "If those varmints come after us again, we'll hand 'em a warm welcome."

Esteban didn't look all that happy about giving Juanita a rifle, but he took one from the wagon, loaded it, and handed it to her, along with a powder horn and a shot pouch. He armed himself the same way, climbed onto the extra horse, and followed Preacher out to a point about fifty yards ahead of the lead wagon.

"How will we go on without the other mules?" he asked.

"Worry about that once we're on top of this here hill," Preacher advised him.

"Perhaps we should have turned around and gone back down."

Preacher shook his head. "Easier said than done. There wasn't room to turn those wagons and teams around. Sometimes the best thing to do is to bull straight on ahead."

"I suspect you know a great deal about bulling ahead, Señor Preacher."

"I been accused o' bein' bullheaded often enough," Preacher said with a chuckle. Despite the lighter moment, his eyes were always moving, roving over the rocky slopes around them, searching for any telltale signs of trouble. His rugged face grew more serious as he asked, "Who do you reckon those fellas were?"

"The men who attacked us? Thieves, of course. They had to be thieves, after whatever is inside our wagons."

The answer came quickly from Esteban. Maybe a little too quickly, Preacher thought as his eyes narrowed. His question had been mostly an idle one. From the start, he had assumed that the bushwhackers were highwaymen of some sort.

But Esteban's reaction made him wonder, and for the first time his instincts warned him there might be more to all of this than he had suspected.

* * *

Hank Sewell wouldn't have to worry about his broken nose anymore. He had a lot more broken now. Probably every damn bone in his body, after that fall into the canyon. That grim thought was in Cobey Larson's brain as he led the men into the camp about a mile from the top of the pass.

Wick Jimpson was there, along with the man they had met the day before, down below the pass. Their employer had shown up on schedule, along with three other men he had hired as guides and bodyguards. Since Wick's wounded leg hampered him too much for him to take part in the ambush, he had assumed the role of bodyguard. He could still get around well enough for that. The extra three men— Hardy Powers, Chuck Stilson, and George Worthy—had been placed under Cobey's command. That gave him seven men, including himself, to stop the wagons carrying those Mexicans. It should have been plenty.

But nothing had worked out, and now Cobey was furious. He had lost Sewell, and Stilson was wounded. A rifle ball had clipped him on the hip. He had bled like a stuck pig, but Cobey thought he was going to be all right. Wouldn't be much good for a while, though, injured like that. Cobey's own wounded arm was still stiff and sore, but it was healing all right and he could handle a gun; that was all that mattered.

The man who had hired them hurried out from the camp to meet them. He was an Easterner, a tall, skinny fella who dressed fancy and liked giving orders too much, especially considering the fact that he didn't know all that much about the West. Still, he had already paid them some decent wages, just for meeting him, and promised more if they helped him get what he wanted.

"What happened?" he demanded as Cobey and the others rode up. "Did you stop the wagons? Where's the Alvarez girl?"

Cobey swung down from the saddle and said wearily, "We stopped the wagons, but then they got away."

"Got away?" the Easterner echoed. "You didn't kill Esteban Alvarez?"

"We didn't kill anybody," Cobey snapped. "Fact is, we lost a man, and got another wounded. You'd know that if you'd just open your eyes."

The man looked angry that Cobey would talk to him that way, but he held his temper. His intense gaze played over the other men for a moment, and he said, "Yes, I see now that one of you is missing. What happened?"

"Somebody else took a hand. We had those greasers and their wagons pinned down, just like I planned. But then some other fella came along and started some rocks rollin' down on us. We had to hightail it outta there, or risk havin' what happened to Hank happen to the rest of us."

"What did happen?"

"One of those rocks knocked him off the ledge where we set up our ambush," Cobey answered grimly. "He fell past the trail and into a canyon a couple of hundred feet deep."

"Did you find his body?"

Cobey snorted in disgust. "We never looked for it. Nobody ever survived a fall like that. Hate to say it, but the wolves'll have to take care of ol' Hank."

The Easterner grimaced. "This is truly a savage wilderness, isn't it?"

"Your choice to come out here," Cobey said.

"So the Alvarezes got away?"

"That's right. They're likely on their way up to the top of the pass now. It'll be a hard climb for them, since we killed two of their mules, but I reckon they can make it."

The other man nodded. "So we'll have to stop them up here. I suppose that'll have to be all right. All that really matters is they don't reach their goal before I do."

"I thought you didn't know exactly how to find what it is

you're lookin' for. That's why you needed us to grab the girl and kill her brother, so you could make her take you to it."

"Finding the location would certainly be easier with her help, but if it becomes necessary, I'll conduct a search of my own. I'm confident in my abilities."

Cobey was glad somebody was confident in the fella. As for himself, he didn't fully trust anybody from east of the Mississippi.

"Well, you'd best tend to your wounded man," the Easterner went on. "There's nothing more we can do today, I suppose." A thought occurred to him. "You said that someone interfered in your plans. Who was it?"

"I ain't sure," Cobey said. "I never got a good look at him. But he's a hell of a shot, I know that. And I know that if I ever find out who it was and cross trails with the son of a bitch . . . I'll take great pleasure in guttin' him, up one way and down the other."

The slow process of climbing to the top of the pass was made even slower by the loss of the two mules. More than once, the two Yaquis who weren't driving had to dismount and put their shoulders against the back of a wagon to help push it farther along the trail. After a while, Preacher called a halt and decided that one of the mules should be taken from the second wagon and hitched into the empty spot in the first team. Then two of the Yaquis' saddle horses were hitched side by side in the second team. Mixing horses and mules often didn't work out, but in this case they didn't have much choice.

That made things go a little faster, and by late afternoon the wagons were finally nearing the top. Preacher sat on Horse and looked back down the trail. To his right, the mountains tailed on farther south. To his left, they petered out and turned into a vast sweep of mostly flat land that stretched all the way over into Texas. That was Comancheria over there, hundreds of miles where few if any white men had ever set foot. Bands of fierce Comanches roamed that territory, hunting buffalo and making war on their enemies. Preacher had heard plenty about them, enough to know that they were best avoided. But he was intrigued anyway and told himself that one of these days he would ride through that country, just to see what it looked like.

Beside him, Esteban Alvarez sat on his horse and said, "At times I wondered if we would ever make it. The journey has been a long one."

Preacher grunted. "All the way from Mexico City? I'd say so."

Esteban turned to him and went on. "I cannot express my gratitude enough, Señor Preacher. If not for your help, we would have died today. Those bandits would have killed us all and looted our wagons."

There he went, talking about thieves again. Preacher still wasn't convinced that was all there was to it. But he didn't want to press the issue at the moment. It was more important that they finish the job of getting the wagons through the pass and then make camp for the night.

The wagons trundled up the last few hundred yards of the trail and came out on a high, windswept plateau. The Sangre de Cristos continued to rise to the west. To the east were some ranges of smaller mountains and hills, with more flat land visible beyond them. Ahead, to the north, were the ruts of the Santa Fe Trail. Though Preacher had never been over it, he knew the trail continued in that direction until it reached the Arkansas River, where Bent's Fort was located. The trail turned east there and followed the river for a good long distance before it veered off to the northeast toward the Missouri settlements where it originated. While he was in Taos, Preacher had talked to several men who were familiar with the trail, and he had filed away in his brain the details of everything they said. Out here on the frontier, information was a little like gold: A man could never have too much of it.

"It's late enough in the day we'd better think about findin' a good place to camp," Preacher told Esteban. "Stay with the wagons and keep them movin' north. I'll find us a likely spot and ride back to show you the way."

"Do you think those men will come back?" Esteban asked worriedly.

"You don't never know," Preacher answered bluntly and honestly. "But this is pretty open country right around here. If they show up, you ought to be able to see 'em comin'. Use the wagons for cover and put up the best fight you can. I'll hear the shots and come a-runnin'."

"I hope it does not come to that," Esteban said with a frown.

"You and me both." Preacher turned Horse and trotted off to the north with Dog following.

He rejoined the wagons in less than half an hour with news that he had found a good campsite. He led the party off the trail to a small hollow ringed with trees. "They'll give us some cover, in case we have to fight off an attack," Preacher explained to Esteban.

"Do you think that is likely?"

"Don't matter whether it's likely or not. I figure to be ready in case it does happen."

After the wagons rolled through a gap in the trees into the hollow, Esteban dismounted and helped his sister and Father Hortensio climb down from the lead vehicle. The Yaquis set about efficiently caring for the animals and getting ready to spend the night here. One of them arranged some rocks in a circle and soon had a fire going. Preacher wasn't sure that was a good idea. The group had been ambushed once already today, and with the exception of the man who had been knocked into the canyon, the varmints responsible for the attack were still out there somewhere. A fire would tell them exactly where the wagons were.

Preacher soon saw that the Yaquis didn't intend to leave the flames burning, though. One of the Indians quickly prepared supper and heated a pot of coffee, and then put out the fire before full darkness settled down. That came closer to meeting with Preacher's approval.

As they all gathered around the remains of the fire, which still gave off a little warmth, and began to eat, Juanita said, "It seems that you are now a member of our little company, Señor Preacher."

"Impossible," Father Hortensio snapped before Preacher could respond.

Esteban said, "We cannot ask Señor Preacher to inconvenience himself by traveling with us. I'm certain he has other destinations in mind."

"Well, I can't rightly say," Preacher drawled, "seein' as how I don't really know where you folks are bound. But it might be a good idea if I was to stick with you for a while. The bunch that jumped you is liable to try again, and you'll likely need every gun you can get to help fight them off."

"I am sure they will find some other group of travelers to rob—"

Preacher interrupted Esteban by saying, "That's another thing. I don't reckon those fellas were regular thieves. I think they were after something mighty particular—and I think you know what it is." Ignoring the surprised looks on the faces of Esteban, Juanita, and Father Hortensio, he went on stubbornly. "I reckon it's time one of you told me the truth."

7

Father Hortensio glared at Preacher and sputtered, "I will not be called a liar by an uncouth heathen—"

"I wasn't really talkin' to you, Padre," Preacher broke in, silencing the priest with a look. He switched his gaze to Esteban and Juanita. Most of the light had faded from the sky, but enough remained for Preacher to make out the expressions of surprise and confusion on their faces. "I'm talkin' to these two."

"I . . . I take offense at your words," Esteban began. "To imply that we have somehow concealed the truth from you . . ."

"Those men were thieves, bandits," Juanita put in. "Why would you think otherwise?"

Preacher took a sip of his coffee and then said, "Mainly, it's the way you've been tryin' to convince me they were just *bandidos*. I've knowed fellas who could quote most of Mr. Bill Shakespeare's plays, and I recollect one of 'em sayin', *Methinks thou doth protest too much*. That's the way it sounds to me when you start talkin' about those bushwackers bein' simple thieves. On top of that, you've got the fact that a couple of rich young folks would come all the way up here from Mexico City, draggin' along a priest and some

Injun servants. Seems to me like you'd have to have a mighty good reason to make such a trip. And then there's the way the whole lot of you acted just now, when I brought it up. You folks are after something, and those bushwhackers were tryin' to stop you from gettin' to it." Preacher leaned back on the log where he was sitting. "If I had to make a guess, I'd say we're talkin' about gold."

Father Hortensio caught his breath with a sharply indrawn hiss. "He knows!"

"I reckon I do now," Preacher said dryly.

With a sigh, Esteban said, "No, you had figured it out already, Señor. But it is not just gold we seek. It is silver, too, and precious gems."

"It is more than that," Juanita added quietly. "It is our history, our legacy."

"Why don't you start from the beginnin'?" Preacher suggested.

The Alvarez siblings looked at each other, but before either of them could speak, Father Hortensio said, "No! Tell him nothing more! I forbid it!"

"With all due respect, Padre, it is not your place to forbid me to speak," Esteban said.

"I am an instrument of the Lord! Defy me and you defy Him!"

"I am sorry," Esteban said with a shake of his head, "but I think Señor Preacher has a right to know."

Father Hortensio glared for a moment, then folded his arms across his chest. "It is your decision, Esteban," he said coldly. "I wash my hands of the matter."

"I remember hearin' about another fella who was big on hand-washin'," Preacher said. "Name of Pilate."

Father Hortensio puffed up until Preacher thought he might bust a blood vessel. The priest didn't say anything else, though. He just stood up and walked stiffly over to one of the wagons, where he stood and glowered off into the growing darkness.

"The father means well," Esteban said in a low voice. "He takes his responsibilities to the Church very seriously."

"Nothin' wrong with that. I just think it's best that I know what we're dealin' with here, so I can lend you young folks a hand."

"You would join us in our quest, Señor?" Juanita asked.

"Suppose you tell me about it, and then we'll see."

"Very well." Esteban took a deep breath. "The story goes back a little more than a hundred and fifty years, to a time when one of our ancestors, Don Francisco Ignacio Alvarez, was a military commander here in the province of Nuevo Mexico. Word reached the governor in Santa Fe that the Pueblo Indians were planning an uprising that would force out all the Spaniards in the province and destroy the missions that had been set up by the priests."

Preacher nodded. "The Pueblo Uprisin'. I've heard tell of it. Led by an Injun name of Popé, or somethin' like that."

"Yes, that is right. You know the story, then. You know how the Indians did rise up as they planned and drove out the Spanish soldiers, forcing the settlers to flee all the way to El Paso del Norte."

"I've heard yarns about it. I ain't an expert on the subject or nothin' like that."

"We are experts," Esteban said. "The story has been in our family for many generations of how the Indians fought with the soldiers and slaughtered every priest they could lay their hands on, desecrating and destroying the missions as well. It was a time of blood and fire, Señor Preacher, of torture and death."

"What's it got to do with you now?" Preacher asked bluntly, knowing that with Esteban's Latin flair for the dramatic, the story would probably take a long time in the telling if he didn't speed things up.

"As I said, our ancestor Don Francisco was a soldier. Before the uprising, the governor sent him to this area, to the Sangre de Cristos, to see if there was anything to the rumors of trouble. When he got here, he met a priest named Father Alberto."

Over by the wagons, Father Hortensio had turned around and was listening to the story, Preacher noticed. At the mention of his fellow cleric, Father Hortensio crossed himself and muttered something in Latin that Preacher took to mean *rest in peace*. Old Father Alberto must have come to a bad end.

"Some of the priests believed that the Indians would never rise against them," Esteban continued. "But Father Alberto knew there was great danger. He had established a mission near here. He sent word to the other missions in the area that the priests should bring all their holy artifacts to his mission."

"And them artifacts was made of gold and silver, I reckon," Preacher murmured.

Esteban nodded. "Of course. Some of them were even encrusted with gems. And there were many gold bars as well. Father Alberto gathered them all at his mission, and when our ancestor arrived with a troop of soldiers, he placed the responsibility for the safekeeping of this fortune in his hands. It was up to Don Francisco to save those things for the Church and keep them out of the hands of the marauding Indians, Father Alberto said. Our ancestor had no choice but to comply."

"What did he do with the stuff?"

"The Indians had not yet risen, but violence was imminent. There was no time to take the artifacts and the gold back to Santa Fe or even to Taos. So with a small group of his men, Don Francisco rode west into the mountains and concealed them, thinking to come back later and retrieve the cache once the uprising had been put down."

"Only it wasn't put down, was it?" Preacher asked. "Not for a good many years, anyway."

"*Sí,* that is correct. By the time Don Francisco and his men returned to Father Alberto's mission, the place was already under attack. The Pueblos killed Father Alberto and his servants, and the soldiers were forced to flee, fighting a running battle as they tried to reach the pass. Many of them were killed. Don Francisco was badly wounded. The few survivors from his troop finally got him to safety, and none of them were from the group that accompanied him into the mountains."

"So this Don Francisco was the only one who knew where he had cached all the mission loot."

Father Hortensio sniffed a little at Preacher's use of the word "loot," but he didn't say anything.

"Yes, and he was too badly hurt to do anything about it. He almost died, and he was never the same after that. He returned to his family home in Mexico City after being discharged from the army due to his injuries. No one knew what he had done except him."

"But he must've told somebody sooner or later, else you wouldn't know about it now."

Juanita said, "Don Francisco was an educated, cultured man, despite being a soldier. His health was always poor after that, but not so poor that he could not write."

Preacher nodded. "So he wrote it all in a book, includin' where to find the gold, and that book has been passed down from generation to generation, until now you two have decided to go after it."

"An excellent supposition, but it is not *quite* that simple," Esteban said. "No one in our family knew about Don Francisco's manuscript until fairly recently."

"That makes sense. Otherwise somebody would've likely tried to find the loot before now."

"Indeed. The Alvarez family has always been wealthy, but

not so rich that it would have turned its back on such a fortune. Don Francisco never told anyone about what he had done or what he had written. Why he kept it a secret, we do not know. Shame, perhaps. A feeling that he had let down Spain and the Church."

"Pride's a good thing sometimes, but it's easy for a fella to have too much of it."

"Es verdad. Don Francisco's manuscript only recently came to light, and the secret was discovered at last."

"So the family sent you up here to recover the treasure," Preacher guessed.

Esteban laughed, but the sound had a bitter edge to it. "My sister and I are all that remains of a once-proud family, Señor Preacher. And our wealth was almost gone. We spent almost all we had left to buy these wagons and outfit them for the journey. Now we must find the treasure, if we are to have anything."

Preacher shot a glance at Father Hortensio. "I ain't sure I understand. Seems to me that when you get right down to it, all that loot really belongs to the Church. It was just turned over to your ancestor for safekeepin', not given to him."

Father Hortensio left his spot by the wagons and walked over to join them again. "This is true," he said in response to Preacher's comment, "but the Church is more interested in recovering the holy relics than in the gold bars. An arrangement has been made to give Señor and Señorita Alvarez a portion of the gold in return for their assistance in recovering the other things."

"Because they've got the book that their great-great-whatever-granddaddy wrote tellin' where the cache is."

Father Hortensio nodded solemnly. "Exactly."

"Unfortunately," Esteban said, "Don Francisco drew no map, and the directions he gives in his manuscript are rather vague. It may not be easy to locate the place where he hid the treasure. We will have to search for it, using the manuscript to give us clues where to look." Esteban sighed. "He was a bitter old man when he wrote it, and I think perhaps he was not quite right in the head."

Preacher rested his hands on his knees and said, "Well, that's all mighty interestin', and I appreciate you tellin' me the truth. But that don't answer all the questions. Who else knows about this?"

Esteban shook his head. "As far as we are aware, no one."

"But you're afraid somebody might have found out," Preacher said. "Otherwise you wouldn't think that the hombres who jumped you in the pass might be after the loot themselves."

"Don Francisco's manuscript was found by scholars from the university," Esteban explained. "It was among several trunks of old papers that . . . that we had sold to the university."

"Do not think badly of us for selling parts of our family heritage, Señor Preacher," Juanita said softly. "As Esteban told you, our fortunes have greatly declined."

Preacher shook his head. "I ain't here to pass judgment on nobody. That's more in the padre's line." He paused and then went on. "If you gave the manuscript to the university, how'd you get it back?"

"One of the teachers there recognized it for what it seems to be at first glance, merely an accounting of Don Francisco's life, and returned it to us, thinking that it might be of great sentimental value. That is when I read it and discovered what it really contained."

"You think somebody else could have read it before you got it back," Preacher speculated.

"It is certainly possible, though the teacher who brought it to us thought that no one had examined it thoroughly."

"No way of knowin' that for sure, though."

"No," Esteban agreed. "There is not."

Preacher thought about everything they had told him. He

tugged on his earlobe and ran a thumbnail along his bearded jawline. It all made sense, except . . .

"How come you went to the Church?" he asked. "You could've gone after the treasure yourselves without bringin' Father Hortensio along."

"As you said," Esteban replied quietly, "everything truly belongs to the Church. It was our thought only to retrieve it and return it to its rightful owners. Don Francisco considered his failure to be a stain on his honor, and therefore on the honor of the Alvarez family. Juanita and I wished only to cleanse that stain. The bishop was the one who suggested that some of the gold be given to us in return for our service."

Preacher listened closely, but he didn't hear anything in the young man's voice except sincerity. He had known all along that Esteban and Juanita seemed like pretty good youngsters. It looked like his hunch about them was right.

"What will you do now, Señor Preacher?" Juanita asked. "If it is true that someone else opposes us and seeks the treasure for themselves, there may be great danger in attempting to recover it."

"Yeah, I reckon you're right about that."

"No one will think unkindly of you if you decide to leave," Esteban said. "We would not ask you to help us."

"We most certainly would not request the assistance of a heathen," Father Hortensio added.

Preacher chuckled. "You know, I'm right glad you said that, Padre. You helped me make up my mind." He came to his feet and tucked his rifle under his arm. "Right now, I'm goin' to scout around a mite and make sure nobody's lurkin' close by. Set up some watches with them Yaquis. We need somebody standin' guard all night."

"You mean. . . ." Esteban began.

"I mean, come mornin', we're goin' after that treasure, and this here heathen's gonna do whatever he can to help you find it."

8

The night passed quietly enough. Preacher's foray around the camp didn't turn up signs of anyone sneaking around and watching them, but that didn't mean they were in the clear. Despite everything Esteban and Juanita had said about no one else being aware of the treasure's existence, Preacher's gut told him otherwise.

While the Yaquis were preparing breakfast, Preacher stood at the edge of camp and looked toward the mountains in the west. They rose steeply, and as his experienced eyes searched them, he didn't see any passes.

"You look troubled, amigo," Esteban said as he came up to stand beside Preacher.

"I am, a mite," Preacher admitted. "We don't know how far into the mountains we'll have to go to find that loot. It's gonna be hard goin' with wagons."

"What would you suggest?"

"If there was a safe place to do it, I'd say we ought to leave the wagons and your sister and the padre somewhere with a couple o' them Yaquis for protection, whilst you, me, and the other two Injuns ride into the mountains on horseback to search for the treasure."

Before Esteban could respond to this suggestion, a growl

from Dog warned Preacher that someone unfriendly was approaching. As usual, Dog's instincts were good. Father Hortensio, who had been close enough to overhear the conversation, came up behind Preacher and Esteban and snapped, "This is impossible! I must be there when the holy treasure is found in order to take proper charge of it."

Preacher turned to look at the priest. "That sounds like you don't trust this boy," he said, inclining his head toward Esteban. "You best remember, after he found the old don's manuscript, him and his sister didn't even have to come to the Church and say anything about the loot. They could've gone after it and kept it all for themselves."

Stiffly, Father Hortensio said, "The Church commends Señor and Señorita Alvarez for their devotion and willingness to do the right thing. That is why the bishop proposed allowing them to retain some of the gold."

"But if it was up to you, you wouldn't give 'em nothin', ain't that right?"

"Such decisions are not mine to make."

"It is all right, Señor Preacher," Esteban said. "Father Hortensio is right. He should be there when the treasure is found. As for my sister . . ." He shrugged. "I would not want to try to persuade her that she should remain behind after coming this far. She has a mind of her own, that one, and is very headstrong in her opinions. I fear that is what has made it difficult for her to find a suitable husband."

Preacher thought that any man who wouldn't be interested in a gal as beautiful as Juanita Alvarez just because she held an opinion or two was a damned fool. He kept that to himself, however, and said instead, "Sooner or later, it'll come to that, because there's only so far you can take the wagons into the mountains. And unless we come across some horses, we've got only so many mounts. Somebody'll have to stay behind."

"What is it you Americans say?" Esteban asked. "We will cross that river when we come to it?"

"Close enough," Preacher said.

They pulled out a short time later, after a quick breakfast, leaving the Santa Fe Trail and striking out across country toward the Sangre de Cristos. By midday they were in the foothills, with the gray, snowcapped peaks looming ever higher above them. The air was cool, not summerlike at all despite the season.

Esteban liked riding one of the horses instead of a wagon. He willingly turned over the chore of handling the team to one of the Yaquis and positioned himself and his mount up front, riding along about fifty yards ahead of the wagons with Preacher.

"Them Yaquis ever talk except amongst themselves?" Preacher asked.

"Not often," Esteban replied. "They are a strange people, known far and wide for their cruelty to their enemies. But as I mentioned, they are also very loyal. These four have abandoned their heathen beliefs and converted to Christianity. They greatly admire Father Hortensio."

Preacher glanced over his shoulder toward the wagons, where the priest now rode with Juanita. "Seems more like a horse's ass to me," he muttered.

"You are not a religious man, Señor Preacher, despite your name?"

"I never said that. It's true I ain't a Catholic like you folks, but when I was a boy my ma took me to a few brush arbor meetin's whenever the circuit-ridin' preacher came through those parts. And since I come to the mountains, I've knowed fellas who could spout Scripture just like some can quote Shakespeare. I swear, there's some old boys who have got pretty much the whole Bible memorized. I've heard plenty of it around campfires here and there."

"But that is the extent of your religion?" Esteban persisted.

Preacher tilted his head back a little and squinted toward the mountains ahead of them. "Look up yonder," he said, pointing.

"What am I looking at?"

"You see that peak . . . that one right there . . . with the snow on top and all the different colors on its slopes and the big blue sky above it?"

"Of course."

"Mighty pretty, ain't it?"

"Beautiful," Esteban agreed.

"Well, the way I look at it," Preacher drawled, "man could never build somethin' that big and that pretty. The biggest, fanciest buildin' in the world is nothin' next to a mountain like that. And no matter what anybody says, I can't believe that it just happened that way. Somebody built that there mountain, and all the other mountains and deserts and forests and oceans, and whoever's responsible for all that has to be a whole heap bigger an' more powerful than folks like you and me—and the padre—can even imagine. That right there . . ." Preacher pointed again to the mountains. "That's my church. That's where I see the face of God in those slopes and hear His voice in the lonesome wind."

Esteban was silent for a moment, then said respectfully, "I see your point, Señor Preacher. And I believe you are a religious man, no matter what Father Hortensio may think."

"Why don't you just call me Preacher? No need to tag the señor on there."

"All right. Men who have fought side by side need not stand on ceremony, eh?"

Preacher nodded, even though he and Esteban hadn't really fought side by side . . . yet.

He would be mighty surprised if it didn't come down to that before all this was over, though.

The group pushed on, and during the afternoon they came to a river that flowed on a slightly southwest-to-northeast axis in a beautiful green valley. Preacher reined in, studied the narrow, fast-flowing stream for a moment, and then said, "I reckon this must be the river folks call the Picketwire. That ain't the real name of it, from what I understand. French trappers called it the Purgatoire, which I reckon must mean Purgatory. But since Americans come to this part of the country, it's been the Picketwire. We'll ride alongside it for a ways, but from what I've heard, we won't be able to follow it all the way up into the mountains. This little valley it's in narrows down to a canyon the wagons would never get through."

Esteban looked at him in admiration. "How can you know so much about this land if you have never before been here, Preacher?"

"I've talked to fellas who have, and I listened. A fella who keeps his ears open and pays attention lives a lot longer out here than one who don't."

They waited for the wagons to catch up to them, and as the vehicles pulled alongside, Father Hortensio said excitedly, "Is this the Purgatoire River?"

"That's what we was just talkin' about, Padre," Preacher replied. "There ain't no signs, of course, but I think this is the Picketwire, sure enough."

"That means we are not far from the Mission Santo Domingo. It was built on the banks of the Purgatoire River, in the shadow of the mountains."

"That's the mission where ol' Father Alberto worked?" Preacher asked.

Esteban nodded. "There are quite a few references to the mission in Don Francisco's memoir. Of course, there will be nothing left of it now, except perhaps some ruins."

"Once the matter of the treasure is settled," Father Hortensio said, "I would like to reestablish the Mission Santo Domingo. That is another part of my charge from the bishop, to investigate such a possibility."

"If you did, I don't know where you'd get your parishioners,"

Preacher commented. "In case you ain't noticed, this is a big country, and it's mostly empty. We ain't seen hide nor hair of anybody since we left the Ojeida tradin' post, except those bushwhackers. And they didn't strike me as the churchgoin' sort."

"I am told there are many Indians in these mountains," Father Hortensio said. "Perhaps they are staying out of sight because we are strangers."

"Last time a bunch of priests tried to convert the Injuns up here in these parts, it didn't work out so good. That's the reason we're here, remember?"

"Things are different now. In those days, the Indians were still too close to their savage roots to fully embrace the Word of the Lord."

Preacher didn't figure things had changed all that much, but the priest wouldn't want to hear that. He would just sneer at whatever Preacher had to say.

"Maybe you're right," he muttered. "Anyway, we'll be pushin' on."

They followed the river, stopping a short time later for the noon meal, then pushing on westward. In the middle of the afternoon, they came in sight of something that, to Preacher's keen eyes, looked unnatural and out of place in these surroundings. After a moment he realized what he was seeing was the remains of some tumbled-down stone walls. It was seeing something man-made in the midst of all these natural wonders that struck him as odd. He knew he had to be looking at the ruins of Mission Santo Domingo.

None of the others had noticed the old walls yet. He drew back on the reins and brought Horse to a halt. Esteban stopped, too, and asked, "Is something wrong?"

"Nope," Preacher replied. "If you look up yonder, you'll see what's left of that ol' mission the padre was talkin' about."

Esteban looked where Preacher pointed, and his face grew excited. He turned in the saddle and called, "Juanita!

Father Hortensio! It is the mission!" He rose in his stirrups and leveled an arm toward the ruins.

Father Hortensio urged the Yaqui driving the lead wagon to hurry. The stolid-faced Indian flapped the reins against the backs of the mules and struck them with a long, slender stick he used as a whip. The wagons quickly caught up with Preacher and Esteban. When they stopped beside the two horsemen, Father Hortensio scrambled down from the seat of the lead wagon and peered at what was left of the fallen mission walls. He looked more excited than Preacher had seen him so far. He made the sign of the cross and then began offering up a prayer of some sort in Latin. Preacher couldn't even come close to following the words.

"Now that we are here, where Don Francisco started when he rode out to conceal the treasure, we can study his manuscript more closely and see where to go next," Esteban said.

"You've got the manuscript with you?" Preacher asked.

"Of course. Did you think we would not bring it with us?"

Preacher shrugged. "For all I knew, you just wrote down the parts about where to find the church loot and left the manuscript someplace safe."

"No, we brought the entire document."

"The only copy?"

"Yes, but—" Esteban stopped short. "I see what you mean. If anything happened to it, our chances of finding the treasure would be much worse."

"That's what I was thinkin'. I reckon we'll stay here tonight and get a good start on the search in the mornin'. Whilst we're here, it might be a good idea to copy down what those old pages say."

Esteban nodded. "Yes, I will do that. An excellent idea, Preacher. We should have thought of it before we left Mexico City."

"Of course, in a way you might've had the right idea," Preacher mused. "If you'd left the manuscript behind, there was always the chance that somebody else could get hold of it and figure out where you'd gone and what you were after."

"This is true. Still, I should make a copy—"

Father Hortensio abruptly broke off his prayer and said sharply, "Listen! Do you hear that? There are cries coming from the ruins!"

Preacher narrowed his eyes and canted his head toward the old mission. He hadn't noticed the sounds before, even with his keen ears, probably because the priest's sonorous Latin had drowned them out. But now he heard them clearly enough. Somebody was up there in those ruins. . . .

And from the way they were hollering, they were in some sort of trouble.

9

"Stay here!" Preacher told the others. "I'll see what's goin' on up there."

"I can come, too," Esteban said.

"Stay here," Preacher said again, "and keep a hand on your gun!"

With that, he heeled Horse into a gallop toward the tumbled-down walls. Dog bounded along with him.

The shouts became louder and more strident as Preacher approached the ruins. Whoever was yelling must have heard him coming, because the sounds took on an added urgency. Preacher could make out the words now, and to his surprise, they were in English.

"Help! For God's sake, somebody help me!"

Preacher couldn't see anybody yet. Parts of all four walls of the mission's main building were still standing, and one of the walls seemed to be mostly intact. Off to the side were what was left of several smaller buildings, but Preacher could see that nobody was around them. The man yelling for help had to be on the other side of that biggest mission wall.

Suddenly, Preacher pulled Horse back to a walk. It had occurred to him that he and his companions probably had enemies in these mountains. He could be riding into a trap.

Instead of charging blindly around the corner of the old building, he stopped, dismounted, and drew both pistols from his belt.

"Hello, the mission!" he called. "What's wrong?"

The frantic shouts stopped for a second as the man heard Preacher's call. Then he said, "Please, sir, help me! There . . . there's a snake . . . I . . . I'm afraid it's going to strike! For the love of God, sir!"

Preacher walked closer with the guns leveled in front of him. As he neared the corner of the building, he heard something that confirmed at least part of what the frightened man had said. The fierce, buzzing rattle was unmistakable. There was a rattlesnake somewhere close by, and it was mad as hell.

Preacher thought the fear in the man's voice was as real as that rattle, too. He took another step and swung to his right, around the corner of the old mission. He saw a man with his back pressed up to the stone wall and his hands splayed against it. The stranger was staring at a jumble of rocks about five feet away from his feet. The snake was coiled in those rocks, his thick, mottled brown body wrapped tightly around itself, his head up and his tongue flickering from his mouth as the rattle at his other end buzzed madly.

."You're doin' fine, pilgrim," Preacher told the man quietly. "Just keep standin' still whilst I draw a bead. That rattler's a big son of a bitch."

Indeed, although it was hard to tell with the snake coiled up like that, Preacher figured it was at least six feet long, which meant that if it struck, it could reach the terrified man who stood by the wall. Moving deliberately, without too much haste but without wasting any time, either, Preacher extended his right arm and aimed the pistol in his hand. It was cocked and primed and ready to fire, just as soon as he was sure of his aim. . . .

The rattling rose to a crescendo. The snake started to strike just as Preacher pulled the trigger.

The pistol roared and bucked in Preacher's hand. He was afraid that the snake's movement had thrown his aim off a little, and as he stepped forward through the smoke, he saw that he was right. The pistol ball had struck the snake just behind the head, severing it from the body. With some momentum already established, the head itself kept going for a couple of feet before dropping to the ground.

"Stay away from that head!" Preacher snapped at the stranger. "That bastard can still bite you! He don't know he's dead yet."

He could see the snake's jaws still working, trying to sink his fangs into something and inject his venom into it. A couple of feet away, the headless body coiled and writhed and thrashed.

Preacher brought the heel of his boot down on the head and felt the satisfying crunch of bones as he stomped it. He ground the head into the rocky dirt, then picked up a stick and used it to flip the grisly remains away. He did the same thing with the snake's blood-dripping body.

The stranger was still leaning against the wall, but it was in relief now, not terror. His face was bathed in sweat despite the coolness. He said, "Thank God you came along when you did, sir!" and started to step away from the wall.

Preacher swept up his left-hand gun and fired again, aiming this time at the stranger's feet. The man shrieked and leaped in the air. When he came down, he landed awkwardly and fell to one knee.

Preacher leaned over and lifted the body of another snake on his pistol barrel. This one was smaller, only half the size of the monster Preacher had first shot, but he had no doubt it was just as venomous. His hurried shot had been accurate, striking the serpent in the head just as it launched itself at the man's leg. The heavy lead ball had completely disintegrated the head.

As Preacher tossed the second snake away, he said to the stranger, "Sorry there weren't time to warn you, friend. That snake come through a hole in the wall right next to your feet. Probably the mate o' that big son of a bitch. Figured I'd best just go ahead and shoot it whilst I had the chance."

The man was shaking. "Are . . . are there any more of those awful creatures around here?"

Preacher glanced around at the ruins of the old mission and said, "I wouldn't be a bit surprised. Snakes like rocky places like this. Plenty o' places for 'em to den up. If you watch where you're steppin', though, and don't start turnin' over rocks, chances are you won't get bit. Most times, a snake'll slither off without botherin' nobody when a man comes around, if he's got half a chance to. They only coil up and get angrified if they feel cornered, or if there's a lot of loud noise. All that yellin' you were doin' probably irritated the hell out o' them snakes."

The man pulled a handkerchief from his pocket and mopped his sweat-drenched face. "I wasn't too happy about it myself."

Preacher started to reload his pistols. As he did so, he glanced at the stranger, taking his measure. The man was tall and slender and dressed like an Easterner, in tight trousers and shoes instead of boots and a tweed waistcoat. He wore a beaver hat on his head and had muttonchop side-whiskers. All in all, he looked about as out of place in the foothills of the Sangre de Cristo Mountains as a man could possibly be.

"No offense, friend," Preacher said as he tucked the loaded pistols behind his belt again, "but what the hell are you doin' here?"

"I . . . I came to study this old mission. I'm a historian and scholar of religion. My name is Rufus Chambers. Dr. Rufus Chambers."

Preacher frowned. "You're a sawbones, too, besides all that other stuff you said?"

"My doctorate is in philosophy, not medicine," Rufus Chambers said. "I'm on sabbatical from Harvard."

"All right," Preacher said, not quite sure what a sabbatical was. Some kind of wagon, maybe. He had heard of Harvard and knew it was a fancy school back East somewhere. He couldn't for the life of him figure out how a greenhorn like Chambers had gotten from there to here without getting himself killed somewhere along the way.

He heard hoofbeats coming from farther west along the river and looked in that direction when Dog growled. "Is . . . is that beast tame?" Chambers asked. "It looks like a wolf."

"Naw, he's a dog . . . mostly," Preacher replied. "And he's tame . . . mostly." He saw two riders approaching the old mission in a hurry. They wore buckskin and homespun. One sported a coonskin cap, the other a trapper's hat with a wide brim, much like Preacher's hat. Each man carried a rifle.

"Ah," Chambers said. "My guides have returned."

So that was how he had managed to survive. He had hired a couple of experienced frontiersmen to look after him. That was a pretty good idea, considering the man's inexperience. Those two should have stayed closer, though, because Chambers had almost gotten himself killed wandering around by himself in these ruins.

The men rode up and reined to a halt, casting wary glances toward Preacher as they did so. "You all right, Professor?" the one in the coonskin cap asked. "We heard a couple o' shots."

"Yes, I'm fine, Mr. Powers," Chambers said. "I had a perilous encounter with a pair of angry reptiles, but this gentleman came along in time to dispose of them for me."

"I shot a couple o' rattlesnakes, is what he's tryin' to say," Preacher put in.

The man called Powers frowned at him. "Who are you, mister?"

"They call me Preacher."

The two guides exchanged a glance, and Preacher knew they had heard of him.

"Well, I'm certainly glad to meet you, Mr. Preacher," Chambers said. "Allow me to introduce my guides, Mr. Powers and Mr. Worthy."

Both men gave Preacher curt nods, which he returned in kind.

"They were scouting along the river and left me here to explore the ruins," Chambers went on. "I didn't think there would be any danger."

"Your guides there should've knowed better."

"How was we supposed to know he'd stumble into a den of rattlers?" the one called Worthy asked in surly tones.

"You never saw any snakes in a place like this before?" Preacher shot back.

"Gentlemen, gentlemen, there's no need to argue," Chambers put in. "The important thing is that no one was hurt. Well, except for the snakes, of course. And I, for one, don't intend to lose any sleep over them."

Preacher turned to the Easterner again. "You plan on stayin' around here for a while?" he asked.

"Yes, indeed. I don't know for how long. I'm conducting a study of Spanish missions, preparatory to writing a volume of history concerning the spread of religion through uncivilized areas and the obstacles encountered in the inevitable collision with more primitive cultures, and I suppose I'll stay as long as my researches require." Chambers looked guilelessly at Preacher. "Why? My presence here doesn't represent a problem, does it?"

"That's one thing about the frontier," Preacher said, not answering the question directly. "A fella can go where he pleases, as long as he can stay alive doin' it."

"Oh. Of course. I thought perhaps you represented the

Mexican government. I have permission from the government to be here, arranged through the university in Mexico City."

"I don't represent nobody but myself," Preacher said. "I sure as hell don't speak for any government, Mexican, American, or otherwise."

Powers spoke up. "Professor, when we were ridin' in, we spotted a couple of wagons parked beside the river a few hundred yards east of here."

"Those folks are with me," Preacher said.

"I suppose you want to move on, then," Chambers said. He extended his hand. "Thank you for stopping and coming to my assistance, Mister . . . Preacher, was it?"

"Just Preacher." He ignored the professor's hand. "Fact of the matter is, we were bound for this old mission, too."

"Oh." Chambers's face lit up. "Are your companions scholars, too?"

"You could say that. One of 'em's a priest."

"Excellent! I can question him directly about the expansion of the Church into the province of Nuevo Mexico. It's quite a bloodstained tale, from what I understand."

Preacher rubbed his chin. He didn't like Powers and Worthy, and Rufus Chambers seemed like the sort of fella who would get mighty annoying to have around after a while. Not only that, but the presence of these three Americans at Mission Santo Domingo could complicate the search for the missing treasure that much more.

Still, Preacher thought that watching the professor and Father Hortensio going at it hammer and tongs might be pretty entertaining to watch. There was nothing he could do about it, either. If he tried to run off Chambers and the two guides, that would likely just make them suspicious.

He and Esteban and Juanita would have to come up with some reasonable story to explain why they were here. Then he and Esteban could carry on with the search while Juanita, Father Hortensio, and the Yaquis stayed here at the mission to keep an eye on Chambers and the other two men. The whole situation was trickier now, but not impossible.

"I'll ride on out and bring the wagons in," Preacher said. "You watch your step, Professor, hear?"

"Indeed I shall! I don't want to stir up any more poisonous snakes."

"Venomous," Preacher said as he gathered Horse's reins.

"I beg your pardon?"

"Them rattlers ain't poisonous. I've eaten rattlesnake meat more'n once in my life. Tastes a mite like chicken. They can't hurt you unless they bite you, so they're venomous."

"I see," Chambers said with a frown. "Perhaps you should be teaching the natural sciences back at Harvard, Preacher."

The mountain man swung up into the saddle. "Professor Preacher?" He shook his head. "I don't reckon that'd be a good idea."

He had his doctorate, whatever that was, in staying alive.

10

Esteban and Juanita were worried about the news that Preacher brought back to the wagons, but Father Hortensio was absolutely livid.

"Impossible!" the priest declared. "Those men have no right to be here!"

"They claim they got permission from the Mexican government."

"Impossible!" Father Hortensio said again. "The government and the Church work closely together. If there was some sort of American expedition bound for Mission Santo Domingo, I would have heard about it."

"Maybe the arrangements were made after we left Mexico City," Esteban suggested. "We have been on the trail quite some time, after all."

That explanation made sense to Preacher. He didn't know how long it took to get from Harvard to Nuevo Mexico. To tell the truth, he wasn't exactly sure where Harvard was. He was a mite foggy on his geography when it came to places east of the Mississippi.

"No matter what the arrangements were," he said, "Professor Chambers and them other two fellas are here, and I don't reckon we can run 'em off without causin' more trouble. We'll just have to keep an eye on 'em, that's all."

Father Hortensio muttered some more, but Preacher ignored him. It was Esteban who asked a more pertinent question.

"What do we tell them about why we are here?"

"I been thinkin' on that," Preacher said. "How about we say that you and your sister have an old land grant from the King of Spain that gives you the right to some land up here, and you're scoutin' it out for the family?"

Esteban nodded. "That sounds like it might be true. There were many such land grants, and they covered much of the territory in Nuevo Mexico."

"That's what I was thinkin'."

Juanita asked, "What if those men ask to see the papers pertaining to such a land grant?"

"Why would they?" Esteban replied. "They have no interest in that. Nor would they have any right to make such a demand. We could reasonably refuse it."

Preacher said, "It ain't likely to come to that. As long as we stay out of their way, I reckon they'll stay out of ours. That professor may talk your ears off, but that's the biggest danger."

"Very well, then," Esteban said. "Let us go."

They got the wagons moving again. By the time they reached the ruins, Preacher saw that Powers and Worthy had a campfire going, well away from the tumbled-down buildings themselves. They didn't want to run into any more rattlesnakes, and Preacher couldn't blame them for that.

"We'll set up our own camp over there," he said, pointing to another spot about a hundred yards away from the ruins of the old mission. There were some trees there to give them a little shade and form a windbreak of sorts.

While the Yaquis pulled the wagons up to the place Preacher had selected as their campsite, Preacher and Esteban rode over to Professor Chambers's camp. The professor had set up a tent for himself. He came out of it when he heard the horses and raised a hand in greeting to Preacher and Esteban.

Preacher performed the introductions. "Professor, this is Don Esteban Alvarez of Mexico City. Don Esteban, Professor Rufus Chambers of Harvard University."

Esteban dismounted and shook hands with Chambers. "It is an honor to meet you, Professor," he said. "I have heard of your great university Harvard. I myself attended the University of Mexico."

"Also known as the Royal and Pontifical University," Chambers said. "The oldest institution of higher learning in the New World."

"You know much about Mexico?" Esteban asked.

"I've studied your country quite extensively, Don Esteban, from the first Spanish colonies to the overthrowing of Spanish rule and the establishment of a sovereign Mexican government less than ten years ago. You come from a fascinating land."

"*Gracias*. I am afraid I know little by comparison about your United States of America."

Chambers waved a hand. "We're upstarts compared to the Spanish. Our country has been in existence a mere fifty years or so." He looked past Preacher and Esteban at the wagons and said, "My word! You have a lady with you. A very beautiful lady, at that."

"My sister," Esteban said, his voice hardening a little. "Doña Juanita."

"Please accept my apologies. I meant no offense. I was just startled to see such a lovely flower out here in the middle of this wilderness."

"I will introduce you to her later," Esteban said. "And to our other traveling companion, Father Hortensio."

"I would be most appreciative. I'm especially interested

in discussing historical topics regarding the Church's development in Mexico with the good father."

Preacher pointed at the wagons with his thumb. "We best go see about gettin' camp set up."

"Of course." Chambers gave them a toothy grin. "So nice to meet you, Don Esteban."

Esteban just nodded and walked back to the wagons with Preacher. Both of them led their horses. Under his breath, Esteban said, "The professor is a strange man."

"He's a fish out o' water, that's for sure," Preacher agreed.

The Yaquis were doing their usual efficient job of setting up camp. Juanita and Father Hortensio were waiting for Preacher and Esteban. "Did they ask questions about why we are here?" Juanita wanted to know.

Esteban shook his head. "No, the professor did not even seem concerned about that. He is very interested in talking to Father Hortensio about the Church, however."

The priest folded his arms across his chest. "I have nothing to say to him."

"You might want to be friendly," Preacher suggested. "That'll keep 'em from wondering about us, maybe."

"There will be no time for such conversation. We will be spending our days searching for the lost treasure."

"Well, now," Preacher said, "I was thinkin' that maybe you and the señorita and them Yaquis might stay here whilst Esteban and I do the searchin'."

Father Hortensio shook his head. "No, I have already said that this is unacceptable. I must be there when the treasure is found."

"What do you reckon Esteban and me are gonna do, run off with it?" Preacher felt himself getting angry, even though he tried to rein in his temper.

Esteban moved between the mountain man and the priest. "Father," he said quietly, "I think Preacher is right. It will be safer if you and Juanita stay here. We cannot forget that we were attacked. The men responsible for that may still be after us. This place will be easier to defend than if we were caught out in the open."

"That's right," Preacher said. "You could fort up in that old mission. You'd just have to be careful and watch out for snakes."

Father Hortensio sniffed and said, "Sometimes the most treacherous serpents are those who go on two legs rather than on their bellies."

For once, Preacher couldn't argue with him.

They were sitting around the remains of their campfire that night when Professor Chambers and his two guides walked over from the other camp. "Hello, there!" Chambers called. "That's the accepted protocol, isn't it? One should always sing out when approaching another man's camp?"

"If you don't want to get shot, it's the smart thing to do," Preacher agreed. He was on his feet, having stood up when he heard the three men coming. His right hand rested lightly on the butt of a pistol.

Esteban stood up, too, and waved toward the log they were using for a bench. "Join us, Señores," he said graciously.

Chambers stopped in front of Juanita and swept off his hat. He bent low in a bow. "Señorita," he said respectfully. "It is my great honor to make your acquaintance."

"My sister," Esteban said. "Doña Juanita Olivera Alvarez. Juanita, this is Professor Rufus Chambers."

"Good evening, Professor," Juanita said as Chambers straightened from his bow. "We did not expect to encounter a man of culture and learning out here so far from civilization."

"Nor did I think to encounter such a charming, lovely young woman."

"You are bold, sir," she said sharply.

"My apologies, Doña Juanita. I mean no offense. We

Americans are plain-spoken, though. We say what's on our minds."

Esteban stepped in, saying, "And this is Father Hortensio."

That distracted Chambers away from Juanita. He turned to the priest and said, "A great pleasure to meet you, Father. I have many questions about the Church."

Father Hortensio grunted and said with ill grace, "I will try to answer your questions, Señor."

Worthy and Powers had sat down at the other end of the log, not making a pretense of being sociable. They had taken out pipes and were filling them from their tobacco pouches. Preacher sauntered over to join them while Chambers kept chatting with Esteban, Juanita, and Father Hortensio.

Preacher sat down on the log, leaving a gap between him and Worthy. He took out his own pipe and pouch, and as he pushed tobacco into the pipe's bowl, he said quietly, "You boys are a long way from home."

"How do you know where we come from?" Powers asked.

"I don't, but I figure it ain't Nuevo Mexico. We're all gringos here, the three of us."

"I'm from Missouri," Worthy said. He seemed to be the slightly friendlier of the two. "Hardy here is from Louisiana."

"Louisiana, eh?" Preacher said. "I been there. I was part o' that dustup Andy Jackson had with the British down yonder at New Orleans, back in '14."

That got Powers's interest. "You was at the Battle of New Orleans?"

"Sure enough."

"You must not've been very old."

"Old enough to pull a trigger," Preacher said. "Never will forget it. We fired our guns and the British kept a-comin', but after a while there wasn't nigh as many of 'em as there was when they started out. After a while they turned tail and run off through the briars and the brambles." Preacher shook his head at the memory. "Hell, them redcoats was so spooked they ran through the bushes where a rabbit couldn't go! We chased 'em all the way down the Mississipp' to the Gulf, and they ain't come back since."

"Yeah, it was a good fight," Powers said. "I was there, too. We give them bloody British what for."

Worthy leaned closer and said, "We heard o' you, Preacher. You've got quite a rep."

Preacher just shrugged.

Powers asked, "How'd you come to be wanderin' around Nuevo Mexico with a couple o' fancy greasers and a padre?"

Preacher's voice was cool as he said, "It's a long story. And that boy and his sister are fine folks, even if they *are,* what you call 'em, aristocrats."

"No offense, Preacher," Worthy said quickly. "You got to admit, though, it's a mite odd, a fella like you throwin' in with the likes o' them."

"No more odd than a couple of ol' boys like you two takin' on the job of guidin' somebody like the professor."

Worthy chuckled. "Yeah, he is a funny duck, ain't he? Pays good, though. I reckon that explains it all right there."

"I reckon so," Preacher agreed.

"So, are them Mexes payin' you?"

Preacher hesitated. Worthy and Powers were being a mite more curious than frontier etiquette deemed acceptable. They were pumping him for some reason. Maybe they were just genuinely curious . . . or maybe they had some other motive for their questions.

"We just happened to be goin' the same direction and fell in together," he said. "They seem like good youngsters, and they could use a hand gettin' around."

"What are they after up here?"

Preacher shook his head. "You'd have to ask them. They ain't said, and I ain't asked."

"Well, it's none of our business," Worthy declared.

"We've got our hands full just lookin' after the professor," Powers added.

"Yeah, it would've been bad if he'd got hisself bit by them rattlers this afternoon." Worthy gave Preacher a friendly nod. "We're obliged to you for takin' a hand. It's a good thing you come along when you did."

Powers chuckled. "Otherwise we might never have got the rest o' the money he owes us."

"Glad I could help," Preacher said. He fetched a still-glowing stick from the fire and used it to light his pipe, then passed it along to Worthy and Powers. The three frontiersmen sat there and smoked in silence. They had already talked more than men of their ilk were accustomed to. The vast, empty distances of the frontier made a man get used to being quiet.

It was a companionable silence the three of them shared, but that was deceptive, Preacher thought. He wasn't sure how Powers and Worthy felt about him. . . .

But he knew that he didn't trust them worth a lick.

11

When Chambers, Powers, and Worthy had gone back to their camp, Esteban called Preacher into the tent that he shared with Father Hortensio. The priest was still outside, talking to Juanita.

"They will say their prayers together before Juanita retires to the wagon for the night," Esteban explained as he lit a candle that sat on a folding table. "Meanwhile, I thought you might like to see this."

He took a wooden box from under his cot. It was old; Preacher could tell that with just one look. The dark wood had a sheen to it that no amount of polishing could achieve. The look came from decades of being handled. The corners were reinforced with brass caps, and a brass strap ran around the center of the box. A brass clasp held it closed. The box was fairly large, a little bigger than the dimensions of a family Bible, and Esteban handled it like it was heavy.

He set the box on the table and reached for an old brass key on a rawhide thong that hung around his neck. He lifted the thong over his head and then bent down to use the key to unlock the clasp. Then he replaced the thong and the key around his neck.

Preacher had a pretty good idea what he was about to see,

so he wasn't surprised when Esteban lifted the box's lid and revealed a stack of old paper. "Don Francisco never had the pages bound into a book," the young man said, "although he could have. Perhaps he thought that would be too vain a gesture. He left them as they were, a manuscript of his life."

The pages were thick vellum, heavily yellowed with age and densely covered with scrawled words in Spanish. Preacher leaned over to take a closer look. The ink had faded since Don Francisco had used it to tell his story more than a hundred years earlier. Preacher could make out some of the words, but some were too dim for him to read.

"There's so many pages, they can't all be about that loot he stashed up in the mountains."

Esteban shook his head. "Of course not. These are memoirs that cover Don Francisco's entire life up to the point when he wrote them. The pages about Father Alberto and the treasure of Santo Domingo are only a small section of the manuscript. In fact, it would be easy to overlook them. The only reason I found them is because I was trying to read the entire manuscript."

"Why'd you do that?" Preacher asked.

"I believe I was destined to do so," Esteban answered solemnly. "I wanted to learn about my ancestor. I learned more than I ever expected."

Carefully, he took the stack of pages out of the box and extracted several of them. Sitting down on a folding stool that went with the table, he went on. "I will copy those pages now, and then I want to give the copies to you, Preacher, for safekeeping."

"I ain't so sure that's a good idea," Preacher said with a frown. "Them pages are mighty important to you. Maybe you'd best hang onto the copies."

"No, in case of trouble, you would be more likely to be able to preserve them than I would be. No matter what happens, in the long run the treasure must be located and returned to the Church."

"Seems like that means a lot to you."

Esteban nodded. "It does. At one time I studied for the priesthood myself. The Church was going to be my life. Eventually, I realized that no matter what I hoped, I simply did not have the calling. But still I am devoted to the Holy Mother Church. Those relics must go back where they belong." He waved a hand in the direction of the ruins. "If their place is in a restored Mission Santo Domingo, I would gladly give my life to bring that about."

"Let's hope it don't come to that," Preacher said.

Esteban took sheets of paper, a pen, and an inkwell from an unlocked box that was also underneath his cot. He put them on the table and spent several minutes copying one of the pages from Don Francisco's manuscript. Preacher watched him, noting the intent, serious look on the young man's face and the care with which he inscribed the words on the fresh sheet of paper.

"I'm curious about one thing," Preacher said.

Esteban looked up from his task. "What is that, *mi amigo*?"

"How come you decided to trust me with all this? I mean, sure I came along yesterday and gave you a hand when those polecats bushwhacked you, but how'd you know I wouldn't double-cross you and go after the treasure myself once you let me in on the secret?"

Esteban smiled. "Why, that is the simplest question of all to answer, Preacher. I knew you would never betray us because I can see the goodness in you. It shines like a beacon in your eyes."

"I got goodness shinin' in my eyes?" Preacher grunted in surprise. "Ain't nobody ever accused me o' *that* before."

* * *

Just as on the previous night, the Yaquis took turns standing guard. Preacher spread his robes under a tree, and several times during the night he got up and prowled around, just to make sure no enemies were lurking. The night passed quietly, and when he awoke the next morning it was to the smell of breakfast cooking.

After he had checked on Horse, Juanita welcomed him to the fire with a smile. "*Buenos dias*, Señor Preacher," she said as she offered him a plate of tortillas and beans and a cup of coffee laced with strong chocolate. Preacher sat down on the log and dug in heartily.

He didn't see Esteban or Father Hortensio. "Where's your brother and the padre?" he asked Juanita.

"Esteban is still asleep. He worked long into the night copying the pages from Don Francisco's manuscript. Father Hortensio has gone over to the mission to pray."

Preacher frowned. "He knows to keep an eye out for snakes, don't he? Them rattlers are liable to be stirrin' around at this time o' day."

"He said that God would protect him from the serpents."

Preacher's frown deepened. Faith was a mighty fine thing, but it was no substitute for being careful. There was an old saying about how God helped those who helped themselves. Preacher would have added that God watched over those who weren't damn fools to start with.

Some folks were funny about snakes and religion, though. When he was a boy, he had heard about people who handled snakes as part of their worshippin'. Never had made much sense to him. As far as he could see, wrappin' a rattlesnake around your arm didn't prove your faith in God; it just proved you were askin' to get bit. He believed that folks had a right to worship however they saw fit . . . as long as they didn't expect him to cuddle up to no rattlers.

He looked over at the other camp, which was located about

seventy-five yards away, and didn't see anybody stirring around it. "Any sign o' the professor and his pards this mornin'?"

"I have not seen them," Juanita said. "Perhaps they are still asleep, too."

Preacher nodded and went back to eating breakfast. Not everybody was used to getting up as early in the morning as he did.

He tossed the last bite of his tortilla to Dog, who caught it out of the air and gulped it down. After draining the last of his coffee, he stood up, motioned for the big cur to follow him, and walked toward the old mission.

He heard Father Hortensio before he saw him. The priest was intoning a prayer, as Juanita had said. The Latin words flowed like a river in Father Hortensio's deep, powerful voice. The mountain man thought that the priest could probably do some mighty fine preachin', if he was of a mind to.

Father Hortensio knelt inside what had been the sanctuary, before the spot where the altar probably had stood. Preacher hoped he had checked for snakes before getting down on his knees. Standing beside the wall, Preacher looked around for rattlers but didn't see any. He studied the old stones that had been crudely mortared together to form the wall. He saw darkened streaks on some of them and figured that must have come from the flames after the Indians set the inside of the church on fire. The walls themselves wouldn't burn, but most of the interior would, and so would the roof. Once it had collapsed, time and the elements had done their job on the walls, although it was possible the rampaging Indians might have been responsible for some of the damage. Stones from the collapsed walls were scattered around the inside of the old church, and grass grew up rankly between them. The ashes that had been left after the conflagration were long gone, having been reclaimed by the earth.

Father Hortensio stopped praying abruptly. Preacher looked at him and saw that the priest had turned halfway around to glare at him. He didn't think he had made any noise when he came up; he was in the habit of walking quietlike. But Father Hortensio had sensed his presence somehow.

"You would spy on me while I am at my devotions?" the priest demanded.

"Wasn't spyin' on nobody," Preacher said. "I just come over here to make sure you was all right. I can see now that you are, so I'll be goin'."

"Yes, a heathen such as yourself must feel uncomfortable in the house of the Lord."

Preacher had turned away, but at Father Hortensio's smug words he stopped and swung back toward the priest.

"How come you got such a burr up your butt about me?" he demanded. "You ain't had a bit o' use for me ever since you laid eyes on me. I never done nothin' to hurt you, and I ain't been disrespectful of your callin'. Well, not too much, anyway."

"You are a heathen, and you are a gringo," Father Hortensio answered bluntly. "All white men are thieves. Esteban was a fool to trust you."

"You think I'm gonna back-stab those young'uns and steal the Church's loot?" Preacher laughed, remembering what Esteban had said the night before about being able to see the goodness in him. "I give you my word, Padre, that ain't never gonna happen."

"Esteban says you should have a share of the gold for helping us."

Preacher's eyes widened in surprise. "I didn't know that, and I sure never asked for it."

"You wanted to know what Esteban and Juanita are getting out of this. The implication is clear. You want to be paid off, as well."

"I never turned down honest money," Preacher said with a shake of his head. "The workman is worthy of his hire. It says that in the Good Book, if I recollect right. But hell, the only reason I come along is because I thought you folks needed help."

"Don't blaspheme," Father Hortensio said coldly.

"It's true my language is a mite rough," Preacher admitted. "I'm tryin' to hold it in these days, on account of I don't want to hurt nobody's feelin's. So I'll apologize for the way I said that, Padre. But what I meant is still true. I may not know these particular mountains, but I've spent a heap o' years on the frontier, and I know how easy it is to get yourself killed if you ain't careful. That's the only reason I come along, so that maybe you and those two young folks—and them Yaquis, too, I reckon—will stand a better chance of comin' through this alive."

"You are most kind and generous," Father Hortensio said, but the look on his face made it clear that the sentiments he expressed weren't genuine.

Preacher shook his head. "I give up," he muttered. He and the priest weren't ever going to get along, and he figured he might as well quit trying. It was like trying to teach a pig to sing—a waste of his time and a danged annoyance to the pig.

He stalked back to camp, leaving Father Hortensio praying in the old mission.

Esteban was awake by the time Preacher got there, and the young man had an eager look on his face. "Today we will ride up into the mountains and begin our search," he said to Preacher.

"I reckon. What about your sister and the padre?"

"They have agreed to stay here." Esteban gave Juanita a hard look. "Is this not true, Juanita?"

"*Sí,*" she said grudgingly. "But the only reason I said that I would stay behind is so that Father Hortensio would, too. I still think I should be with you, Esteban."

"Preacher and I will be fine, and if fortune smiles on us, we will locate Don Francisco's cache today and our quest will be over."

Preacher had a hunch it wouldn't be that easy, but he didn't say anything. It wouldn't hurt to let Esteban feel optimistic for a while.

A short time later, while Preacher was getting Horse ready to ride, the sound of loud, angry voices came to his ears. He glanced toward the mission and saw Father Hortensio and Professor Chambers standing outside the walls, arguing about something. Preacher couldn't catch all the words, but it was something about the Catholic Church's role in helping Spain colonize Mexico. Chambers said something about the Aztecs, and Father Hortensio disputed it.

Preacher shook his head as he tightened the saddle cinch. He looked down at the big wolflike creature sitting near him and said, "I don't know about you, Dog, but I'm mighty glad we're ridin' out and won't have to listen to them two squabble all day."

Dog just sat there, tongue lolling out, but Preacher would have almost sworn that he nodded in agreement.

12

It was still fairly early when Preacher and Esteban rode out. Preacher let Esteban take the lead, since the young man was the one who had studied Don Francisco's manuscript and had some idea where they were going. After they had followed the river for a short distance, though, Preacher said, "Maybe you better give me some idea what the old don had to say, Esteban. I might see some landmark he mentions that you wouldn't notice."

"The same thought had occurred to me," Esteban agreed. "I was just waiting until we got away from camp, so that we could discuss the situation in peace."

Preacher thought about the argument between Father Hortensio and Professor Chambers and grinned. "Probably a good idea," he said with a chuckle.

"Don Francisco knew he did not have much time," Esteban began as he reached inside his short, charro-style jacket and brought out a sheaf of folded papers: the pages he had copied the night before. He unfolded them as he went on. "It was feared that the Indians would attack at any moment, so he had to move quickly. The relics were wrapped in cloth and placed in heavy bags. The gold bars were loaded in wooden chests. Don Francisco picked ten of his most trusted men to go with him, and they loaded the treasure onto pack mules. Then they set off from the mission into the mountains, following this river at first."

Preacher could see it in his mind's eye: the soldiers in their armor and plumed helmets; the proud grandee who was their commander, also wearing armor but set apart by his silks and finery; the line of heavily laden pack mules plodding over the rocky ground, bearing their load of treasure toward the rugged peaks.

"Do them papers say how far they followed the river?" he asked.

Esteban shook his head. "Not exactly. According to the manuscript, the party branched off into a dry canyon that rose steadily, taking many turnings, until it reached a high plateau. There they located a suitable hiding place and concealed the treasure before returning to the mission and the violence that awaited them there."

Preacher frowned. "That's all it says? No offense to your old ancestor, Esteban, but shoot, that ain't much to go on!"

"I know," Esteban said with a sigh. "Don Francisco was writing this not as directions for finding the treasure, but only as part of the story of his life. Therefore he was not as . . . specific . . . as he might have been."

"Any mention of any other landmarks besides the twisty canyon and the high plateau?"

"Only one. Let me see . . ." Esteban turned through the pages he had copied so laboriously, frowning as he searched for the reference he was looking for. His expression cleared a moment later as he said, "Ah, here it is. He says that the treasure will be protected by the wolves of God."

"The wolves of God," Preacher repeated. "Wonder what in tarnation he meant by that."

Esteban shook his head. "I have no idea. There is no explanation in the manuscript."

"Well, whatever he was talkin' about, maybe we'll know it when we see it."

"This is my fervent hope," Esteban said.

He put the papers away inside his jacket, and the two of them got their horses moving again. Preacher kept his eyes open for any likely-looking canyons. Some landmarks might change over the course of a century and a half, but he doubted if an entire canyon would just close up and disappear.

Unfortunately, anywhere there were mountains, there were also lots of canyons. It might take days, even weeks, to search all of them in the area.

But if it took that long, so be it. The Alvarezes had brought along plenty of supplies from the trading post, and if they ran low on food, there was abundant game in these parts, not to mention edible plants. Preacher had lived off the land many times in the past and had no doubt that he could do so again.

About an hour after they rode away from the wagons, Esteban pointed and asked excitedly, "What about that canyon there? Do you think that might be the one?"

"Only one way to find out," Preacher said. He had already noticed the canyon mouth, but had been waiting to see if Esteban would see it, too. He would have spoken up if the young man hadn't, but he wanted to find out just how keen-eyed Esteban was. The canyon mouth was partially concealed by brush, but Esteban had seen it anyway.

They rode around the brush and into the canyon, which cut into the side of a mountain like a knife slash. It didn't look to Preacher like it had any twists and turns, but maybe those started farther up. They couldn't afford to ignore any possibility, so he pushed on and Esteban followed.

After a mile or so, however, the canyon came to an abrupt end against a stone wall. Preacher studied the barrier. In a hundred and fifty years, a rock slide could have blocked the canyon they were looking for. However, this wall appeared to be a solid sheet of stone, making it unlikely that it had been formed by such an avalanche. This canyon had probably come to an end right here in this spot for untold centuries. It couldn't have been the one that Don Francisco and his men had followed with their mule train.

"All right," Preacher said. "Looks like a dead end, so we turn around and head back."

Esteban couldn't conceal his disappointment. "I was hoping this would be the one."

"So was I, but I didn't figure it would be that easy. Most things in life that you're lookin' for take a whole heap o' time and trouble to find, leastways if they're worth havin'."

"What about you, Preacher? What are you looking for in life?"

Preacher flashed a grin. "I ain't quite sure. But like we said before, I'm hopin' I'll know it when I see it."

"That may require a great deal of searching."

Preacher thought about all the places he had never been before and said, "That's all right by me."

From the top of a pine-covered hill overlooking the Purgatoire River, Cobey Larson peered down at the old, abandoned mission through the lens of a spyglass. He followed the movements of Professor Chambers, Hardy Powers, and George Worthy, as the professor poked around the ruins and pretended to be studying them. Hell, thought Cobey, for all he knew, Chambers really was studying what was left of the mission. He was from back East somewhere, and a professor to boot, and everybody knew folks like that were all crazy.

Chambers was set on getting his hands on that treasure, though, and not only was he willing to pay good wages to the men who were helping him, he also didn't care who got hurt in the process, which made things a little easier. He wouldn't get squeamish if they had to get rough with the girl while they were trying to get the location of the loot out of her. Chambers didn't mind if they killed the boy and the priest and those Mexican Injuns, neither.

Preacher, now . . . Preacher might be a problem.

Cobey had heard of the rugged mountain man. Preacher was supposed to be as dangerous as a sack full of wildcats. He had survived numerous Indian fights as well as his legendary hand-to-paw battle with a grizzly bear.

But Cobey was tough, too, and he thought he could take Preacher if it ever came down to that. Maybe it wouldn't, though. Maybe they would be lucky and would find a way to kill him easier than that.

Arnie Ross came up and knelt beside the place where Cobey was stretched out. "What're they doin' down there?" he asked.

"More of the same. The professor's putterin' around, and Powers and Worthy are tryin' to stay out of the way."

"Is Chambers still arguin' with that priest?"

"No, that seems to be over with, at least for now."

"So what the hell are we supposed to do?"

Cobey grunted. "Wait, I guess. We could jump those Yaquis and kill them and the priest, but then we'd have Preacher and the boy to deal with when they get back."

Arnie licked his lips. "You think they went off lookin' for the treasure?"

"No place else I reckon they'd go."

"Maybe they'll find it and bring it back to the mission. Then we wouldn't even have to look for it. We could just take it away from 'em."

"Yeah, that'd be mighty pretty, wouldn't it?" Cobey laughed humorlessly. "I'll believe it when I see it."

Arnie hesitated and then said, "Speakin' of takin' that treasure away . . . we ain't gonna let the professor pay us some piddlin' wages and then ride off with that whole dang fortune in gold and silver and gems, are we?"

Cobey lowered the spyglass and turned his head to look over at his partner. An ugly grin spread across his face as he asked, "What do you think?"

The priest was insufferable, Rufus Chambers thought. Stiff-necked, judgmental, smug, and arrogant . . . Father Hortensio seemed to think that he knew more about the history of the Church in Mexico and South America than he, a professor at the greatest institution of higher learning in the Western Hemisphere, did. Father Hortensio refused to admit that the Church had been responsible for more bloody-handed conquest than the Aztec, Mayan, and Incan empires combined. It was a simple matter of history as far as Chambers was concerned. It did no good to deny the facts.

But soon the priest would be dead, along with the Yaquis and Esteban Alvarez and the man called Preacher. Chambers consoled himself with that thought. Soon he would have not only the fortune that old Don Francisco had hidden in these mountains, but he would have Don Francisco's beautiful great-great-great-granddaughter, too. Was that enough generations? Chambers asked himself with a frown. Well, it didn't really matter. What was important was that he would be rich, and Juanita Alvarez would be his to do with as he wished.

She was a bonus. When Enrique Gallardo, his friend from the university in Mexico City, had written to him about the lost treasure of Mission Santo Domingo, he hadn't said anything about a beautiful young woman being involved. Enrique had read about the treasure in an old manuscript written by Don Francisco Alvarez, and he had immediately thought of his friend from Los Estados Unidos, Rufus Chambers. Enrique could not, or would not, abandon his position in Mexico City just to go on a treasure hunt that might turn out to be futile, but Rufus Chambers might. After all, Chambers was at loose ends after having been dismissed from his teach-

ing position at Harvard following that unfortunate incident
with the daughter of a fellow instructor. He had left Cambridge and crossed the Charles River to Boston, where Enrique's letter had found him. For a percentage of the profits,
Enrique was willing to pass along the secret he had discovered. Chambers had agreed, of course. Whether or not he
would ever live up to that part of his bargain . . . who could
say? Perhaps he would; Enrique, like all Latins, was possessed of a fiery temperament and an easily offended honor.
If Chambers double-crossed him, Enrique might hunt him
down to the ends of the earth. Easier to just pay him, take the
lion's share of the treasure, and the girl as an added treat.

Chambers paused in his study of the tumbled-down walls
and cast a glance toward the camp where Juanita and Father
Hortensio were talking. She was beautiful, as lovely in her
dark, volatile way as any of the more pallid young women
with whom he had dallied in Cambridge and Boston. He
couldn't wait until the first time they were together. Taming
a spitfire like that would be very enjoyable indeed!

Lost in those thoughts, he didn't hear George Worthy until
the man came up behind him and said, "Professor, me and
Hardy been thinkin'."

Chambers jumped a little, then turned and said, "You
startled me."

"Sorry. Anyway, we been thinkin'——"

"Not your strong suit," Chambers cut in. "You should
leave that to me."

The frontiersman frowned. "You got no call to talk to me
that way, Professor. We're part of this business, too, and we
know a lot more about some things than you do."

"Yes, of course, you're right," Chambers said easily. "My
apologies, George. Now, what's on your mind?"

"Well, we were just wonderin'. . . . Seems to us we could
go ahead and kill them Yaquis now, and the priest, too. They
ain't expectin' any trouble, so we could take 'em by surprise."

Chambers nodded. "Yes, yes, no doubt. And Mr. Larson and the other men are close by in case you needed any assistance. But what about Preacher and Señor Alvarez? They might hear the shots and come rushing back."

"We'd have the girl to use as a hostage," Worthy said stubbornly. "They couldn't do a thing, as long as they wanted to keep her alive."

"Didn't we have a long talk about this? The only real threat facing us is Preacher. We don't want him wandering around loose, knowing what we're really after. Right now he believes the lies he's been told. We need to keep him from becoming suspicious of us, and that way we can bide our time and strike at the proper moment, so that we wipe out all of our opposition at once."

"Waitin's all well and good, but sometimes you got to strike while the iron's hot."

"Yes, I've heard that old saying. It's not always applicable."

Worthy looked confused.

"Sometimes it's better to wait," Chambers went on, clarifying his position. "Trust me, George. Before we're through, the lost treasure of Mission Santo Domingo will be ours, and all of our enemies will be dead."

"Includin' Preacher?"

"Especially including Preacher," Chambers said.

13

Preacher and Esteban went up and down several canyons that morning without finding what they were looking for. None of the canyons led to the top of a plateau, and Preacher didn't see anything that looked like it would inspire the name "wolves of God." When they stopped to make a cold lunch on jerky and tortillas, Esteban was discouraged.

Preacher tried to cheer him up by saying, "You didn't really figure you'd find the treasure the very first mornin' you went to look for it, did you?"

"We could have," Esteban said.

Preacher nodded. "Yeah, I reckon we could have. Stranger things have happened, as folks sometimes say. But I ain't disappointed. We'll just keep lookin'."

"Do you really believe we will find the place?"

"Sure I do. Things change in a hundred and fifty years, but the big things are still the same. We'll find the right canyon and it'll lead us to that plateau, and when we get there we'll find the cave."

"I hope so," Esteban said. "I would feel like my life would be justified if I could do this thing."

"I reckon I never felt like I had to justify my life," Preacher said. "I just live it."

They moved on, checking canyons on both sides of the river. Some, they were able to eliminate fairly quickly; other, deeper canyons required them to spend more time riding to the end and back once it became obvious none of these were the one they were looking for.

"Does that manuscript say how long it took Don Francisco and his men to cache that loot and get back to the mission?" Preacher asked.

Esteban shook his head. "Unfortunately, no. Don Francisco speaks of the need for haste, but he does not say whether he means by that a matter of hours or days. He could have been gone from the mission for several days and still considered that acting quickly."

"Could be," Preacher agreed, looking around at the mountains that surrounded them. "Seems to me he would have been in more of a hurry than that."

"Then the canyon should be close," Esteban argued.

"You'd think so. We just don't know."

By late afternoon, it became obvious they weren't going to find what they were looking for on this day. Preacher said that they ought to head back to the camp at the old mission.

"Perhaps we should go a little farther," Esteban urged. "We have time to check one more canyon, surely. And it might be the one we seek."

Preacher thought it over and nodded. "All right. One more."

They rode along until they came to another opening leading away from the river. The canyon was narrow, and sure enough, it took a sharp bend to the right about fifty yards in. After another short distance, it bent back to the left. Preacher frowned, wondering what would cause a zigzag formation like this. In the straighter canyons, it was relatively easy to see that they had been worn out by the action of water flowing through them over the centuries and by the upheaval of the earth's crust in earthquakes and volcanic eruptions and suchlike. He supposed water had carved out the twists and turns of this canyon, too, but he had seldom seen one that twisted around quite this much. Esteban was getting excited, and Preacher's spirits started to lift, as well. Now he was glad they had decided to press on and check one more canyon before turning back.

"We are climbing, are we not?" Esteban asked. "It seems so."

"I reckon we are," Preacher agreed. "If we could look behind us, we could probably tell how far we've climbed. Way this canyon snakes around, though, you can't see very far in any direction."

He reined in suddenly as a sound came to his ears. He held up a hand and said to Esteban, "Listen."

"What is it?" the young man asked eagerly.

"Just listen," Preacher said again.

After a moment, Esteban's eyes widened as he realized what he was hearing. "Wolves!" he exclaimed. "It is the howling of many wolves!"

"The wolves of God," Preacher said softly.

"It must be! But—" Esteban's face fell. "How can it be, Preacher? That sounds like a whole pack of wolves. Even if my ancestor saw them where he concealed the treasure, how could they still be there, over a hundred and fifty years later."

Preacher shook his head. "That ain't real wolves you're hearin', even though it sure sounds like it. Somewhere up yonder above us on the mountain, the wind is blowin' through some sort of rock formation that's causin' those howls. I've heard such things before, though I don't reckon I've ever run across anything that sounds quite so much like real wolves as that does."

"We must go on!" Esteban started to urge his horse forward.

Preacher reached over to lay a hand on his arm and stop him. "Hold on a minute. Look up at the sky. We're losin' the light, amigo. Even if we turn around now and head straight back to camp, it'll be dark before we get there."

"What is wrong with that? Can you not find your way back to the mission after dark?"

"I reckon I can, sure enough. This canyon will take us right back to the river, and all we have to do is follow it to the mission."

"Then we should go on!"

"It may take an hour or more to get to the head of this canyon," Preacher said. "Once we get there, we won't have time to search for the treasure before nightfall. It makes a lot more sense to head back to camp and come here again first thing in the mornin'. We'll have good light and most of the day, and I reckon there's a real good chance we'll find ol' Don Francisco's hidin' place."

"But . . . but . . . to be this close and turn back!" Anguish was easy to hear in Esteban's voice. "I do not know if I can stand it, Preacher."

"It's still possible this ain't the right canyon. That sound could be carryin' for a long way."

"But everything fits with the description in the manuscript!"

"Yeah, it does, and I think there's a real good chance this is the one we been lookin' for. It'd still be better to wait until tomorrow to find out for sure." Preacher glanced at the sky again. "We're burnin' daylight just talkin' about it."

"All right," Esteban said, but he didn't sound happy about it. "I cannot believe I am saying this, but we will go back. Tomorrow, though, we will return here as soon as possible."

"Dang right we will," Preacher agreed.

They turned their horses and started back down the canyon, as somewhere above them, the wolves of God continued to howl.

Juanita didn't care very much for the way she caught Professor Chambers watching her a couple of times during the day. She knew what it was like to have men look at her with lust in their eyes. She had been familiar with that feeling for quite a few years, ever since she had begun to turn from a girl into a woman. She wasn't particularly worried about Chambers, though. He seemed rather mild-mannered, not dangerous at all.

The men called Powers and Worthy, though, they were different. They were frontiersmen, rough and accustomed to taking whatever they wanted. They looked at her with avid gazes, too, and it was because of them that Juanita made a point of staying near Father Hortensio and the Yaqui servants. They would protect her if the gringos tried anything, she thought.

Oddly enough, the most dangerous gringo she had ever encountered, the man known as Preacher, did not frighten her at all. She knew he was aware of her beauty, but she never felt that she might be in any danger from him. Despite his rough exterior, he was a true gentleman, every bit as noble in his soul as any of the grandees she had met in Mexico City. More so, in fact.

So she was glad that evening when Preacher and Esteban returned to the camp near the old mission. When it had grown dark, around an hour earlier, Juanita had begun to worry that something had happened to her brother and Preacher. It seemed unlikely that the mountain man would be caught unawares by anything—he was perhaps the most *alert* man Juanita had ever seen—but an accident of some sort could not be ruled out. However, it was only because of their search that they were late getting back.

Juanita knew as soon as she saw the excitement on Esteban's face that they might have found what they were looking for. Esteban dismounted quickly, came over to her, and took her hands in his.

"We have found it!" he said.

Juanita's eyes widened in joy. "The treasure of Mission Santo Domingo? You have it with you?"

"No, not yet, but tomorrow—"

"We found a likely place to look," Preacher put in as he strolled over, much more deliberate in his movements than Esteban was. He could move very swiftly when he needed to, of course, but the sort of high-strung nervous energy that Esteban was exhibiting at the moment seemed alien to Preacher's very nature. He went on. "We won't know for sure until we've had a closer look."

"But I am sure it is the right place," Esteban insisted. "My heart tells me it is so."

Juanita cast a glance toward the other campfire. "We should be careful how we talk of these things. Professor Chambers and the others do not know why we are really here."

"And that is the way it shall remain," Esteban declared. "This is our business, and none of theirs."

"Tell me about it," Juanita urged. "Sit down and tell me what you found."

They sat on the log, still holding hands, and Esteban explained about their day-long search for the right canyon. While he was doing that, Preacher tended to the horses.

"We were about to give up for the day because it was getting late," Esteban said, "when I asked Preacher if we could check one more canyon. That proved to be the one we were looking for. It matched the description in Don Francisco's manuscript perfectly! We even discovered what the wolves of God are."

"Not real wolves, surely," she said.

He shook his head and explained about the rock formations that caused the howling sounds when the wind blew through them.

"You saw them for yourselves?" Juanita asked.

"No, but Preacher knew what caused the sounds. He said that he has heard such things before."

"I am surprised you turned back and did not continue the search until you found the treasure."

"It was too late," Esteban said, but he sounded disappointed. "Preacher said it would be better if we returned in the morning, when there will be plenty of time and light." He shrugged. "I suppose it makes sense. But I wanted so much to keep going until we found the treasure."

"That settles it," Juanita said. "Tomorrow I go with you."

Preacher came up in time to hear that statement. "I ain't sure that's such a good idea," he said.

"Why not?" she asked as she looked up at him.

"For one thing, those wagons won't be able to make it up that canyon. It's too narrow."

"Could they reach the mouth of the canyon, by the river?"

"Well . . ." Preacher hesitated. "I reckon they might."

"Then we can take the wagons that far, and then I will join you and Esteban on horseback for the final part of the search."

"And I as well," Father Hortensio put in. Juanita hadn't heard him come up, but obviously he had overheard enough of the conversation to know what was going on. As he stepped into the firelight, his normally solemn visage was more animated than Juanita had ever seen it.

Preacher frowned. "I don't know that we need a crowd up there. If you folks stayed down at the mouth of the canyon with the wagons, Esteban and I could bring the loot down a little at a time, and the rest of you could stand guard over it."

"You would deny me the right to be there when those holy relics are uncovered for the first time in over a century? A prayer should be said over them immediately, to bless their rediscovery and to wipe out the stain of the violence that led to their being hidden."

"Well, I don't reckon it'd hurt anything if you went along to the mouth of the canyon," Preacher grudgingly agreed. "After that, we'll see."

Juanita squeezed Esteban's hands. "I can hardly believe that we are so close to our goal at last."

"Believe it," he said. "I do."

She might have asked him for more details, but at that moment Professor Chambers sang out from somewhere nearby, "Hello, the camp!"

"Say nothing more about the treasure," Esteban warned in a low voice.

Juanita nodded. She decided that she wouldn't say anything to Esteban about her uneasiness over Chambers and the two guides. He had enough on his mind already.

Besides, soon they would have the treasure, and they would be on their way back to Mexico City with it. Their quest was almost over.

14

Preacher had heard Chambers approaching before the professor called to them, and so had Dog, growling as he gazed off into the darkness. Preacher had been about to shush the two youngsters when they had quieted down about the treasure on their own. No point in tempting a couple of rough hombres like Powers and Worthy with talk about hidden gold and such.

Chambers came up and said, "Good evening, everyone. I hope you had a productive day. I know I did. I even enjoyed my discussions with the good padre here, spirited though they might have been."

Father Hortensio just sniffed. Evidently it was a toss-up who he liked the least, Preacher or the professor from back East.

Esteban was gracious. "Please join us, Professor. We were about to eat supper."

"I've already eaten, thank you. I certainly wouldn't mind sharing a cup of coffee with you, though, and the cama-raderie that comes with it."

"You are welcome," Esteban said.

Chambers didn't seem to notice that his presence had put a damper on the conversation. He sat down on the log between Esteban and Father Hortensio and filled a cup from the coffeepot that sat at the edge of the fire. Preacher was a little worried about that fire. He hadn't forgotten the ambush and the fact that somebody didn't wish the Alvarez party well. But there was a fire over at the professor's camp, too, so it wouldn't really serve any purpose to extinguish this one. Might as well let folks enjoy it, he decided.

He got a plate of tortillas and beans and sat off by himself while Chambers regaled Esteban and Juanita with stories about life back in Boston and asked them questions about Mexico City.

"Since my area of expertise is the Spanish conquest of the New World, I find everything about your country fascinating," he told them.

"Have you ever visited Mexico?" Esteban asked.

"No, I haven't had that good fortune as of yet, but I hope to someday."

Father Hortensio asked, "How can you claim to know anything about a land where you have never been?"

"Well, there are a great many books about the conquest—"

"Bah! The only book from which one can truly learn is the Holy Word of God."

"Perhaps you're correct as far as spiritual matters go, but when it comes to history, one has to rely on other books."

Preacher couldn't resist putting in a comment of his own. "There ain't been a history book yet that wasn't written by a fella who wanted you to believe his version of the way things were."

"History is written by the victors, is what you're saying," Chambers responded.

"Yep. Except when other folks come along years later and try to twist things around so that the way they tell the stories ain't exactly the way they really happened. Wouldn't surprise me a bit if someday you professors tried to say that these days was completely different than the way they really are."

"Oh, surely not. Scholars are supposed to be devoted to the truth, not to some distorted version of the facts concocted simply to support some dogma of their own."

Preacher shrugged. "Wait and see, that's all I can say. It could happen . . . and it'll be a mighty sorry day for this country when it does."

He went back to eating, having put in his thoughts. When he was done, he got up and strolled around the camp, rifle tucked under his arm. Dog went along with him, sniffing the night air. If there were any predators out there, four-legged or otherwise, Dog would smell them out.

The night seemed quiet, though, and when Preacher went back to the camp, he saw that Chambers was gone. The professor had said his good nights and returned to his own camp. Esteban and Juanita sat with their heads close together, talking quietly but excitedly, and Preacher knew they were talking about the treasure again.

He hoped for their sake that he and Esteban had found the right place and the lost loot would soon be recovered. Then he could see them on their way safely and get back to his own business. He was starting to long for more northern climes. If he didn't know better, he would say that he was starting to get homesick for his old stomping grounds. It would be good to get back and start running his trap lines again, maybe see some old friends, or even some old enemies.

The mountains were calling him, no doubt about that, and Preacher hoped he would soon be able to answer.

It was far into the night when a hand touched Rufus Chambers' shoulder and shook him awake. Instinct took over and made Chambers react instantly. His hand snaked under his coat and came out with a little pocket pistol he kept loaded and primed. His thumb looped over the hammer as he withdrew the weapon from his coat, and it was ready to fire as it flashed into the open.

A big hand clamped over his, trapping the pistol's hammer. "Take it easy, you damn fool!" an angry voice hissed. "You almost blew my head off!"

"Larson?"

"That's right. Now give me that gun." Cobey wrenched the pistol out of Chambers's hand.

Chambers sat up. The fire had died down to just embers, and the night was cold. The good thing about the chill was that the snakes would be dormant until the sun rose and warmed them in the morning. Cobey hunkered next to the professor's bedroll. The big frontiersman carefully lowered the hammer on the pistol and gave it back to Chambers.

"Be careful with that," he warned.

"I know how to handle a gun," Chambers said coldly. "Don't underestimate me, my friend."

"I don't intend to. Listen, Powers and Worthy tell me those pilgrims found what they were looking for."

"We don't know that for certain yet. Worthy was able to sneak up and eavesdrop on them while I approached more openly, as a distraction, so to speak. He heard them saying something about a canyon and the wolves of God—"

"What in blazes is that?"

"According to my friend in Mexico City, the phrase 'wolves of God' is connected somehow to the hiding place of the treasure, according to Don Francisco's manuscript. I believe, based on what Worthy overheard them saying, that Preacher and the Alvarez boy have solved the mystery of that phrase and have either actually located the treasure or have a good lead to it."

"Then we could go ahead and make our move, right? I got the rest of the boys close by, and we can wipe out all that bunch except the girl. She can tell us what we need to know,

I reckon. Her brother will have filled her in on everything they've discovered."

Chambers shook his head emphatically. "There's no need for haste. Why not let them go ahead and recover the treasure? That way our work will be done for us. All we'll have to do is kill the others and take the treasure."

"And the girl," Cobey said.

"And the girl, of course. We shan't forget her."

Cobey thumbed his hat back on his head and thought about it. "I reckon that might be best. I got to tell you, though, the boys are gettin' a mite impatient, and so am I. We're ready to see that gold and get our share that you promised us."

"Soon, my friend, soon," Chambers assured him. "We'll all be rich men before too many more days go by."

"We'd better be," Cobey said, and there was no mistaking the threat in his voice.

As usual, Preacher and Dog made several patrols around the camp during the night. Several times, Dog looked off toward the other camp and growled. Preacher ruffled the thick fur at the big cur's neck and said, "I agree with you, fella. Somethin' about them hombres don't smell right to me, neither."

Chambers and the other two hadn't done anything openly suspicious, though, so there was nothing Preacher could do except to keep an eye on them.

Early the next morning, the Alvarez party began making preparations to break camp. Professor Chambers must have noticed the Yaquis hitching up the mules and the horses, because he walked over and said, "What's this? You're leaving?"

"Yes, there is more of the old land grant we must explore," Esteban said, falling back on the story they had told Chambers to explain their presence here in the Sangre de Cristos.

"Well, I'll certainly miss your company. Especially the lovely Señorita Alvarez, and the stimulating discussions with Father Hortensio. Will you be coming back this way?"

"Probably," Esteban said.

Chambers smiled. "Perhaps my companions and I will still be here then. I hope so."

He shook hands with Preacher and Esteban, tipped his beaver hat to Juanita, and said to Father Hortensio, *"Vaya con Dios, padre."*

"I will go with God," Father Hortensio said. "Can you make the same statement?"

Chambers didn't answer, but just smiled instead. He waved as Preacher and Esteban mounted their horses and the others climbed onto the wagons. The group moved off to the southwest, following the river. Preacher glanced back from time to time and saw Chambers, Worthy, and Powers moving casually around the old mission. The three men didn't seem to be making any effort to follow them.

They might later, though, after Preacher and the others were out of sight. Preacher didn't have to warn himself to remain alert. That was just a way of life with him.

Traveling with the wagons meant that they had to go slower than he and Esteban had the day before. They weren't wasting any time now on fruitless trips up dead-end canyons, though, so it tended to even out. It was still past midday before they reached the canyon that appeared to lead to the hiding place of the treasure. They wouldn't know for sure until they explored all the way to the end of it.

"This is it," Preacher said as he called a halt. "Esteban and I will ride up and see what we can find. Might take as long as an hour to reach the head of the canyon, so it'll be fairly late by the time we get back."

"I must go with you," Father Hortensio declared as he started to climb down from the lead wagon.

"There ain't an extra horse," Preacher pointed out.

"There are the two hitched to the other wagon," the priest said. "One of them can be unhitched and saddled so that I can ride."

"It'd be better to leave 'em both where they are," Preacher argued, "in case we had to move these wagons in a hurry."

"Please, Padre," Esteban said. "Preacher and I can handle this part of the task."

Stubbornly, Father Hortensio shook his head. "I must go. If you refuse, I will wait until you are gone and then order the Yaquis to prepare a horse for me to ride. They are good Christians and will do as I command."

Esteban sighed and looked over at Preacher. "He is right, amigo. The Yaquis are more his servants than mine. It appears we must allow him to accompany us."

"Maybe so," Preacher said with a frown, "but that don't mean I've got to like it."

With a self-satisfied smirk, Father Hortensio told the Yaquis to get one of the extra horses unhitched from the second wagon and put a saddle on it. The chore was performed quickly, and the sun was still high in the sky when Preacher, Esteban, and Father Hortensio were ready to start up the canyon.

Esteban rode over to the lead wagon and reached across to take his sister's hand for a moment. "You will be all right here with the Yaquis?" he asked.

Juanita nodded. "I wish I was coming with you, but I do not want to slow you down. Just be careful, Esteban, and I pray you find what we have so long sought."

"I will," he said. "I am certain of it."

He turned his mount and joined Preacher and Father Hortensio, who looked a bit ridiculous with his robe hiked up so that he could sit astride the horse. With Preacher leading the way, the three men started up the canyon. Dog trotted in front of them. The first turn took them out of sight of the wagons.

Preacher's nerves were taut. He rode with his rifle across

the saddle. The twisting and turning of the canyon grew more and more pronounced, until it seemed almost like they were going around in circles.

"It is enough to make one dizzy," Esteban commented. "This must be the right canyon. No wonder its serpentine path impressed itself so strongly on Don Francisco, and he remembered it years later."

Father Hortensio said, "I hear no howling of wolves."

"The wind ain't blowin' hard enough, I reckon," Preacher explained. "You won't be able to hear the howlin' all the time, just when conditions are right."

"To refer to such a phenomenon as the wolves of God is a bit irreverent," the priest said disapprovingly. "Perhaps even blasphemous. To the best of my recollection, nowhere in the Holy Scripture is the Lord linked with savage creatures such as wolves."

"Don Francisco heard howlin', and it came from somewheres high up," Preacher said. "I reckon that's why he came up with the name he did."

"Still, a truly pious man would not think of such a thing."

"My ancestor was a soldier, not a priest," Esteban said rather sharply. "I'm sure he never considered things from your perspective, Padre."

Father Hortensio sniffed, and as usual, that marked the end of the conversation. If anyone ever dared to argue with him, he ignored them to the best of his ability.

A short time later, Preacher chuckled as the wind picked up and the distant howling could be heard. It sounded just like a pack of wolves baying at the moon. "There you go," he said.

"I wonder if we are getting close." Esteban sounded excited as he spoke.

"Ought to be. We've climbed quite a distance."

Preacher wasn't surprised when, a few minutes later, they rounded another bend in the canyon and saw that it emerged onto a broad stretch of flat land. Don Francisco had described it as a plateau, but it wasn't, not really. It was more of a shoulder that stuck out from the side of the mountain, maybe a mile long and half a mile deep. A rocky slope jutted up on the far side, and steep drop-offs bordered the other three sides. The only reasonably easy way to get up here was by following the zigzag canyon up the side of the mountain.

"This is it!" Esteban said. "It must be!"

"Looks like it, from the description you read," Preacher agreed.

"But where is the treasure?" Father Hortensio asked anxiously.

Esteban's hands shook a little as he dug out the pages he had copied from the old don's manuscript. He studied them for a moment, flipping through the pages, before he said, "There is nothing else. Only the canyon, the plateau, and the wolves of God."

"Look up yonder," Preacher said.

He pointed to the cliff on the far side of the open ground. It rose almost sheer for a couple of hundred feet, and on top of it were a dozen or more rocky spires pointing toward the sky. Preacher's keen eyes had spotted holes worn in the spires by time and the elements, and he knew that was what produced the sounds that so resembled the howling of wolves.

"I don't see what you mean," Esteban said.

"Them rocks up there don't just sound like wolves, they look a little like 'em, too," Preacher explained. "Them spires are like the snouts of a bunch of wolves, thrown back and pointed toward the moon."

"Toward heaven," Father Hortensio corrected. "That is why Don Francisco named them as he did. They sing their homage to God."

Preacher shrugged. "That explanation makes as much

sense as any other," he said. "And seein' them so-called wolves up there is good enough for me. I'm convinced this is the right place."

"Then the treasure is here," Esteban said.

Preacher nodded. "Yep. Now all we got to do is find it."

15

That proved to be easier said than done. Even though the area was relatively small, there could be any number of hiding places here. Preacher suggested that they split up, so that they could cover the ground more quickly.

"See," Father Hortensio said. "It was a good thing that I came with you. Three men can search more places than two."

"You're right, Padre," Preacher said. He pulled one of the pistols from behind his belt and held it toward the priest.

Father Hortensio recoiled as if Preacher had just tried to hand him one of the rattlesnakes that made its home in the old mission downriver. "I have no need of a gun," he said. "The Lord will protect me from any danger."

"I ain't givin' it to you for protection. If you find the cache, fire off a shot into the air, and we'll come a-runnin'."

Father Hortensio hesitated. "I am not sure I know how to fire such a weapon."

Preacher reined in the frustration he felt. He had almost said *For God's sake*! but he knew that wouldn't have gone over well. Instead, he said patiently, "It's already loaded and primed. All you have to do is pull back the hammer until it locks, then point the barrel into the air and pull the trigger. Don't point it straight up above you, though. If you do that, the ball's liable come back down and hit you. Aim off to the side a little."

Reluctantly, Father Hortensio reached out and took the pistol. "Very well. But I feel a bit unclean having such a weapon in my possession."

The old padres hadn't felt that way about having conquistadors armed with swords, pikes, and blunderbusses along with them when they first came over here from Spain to take over the place, Preacher thought, but again, he kept it to himself.

He looked at Esteban instead and said, "Same goes for you. If you find anything, fire a shot in the air and we'll come to you. I'll do likewise if I'm the one who runs across the hidin' place first."

"Of course," Esteban said. "Good luck, amigo."

Preacher said, "Padre, you take the near end of this shelf. Esteban, you've got the middle. I'll go down yonder to the far end."

The other two men nodded in agreement. Preacher wheeled Horse and put him into a trot that carried him toward the far end of the flat stretch of ground. Dog followed.

This shelf might look flat, but that was only in comparison to the mountains that rose around it. As Preacher rode over the ground, he discovered that it was more rugged than it appeared and was cut in places by gullies and ravines. They were dry now, but when it rained higher up, he imagined all those ditches ran full of water.

There were also patches of hardy grass and stands of pine trees. The elevation kept the trees from growing quite as well as those lower down, so they were a bit smaller.

Preacher didn't see any likely hiding places for the treasure out in the open. When he reached the far end of the shelf, he turned Horse and rode toward the cliff. The shelf had narrowed down here to no more than a quarter of a mile wide, so it didn't take him long to reach the wall of stone that reared up at the back of the shelf. He started along it, watching for clumps of boulders or cave mouths. The face of the cliff was almost sheer and appeared to be featureless, however. Preacher remembered Esteban saying that the relics from the missions had been placed in bags, and the gold bars in wooden chests. He didn't know how many of either there were, but it seemed to him that a good number would be required. That would take some room if they were going to be properly hidden.

He couldn't see Father Hortensio from where he was, but he could pick out the figure of Esteban in the distance, still mounted and poking around a grove of trees. Preacher stuck close to the cliff, figuring that would be the most likely spot for the cache. A couple of hundred feet above him, the wind blew harder and the "wolves" howled louder. The sound had a faintly mocking quality to it. Preacher felt his frustration growing as the minutes dragged by and his search continued to turn up nothing.

He kept one eye on the sun as that glowing orb dipped closer and closer to the peaks of the mountains on the western horizon. It had taken an hour to reach the top of the zigzag canyon, and it would take about that long to get down. Preacher wanted to get back to the wagons by nightfall so that Juanita and the Yaquis wouldn't be by themselves once it was dark. The Yaquis had a reputation as fierce fighters, but Preacher didn't know firsthand just how much they could be depended upon.

He crisscrossed his search area several times before he decided that it was getting too late. Knowing that Esteban was going to be disappointed, Preacher looked around until he spotted the young man about three hundred yards away. He rode toward Esteban.

With an eager expression on his face, Esteban came to meet Preacher. "Did you find anything?" he called when twenty yards still separated them.

Preacher shook his head. Both men reined in as their horses trotted up to each other. "I didn't see hide nor hair o' that loot, nor any place that looked like a good spot for a cache," Preacher said. "Don't seem to be nothin' up here except some grass and trees and a few rocks. Didn't even see any animal sign."

"But it must be here!" Esteban waved his arms. "The canyon that twists back upon itself, the rocks that look and sound like wolves . . . everything fits! This must be the place Don Francisco described."

"Sure seems like it," Preacher agreed. "Let's go see if the padre found anything."

"He would have fired a shot if he had, would he not?"

"I hope so, but you can't never tell with a fella like him."

Together they rode along the shelf, which led them in a generally easterly direction. Preacher kept his eyes open. Just because Esteban had already searched this area didn't mean that the young man couldn't have missed something.

By the time they found Father Hortensio, however, Preacher still hadn't seen anything promising. Esteban hailed the priest.

"Please tell us you have found something, Father," he said.

"No, if I had, I would have shot the gun that Señor Preacher gave me," Father Hortensio answered. "Am I to assume that neither of you found the lost treasure of Mission Santo Domingo, either?"

"You can assume that, all right, Padre," Preacher drawled.

Esteban dismounted, took off his sombrero, and walked around for a moment with a frustrated, pained expression on his face. He burst out, "I do not understand it! Everything is perfect! The treasure should be here!"

"It ain't like we found the hidin' place and the loot was gone," Preacher pointed out. "Then it really would be lost.

Either this ain't the right spot . . . or we just ain't found the stuff yet and it's still here."

Father Hortensio said, "I searched everywhere in this area and found nothing. Are you saying that I overlooked something?"

"Nope, I'm sayin' one of us maybe overlooked somethin', but until we find it, there ain't no way of tellin' which one of us missed it the first time around." Preacher swung down from Horse's back and went over to Esteban. He laid a hand on the young man's shoulder. "I know you're disappointed, but maybe the ol' don just hid the loot really good. Like I've said all along, sometimes it takes a while to find what you're lookin' for. We'll head back down to camp for the night and come up here again in the mornin'. We'll spend the whole day searchin' on foot, takin' a closer look at everything. Might take a few days, but if that cache is here, we'll find it."

Esteban looked at him. "You sound certain."

"I am certain. And if it turns out this ain't the right spot, we'll push on and see if we can't find somewheres else to look."

Esteban smiled faintly. "You seem almost as devoted to our cause as the father and I, Preacher, and yet you have no stake in this."

"Oh, I got a stake, all right," Preacher said. "Once I get started on somethin', I'm about as stubborn as one o' them mules down yonder. That's my stake!"

Juanita was disappointed, of course, when they didn't return with the treasure. She smiled bravely, though, and told Esteban, "I am sure you will find it tomorrow."

"I pray you are right," he said.

While Preacher and the others were gone, the Yaquis had set up camp just outside the mouth of the canyon. There was grass for the mules and horses, and the river was close enough so that fetching water wasn't a problem. They could stay here for a week if they had to.

But it wouldn't take a week to thoroughly search that shoulder of ground at the top of the canyon, Preacher knew. If they hadn't found the treasure in another couple of days, they would have to consider giving up on this location and moving on. That meant he and Esteban would have to start searching the canyons again for another one that matched Don Francisco's description.

He warned himself not to borrow trouble. Tomorrow they might be lucky.

As usual, through Esteban he instructed the Yaquis to take turns standing guard during the night. Preacher rose several times to check on everything, and the rest of the time he slept lightly, with Dog beside him and Horse nearby. He knew that if there was trouble, his four-legged friends would probably be aware of it before anyone else and would warn him. The night passed quietly, however, and Preacher was fairly well rested when he rolled out of his robes the next morning.

Esteban didn't look so chipper, and Preacher figured he'd had a hard time sleeping. The young man confirmed it over breakfast. "I spent a long time studying Don Francisco's manuscript again," Esteban said. "I hoped that I had overlooked something that would give us more of a clue where to search. I was wrong, though. There is nothing more in the manuscript than I have already told you, Preacher."

"Then we just keep lookin'," Preacher said.

"And today I will come with you," Juanita declared.

Esteban was about to argue with her, but Preacher stopped him with a raised hand. "That probably ain't a bad idea," he said. "That'll give us another pair of eyes. Fact of the matter is, I was wonderin' if we ought to leave a couple o' them Yaquis here to watch the camp and take the other two with us to help search. They could double up on that extra hoss."

"I think that is an excellent idea," Juanita said, clearly glad that Preacher wasn't going to object to her accompanying them to the top of the canyon.

Esteban shrugged, still in the grip of his discouragement. "If you think that is for the best, Preacher, then we shall do it."

"The more eyes we got lookin', the better," Preacher said.

After they had eaten, the group got ready to ride. Esteban picked two of the Yaquis to go with them. Preacher thought their names were Pablo and Joaquin. Those were the names they had taken, anyway, when they converted to Christianity. Preacher doubted if they had been born with them. To tell the truth, though, he had trouble keeping the Yaquis straight. They were all grim, stocky, unfriendly-looking cusses, as far as he was concerned.

The group that rode up the canyon was twice as big as the one the day before. Preacher hoped that would make them twice as lucky, but he wasn't going to hold his breath waiting.

When they reached the top of the canyon, he split them up, telling Juanita to stay close to her brother. One of the Yaquis he sent with Father Hortensio, and he took the other Indian with him. Again they divided the shelf into rough thirds, but today there would be two people searching in each area, and on foot rather than from horseback.

"Which one are you?" Preacher asked his companion as they started their search along the face of the cliff.

"Pablo, Señor," the Yaqui replied.

"Well, keep your eyes open, Pablo. We're probably lookin' for a cave, or somethin' like that. It's a cinch all that loot ain't stashed right out in the open."

Preacher didn't know how much Pablo understood of what he was saying, but the Yaqui nodded and seemed to know what Preacher meant. They spread out. Preacher poked under rocks and prodded at the ground and pulled aside the scrubby bushes that grew out of the cliff in places.

Dog bounded around enthusiastically at first, but then sat down and looked puzzled when he realized there weren't any rabbits up here for him to chase.

Why *weren't* there any rabbits up here? Preacher suddenly asked himself. He hadn't seen any birds in the trees or any varmints of any kind, not even a lizard. There were no tracks to indicate that deer or bears ever came up here to forage. Why not? There had to be a reason for animals to avoid the place, didn't there?

He sniffed the air. He hadn't really noticed it the day before, but there was a lingering trace of brimstone in the air. It was very faint, so much so that if he hadn't been looking for something odd, he might not have smelled it even now.

More than once, he had been to the area up north of the Tetons known as Colter's Hell, because John Colter had been the first white man to lay eyes on the place. It suited its name. Boiling water shot up out of the ground, and there were molten pools of mud and ash that gave off such a noxious scent that they sure seemed like doorways to Hades. The scent that Preacher smelled now was a little like that, only nowhere near as strong.

He knew that the geysers and the stink in Colter's Hell came from volcanic action far below the earth. Maybe something was going on, on a much smaller level, in these mountains. Though he hadn't seen it for himself, he had heard about an area somewhere here in Nuevo Mexico where an ancient volcano had erupted far in the past and left a layer of black, razor-sharp lava all over the ground for miles around. Maybe there was another volcano around here, long dormant but still bubbling deep in its bowels, and from time to time some of the pressure that built up was vented off through fissures in this cliff. That might be enough to make animal life avoid the place.

That was interesting as all get-out, Preacher told himself, but it didn't put him any closer to finding the treasure.

He looked along the cliff toward Pablo, who was poking around at the base of the cliff about a hundred yards away. As Preacher watched, the Yaqui suddenly straightened—

And then he was gone, vanished as if he had never been there.

16

Preacher stared for a second, unable to believe his eyes. Folks didn't just disappear like that. But Pablo sure had, and there was only one explanation Preacher could think of. A moment later, as he heard faint, muffled shouts for help, that guess was confirmed.

The mountain man's long legs carried him quickly toward the spot where Pablo had vanished. Preacher was running by the time he got there. When he reached the place, he dropped to his knees beside a hole in the ground, an irregular circle a little less than three feet in diameter. It was located right against the base of the cliff, and enough sunlight penetrated the hole so that Preacher could see that it sloped backward, underneath the huge stone wall.

He couldn't see Pablo. He could hear the Yaqui's frantic cries, however. He leaned over the hole and called, "Pablo! I'm here! Hang on, dang it!"

Preacher turned his head and saw that Horse and Dog had followed him over here, as he expected. There was a rope coiled on the big horse's saddle. Preacher sprang up and ran to get it.

He was uncoiling the rope as he reached the hole again.

He said, "I'm gonna throw a rope down to you, Pablo. Grab onto it, and I'll haul you out of there."

"H-hurry, Señor!" The Yaqui's usual stolid demeanor had deserted him. "I cannot hold on much longer! My hands . . . they slip!"

Preacher tossed the rope down the hole, paying out as much of it as he could and still keep a good grip on it. "There it is! Grab hold!"

"I . . . I cannot! Señor—!"

Pablo screamed as he slipped and fell. Preacher grimaced, knowing that this hole in the ground might be hundreds of feet deep. He expected to hear Pablo screaming for a long time as he fell. . . .

But a mere heartbeat later, there was a heavy thud and a pained grunt that echoed in the narrow shaft. After a moment, Pablo said, "Señor?"

"You all right, Pablo?"

"*Sí.* The fall, she was a short one."

"Can you see anything?"

"No, Señor. All is dark."

Preacher began pulling up the rope. "Well, if you're set good, don't move. No tellin' if there are any other holes down there. You go to rustlin' around and you might fall again."

"I will not move, Señor."

Confident that Pablo would be all right if he just stayed calm and still, Preacher hurried over to the nearest trees and found a branch that had broken off sometime in the past. He brought it back to the hole and pulled up some dry grass that he wrapped around one end of the branch and tied in place. He tied the rope to the other end of the branch. Then he gathered some more grass, took flint and steel from his pouch, and quickly struck some sparks to get a fire going. When he had a tiny flame and a little curl of smoke, he leaned over and puffed on it until it grew into a large enough fire so that he could light the makeshift torch.

He turned to the hole in the ground and called into it, "I'm gonna lower a torch to you, Pablo, so you can see where you are."

"Sí, señor."

Preacher lowered the torch into the hole. The glare from it lit up the slanting shaft. The rough walls told Preacher that it was a natural opening in the earth, not man-made.

But a man could have taken advantage of it. Don Francisco Alvarez, to be precise.

Preacher was trying not to think about that. The important thing right now was to get Pablo out of there. The torch dropped out of sight, but a second later he felt the tension in the rope change. "I have the torch, Señor," Pablo called, his voice echoing. *"Madre de Dios!"*

"What is it?"

"Señor," Pablo said, his voice shaking a little now, "we have found the treasure."

Preacher's heart pounded harder. "You're sure?" he called down.

"There are wooden chests and big bags, just as the padre told us there would be. What else could it be? Do you want me to open some of them?"

"No, just hang on a minute," Preacher said. "What's the cave like?"

"Not too big. Large enough for the treasure, but not much more."

"Any other holes that lead deeper?"

"No, only some small cracks in the rock." Pablo paused. "It smells bad in here."

Preacher could smell it, too, wafting up from down below. Gas from somewhere deeper in the earth had to be seeping through those cracks in the cave wall. If a fella was shut up in there, it might be potent enough to choke him to death. As long as the shaft to the surface was open, though, Preacher figured they could stand to breathe the stuff.

"Untie the rope from the torch," he told Pablo. While the

Yaqui was doing that, Preacher tied the other end to Horse's saddle.

"It is loose, Señor."

"All right. I'm comin' down. I'm gonna fire a shot first, though, so the others will come on over here. Just in case somethin' goes wrong and we need some help."

He pulled out one of his pistols, cocked it, and fired into the deep blue sky. Then he reloaded the pistol and tucked it behind his belt again.

With that done, he positioned Horse near the hole in the ground and ordered, "Stay right there, old hoss. Don't move."

He gripped the rope tightly and started lowering himself into the hole. Dog whined worriedly as his master disappeared into the earth.

The rocks scraped a little hide off Preacher as he slid over them. When he looked over his shoulder he could see a red glow in the darkness that came from the torch Pablo held. About fifteen feet below the surface, the slanting shaft turned and dropped straight down. Preacher's legs dangled over the edge, and the feeling of empty air underneath him made his hands tighten instinctively on the rope.

"It is not far, Señor," Pablo said. "Only a few feet."

Preacher hung over the edge, looked around, and saw that Pablo was right. The floor of the cave was only a couple of feet below his boots. He let go of the rope and dropped the rest of the way, landing lithely.

As he straightened, he looked around. The cave was a rough square, about fifteen feet on a side. Pablo stood holding the torch in front of a stack of about a dozen wooden chests. Next to the chests was a pile of sailcloth bags. Preacher stepped over to them and rested a hand for a moment on one of the bags. He could feel some sort of solid object through the cloth.

He had known about the lost treasure of Mission Santo Domingo for only a few days. Finding it had not been a long-held goal for him, the way it was for Esteban and Juanita and Father Hortensio. Yet Preacher still felt a fierce sense of exultation for a moment. As he had tried to explain to the priest, he was not an overly religious man in the traditional sense, but it would give him some satisfaction to see these artifacts returned to their proper place, instead of being hidden away underneath the ground.

"It is the treasure we seek, Señor?" Pablo asked.

"Yep, it sure is," Preacher replied. He moved over to one of the wooden chests. At this elevation the air was fairly dry, even in the cave, so the wood hadn't deteriorated much in a hundred and fifty years. A simple brass latch held the lid closed. There was no lock. Preacher turned the latch and lifted the lid. The guttering light from the torch shone dully on the gold ingots stacked inside the chest.

"Madre de Dios," Pablo said again, this time in a breathless half whisper.

"Yeah," Preacher agreed.

He lifted his head as he heard the swift rataplan of hoofbeats on the surface. A moment later, Esteban called, "Preacher! Are you down there?"

"We're here," Preacher said, raising his voice so that it echoed in the close confines of the cave. "And so is the treasure!"

"Praise be to God!" That exclamation came from Father Hortensio.

Juanita asked, "Are you all right?"

"And where is Pablo?" Esteban added.

"Pablo's here with me, and we're both fine," Preacher replied. "Hang on a minute, and we'll climb out."

"We leave the treasure here, Señor?" Pablo asked, sounding surprised.

"Just for now," Preacher assured him. "That torch ain't gonna last much longer. We'll have to get some better light down here, and then we'll figure out how to get the treasure

up to the surface." He smiled. "Don't worry. . . . It ain't goin'
anywhere until we move it."

At Preacher's urging, Pablo climbed out of the cave first.
He set the torch aside and grasped the rope, and Preacher
gave him a boost that enabled him to reach the slanted part
of the shaft. From there he was able to scramble to the surface on his own, although Esteban and Joaquin stood ready
to help him if need be. Preacher went up next. When he
emerged from the hole, Juanita threw her arms around his
neck and hugged him.

"Please, Señorita," Father Hortensio said stiffly in disapproval, "there is no need for such a display."

"Without Preacher we might never have found the treasure, Father," Esteban said. He extended a hand to the mountain man. "He deserves our thanks."

Preacher shook hands with the young man. "It was Pablo
who found the cave," he pointed out.

The Yaqui grunted and said, "By falling into it, Señor. I
thought I was a dead man."

"I was a mite concerned about you when you slipped off
that edge," Preacher admitted. "Without any light down
there, there was no way of knowin' just how deep the cave
was or how far the drop was gonna be."

"Just far enough to twist my ankle a bit when I landed . . .
a price I will gladly pay to do the Lord's work."

Juanita hugged him, too, making the grim-faced Yaqui
look a little uncomfortable, and Esteban slapped him on the
back. Father Hortensio was too busy praying to issue any
congratulations.

Preacher knelt and studied the hole. Now that they knew
where the treasure was, there was no hurry about retrieving
it, so he decided to indulge his curiosity. "I rode along here
yesterday," he said to no one in particular. "I should've noticed a hole this big."

"But it was not that big, Señor," Pablo said. "It was small, like the burrow of an animal, and I had to move a rock aside to get a good look at it. When I did, the ground gave way beneath my feet and I fell."

"Yeah, the way you dropped out of sight, I figured somethin' like that must've happened. Maybe ol' Don Francisco and his men filled in most of the upper part o' the openin' and rolled that rock over it as a landmark. They could've figured that they would dig back down to the cave when they came back for the loot."

Esteban took up the speculation. "But they never returned, and over the years rain washed out some of the earth they used to block the tunnel, until it was open again except on top."

Preacher nodded and said, "That's the way it looks to me. Pablo came along and moved the rock, which changed the stress on the ground, and then stepped where he shouldn't and it all went out from under him."

Father Hortensio stopped mumbling prayers and sniffed. It wasn't a sound of disdain this time, however. "What is that smell?" he asked.

"Volcanic gas would be my guess," Preacher said. "It's comin' up from underground somewheres. There are cracks in the cave wall down there, and the stink is comin' through them."

"It smells like the very fires of Hades itself," Father Hortensio said darkly. "To think that relics dedicated to the Lord have been sealed away in that hellhole for all these years. It is shameful!"

"Yeah, well, them Pueblo Indians would've melted 'em down if they'd got their hands on 'em," Preacher pointed out. "Then they would have been gone for good."

"Es verdad," the priest admitted grudgingly.

"What do we do now?" Juanita asked. "How do we get the treasure out of there?"

"First thing we need to do," Preacher said, "is to gather

some dead branches and some brush and toss it down the hole. That way we can make a little fire down there so we can see what we're doin'. The torch we had down there is burned out by now. Once we've done that, somebody can climb down, get the fire started, and tie the rope to one of those bags. The rest of us can pull it up. It'll take a while, and we might have to use Horse to lift them chests full o' gold bars, but we'll get it all done."

"It is hard to believe we finally found it," Esteban said. "This has been a dream of mine ever since I first read that old manuscript, penned so long ago by my ancestor."

Preacher clapped a hand on Esteban's shoulder and grinned. "You can believe it, amigo. Now, let's get to work."

17

Esteban and Father Hortensio both insisted on going down into the cave so that they could see the treasure where it had been hidden for the past century and a half. Preacher figured it wouldn't hurt anything, so he didn't argue the matter. Once they had thrown enough branches and dried brush into the hole, he shinnied down the rope again and got the fire started. He kept it small, not wanting the air in the cave to get stifling hot. Then he called up and told Esteban and the priest it was all right to descend the rope.

Father Hortensio came first, and Preacher looked away, not particularly enchanted by the view of the priest's hairy legs under the robe. When Father Hortensio reached the bottom, he dropped to his knees in front of the treasure, crossed himself, and began to pray as if he were kneeling in front of an altar. That made Preacher frown. It didn't seem right somehow for a holy man to be so impressed by a pile of riches.

Esteban climbed down and dropped easily to the floor of the cave. He crossed himself, too, and said a prayer of his own as he looked at the heaped-up treasure, but at least he stayed on his feet. He went over to one of the bags and untied the rawhide thong that held it closed. The thong had been in place for so long that Esteban had to struggle with it for a moment, but finally he got it loose. He opened the bag and reached inside to withdraw an object wrapped in oilcloth.

Father Hortensio got to his feet and said, "Esteban, what are you doing? It is not our place to disturb these relics. They should not be unwrapped until we have returned them to the mission where they belong."

Esteban shook his head. "I understand, Father, but after all this time, I must see for myself that we have succeeded. I will do nothing to dishonor whatever artifact this may be." He ignored Father Hortensio's scowl and continued unwrapping the object in his hands.

Underneath the oilcloth was another layer of coverings, this one of fine linen. Esteban unwound it carefully, and the firelight suddenly gleamed on the heavy candlestick that was revealed. It appeared to be cast of solid gold. Esteban's hands shook a little as he peered down at what he held.

"That candlestick should be on an altar, not in this cave that stinks of the very devil himself," Father Hortensio said. "Please, Esteban . . ."

Slowly, Esteban nodded. "You are right, Father." He began to carefully wrap up the candlestick again. Father Hortensio helped him.

Meanwhile, Preacher tried to heft one of the chests. He was able to lift it slightly, but he knew he could never climb up the shaft with it. He was confident that Horse could raise it, though. They would probably need a second rope, so that two of them could be fastened around the chest.

"We'll get the bags out first," he said as he brought the end of the rope over to where Esteban and Father Hortensio stood. Esteban had replaced the candlestick in the big sail-cloth bag. Now he tied the rawhide thong around the bag again, closing it, and Preacher tied the rope to the bag.

He stepped over to the opening of the shaft, carrying the

bag. He set it on the ground, cupped a hand at his mouth, and called up, "Haul away!" The rope grew taut as Pablo and Joaquin began pulling it up hand over hand. The bag of holy relics rose from the floor of the cave. Preacher took hold of it and reached above his head to guide it into the shaft. The bag disappeared from sight.

"You fellas might as well climb out when the rope comes back down," Preacher told his two companions. "I can handle this part of the chore, at least for now. Might need a hand when it comes time to boost those chests up."

Esteban shook his head. "I think you should go back to the surface, Preacher. It is still possible that the men who attacked us several days ago could have been trying to stop us from reaching the treasure, rather than simply intending to rob and murder us. If that is true, they could still be around, waiting to, how do you say, jump us again. I would feel better if you were up there to protect us while we work."

"Well, you might be right about that," Preacher allowed. "I'll climb up and keep an eye on things."

A few minutes later, the end of the rope came slithering down the shaft again and dropped into the cave. Preacher nodded to Esteban and Father Hortensio, then grasped the rope.

"I'm comin' up," he called, and he started to climb.

Professor Rufus Chambers could barely contain his excitement as he lowered the spyglass. "They've found the treasure!" he said. "I'm certain of it!"

Cobey Larson reached for the glass. "Lemme see."

"There's some sort of tunnel," Chambers went on. "Preacher and one of the Indians climbed out of it. There must be a cave down there, below the cliff. What better place for Don Francisco to have concealed the treasure?"

Chambers and his group of hired gunmen had followed

the Alvarez party along the river that morning, and when everyone except the two Yaquis who had remained with the wagons had started up the canyon across the way, Chambers had suspected that was the one Don Francisco had talked about in his manuscript. Arnie Ross, who seemed to be more intelligent than he appeared, had suggested that some of them climb to this ledge on the opposite side of the river where they might be able to see what was going on at the head of the canyon where Preacher and the others had gone. The climb had been long and hard, but it had been rewarded. From this vantage point, with the help of the spyglass, they could see what was going on over there, a good half mile straight across the valley of the Purgatoire. A distant shot had drawn their attention and helped them to focus on the right place. Chambers, accompanied by Larson and Ross, had watched as the Alvarez siblings, the priest, and one of the Yaquis had converged on the spot. The professor had wondered where Preacher and the other Indian were, when lo and behold, the two of them had climbed into sight, apparently from out of the ground.

From there, it took no great reasoning skills to deduce that there was a cave over there, and from the excited attitude of the individuals gathered around it, Chambers knew they must have located the lost treasure of Mission Santo Domingo. That was the only thing that would produce such a reaction.

"Yeah, you're right," Cobey said. "They're throwin' branches and such down the hole, so they must be plannin' to build a fire in that cave."

"There's no point in waitin' any longer," Ross put in. "We need to climb back down, join up with the rest o' the fellas, and get over there to jump those folks before they know we're anywhere around."

Cobey nodded in agreement. "Sounds good to me."

"Wait just a moment," Chambers said. "Perhaps it would

be better to wait and let them bring all the treasure out of the cave before we make our move."

"Hell, no," Cobey said emphatically. "I didn't have a problem with lettin' them find the cache, but there are plenty of us to haul it up outta that cave. We need to jump 'em now, while all their attention is on what they're doin'. If we wait until they've brought the treasure out and loaded it on the wagons, Preacher will be on his guard even more than he was before." He clenched a fist. "I want that son of a bitch dead before he knows what's hit him."

Chambers thought it over for a moment and then nodded. "I think you're right, my friend. Let's go. It will take us a while to climb down, and then we have to get up that canyon and take them by surprise."

"That'll mean killin' the two Yaquis they left with the wagons," Arnie pointed out.

Chambers just smiled and said, "Yes. So it will."

Preacher climbed out of the hole and saw that the first bag of treasure had been tied to the saddle of the horse that had carried the two Yaquis up here. Juanita said, "I thought we could go ahead and send Joaquin down to the wagons with it, but I wanted to be sure you approved of that first, Preacher."

After a moment's thought, Preacher shook his head. "We need to get all the loot out first, so we can carry as much down as we can at one time. We'll want to ride guard on it, too, in case anybody tries to take it away from us."

Juanita frowned. "You think that is possible?"

"Anythin's possible," Preacher said. "Especially when you're dealin' with a fortune in gold."

"Very well. I trust your judgment, Preacher."

He hoped she was right in doing so.

For the next hour, they worked steadily. Preacher checked the other horses, but none of them had a rope tied to the saddle, which put a minor crimp in his plans. They could pull the chests out with only one rope, but it would be a trickier chore and they would have to be careful not to break the rope or to let any of the chests slip out of the loop and fall while they were being hauled up. He was sure they could manage, though.

In the meantime, raising the bags of relics to the surface one at a time was fairly easy, though time-consuming. They had to take a break from the work, too, while Father Hortensio climbed out of the cave. He was rather pale and claimed that the smell bothered him.

"I do not know what is sickened more, my stomach from the fumes or my soul from the reminder they carry of the infernal realm ruled by El Diablo."

"You figure Hell is really down there under the ground, Padre?" Preacher asked.

"Where else would it be?" Father Hortensio snapped.

Preacher scratched his bearded jaw. "I dunno. Don't reckon I've ever really thought about it that much."

"You should spend more time in religious contemplation."

"I'll keep that in mind," Preacher said dryly. Father Hortensio's skeptical expression made it plain that he didn't believe the mountain man for a second.

They got back to work, and the pile of bags on the ground near the entrance to the cave continued to grow. Finally, Esteban called up, "This is the last bag, Preacher."

"All right," Preacher replied. "We'll haul it up, and then I'll climb down and we'll see about bringin' those chests outta there."

A few minutes later, the bag was on the surface and added to the pile that had grown over the past hour. Preacher took hold of the rope and let himself down into the cave.

He found Esteban waiting for him with one of the chests open. The young man reached into it and took out one of the heavy bars of gold.

"I have been thinking, Preacher," he said. "You should take this." He held out the ingot.

Preacher frowned. "Why would I want to do that?"

"You deserve it for all the help you have given us. The Church is willing to let Juanita and me keep some of the gold, so that we can revive our family's fortunes. You are equally deserving."

Preacher shook his head. "A bar o' gold would just weigh me down. Anyway, it ain't like I'm headin' back to St. Louis or some other place where I could do anything with it. Once I get back to my old stompin' grounds in the Rockies north o' here, I wouldn't have no use for any gold."

"You are certain?"

"Certain sure," Preacher said. He added, "I might let the Church buy me some supplies once we get back down to the tradin' post, if Father Hortensio will go along with it."

"I will see that he does," Esteban promised.

Preacher knew the youngster meant well by that, but he wasn't sure Esteban was in any position to deliver on that promise. When Father Hortensio didn't want to do something, he seemed to be harder to budge than a Missouri mule.

Esteban replaced the ingot in the chest and closed it. He and Preacher got at each end of the chest and lifted it, carrying it over to where the rope waited. They set it down, and Preacher looped the rope around the chest so that it crisscrossed itself before he tied it securely. The chest couldn't slip out of that arrangement. The only question was whether a single rope was strong enough to lift the great weight of the chest.

"All right, somebody lead Horse away from the shaft!" he called to those on the surface. "The rest of you haul on the rope, too!"

As the rope grew taut, Preacher and Esteban lifted the chest as well, boosting it toward the opening of the shaft. They had to raise themselves on their toes to guide the heavy box into the opening. Then Preacher stepped back and motioned for Esteban to do the same.

"If that rope was to snap, we don't want that chest fallin' back down on us," he explained. "It's heavy enough to bust a fella's head wide open."

They heard the chest scraping against the sides of the shaft as it rose steadily. After a few moments, the noises stopped and Juanita called excitedly, "The chest is here. We have it!"

"Good!" Preacher replied. "Untie the rope and toss it back down, and we'll get the next one ready to haul up."

He stood underneath the opening now, waiting for the end of the rope to tumble back down to the cave. When it didn't appear after a moment, he began to frown.

"Juanita? Somethin' wrong up there?"

Suddenly, there was a muffled half scream, cut off abruptly, and somewhere above them a gun roared, the blast echoing down the shaft to the two startled men below the surface.

18

For a moment, while they were on that ledge high above the river, Cobey Larson had considered pushing the professor over the edge. It would have been pleasurable to watch the arrogant bastard flail his arms and legs and listen to his terrified screams as he plummeted through empty air to his death. Cobey had kept Chambers alive until they found the treasure, but they didn't really need him anymore.

Still, you never could tell what might happen. A situation could arise in which it would be handy to have Chambers around, although for the life of him, Cobey didn't know what it would be. He supposed they could let the professor live a while longer.

They climbed down and rejoined Bert McDermott, Hardy Powers, George Worthy, Wick Jimpson, and Chuck Stilson. Wick and Chuck were still the walking wounded, and Stilson didn't mind bitching about how bad his hip hurt where one of Preacher's bullets had grazed it during the fight a few days earlier. Wick limped around in silence. He had complained about his wound at first, but after Cobey had lost his patience and snapped at the dim-witted giant to shut his pie hole, Wick had stayed quiet for the most part. In his dog-like loyalty, he didn't want to upset Cobey.

"What did you find out?" Bert asked eagerly. "Have they found the treasure?"

"Yeah," Arnie Ross replied. "We saw 'em bringin' it up out of a hole in the ground, on a shelf up at the head of that canyon."

"Are we goin' to get it?" Powers asked.

Cobey nodded. "Yeah, mount up. They left a couple of the Yaquis with the wagons at the mouth of the canyon. We'll take care of them first and then sneak up on the others."

The men swung up into their saddles. Chambers was a surprisingly graceful rider for an Easterner. They started along the river toward the spot where the Alvarezes had left the wagons.

Cobey called a halt before they got there, and the men dismounted. "Arnie an' me will take care of those Yaquis, quietlike so the ones up at the other end of the canyon won't hear anything. Hardy, you and Bert come along, too, in case we need a hand."

"Yaquis are supposed to be pretty tough sons o' bitches," Arnie pointed out.

"That's why we're takin' Hardy and Bert along."

Arnie nodded, but still looked worried.

They set off on foot, slipping quietly through the trees. The Yaquis were from farther south in Mexico, Cobey reflected. They weren't at home up here in the Sangre de Cristos any more than the gringos were. He hoped that unfamiliarity with the territory would even the odds a little. It was important that they dispose of the Indians without warning the others.

Using every bit of cover they could find and moving with all the stealth they could muster, the four hard cases snuck up on the wagons. Cobey lifted a hand to signal a stop when they were about fifty yards away, crouched behind some brush. He peered through a gap in the dense foliage to study the layout.

The Yaquis had left the teams hitched and had hobbled the mules. One of the Indians sat on the lowered tailgate of the second wagon, a rifle across his knees. The other redskin prowled near the mouth of the canyon. He carried a rifle, too.

"How we gonna get 'em?" Arnie whispered in Cobey's ear. "We can't get close enough to jump 'em without them seein' us."

Cobey had already realized the same thing. He frowned as he tried to figure out what to do next. He and Arnie and Bert were good shots, he knew, and he supposed Hardy Powers was, too. If they all fired, they could cut down the two Yaquis before the Indians knew what was happening.

But the sound of those shots probably would reach the top of the canyon with little trouble in this thin air. That would alert Preacher and the others that something was wrong down here. Surprise was vital if they were going to deal with the deadly mountain man.

"We gotta lure 'em over here some way," Cobey breathed. "And when we jump 'em, we gotta kill 'em quick, so they don't even have time to yell."

Arnie and the other two nodded in understanding.

Cobey began making a faint rustling sound in the brush, the sort of sound that a small animal might make. He had to be careful not to make too much noise. If too many branches began to crackle, the Yaquis might decide there was a bear or a wolf or some other big varmint in here and just blaze away at it. He had to get them curious enough to investigate, but not worried enough to shoot first and check to see what they were shooting at later.

The Yaqui sitting on the tailgate heard the noise first. He looked toward the brush and frowned. Arnie, Bert, and Hardy lay utterly still while Cobey continued to shake the brush a little. Cobey stopped for several seconds while the Yaqui was watching, then started again, like an animal that had paused briefly in whatever it was doing.

After a minute the Yaqui said something to his companion. Cobey didn't understand the language. It just sounded like a bunch of grunts to him, mixed with a few barely recognizable Spanish words. The Yaqui at the wagon stood up. The one over by the canyon mouth walked toward him. Together they started toward the brush where the gringos were concealed.

Cobey slid his knife out of its sheath and motioned for the others to do likewise. He gripped the weapon tightly, ready to throw it. Beside him, Arnie was tense with anticipation. Cobey knew that Arnie Ross was deadly with a knife; that was just one of many ways in which folks usually underestimated the round little man who was so much more dangerous than he appeared.

Cobey stopped making the rustling noise when the Yaquis were about ten feet away from the line of brush. The two Indians stopped as well and waited to see if the rustling would resume. When it didn't, one of the Indians shrugged, said something to his companion, and started to turn away. They thought that whatever was in the brush had gone on.

With a nod to Arnie, Cobey suddenly burst out of the brush and flung his knife. Beside him, Arnie did the same.

Cobey's knife buried its blade deep in the chest of one of the Yaquis. Arnie's throw was even better, the blade lodging in the other Indian's throat so that he couldn't cry out. The two white men followed their knives with a rush that bulled into the Yaquis and knocked them off their feet. McDermott and Powers charged out right behind them in case they needed help subduing the Yaquis.

Cobey ripped the rifle out of his man's hands and threw it aside. He slammed his knee into the Yaqui's groin and locked his hands around the man's neck.

A few feet away, Arnie Ross grabbed the knife he had thrown and ripped it across the other Yaqui's throat. Blood fountained high in the air, and the Indian's heels beat a grotesque tattoo against the rocky ground as he died.

Cobey kept choking his man until the Yaqui went limp underneath him. A fierce sense of satisfaction went through Cobey. Both of the Yaquis were dead, and neither of them had let out a shout or gotten a shot off. The small sounds of the deadly struggle could not have been heard up above on the shelf where the rest of the Alvarez party worked at recovering the lost treasure.

Cobey pushed himself to his feet and motioned the others forward. Arnie went back to fetch Wick and Chuck and the horses, as well as Professor Chambers.

When they were all together again, Cobey said quietly, "We'll leave the horses down here and go up the canyon on foot. We don't want the others to hear horses comin' and get spooked."

Chuck Stilson whined, "I don't know if I can make it that far on foot, Larson."

"You'd damned well better if you want a share of the loot," Cobey growled. "We're all goin' up there, so the odds will be as much on our side as possible. You, too, Professor."

Chambers nodded. "Of course. You can count on me. I'll do my part."

Cobey wasn't sure about that. He figured the professor might "accidentally" catch a stray bullet before all the shooting was over. He'd just have to wait and see about that.

Bert said to the giant, "Reckon you can make it, Wick?"

"I can go anywhere Cobey says to go," Wick replied without hesitation.

Cobey slapped him on the arm. "That's the spirit. Everybody check your pistols, and then let's go kill us some pilgrims and get us some gold."

"But not the girl," Powers spoke up. "We won't kill her."

"No." Cobey shook his head, thinking of Juanita Alvarez's thick dark hair and ripe figure. "We won't kill the girl."

* * *

The Yaqui's name was Benedicto. He had been born with a name that translated to Blue Eagle, but Benedicto he had become when he converted to Christianity and accepted the Spaniards' God. Now he called on Jesus, Mary, and Joseph to give him strength and help him ignore the pain that filled his body. Far in the back of his mind, he called on older, more savage gods as well. He would take whatever help he could get, as long as it allowed him to have his revenge on those who had done this to him.

He had no idea how much time had passed since blackness claimed him. When the gringo's choking hands had sent him into oblivion, Benedicto had believed that he was dying. He might die yet, of course, but somehow he had clung to life and now had made the long, slow climb back to consciousness. He drew rattling breaths through his bruised and painful throat, and each of those breaths seemed to add fuel to the fire that burned in his chest. The knife that had penetrated his body was gone, pulled back out by the man who had thrown it. Blood had followed, welling out of the wound so that the front of Benedicto's shirt was soaked with the stuff. Even though his chest was on fire, the rest of him was cold, as cold as a winter morning high in the mountains. He could barely feel his hands and feet.

But he managed to pull himself upright anyway, and as he stumbled to his feet he lifted his pain-blurred eyes and looked around.

The gringos were gone.

He did not know how many of them there had been. He remembered seeing two, perhaps more. They had killed Ismael and wounded him, then left.

Even through the fog of pain that shrouded his brain, Benedicto was able to think clearly enough to realize what must have happened. The gringos had sneaked up, attacked him and Ismael, and then gone up the canyon to kill the others and steal the holy treasure.

"Padre," he murmured, thinking of Father Hortensio. It was Father Hortensio who had shown him the light and led him to the Lord. Benedicto owed everything to Father Hortensio. He would gladly give up his own life to save the priest. Señor Esteban and Señorita Juanita were in danger, too, and Benedicto wanted to help them. He cared nothing for the man called Preacher. Preacher was a gringo and a heathen, and therefore less than nothing. But the others, including Pablo and Joaquin . . . Benedicto had to help them.

He looked around for his rifle, but even after he found it, he knew he lacked the strength to lift it and carry it up the canyon. His hand went to his waist. His knife was still there in its sheath. He could handle the knife. He drew it and stumbled toward the mouth of the canyon.

It never occurred to him to pick up the rifle and fire a warning shot. He merely shuffled along, clutching his knife, grimly determined to catch up to the evil gringos and avenge himself.

With each step, more of his life's blood dripped onto the canyon floor.

In the twisting canyon, men could move just about as fast on foot as on horseback. Cobey led the way, setting a quick pace. He had known the canyon twisted and turned, but he was surprised that it snaked around as much as it did. It was almost enough to make a man dizzy.

It took them over an hour to reach the top. That was longer than it had taken him and Arnie and the professor to get to the ledge on the other side of the river, but that had been a straight, relatively easy climb. As they trudged up the canyon, he heard Chuck Stilson muttering curses under his breath. Stilson was another one, like the professor, that they could probably do without, Cobey decided. Wick still didn't complain, even though he was really hurt worse than Chuck was.

When they neared the top, Cobey called a halt while they were still out of sight of the people on the shelf. For ten or fifteen minutes they waited there, catching their breath from the long climb. That gave Cobey a chance to go over the plan with the other men.

"Arnie, you and me'll take Preacher. He's got to go down fast and hard, since he's the most dangerous of the bunch. We'll fire at the same time. Bert, you'll line your sights on Preacher, too, and if Arnie and me don't drop him right away, it'll be up to you."

McDermott nodded in understanding.

Cobey turned to Powers and Worthy. "It'll be up to you two to get them Yaquis, since they're probably the biggest threat after Preacher."

The two men gave grim nods of assent.

"That leaves you and Wick to take care of the Alvarez boy," Cobey said to Stilson. "I don't know how good a shot he is, so aim good and we won't have to find out."

"Yeah, I got it," Stilson said in surly tones.

"Wick, you understand?" Cobey asked the big man. "You're gonna take your gun and shoot at Esteban Alvarez. He's the young fella who'll probably be wearin' a sombrero."

"I understand, Cobey," Wick said with a frown, "but I don't know why we're doin' this. Why would I want to shoot at somebody who ain't shootin' at me?"

"Because we want what he's got. You remember me tellin' you about the gold?"

"Oh, yeah," Wick said, his expression clearing up a little. "The gold. I remember now."

"You just do what I tell you, and you'll get some of the gold."

"All right," Wick said. "I'll be good, I promise, Cobey."

"What about me?" Chambers asked. He took his pistol out of his coat pocket. "I can shoot, too, you know."

"You're like Bert, Professor," Cobey said. "If any of the rest of us miss with our first shots, it'll be up to you to step in and finish the job." But that wasn't likely to happen, of course, and anyway, Cobey didn't want to think about how badly things would have to be fouled up before their fate would rest in the hands of a professor from back East.

"Excellent," Chambers said. "Are we ready?"

"I reckon we are. It's half a mile or more to that cliff where the cave is. There are plenty of trees between here and there for us to use as cover, though. I figure we can get within fifty yards of them without 'em knowin' we're there. That'll be close enough to cut 'em down without any trouble." Cobey looked around at the other men, saw the greed and ruthlessness on their faces—well, with the exception of Wick, of course—and he was pleased. "Let's go," he said.

The gringos were fools, Benedicto thought an eternity later as he reached the top of the canyon and staggered after his quarry. They believed him to be dead, and they never looked behind them. All their attention was focused ahead.

They had no idea that death was dogging their trail, he thought as he smiled grimly and tightened his grip on the knife in his hand.

19

Everything had gone as planned so far. Cobey, Arnie, and the others crouched in the trees, watching the people gathered around the mouth of the cave. No one had noticed their presence.

But now things began to go wrong. Cobey realized with a scowl that he didn't see Preacher anywhere, or the Alvarez kid, either.

That meant the two of them had to be down inside the cave.

There was a big pile of sailcloth bags near the horses. Professor Chambers slipped up next to Cobey and clutched his arm. He pointed with his other hand at the bags and whispered, "The artifacts from the missions. The gold ingots are supposed to be in wooden chests."

Cobey nodded. "They're still bringin' the stuff up. Haven't gotten to the gold yet."

That wasn't a problem. Once everybody except the girl had been disposed of, some of Cobey's men could climb down in that hole and see to bringing the gold out. The problem was that Preacher wasn't out in the open where they could shoot the son of a bitch first thing. Cobey didn't figure that Esteban Alvarez represented much of a threat, but Preacher, now . . . Preacher was different.

Cobey leaned over to Arnie and whispered, "Preacher's down in that hole. We'll have to wait for him to come up."

Arnie nodded. "Yeah. We got to kill him first."

Cobey motioned for the other men to just wait and be quiet. They had waited this long; they could be patient for a little while longer.

Meanwhile, the two Yaquis hauled on a rope that went down into the hole and brought up several more bags of loot, one at a time. The watchers were close enough so that Cobey could hear the girl calling down the hole to Preacher and Esteban. He couldn't hear what they said back to her, though. But he made out enough of the conversation to know that all the bags were now on the surface. That left the chests full of gold bars. Cobey licked his lips at the thought of all that gold. . . .

Juanita Alvarez lowered the rope into the hole in front of the cliff again and then waited. The other end of the rope was tied to the saddle of the big rangy horse that Preacher normally rode. One of the Yaquis went over to the horse and grasped its reins, being careful because the animal bared its teeth at him. That was a one-man horse, Cobey thought, but it looked like the animal was willing to let the Yaqui lead it, even though it wouldn't have tolerated taking the Indian on its back.

Didn't Preacher have a dog? That thought suddenly occurred to Cobey. He had forgotten about the damned dog! Where was the shaggy beast? Off chasing varmints somewhere, Cobey hoped.

"Look how taut that rope is," Arnie said as the Yaqui began to lead the horse away from the hole. "There's somethin' heavy on the other end!"

"Damn right," Cobey said. "A fortune in gold." Instinctively, he lifted his rifle.

That was when a blood-covered apparition reeled out of the brush behind Cobey, lunged toward him, and drove a knife at his back.

Instinct and keen hearing warned Cobey in time for him to turn halfway around toward the unexpected threat. Horror shot through him at the sight of the pain-crazed Yaqui who was supposed to be dead down at the mouth of the canyon. Pain jolted Cobey the next instant as the Yaqui's knife lanced into his upper left arm. The thrust would have gone into his back if he hadn't turned sharply when he did. The rifle slipped out of his hand and clattered to the rocky ground, and he let out a choked groan, unable to hold it back.

Over by the cliff, a heavy wooden chest had just emerged from the hole on the end of the rope. The priest and the other Yaqui grabbed it and wrestled it to the side. Evidently, they hadn't heard the disturbance in the trees.

But Juanita Alvarez had, and as she turned swiftly, she saw Cobey stumble into the open, knocked forward by the collision with the Yaqui who had just stabbed him. She opened her mouth to scream.

Cobey wasn't sure until later exactly what happened next. Arnie Ross streaked forward, moving faster than a short-legged fat man had any business moving. He covered the ground between the trees and the cliff in a flash and tackled Juanita, clapping a hand over her mouth as he bore her to the ground. Fast as he was, though, he was too late. She had already gotten out part of a scream.

Snarling, Cobey jerked his pistol from behind his belt and raised it, cocking the hammer as he did so. The blood-covered Yaqui ripped his knife from Cobey's arm and brought it back to strike again.

Cobey jammed the pistol in the Indian's face and pulled the trigger.

The fire that geysered from the pistol's muzzle burned the Yaqui's right eye out. The heavy lead ball shattered his cheekbone and bored on through his head to burst out the back of his skull in a grisly shower of gray matter and glistening white bone fragments. The Yaqui flopped to the ground, dead at last. Cobey breathed hard as he looked down at the corpse. The reaction was partially from the pain in his arm and partially from the atavistic fear that the Indian would rise again, shattered skull and all, and come after him again. He would have sworn the Yaqui was dead when they left him down below.

He was dead now, sure enough, and didn't move except for a few final twitches. Cobey twisted around as more shots blasted out. The whole plan had gone to hell.

And any second, Preacher might crawl up out of that hole and go to killin'.

Juanita Alvarez struggled madly in the stranger's grip, but he was much stronger than her and his hands were like iron as he grasped her. She managed to get one hand loose and clawed at his face, trying to gouge out his eyes. He jerked his head to the side so that she merely scratched his cheek. He grunted in pain but didn't loosen his grip. She felt her feet leave the ground as he lifted her and carried her toward the trees.

Several other men stepped out of those trees and fired rifles at Father Hortensio and the two Yaquis. Those shots were hurried, however, and all but one of them missed. The only one that hit its target just grazed Joaquin's upper left arm. The impact was still enough to slew him around sideways. He recovered and snatched his rifle from the ground. Pablo had already grabbed his rifle and was drawing a bead on their attackers.

Father Hortensio was behind the horses, using the animals as cover from any more shots.

Pablo's rifle blasted and one of the strangers cried out and went over backward. Joaquin knelt behind the pile of bags, knowing their contents might stop a rifle or pistol ball. Father Hortensio saw what he was doing and shouted, "No! The holy relics must be protected!"

Joaquin thought the world of Father Hortensio, but the priest did not always see the practical side of things. How could he, Joaquin, protect the holy relics if he allowed the gringos to shoot him? It made no sense.

So he dropped to a knee behind the sacks, raised his rifle to his shoulder, and fired. At the same time, one of the men loosed a round at him from a pistol. Sure enough, the ball smacked into the pile of sacks but didn't penetrate all the way through it. Father Hortensio let out a cry as if the ball had struck him instead of the relics.

Joaquin's shot passed close enough to the head of one of the men to make him duck frantically into the trees. All of the gringos were retreating now, including the one who had hold of Juanita. She continued to struggle until the fat gringo holding her drove a fist against the side of her head. Pain flashed through her skull, and she went limp in his arms, knocked unconscious by the blow.

There were two loaded pistols holstered on the saddle of Señor Preacher's horse. Joaquin grabbed the butts of the guns and jerked them from their holsters, but as he spun toward the trees and lifted them, Pablo caught one of his arms and stopped him from firing.

"They have the señorita!" Pablo said. "If you shoot, you risk hitting her!"

Joaquin hadn't thought of that. He nodded and lowered the pistols. Now that the shooting had stopped, Father Hortensio came out from behind the horses and began to harangue them.

"The gringos have stolen Señorita Juanita!" the priest said. "What will we do?" He crossed himself. "At least the holy relics and the gold are safe!"

But for how long? That was the question none of them could answer.

And from behind the three men came Preacher's outraged bellow. "What the hell!"

The moment when Juanita screamed and the shooting started was one of the worst in Preacher's life. He was used to trouble, having lived with it for many years, but in the past he had always been able to strike back at whoever was trying to hurt him and his friends. He had never been trapped down in a hole in the ground, able to hear what was going on but unable to do anything about it or even to be sure exactly what was happening.

The situation was intolerable, that was all there was to it. "Gimme a boost," he said to an equally worried Esteban.

"What?"

"Help me get up to where the shaft starts."

"But there is no rope—"

"That ain't gonna stop me," Preacher vowed grimly.

As more shots rang out on the surface, Esteban made a stirrup of his hands. Preacher put his foot in it, and Esteban grunted from the effort as he heaved Preacher upward. The mountain man was heavier than his lanky frame would indicate, since it was so packed with muscles. He reached for the lip of the shaft, stretching as high as his long arms could reach. His fingers closed over the edge and took some of the weight off Esteban. The young man lifted Preacher higher. Preacher's foot came off Esteban's hands as he pulled himself into the shaft.

It angled toward the surface, seemingly too steep to climb without a rope or anything else to hang on to. The shaft was a little less than a yard wide, however, and Preacher's arm span was wider than that. He pressed his hands against the sides and pushed with his feet. That allowed him to inch upward. It took an incredible amount of strength to brace himself against the walls of the shaft like that and keep himself from falling, but it was strength that Preacher had. His progress was slow but steady. He kept his head back and his eyes fastened on the ragged circle of light that marked the upper end of the shaft.

The shooting came to an end just before he reached the top. Not knowing if that was good or bad, he was prepared for anything as he levered himself out of the shaft and sprawled on the ground. As he scrambled to his feet, he jerked his pistols from behind his belt. The muscles of his arms and legs tried to tremble from the exertion they had just gone through, but he willed them to an iron steadiness as he shouted, "What the hell!"

Father Hortensio and the two Yaquis were standing beside the pile of sacks containing the artifacts that had been hidden below. One of the Yaquis—Joaquin, Preacher thought—had a couple of pistols in his hands. Preacher recognized the weapons as the ones from his saddle.

The only person missing was Juanita Alvarez. "Where's the señorita?" Preacher snapped.

"They . . . they took her," Father Hortensio said.

"Who took her?"

"The gringos!" The priest leveled an arm toward some nearby trees.

Preacher swung in that direction, his pistols held ready to fire. He didn't see anything moving in the trees, however. "Where are they?"

"They fled," Father Hortensio said. He seemed to be getting some of his wits back about him now. "After they took Señorita Alvarez and tried to kill the rest of us, they ran off."

"We tried to stop them, Señor," Joaquin said. He lifted his left arm. Blood stained the sleeve of his shirt. "I was wounded."

"You hit bad?" Preacher asked.

The Yaqui shook his head. "The ball barely touched me."

Preacher grunted. "You were lucky. Get the rope back down the hole and help Señor Esteban outta there. And gimme back my guns."

He replaced the pistols behind his belt and took the ones that Joaquin had been holding. All four guns were double-shotted and loaded with a heavy charge of powder. They gave him considerable firepower as he stalked toward the trees.

He saw quickly that he wasn't going to need it. Juanita's kidnappers were gone. The tracks they had left headed off straight toward the top of the canyon, and Preacher had no doubt they were on their way back down now, taking Juanita with them as a prisoner.

They had left behind a couple of dead men. One of them was a Yaqui. He had been shot in the face at close range, destroying most of his features. Preacher was still able to recognize him as one of the Indians who had been left with the wagons.

The other man's identity was a mite more interesting. He was Hardy Powers, one of the so-called guides who worked for Professor Rufus Chambers.

20

By the time Preacher stalked back to where the others waited, Esteban was on the surface, having climbed up the rope that the Yaquis had dropped down the shaft to him. He hurried anxiously to meet Preacher and asked, "Where is Juanita? Did you see her?"

Preacher shook his head, and he hated to see the devastated look that settled on Esteban's face in response. The young man had to know what the situation was, though. Preacher said, "They've got her, all right."

"But who are they?" Father Hortensio asked.

"I don't know about all of 'em, but I've got a pretty good idea one was that Professor Chambers."

"I knew it!" the priest burst out. "I thought I saw him for an instant in the trees. He had a pistol and fired at us, as did the others."

Preacher jerked a thumb toward the trees. "Hardy Powers is dead over yonder. I reckon that fella Worthy was probably with 'em, too." He looked at Pablo and Joaquin. "I hate to tell you fellas this, but one of your pards is over there, too, shot dead."

They looked a little puzzled, so in rapid Spanish Esteban

clarified what Preacher had just said. Both of the Indians gave guttural exclamations and then hurried toward the trees.

Preacher turned back to Father Hortensio. "Tell me exactly what happened," he ordered the priest.

Before Father Hortensio could answer, Esteban said, "Should we not go after Juanita? Can you follow the trail they left?"

"I reckon I can," Preacher said. "First, though, we need to know what we're up against. Tell me what happened, Padre."

"I . . . I am not sure," Father Hortensio said.

That was probably the first thing the priest hadn't been absolutely certain of since Preacher had known him, the mountain man reflected.

"We had just brought up the first chest of gold," Father Hortensio went on. "Then Señorita Alvarez screamed, and when I looked around I saw a gringo running toward her. A fat little gringo, but he moved very fast."

That rang a faint bell in Preacher's memory, but he passed over it for now. "Go on."

"At the edge of the trees, there was another gringo struggling with one of the Yaquis. I think it was Benedicto."

"The Yaqui, you mean?"

"Sí. The gringo, I had never seen before."

"What did he look like?"

Father Hortensio frowned in thought. "He was tall. A big man, strong-looking. He wore buckskin clothing, much like yours, but with more beads and decoration on them. He had long, fair hair and a beard."

Preacher nodded. That jibed with the memory that had cropped up at Father Hortensio's mention of the fat man. "The bunch from the trading post," Preacher said.

"Que?"

Preacher shook his head. "Never mind. Go on."

Father Hortensio rubbed his hands over his clean-shaven face and took a deep breath. "The tall gringo shot Benedicto. Then other gringos stepped out of the trees and began shooting at us. I could not say how many there were. A half dozen, perhaps. I thought one of them was Professor Chambers, but I was not sure. We tried to fight back . . . or rather, Pablo and Joaquin did. I, of course, could not."

"You let them steal Juanita while you stood by and did nothing?" Esteban asked.

Father Hortensio drew himself up straighter. "I am a man of God," he said. "A man of peace. I cannot allow my hands to be stained with blood."

Esteban's face darkened angrily, and Preacher felt more than a mite irritated himself. But they didn't have time to waste, so he put a hand on the young man's shoulder and said to the priest, "Go on, Padre."

Father Hortensio shrugged. "There is not much left to tell. The fat man carried Juanita into the trees, and then all of the gringos fled."

"Why would they take her?" Esteban asked, his voice shaking. "Why?"

There was one pretty obvious reason, but Preacher figured there was a lot more going on here. He might be lacking much of a formal education, but he had a keen native intelligence and the ability to put things together quickly.

"Don't worry, Esteban, we're gonna get her back."

The young man turned an anguished look on him. "How can you know this?"

Preacher nodded toward the sacks of artifacts and the single chest of gold that had been brought up so far and said, "Because we've still got something that they want."

Never in his wildest dreams would Cobey have thought that so much could go so wrong so fast. They had lost another man—Hardy Powers, drilled dead center by a lucky shot from one of those damned Indians—and they didn't have any of the treasure they had set out to steal. Worst of all, Preacher was still alive. At least, Cobey supposed he was. From what they had seen before all hell broke loose, it had looked like Preacher and the young Mex were down in the hole under the cliff where the loot was hidden.

The only good thing to come out of this debacle was that they now had the girl.

That had been quick thinking on Arnie's part to rush out there and grab her like that. Once Cobey had seen that, he'd realized that their best course of action was to cut their losses and get out of there, taking Juanita Alvarez with them.

Unfortunately, Hardy Powers had been hit and killed by that shot before they could pull back. Cobey hadn't known Powers for long, but he had seemed like a good enough fella. Too bad it couldn't have been the professor who caught that ball through the guts. Cobey wouldn't have minded that at all.

They were about halfway down the canyon when Cobey called a halt. Chambers objected, saying, "Shouldn't we keep moving? What if Preacher comes after us?"

"He knows by now we've got the girl," Cobey replied. "He's not gonna crowd us too much. From everything I've heard about him, he's a smart bastard. He'll have figured out by now that we're gonna have to work a swap."

"A swap?" Chambers echoed.

Cobey nodded. "That's right—the treasure for Señorita Alvarez."

The light of understanding dawned on Chambers's thin face. For a professor, he was dumb as a rock sometimes. The idea of trading Juanita for the treasure had sprung fully formed into Cobey's brain as soon as he saw Arnie grab her.

It wasn't as good as killing everybody else and just taking the girl and the loot . . . but once things had fallen apart, it was the best option they had left.

Juanita was starting to come around now. While Arnie hung onto her, Cobey took some rawhide thongs from his possibles bag and used them to tie her wrists. That would make her easier to handle. As consciousness returned to her and she realized what was going on, she began to spout a torrent of furious Spanish at them. Cobey put his face a couple of inches from hers, glared at her, and warned, "You better shut up, gal, or I'll gag you, too!"

That made her fall silent, although she still looked daggers at Cobey and all the other men. When her gaze reached Chambers, her eyes widened and she gasped, "Professor! You must help me!"

Chambers smiled and said, "I'm sorry, my dear, but I'm afraid I can't do that. You see, these men are my business associates."

"Then . . . you are a thief and a murderer, too!"

"Sadly, true."

"Why have I been abducted? I have never done anything to harm any of you men."

"You know better than that," Cobey snapped. "You know damned good and well why we grabbed you."

"You're our key to obtaining the lost treasure of Mission Santo Domingo, Señorita," Chambers said. "Surely, in order to insure your safety, your brother will turn over the treasure to us."

"You want to . . . trade me for the treasure?"

"That is essentially correct."

Juanita began to laugh. Cobey and Chambers frowned. "What's so damned funny?" Cobey demanded.

"You do not know Father Hortensio. He will not allow anything to divert him from his holy quest, not even my life."

"You're saying he won't turn over the treasure?" Chambers asked.

"Of course not. My life means nothing to him, in comparison to his devotion to the Church."

"He's just one man, and a priest, to boot," Cobey growled.

"He won't be able to stop your brother from dealin' with us, and he sure as hell won't be able to stop Preacher."

"And do you think Señor Preacher will meekly go along with your plan?" Juanita asked.

To tell the truth, Cobey was worried about that very thing. Preacher was just the sort to try to figure out a way to rescue Juanita and save the treasure. But he could try all he wanted to, because in the end Cobey and his companions held all the aces in this game.

"He'd damned well better go along with it," Cobey said. "Otherwise, you're gonna be one dead señorita."

Preacher rode slowly down the canyon, guiding Horse with his knees because he had both hands on his rifle, ready to fire at the first sign of a threat. Dog walked in front of him, ears pricked forward. The big cur had wandered up after all the trouble was over, one of the few times since he'd been with Preacher that he had missed a fracas. Now, though, Preacher was mighty glad to have Dog with him. His senses were even sharper than Preacher's.

So when Dog suddenly stopped short and the fur around his neck bristled and he started to growl deep in his throat, Preacher knew trouble was waiting for him.

The fat man eased around the bend in front of Preacher. Not for a second, though, did Preacher believe that he was alone. One or more of the other hard cases would be with him. They might even have guns lined on Preacher at this very moment.

Dog would have lunged at the fat man and torn out his throat, but Preacher stopped him with a soft-voiced command.

"First thing I got to say to you," Preacher told the fat man, "is that if your pards try to bushwhack me, you won't never get your hands on that treasure."

"Why not?" the fat man asked with a wily smile. "Seems

to me like it'd be smart to get rid of our most dangerous
enemy while we've got the chance."

"Because if I don't come back, Esteban Alvarez will make
sure nobody ever gets it. He's gonna blow it to kingdom come."

The fat man's eyebrows rose in surprise. "What? How in
blazes is he gonna do that?"

"There are fumes down in the cave where the loot is. They
seep up from somewhere deep in the earth, and if they build
up enough, a spark will set 'em off and blow the whole side
of that cliff off."

The fat man shook his head. "That's crazy."

"No, just a fact." Preacher paused and then added, "Ask the
professor about it if you don't believe me. He ought to know
enough about such things to know that I'm tellin' the truth."

"It couldn't be that bad," the fat man protested. "You and
the Mex been climbin' up and down outta that hole all day."

"Yeah, but that shaft lets fresh air into the cave. It stunk a
lot worse when we first opened it up and damned near
knocked out one o' them Yaquis, and it had a small hole to
let in fresh air even then. Now it's sealed up tight with rocks
on top of the hole."

"You did that?" The fat man sounded like he couldn't
believe it.

"Damn right we did," Preacher said. "But before we closed
it up, we put a pistol down there, cocked and primed, with a
string tied to the trigger. The string runs up the shaft to the surface. We left just enough room for it when we piled up the
rocks to close the entrance. By now them fumes have probably built up to where they'd make a mighty big blast if somethin' set 'em off. And all it'll take is one pull o' that string."

The fat man was pale now, and worried-looking. "Whoever pulled on it would blow himself up, too."

Preacher smiled and shook his head. "Nope, because we
tied several ropes to the end of the string. It can be pulled

from a far enough distance so that whoever yanks on it will have a chance to get clear before the cliff comes down."

The fat man scrubbed a hand over his face. He turned and made a slight motion, and Preacher knew he was telling his companions not to shoot. He didn't want to take a chance that Preacher was telling the truth.

Which he wasn't—it was all a pack of lies—but the fat man didn't have to know that. The man glared at Preacher and said, "All right. Say what you came down here to say."

Preacher kept his face expressionless, but inside he was glad that the bluff had worked. He had thought of the whole rigmarole, and Esteban had agreed that it sounded plausible enough so that the men who had kidnapped Juanita might not want to risk a double cross.

Now Preacher said, "I reckon you want to trade the girl for the gold."

"Not just the gold. The whole treasure. All of it."

"That's what I meant. How do we know Señorita Juanita is still all right?"

"You'll have to take my word for it . . . but we can't very well expect to trade her if she ain't, now can we?"

"She better not be hurt in any way." Preacher's hard stare made it clear what he meant.

"Don't worry, ain't nobody bothered her. Cobey's seein' to that."

"He's your boss, is he?"

"He's the one runnin' things, yeah. And he's a mighty dangerous man, so you'd better not try any tricks."

Preacher shook his head. "No tricks, just a straight swap. You bring the girl back up and give her to us, and we'll ride away and leave the treasure in the hole for you."

"You'd already brought some of it up," the fat man protested.

"Yeah, we had," Preacher drawled, "but it's back in the hole now, along with that cocked pistol."

The fat man looked like he wanted to cuss, but he held it in. "How are we supposed to get the treasure if it's primed to blow up?"

"All you have to do is move the rocks coverin' up the top of the hole. Then the gas will come out and it'll be safe to climb down there and haul the stuff out. We did it without much trouble."

The fat man rubbed his jaw. "Yeah, I reckon."

"Just be careful not to pull that string until you've aired out the place," Preacher warned. "Might get more than you bargained for if you did."

After a moment, the fat man nodded. "All right. You got a deal, Preacher. The girl for the treasure, straight up. We'll bring her up here and give her to you, and you and the others ride off. We'll have you covered the whole time, though, in case you try anything."

"No tricks," Preacher said. "Juanita's life is worth more than a bunch o' old relics and some bars o' gold."

"I'm glad you feel that way," the fat man said with a grin. "How's that little priest feel about it?"

"He ain't happy," Preacher admitted, "but he'll go along with the plan."

"All right." The fat man backed toward the bend. "We'll be back in an hour with the girl. Don't try to sneak any o' them gold bars out, neither. You do and the deal's off."

"How many times do I have to tell you . . . there won't be any tricks."

"Remember that, or the girl's blood will be on your hands."

With that, the fat man ducked back around the bend and was gone. Preacher waited a minute to be sure, then said, "Come on, Dog." He turned Horse and started back up the canyon. The next hour was going to be a busy one.

21

Juanita's captors had stuck her in the back of one of the wagons and left the man they called Wick to guard her. Wick was probably the biggest man she had ever seen, close to seven feet tall and perhaps over three hundred pounds. The sleeves and shoulders of his buckskin shirt bulged with massive muscles. Juanita could tell when she looked at him, however, that he had the mind of a child. That gave her some hope. Perhaps she could convince him to let her go. She knew that she would have to befriend him first, though.

She wasn't sure where the other men were. The fat man and a couple of the others had gone back up the canyon. Professor Chambers and the one called Cobey, who seemed to be the real leader of the group, had disappeared somewhere, perhaps to plan their next move.

Juanita's hands were tied together in front of her. The rawhide thongs were tight enough so that her fingers had gone partially numb. She wasn't lying when she said through the open back of the wagon, "Señor Wick, my hands hurt. These bonds are too tight. Could you loosen them a little?"

He sat on a rock just outside the back of the wagon, with his knees sticking up because his legs were so long. He shook his head and said, "No, ma'am, I can't. Cobey told

me to watch you and not do anything that you asked me to
do, and I got to do what Cobey says."

"Why? Is he your father?"

Wick laughed. "My father? Cobey? No, ma'am, he ain't.
I don't rightly remember my pa. I don't think my ma really
knowed who he was."

"Your brother, then?"

"Nope. Ain't got no brother. Ain't had nobody since my
ma died. Except for Cobey. He's my friend. He's my good
friend. He looks out for me."

"How did you meet?" It was a strain for Juanita to keep her
voice so affable and sound as if she were genuinely curious,
but she had to do so.

"I don't know." Wick frowned in thought. "It's been a while.
Cobey's been takin' care o' me for a long time." He scratched
his jaw. "I think it was in St. Louie, or maybe Pittsburgh. Some
town on a river. It's comin' back to me now. I was on a dock,
unloadin' some boxes from a boat . . . an' I dropped one of 'em.
I didn't mean to, but I dropped it and it busted open, and this
fella laughed at me, and it made me mad so I hit him."

"You don't like for people to laugh at you?" Juanita asked
gently.

"No, ma'am, I don't. It makes me mad. So when that fella
laughed at me, I hit him in the head and he fell down, and a
bunch o' blood come outta his ears and his nose, and some
other fellas run up and looked at him and said he was dead.
They said I had to go to jail." Wick shook his head. "I didn't
want to go to jail. But they made me, after I hit some more
fellas and made their heads bleed, too."

Juanita suppressed the shiver that ran through her as Wick
recounted his gruesome tale. Obviously, he possessed
enough strength to kill a man with a mere blow from his fist.

"They said they was gonna put a rope around my neck and
string me up, whatever that means," Wick went on. "But that
night, before they could do it, Cobey came and let me outta

jail and said I was gonna go with him and he'd look after me
from then on. He'd stuck a knife in the fella that was in
charge o' the jail so he could get me out, so I knew he really
likcd me. Ever since then, I've stayed with Cobey and done
whatever he told me to do. He's my friend."

Juanita knew that friendship had nothing to do with it.
Cobey had recognized the opportunity to insure this giant's
slavish devotion, and he had seized it. No doubt they had
robbed and murdered their way all across the frontier, with
Wick probably handling most of the violence while Cobey
planned their crimes. Cobey had gathered other ruthless
men around him, but Wick was his own personal tool, an im-
plement of death as surely as a gun or a knife was.

Surprisingly, she found herself feeling some genuine
sympathy for the huge man. There was no telling how many
bloody-handed deeds he had carried out at his mentor's
command, but Wick didn't really know he was doing wrong.
He was just doing what his "friend" told him to do.

"I understand why you feel the way you do about him,"
she said. "I really don't think he would mind, though, if you
loosened these bonds on my wrists."

Wick scowled. "He said you might try to trick me, so that
you could run away. He don't want you to run away."

Juanita swallowed her frustration and kept her tone calm
and gentle. "I cannot run away as long as I am in this wagon,
and if I try to get out of the wagon, you can stop me. That
has nothing to do with my hands hurting because my wrists
are tied too tightly."

"Well . . . I reckon that's true."

"If you will loosen the thongs, I give you my word I will
not try to run away." She felt bad about lying to him—no
doubt he had been lied to a great deal in his life—but there
were greater concerns here. She knew her captors were
going to try to trade her for the lost treasure of Mission
Santo Domingo. And Esteban would make such a trade, too,

even though losing the treasure would be a terrible blow to him. She could not let that happen if she could prevent it.

Wick put his hands on his knees and pushed himself to his feet. "I guess I could look at your hands," he said grudgingly. "Cobey didn't tell me I couldn't talk to you, or look at you, or touch you. He just said for me to keep you here and for me not to hurt you."

Juanita smiled at him and said, "If he told you not to hurt me, then I think he would want you to loose my bonds so that I am not in pain."

"You think?"

"It seems to me that it would be so."

His huge body almost filled up the opening at the rear of the wagon. "Let me see."

She thrust her hands out toward him. He started to look at them, but then he got distracted. His gaze strayed to her breasts. His eyes widened and his breathing got faster. Juanita felt a chill go through her, but tried not to show the revulsion she felt as he stared at her.

"Them are mighty pretty bosoms, ma'am," he said.

"Th-thank you."

"Can I touch 'em? Cobey says I got to ask 'fore I touch a lady's bosoms or do anything else like that with her."

"I . . . I don't think you should. It would not be proper."

"Oh." Wick's eyes fell. "All right, then."

"Wait," Juanita said hastily. She steeled herself and went on. "I think it would be all right if you touched them, Wick. Just a little, though."

His face lit up again. "Really?"

"Really," she assured him. "I do not think you should tell Cobey about it, though."

"You reckon he'd mind?" Wick asked in a whisper.

"Oh, no," Juanita said. "He wouldn't mind. I would just prefer that it was our secret. Don't you ever keep secrets, Wick?"

"Not from Cobey."

"Well, this time you have to, otherwise you cannot do it. All right?"

He stared at her breasts for a long moment before he finally nodded his shaggy head. "All right."

"You promise?"

"I swear."

Juanita took a deep breath. "Go ahead, then."

He leaned closer and reached out with one huge hand. His fingertips touched the underside of her right breast through the fabric of her dress. He slid them forward gingerly until the whole thing was resting in the palm of his hand. His touch was gentle as he cupped that breast and then eased his hand over to the other one. Somehow, despite the riot of emotions going on inside her, Juanita kept a smile on her face and didn't shudder as he caressed her.

After a couple of minutes, she said, "That's enough, Wick," and he obediently took his hand away. She went on. "You said you would loosen these thongs around my wrists."

"Oh, yeah." He bent to that task, his sausagelike fingers fumbling as he worked with the knots. He poked the tip of his tongue out of his mouth as he frowned in concentration. Finally, the knots loosened, and Juanita tried not to grimace as feeling flowed painfully back into her hands.

"Is that better?" Wick asked.

"Much better," she told him, still smiling. "Thank you."

"I won't tell Cobey I loosened 'em. And I won't say anything to him about, uh, feelin' your bosoms."

She nodded and whispered conspiratorially, "Yes, I think that would be best."

"You're a really nice lady." He started to go back and sit down on his rock again, but he stopped and added, "I sure hope Cobey don't decide we got to kill you."

* * *

"It's agreed, then?" Chambers asked. "We don't let any of them live except the girl?"

"Of course not," Cobey said. "What sort o' dumb bastards would we have to be to do that?"

"I just don't want this coming back to haunt us later."

"It won't." Cobey rested a hand on the hilt of his knife. "And as soon as we've had our fill of the girl, she'll have to die, too."

With a regretful look on his face, the professor nodded. "That's all too true," he agreed. "No witnesses to testify against us."

"No witnesses," Cobey repeated.

Chambers didn't know it, but he wasn't going to survive this incident, either. Sure, he had been the one to find out about the treasure, through some friend of his in Mexico City, but that had been pure dumb luck. Chambers hadn't done anything to actually earn any of that loot. Cobey and his partners, on the other hand, had done the real work. They had risked their lives more than once for a shot at the treasure, and they were the ones who deserved to have it, not some fancy Easterner.

The two men stood under a tree near the mouth of the canyon. Cobey heard somebody coming, and wasn't surprised when Arnie Ross, Bert McDermott, George Worthy, and Chuck Stilson came into view, trudging out of the canyon. Cobey went to meet them.

"Somebody come down to parley?" he asked.

Arnie nodded. "Preacher his own self."

Cobey felt his pulse quicken. "Didn't the rest of you get a chance to bushwhack him? I didn't hear no shots."

"We couldn't shoot him," Arnie said disgustedly. "Before he came down to meet us, he put all the loot back in that cave and rigged the whole place to blow up if he didn't come back."

"What?" Cobey exploded. "How in hell did he do that?"

Quickly, Arnie explained about the gas building up in

the cave and the pistol Preacher had set up to explode it if the string tied to its trigger was pulled.

Chambers listened to what Arnie had to say and then nodded solemnly. "It could well be true," the professor said. "Such volcanic gas will explode if a sufficient concentration builds up. Plugging the shaft down into the cave might accomplish that. It's rather an ingenious thing to do, actually."

"Yeah, but he was bluffin'," Cobey growled.

Arnie asked, "How do you figure?"

"That Alvarez kid ain't gonna blow up the loot while we've still got his sister, no matter what happens to Preacher!"

Arnie frowned, took off his hat, and scratched his mostly bald head. "Damn it, you're right," he muttered.

"Preacher just wanted to throw you off balance long enough so that he could get out of there alive." Cobey snorted. "Looks like he did it, too."

"Yeah, but it don't matter," Arnie argued. "He agreed that they'd trade the treasure for the girl, and after we've made the swap we're gonna kill 'em all anyway, ain't we?"

"Yeah, but it would've been easier if Preacher was already dead."

There was no disputing that, so Arnie just shrugged.

"Well, what's done is done," Cobey went on. "What's the deal?"

"We bring the girl up to the top of the canyon and turn her over to Preacher and the others. They ride away, leavin' the treasure down in the hole so that we can take it out again."

"I thought you said the cave was full o' gas," Cobey said with a frown.

"We got to open up the shaft again and let it air out for a while. Then it'll be all right to go down and get the loot."

Cobey looked at Chambers, and the professor nodded and said, "Yes, it should be fine. They had a fire down there at one point, so the gas concentration must be very low when the shaft is open. We should probably wait an hour or two after it's opened up, just to make sure."

"All right," Cobey said. "We give 'em the girl, they start to ride away, and we shoot 'em. That's simple enough."

"Preacher's liable to be watchin' for a double cross," Arnie warned.

"I don't care. We'll have 'em outgunned."

"We're liable to have a fight on our hands."

"Think about all that gold and silver," Cobey said. "And think about that girl." His lips drew back from his teeth in a savage grin. "If all that ain't worth fightin'—and killin'—for, then I don't know what is."

22

Preacher had some figurin' to do, because he was damned if he was going to hand that treasure over to Chambers and those other bastards. He knew there was no way the thieves would let him and the others just ride away. The fat man had lied to him. A double cross was a certainty. Probably at the moment when Juanita was handed back over to them, or right after that, he decided.

There were steps he could take to make that less likely. For one thing, they would put all the treasure back down in the cave and make things look like the place was rigged to blow up, just as Preacher had told the fat man. The possibility of the cave and all the treasure being blown to kingdom come would certainly make the thieves think twice about trying anything.

In the end, though, Chambers and Cobey would feel like they couldn't afford to let Preacher and his companions live. They would have to do *something*. . . .

Preacher reached the top of the canyon and started across the shelf toward the cliff and the cave beneath it. Dog ran ahead of him. Before Preacher got to the cave, though, Dog was back, barking and running in circles like something was wrong. Preacher frowned at the big cur and said, "What the hell is it, Dog?"

With a nudge of his heels, Preacher sent Horse trotting forward at a faster pace. Within a few moments, he came in sight of the area around the cave. He noticed right away that Esteban's horse, and the other two horses, were gone. Alarm bells rang in his brain.

The horses could have pulled loose from where they were tethered and wandered off, although Preacher figured that was unlikely. But he didn't see anybody moving around the site, either. He expected Esteban would have come hurrying out to meet him, to see how the parley with Juanita's kidnappers had gone, and he should have been able to see Father Hortensio and the two Yaquis, as well.

"Esteban!" he shouted as he rode closer. "Padre!"

Where the hell had everybody gone?

That unanswered question made a bizarre thought flash through Preacher's brain. Father Hortensio had talked about the smell of brimstone and how that shaft leading down into the earth was like a portal to Hades itself. Maybe Lucifer and his imps had crawled up out of the hole and dragged Preacher's companions back down to Hell. . . .

He gave a little shake of his head. That was crazy. Preacher had no doubt Hell existed, but you couldn't get there by going down a hole in the Sangre de Cristo Mountains. Something had happened to the others, all right, but it wasn't the hand of Satan that had caused the trouble.

Spotting a limp figure sprawled on the ground near the opening of the shaft, Preacher reined in and flung himself out of the saddle before Horse had completely stopped moving. Preacher ran over to Esteban Alvarez and dropped to a knee beside the young man's motionless body. Esteban lay face-down. His sombrero had fallen off and lay next to him. Preacher saw blood welling from a swollen gash on the back of his head. Somebody had clouted the youngster a good one.

Carefully, Preacher turned Esteban over, wadding up the young man's sombrero and placing it under his injured head to cushion it. Preacher's fingers pressed against Esteban's neck, searching for a pulse. He found one beating strong and fairly regularly. Esteban's eyelids flickered and he stirred slightly as consciousness began to creep back into him.

"Esteban!" Preacher said urgently. "Wake up, hombre, and tell me what happened."

Preacher's gaze darted around the area, searching for any sign of Father Hortensio, Pablo, or Joaquin. The three men were gone, vanished just like the horses. Preacher's eyes narrowed as he noticed that the pile of sacks containing the holy relics from Mission Santo Domingo wasn't there anymore, either. Nor was the chest that had contained gold ingots. The suspicion that began to lurk in his head wasn't a pretty one.

Esteban groaned and opened his eyes. He stared uncomprehendingly up at Preacher. The mountain man leaned over him and said sharply, "Better get your wits back about you, son. We got all kinds o' trouble here."

"P-Preacher?"

"That's right. You remember me, but do you know what happened here whilst I was gone?"

Esteban lifted a hand toward his head, but stopped before he touched it. "Someone . . . hit me."

"I figured as much. Did you see who it was?"

Esteban hesitated. "Not . . . sure. I had been arguing . . . with Father Hortensio . . . when I saw one of the Yaquis . . . step behind me . . . Then . . . I was struck down . . . and I remember nothing more until . . . just now."

"One o' the Yaquis hit you?" That didn't come as a complete surprise to Preacher since he hadn't seen any sign that anyone else had been up here. Still, it was something of a shock, considering what devoted servants the Indians had seemed to be.

But they were actually Father Hortensio's servants,

Preacher reminded himself. It was the priest they were devoted to, along with the Church itself.

"I . . . I cannot be sure," Esteban said. "But no one else was around." His voice strengthened a little and sounded certain as he went on. "It must have been Pablo or Joaquin. No one else was here except me and Father Hortensio, and he was in front of me. He motioned to whoever was behind me." Esteban paused and then said grimly, "He gave the order."

Preacher's jaw clenched in anger. "The padre betrayed you."

"Sí." Esteban closed his eyes for a second, then opened them and said, "Though it pains me to admit it, Father Hortensio betrayed me. He told the Yaqui to strike me down."

"Why would he do that? What had the two o' you been arguin' about?"

"The treasure." That answer didn't come as a surprise to Preacher, either. "He said it belonged to the Holy Mother Church, and that he could not allow it to fall into the hands of heathens."

"What about your sister?"

"He said that he was sorry about Juanita, but that the needs of the Church came first." Esteban struggled to a sitting position, clawing at the sleeve of Preacher's buckskin shirt as he did so. Preacher put an arm around his shoulders to help him sit up. "He had one of the Yaquis knock me unconscious so that he could steal the treasure!"

"It sure looks that way," Preacher agreed. His face was set in bleak lines. "The padre wouldn't see it like that, though. To his way o' thinkin', he was savin' the treasure, not stealin' it."

"But how . . ." Esteban looked around wildly. "How did he get away? Where did he go?"

"I ain't sure about that," Preacher admitted, "but he sure as blazes went somewhere. Him and those Yaquis didn't just flap their arms and fly off like big ol' birds."

Esteban clutched at Preacher again. "What about Juanita?

How can we trade the treasure for her if Father Hortensio has taken it?" His voice went up in a note of panic.

"Don't start worryin' about that yet," Preacher told him. "Just lay back and rest for a minute whilst I take a look around."

Esteban didn't want to rest. He wanted to get up and rush around, looking for Father Hortensio and the Yaquis. But Preacher wouldn't let him, and Esteban was still too weak to stand. With a worried sigh, he lay down again.

Preacher stalked over to the spot where the bags of loot and the chest of gold had been left earlier. The rope was missing, too. Preacher stared at the hole for a moment, then grimaced and lowered himself into it, bracing himself against the walls and inching down the shaft as he had climbed up it earlier.

He reached the drop-off and let himself slide, catching the edge with his hands just long enough to break his fall before he let go and dropped the rest of the way to the floor of the cave. He was in darkness; the fire had gone out. But working by feel, he was able to gather up enough unburned brush to start a small fire with his flint and steel.

Looking around by the flickering glow, he saw that the other chests had been emptied of gold ingots as well, just as he expected. They were lying around haphazardly, wherever they had landed when they had been tossed back down the hole. Preacher counted the empty chests. There were eight of them, and he was pretty sure that was how many had been down here to start with. Father Hortensio and the Yaquis had been busy while he was gone. After knocking out Esteban, they had hauled up the rest of the chests, taken out the gold, and thrown the chests back down the hole. Preacher wondered about that for a moment, but then he realized it had been a shrewd move on Father Hortensio's part. Preacher had been forced to spend some time climbing down here, just to make sure the gold was gone. That was time he hadn't been able to use getting on the trail of the priest and the two Indians.

Moving quickly, well aware that minutes were ticking by, Preacher stacked up the looted chests so that he could climb on them and reach up to grasp the edge of the slanting shaft. With a grunt of effort, he pulled himself into the shaft and started the laborious climb one more time. It would be the last time, because there was no longer any reason for him to come down here. The treasure chamber where Don Francisco Alvarez had cached the loot a century and a half earlier was now empty.

When Preacher reached the top and crawled out of the opening, he found Esteban sitting up again. The young man asked anxiously, "The gold?"

"All gone," Preacher told him bluntly.

Esteban's face fell. "But how?" he wondered. "How could they carry it all away? Where did they go?"

"They had three horses and some rope," Preacher said. "I reckon they tied the bags of relics together and slung them over the backs of the horses. Somehow they rigged some other bags for the gold and tied those to the horses so that they could drag 'em."

"But the weight would be tremendous!"

Preacher nodded. "Yeah, it would, and it would wear out the horses pretty quick, too. But I reckon Father Hortensio figured if he could get away from here, he could stop and let the horses rest as often as he needed to."

"They did not go down the canyon. You would have seen them."

"Yep, and they wouldn't go that way to start with, because Chambers and the others are down at the bottom. They went somewheres else." Preacher got hold of Horse's reins and swung up into the saddle. "I aim to go find out where."

Esteban started to get up. "What can I do to help?"

"Stay here," Preacher said. "You've still got a pistol and a rifle, in case Chambers and his bunch show up. Take cover and try to hold 'em off, and if I hear shootin' I'll light a shuck back here. With any luck, though, I'll find what I'm lookin' for and be back here before they show up to make the trade."

"Ah, Juanita!" Esteban said anxiously. He was muttering to himself in Spanish as Preacher rode off.

Horses didn't leave much sign on this dry, rocky ground, but it didn't take much for a man with eyes as keen as Preacher's. He found tracks that indicated three men on foot and three horses had started off toward the eastern end of the shelf. As he followed the tracks, he saw some scuff marks on the ground that confirmed his earlier guess: The horses were dragging something heavy behind them. Bags full of gold bars, no doubt.

Preacher hadn't been on this part of the shelf. His searching had been concentrated on the other end, and the actual location of the treasure cave was more toward the middle of the flat land that shouldered out from the side of the mountain. So it came as a surprise to him when he found a narrow trail leading off around the mountain. He wasn't too surprised, though. He had known that Father Hortensio and the Yaquis were heading somewhere, so there had to be another way off this shelf.

The trail was nothing more than a ledge that was just wide enough for a horse to negotiate it. The men had led the horses along it, with a sheer rock wall to their left and a drop of several hundred feet to their right. It must have been a harrowing trip, where one misstep would mean a long plunge to a crashing death. Preacher looked down the cliff, searching for any smashed bodies of man or horse. He didn't see any. Father Hortensio and the two servants had made it without falling at least farther than Preacher could see.

He wheeled Horse around and galloped back to where he had left Esteban. There was no sign of Chambers, Cobey, and the others. Without dismounting, Preacher held out a hand to Esteban and said, "Come on."

"Come on?" the young man repeated as he climbed unsteadily to his feet. "Where? Did you find out what happened to Father Hortensio and the Yaquis?"

"There's another trail over yonder." Preacher inclined his head toward the eastern end of the shelf. "It ain't much of one, but it was enough for them to be able to get out of here. We got to do the same thing."

"But what about Juanita? We . . . we cannot abandon her to being a prisoner of those men." Horror tinged his voice at the very idea.

"We ain't abandonin' her," Preacher said, "but we can't do her any good by stayin' here. There's only one way we can help her, and that's by gettin' that loot back and usin' it to bargain with the bastards who've got her."

"I . . . I suppose you are right, Preacher." Esteban passed a trembling hand over his face. Then he reached up, grasped the mountain man's wrist, and climbed onto Horse's back behind him. "But when they come up here, expecting to make the trade, and find us gone . . . what will they do then?"

"I ain't sure," Preacher said, "but they know the only chance they've got of swappin' for the treasure is to keep Juanita alive and unharmed. You hang onto that hope, Esteban, and I will, too."

They rode away, trailed by Dog, leaving the now-empty cave behind them.

23

Juanita saw the man called Cobey stalk toward the wagons. Wick got up from the rock where he had been sitting and greeted his friend by saying, "She's still in there, Cobey. She ain't tried to get away. I watched her real good, just like you told me."

Cobey brushed past the giant with a curt nod and didn't say anything to him. Perhaps stung by being ignored, Wick went on. "I didn't touch her bosoms or loosen them thongs around her wrists or nothin' like that."

Juanita closed her eyes for a second in despair. She had been working at her bonds for the past half hour, trying to loosen them even more, but so far she'd had little success. Now she wouldn't get a chance to continue the effort, because Cobey stopped short and swung around to glare at Wick.

"Damn it, Wick, what'd I tell you—"

Wick looked like he was going to cry. Cobey shook his head and went on. "I don't reckon it matters. We'll be tradin' her for that treasure in a little while, so she won't have time to try to get away. Get her out of the wagon."

"Sure, Cobey," Wick said eagerly, his expression happy again after having been given a job to do by his friend. He came over to the wagon and reached in toward Juanita. Instinctively, she shrank back from his grasping, hamlike hands. "Don't be scared," he told her. "I ain't a-gonna hurt you."

He slipped his hands under her arms and lifted her out of the wagon as if she had been nothing more than a child's doll. She couldn't help but gasp at the enormous power in his grip. As he had promised, though, he was gentle with her and didn't hurt her. He just set her feet on the ground and then let go of her.

Cobey stood in front of her and grinned. "Your brother must think a lot of you, Señorita. He's willin' to trade all that hidden loot for you." He brought his hand up and brushed his rough knuckles against the smooth skin of her cheek. "Too bad we ain't got time to get better acquainted before we make the swap."

Juanita wanted to spit in his leering face, but she suppressed the impulse. She didn't want to anger him or test the limits of his patience. She just wanted to be back with Esteban.

But could these men be trusted? The obvious answer was no. They would try some sort of trick, rather than sticking to whatever agreement they had made. Treachery would be second nature to them. But surely Esteban would realize that.

Even if he didn't, Preacher would. The mountain man would not be fooled, Juanita told herself.

She looked past Cobey as Professor Chambers walked up. Seeing a civilized man like him gave her hope, even though she knew it shouldn't. "Professor," she said, "are you sure you want to do this thing? There is no honor in it."

"No, perhaps not," he agreed. "But only a rich man can afford honor, my dear. Unfortunately, I've never fallen into that category."

Her hopes fell yet again. She couldn't look for any help from Chambers. Indeed, the look in his eyes when he gazed at her was just as lustful as that of any of the other men. Despite his background, he was just as evil as they were.

Cobey gestured curtly toward the mouth of the canyon. "Let's go," he ordered. "Wick, put the girl on my horse."

Again the giant sprang to obey. He lifted Juanita onto the back of one of their mounts, just in front of the saddle. She had to straddle the animal, which meant her dress was pulled up, revealing her boots and the stockings above them. She burned with shame at that indecent display, and her flush deepened as Cobey swung up behind her and slid an arm familiarly around her waist.

The other men mounted up as well, and the entire party started riding up the canyon toward the shelf where the cave was located. The rocking motion of the horse and the pressure of Cobey's arm around her waist meant that Juanita spent most of the time pressed tightly against her captor. "You're a sweet one, you are," he hissed in her ear. "I'll bet you're a real wildcat when it comes to lovin', too."

She ignored him as best she could and distracted herself from the humiliation he was putting her through by thinking about what Preacher might do to him. Preacher would find some way to prevent these men from getting away with their villainy, and then he would dispense frontier justice to them. That justice would be swift and ruthless. At least, Juanita hoped so.

It was late afternoon by the time the riders neared the top of the canyon. Despite the harrowing situation in which she found herself, Juanita was aware that she hadn't eaten since early that morning. Her stomach growled and complained. She ignored that, too.

Cobey called a halt while there was still one more bend between them and the top. "Remember, don't open fire until we've made the swap," he told the others.

Juanita stiffened at those words and tried to turn around to stare at him. He was going to betray the agreement, just as she had feared. That meant Esteban, Preacher, and Father

Hortensio would be riding into a trap. Perhaps they were close by. She opened her mouth to scream a warning.

Before any sound could come out of her throat, Cobey looped a twisted bandanna around her head from behind. He jerked it tight, so that it closed off her mouth. All she could do was make incoherent noises. He tied the bandanna in a knot at the back of her head.

"Thought you was gettin' away from me, didn't you, gal?" He chuckled. "Well, you ain't. We're gonna have you, and the loot, too. You might as well get used to the idea."

Juanita made strangled noises.

"Don't worry about your brother and Preacher, though," Cobey went on. "They'll both be dead, along with the priest and them Indians of yours."

He was wrong about the Yaquis, of course. They were Father Hortensio's servants, not hers and Esteban's. Not that it mattered now. Pablo and Joaquin would be gunned down just like the others. Killed as Benedicto and Ismael had been. The slaughter would be complete. . . .

Unless Preacher had a few tricks of his own waiting for them. Juanita clung desperately to that hope.

Cobey nudged his horse ahead again, around the bend and up the last slope to the shelf. The others followed. They emerged from the canyon onto the shelf. Cobey reined in as Professor Chambers rode up beside him.

"Where are they?" the professor asked worriedly. "Weren't they supposed to meet us here?"

"I thought so," Cobey said. He looked around at the other men. "Arnie, didn't you say they'd be waitin' for us?"

The fat man edged his mount up on Cobey's other side. "That's what I thought we'd agreed to," he said. "Maybe Preacher took it different. Maybe they're waitin' for us over by that cave."

"And maybe they've set a damned trap for us!" Cobey snapped. "Spread out! Keep your eyes open!"

He rode forward slowly as the other men dispersed. All of them had guns drawn now, Juanita saw, except for Cobey. He held the reins in one hand and still had the other arm around her, holding her tightly. She was a human shield, she realized. Anyone taking a shot at Cobey would stand a greater likelihood of hitting her. Esteban and Preacher would not take that chance.

Even Professor Chambers had a pistol in his hand. The intent, avaricious expression on his lean face made him resemble a hawk searching for prey. Juanita asked herself how she could have ever considered him a civilized man. He was a brigand, just like the others.

They came in sight of the cave entrance, and Juanita stiffened as she realized that all the horses were gone. So were the five men who should have been there. Everyone was gone.

Cobey had seen the same thing. "Damn it," he grated. "Where'd they go?" Lifting his voice, he called to the others, "Watch out for an ambush!"

No shots shattered the late afternoon stillness, however. Gradually, the men all converged on the cave. "Take a look around!" Cobey snapped at them.

A few minutes later, Arnie reported, "There's nobody here, Cobey. They've lit a shuck."

"I can see that, damn it! What about the treasure?"

Arnie turned to one of the other men and said, "Get a rope and shinny down into that hole. See if they put it back down there before they left."

"Why me?" the man protested.

"Because you're the skinniest of us, Bert," Arnie said. "Now get movin'."

Grumbling, the man took a rope from his saddle and tied it to his horse. One of the other men fashioned a makeshift torch and lit it, then handed it to Bert as he got ready to lower himself into the shaft. Carefully, holding the rope in one hand and the torch in the other, he backed into the hole and let himself down.

"Weren't the bags with the old relics in 'em already up here when we snatched you?" Cobey asked Juanita.

She pointed with her bound hands, seeing no point in lying right now. "They were right there, along with one chest full of gold ingots."

"Well, what happened to all that loot?"

She shook her head. "I have no idea."

A few moments later, Bert called from down in the cave, his voice echoing hollowly up the shaft. "The chests are down here, but they're all empty! And there ain't no relics, neither!"

"It was all a lie," Cobey snarled. "They didn't rig the damn cave to blow up! They just loaded the loot and took off with it."

Juanita shook her head, unable to believe that Esteban would do such a thing. He would never abandon her like that, leaving her in the clutches of these cutthroats. . . .

"Looks like that brother o' yours is more attached to the treasure than he is to you, Señorita," Cobey said.

"No. No, it cannot be."

"What are we going to do now?" Professor Chambers asked.

"I don't know, but I ain't givin' up," Cobey said. "They didn't come down the canyon with that loot, so they must've gone somewheres else." His voice grew fierce with anger and frustration as he ordered, "Find 'em! Find out how they got outta here! I'm gonna have that treasure, by God!" He paused and then added, "And I'll have that bastard Preacher's head to go with it, too!"

24

Preacher led the way along the ledge, with Horse right behind him. Esteban came next, followed by Dog. Preacher figured that if any pursuit started closing in on them, Dog would let him know.

Esteban was still a little unsteady on his feet, so he held onto Horse's tail. Horse didn't like it, but Preacher patted him on the shoulder and spoke to him in soothing tones until the big stallion accepted the indignity. The little party of two men and two animals made its way along the ledge at as fast a pace as Preacher dared to set.

Heights didn't bother him much, but just to make sure he didn't get dizzy, he kept his eyes on the trail in front of him or the wall of stone to his left, and advised Esteban to do the same thing. "I've seen fellas practically jump off the side of a mountain 'cause they got to lookin' down too much. All that empty space does somethin' to a man's brain."

"Don't worry," Esteban assured him. "I am not looking anywhere except at the tail end of this horse of yours."

Preacher chuckled. "Let's just hope you ain't followin' two horses' asses."

After a few minutes, Esteban asked, "What do you think is happening to Juanita?"

"I imagine she's scared, but I don't reckon she's been hurt. Like I said, those sons o' bitches stand a lot better chance of gettin' that loot if she stays unharmed."

"You would truly give the treasure to them in order to save her life?"

Preacher didn't hesitate before answering, "Sure I would. I'd hate like the devil to just turn that much loot over to them, but to save Juanita's life I'd do it. I don't reckon it'll ever come down to that, though."

Esteban sounded alarmed as he said, "You do not think we will recover the treasure from Father Hortensio?"

"Oh, we'll get it back, all right," Preacher said confidently. "But no matter what Cobey and Chambers say, they ain't gonna abide by any deal they make. They'll try their damnedest to kill us, even if we swap the loot for Juanita."

"Then why would we even try?"

"Because we don't have any other choice. We got to make them think we're playin' along with 'em, and to do that we got to have the treasure. Then, when they try to betray us, we'll turn the tables on them some way."

Esteban shook his head. "It all sounds hopeless to me."

"As long as we're drawin' breath, we got reason to hope," Preacher told him. "I've gotten out of plenty of worse scrapes than this."

"I pray you are right, Preacher. And I pray for Juanita's safety."

"That's a good idea. You keep it up, and I'll say a prayer myself."

The ledge curved on around the mountain. Shadows began to gather. Preacher felt like they had been following the narrow trail for hours, but he knew that was because his nerves were drawn taut. It really hadn't been that long. He began to wonder, though, what they would do if darkness caught them up here in this precarious position.

A short time later, the ledge began to slope downward.

That was what Preacher had been hoping for. The ledge had to provide a way down off the mountain, otherwise it wouldn't have done Father Hortensio and the Yaquis any good to take it. But how had they known the ledge was truly an escape route? It could have just as easily petered out and left the fugitives stranded on the side of the mountain.

It had been a matter of blind faith, Preacher realized. Father Hortensio had trusted in the Lord to get them out of here.

The ledge curved sharply to the left, around a blind corner. Preacher stepped around it and then came to an abrupt halt. He couldn't go any farther. The way was blocked by a wall of rock.

"Damn it!" The sight of the unexpected obstacle jarred the curse out of him.

"What is it?" Esteban asked anxiously. "Why have we stopped?"

"Because we can't go any farther," Preacher explained. "There's been a rock slide. The ledge is covered up."

"No! We must get through! Juanita's life could depend on it."

That was true enough, but it didn't change things. Preacher studied the rocks that blocked the trail, then turned his head to look up at the cliff where a whole section had broken off and slid down here. The scars left behind by the rock slide looked very recent.

"The padre did this," he said. "That's the only explanation, because they came this way and we sure ain't run across 'em. They got past this spot with the horses and the treasure, and then the padre started a slide somehow and blocked the trail."

"How could he do that?"

"Sometimes all it takes is pullin' one piece of rock loose. That unsettles everything enough for more to come down. Maybe he used the rope and threw a loop over some out-croppin', then hitched it to one o' the horses and yanked it outta place. That might have been enough."

"But what do we do now?" Esteban asked. "We cannot go back."

"No, that'd be a big chore, all right. There ain't room for Horse to turn around, so he'd have to back all the way, and I don't reckon he'd take kindly to that." Preacher rubbed his bearded jaw and frowned in thought. "I reckon the only thing we can do is clear away the rocks so we can keep on goin'. And that's gonna be a job, too."

"I will slip past the horse and help you."

"Not just yet," Preacher said. "Stay where you are for now. You may have to come up and spell me later on, but we'll wait and see about that."

He hung his hat on the saddle and went to work, picking up the smaller rocks and tossing them over the edge. Some of the chunks of stone were too big for him to lift, but if he cleared away most of the smaller ones he thought he could roll the larger ones off the ledge.

It was hard work, but Preacher's corded muscles were accustomed to such labor. The air was cool at this altitude, too, which helped. Once the sun set, it would be downright cold, but Preacher didn't plan on stopping for long enough to let the chill stiffen up his muscles.

He lifted and shoved and rolled and threw, and slowly the barrier of stone began to diminish. The sun went down and the sky turned from blue to purple to black, with the stars winking into life one by one overhead. Preacher continued working as the moon rose and cast a pale silvery glow over the rugged landscape. He wedged his way behind one of the larger boulders and got his hands and feet on it, bracing his back against the cliff as he pushed. The boulder rocked a little, and Preacher pushed harder. It began to move even more, and then gravity and the boulder's own weight took over. It toppled over the edge, leaving Preacher sprawled dangerously close to the brink. He crabbed backward as a booming crash came floating up from far below. The boulder had landed.

"A couple more o' those out of the way, and I think we'll be able to pick our way past," Preacher said.

"Yes, but this delay has given Father Hortensio enough time to get far ahead of us," Esteban said. "I fear we may never catch him."

Preacher snorted. "You're givin' up too easy, amigo. One thing I've learned out here on the frontier is that if a fella keeps on goin' after what he wants, he finally gets it more often than not. You just got to be stubborn as a mule, and don't never give up."

"All right, Preacher. Perhaps you should have been a real preacher, since you are eloquent in your own rough way."

"Thanks . . . I think," Preacher said with a chuckle. "I'll leave it to other folks to spread the Gospel, though. They're better at it than I am." He pushed himself to his feet, this brief breather over. "Right now I got to get back to work on these rocks."

Cobey stalked back and forth, waiting for his men to come back and report whatever their search of the area had turned up. Chambers sat under a tree watching him, and not far away, Juanita sat on a log with Wick perched beside her. The giant was still charged with keeping an eye on the prisoner, as Cobey had ordered.

After a while, Wick spoke up tentatively when Cobey's pacing brought him close to the log. "Cobey, you reckon it'd be all right to take this gag off the lady now?"

Cobey stopped and glared at him. "What?"

"I said, you reckon we could take this gag off—"

Cobey gestured curtly and said, "Yeah, sure. Those bastards have already flown the coop with the treasure. She can yell her head off and it won't hurt anything now."

"Thanks, Cobey." Wick turned to Juanita and began fumbling with the knotted bandanna at the back of her head.

"Oh!" she said in relief as the bandanna came loose, allowing her to close her mouth and easing the ache in her jaws.

"I'm sorry, ma'am," Wick said. "I know that must've hurt."

Juanita worked her jaws from side to side. She couldn't even speak for a moment. When she could, she said, "Thank you, Wick."

He blushed and looked down at the ground. "Why, you're sure welcome."

Cobey ignored them and said, "Damn it, the boys oughtta be back by now."

A few minutes later, in fact, the searchers did return, led by Arnie Ross. The fat man swung down from his saddle and said, "Well, we found out where they went." He jerked a thumb toward the eastern end of the shelf. "There's another trail over yonder that leads off around the mountain. Just a little ledge, really, about wide enough for a horse to walk on."

"How do you know they went that way?" Cobey demanded.

Arnie shrugged. "Found a few tracks. And where else could they have gone? We've covered the whole shelf. There ain't no other way down, at least that a horse could take, except the canyon. And we know they didn't leave that way. Since they ain't here anymore . . ."

"Yeah, yeah, I guess you're right," Cobey muttered. He took off his hat and ran his fingers through his tangled hair. "Lemme do some figurin'."

Arnie went on. "The trail's got to go somewhere. I think we ought to send a couple o' men along it to see where it comes out. The rest can go back down the canyon to the wagons. Once we know where that ledge leads, we can pick up the trail, and one of the fellas can come back to get the rest of the bunch. It may take some time, but we'll track 'em down one way or the other."

"Damn right we will," Cobey said. "Are you volunteerin' to follow the ledge?"

Arnie shrugged again. "I reckon I can. Ain't that fond o' heights, but they don't bother me that awful much."

"Take Worthy with you."

Arnie nodded. "All right. Come on, George."

The two men rode off. That left Cobey, Chambers, Wick, Bert McDermott, and Chuck Stilson, along with Juanita, to return down the canyon to the wagons. Cobey got them moving quickly, since it was already late enough in the day so that it would be dark by the time they returned to the valley of the Purgatoire River.

Once again, Juanita was set on the back of Cobey's horse, and he climbed on behind her. This time, when he put his arm around her, he pressed it up against the undersides of her breasts. "Looks like we're gonna have plenty of time to get to know each other, Señorita, thanks to your brother desertin' you like this."

Juanita sat stiffly in silence and stared straight ahead, ignoring Cobey's touch and his leering comment. She was thinking about Esteban, and she was filled with fear for him. She knew that he would not have abandoned her to her captivity by choice. Something had happened to him. It must have. She hoped that his disappearance meant that he was still alive. If he were dead, his body surely would have been left behind when the others departed on the narrow ledge. But was he a prisoner, too? Who could have captured him? Were there hostile Indians in this region? Preacher had not seemed worried about such a threat.

Of course, it might take a lot to worry a man like Preacher.

The questions kept Juanita's mind occupied so that she was able to ignore the vile things Cobey whispered in her ear as they rode down the canyon. She knew that before she escaped from this man—as she was sure she would eventually—her honor might be forever compromised. Time would tell. If this ordeal left her indelibly stained, she would enter a convent when she returned to Mexico City. She had already given much thought to spending the rest of her life inside the walls of a nunnery. Right now that prospect seemed almost appealing.

Darkness settled down as the group of riders followed the twists and turns of the canyon. At one point, Cobey reined in sharply as the sound of a distant crash came to them. "What was that?" Chambers asked.

"Sounded like a big rock fallin'," Cobey replied. "Hope it didn't fall on Arnie and George."

They pushed on, and a short time later they neared the bottom of the canyon. The moon was up now, flooding the valley with pale illumination. Between that lunar glow and the light from the stars, it was almost as bright as day.

Plenty bright enough, in fact, for them to see that the wagons were gone.

25

It took Preacher another half hour to clear away enough of the rock slide so that he and Esteban, along with Horse and Dog, could pick their way along the ledge past the obstruction. It was tricky working the big stallion along an even narrower path than the ledge had provided so far, but Horse was almost as sure-footed as a mountain goat and made it just fine.

Other than a lingering headache, Esteban claimed to feel much better now, too. Once they were past the rock slide, he moved along the ledge easily, keeping one hand against the cliff to the left.

The trail dropped at an even steeper angle now. Preacher checked the stars now and then and could estimate the time fairly closely by their position as they wheeled through the sky. He figured it was close to midnight when he and Esteban reached the bottom of the ledge and found themselves in some knobby foothills.

Preacher pointed and said, "I don't reckon the river is more than half a mile over yonderways. That's probably the way Father Hortensio and them Yaquis went, but it'll be hard to know for sure until mornin', when we can see better."

"We are not going to try to keep on following them tonight?" Esteban asked, sounding surprised.

"There are some situations where you can track somebody at night, especially if there's plenty o' moonlight, like tonight," Preacher explained. "But that don't hold true where there are so many stretches o' rocky ground, like there are in these parts. Unless we want to risk losin' the trail completely, we got to wait for the sun to come up."

Esteban heaved a sigh. "I suppose if we must . . . but it is hard to wait, knowing that Juanita is still in the hands of those . . . those . . ."

"Yeah, I can't hardly think of a name bad enough for 'em, neither," Preacher said. "Why don't you hunt you a soft place to lay down under them trees, and you can get some sleep. I'll stand watch."

"I should take a turn, too," Esteban protested. "You must be exhausted after all the work you did moving those rocks."

"I'll be a mite sore in the mornin', I reckon, but you're the one who got walloped in the head. You prob'ly need the rest more'n I do."

"We will trade," Esteban said stubbornly. "Wake me in a few hours."

"We'll see."

Esteban stretched out on a patch of grass. Horse grazed a little on the same grass, and Dog lay down there, too. Taking his rifle from its sling attached to the saddle, Preacher walked over to a rock that was in a dense shadow cast by a tree and sat down. He wouldn't be very noticeable here if anybody tried to slip up on them. Resting the rifle across his legs, he drew several deep breaths and willed his muscles to relax. His brain stayed keenly alert, though, and his eyes never stopped moving as his gaze roved over the surrounding countryside.

He thought about Juanita Alvarez and hoped that things weren't going too rough for her. Earlier, he had been fairly confident that her kidnappers wouldn't molest her while they were still planning to swap her for the treasure. Now, with all that loot maybe gone for good, they might decide they didn't have to treat her so gently. She could be in for a hard time of it at their hands. Preacher wasn't sure how well she would be able to cope with something like that. Frontier women had always known there was a real danger of such things happening to them if they were captured by Indians. Juanita hadn't been raised on the frontier, though. She had lived, for the most part, a pampered and sheltered life in Mexico City.

But while he had been around her, Preacher had sensed that she had a core of strength in her, the same sort of inner steel that was present in women who had spent their lives in much harsher surroundings. He hoped for Juanita's sake that she really did possess such strength.

Because before all this was over, she was liable to need it.

Cobey was livid. He leaped down from his horse and ran back and forth. "We left them wagons right here, damn it!" he shouted. "I know we did!"

Chambers looked around and said, "I believe you're right." He pointed. "That clump of brush right over there is where we hid when we ambushed those first two Indians. And I remember those trees as well, not to mention the fact that the mouth of the canyon is right over there. This is the place, certainly."

Cobey stared up at him. "Then where are the damn wagons?"

Chambers could only shake his head and say, "I don't know."

Bert spoke up. "What about that other Yaqui? If the one lived who jumped you later on, Cobey, and ruined ever'thing, maybe the other'un did, too. He could've run off with the wagons."

"Only if he sewed up his own throat where Arnie cut it!"

Cobey shook his head in disgust. "No, that Injun's dead, no two ways about it. Poke around over there in the brush where we slung the body and you'll probably find it. Somebody else had to come along and steal the wagons."

On the back of Cobey's horse, Juanita sat, still silent, and thought that from the way he was carrying on, anyone would have thought that the wagons belonged to him. In truth, of course, Cobey had stolen them from Juanita and her brother.

She was puzzled by what had happened to the vehicles and their teams, too. All sorts of odd things were happening here in these mountains named after the Blood of Christ. Father Hortensio had talked about how the cave where the treasure was hidden smelled like brimstone. Perhaps the area was cursed. Perhaps the treasure itself now had a curse on it. Juanita didn't know. All she could be certain of was that she was cold and frightened and so very, very tired. Even though she couldn't forget that she was a prisoner, all she wanted to do right now was lie down and rest.

She turned to the giant and asked quietly, "Wick, would you help me down?"

"Just a minute," he rumbled. "Cobey, is it all right if I take the señorita off your horse?"

Cobey flapped a hand dismissively. "I don't care what you do with her. Just don't let her run off."

"She won't. I promise." Wick dismounted and stepped over to Cobey's horse. He reached up and scooped Juanita into his arms. He carried her like she was a baby, limping a little on his still-healing leg as he walked over and sat her down on a large, flat rock. It still held a little of the heat it had absorbed from the sun during the day.

"You sit right there," he told her.

"I will," she promised.

"You want a drink?"

Juanita nodded. "That would be very nice. I'm thirsty."

Wick stepped over to his horse and got a canteen from the

saddle. He uncorked it and handed it to Juanita, who had to take it in both of her hands because her wrists were still tied together. She lifted the canteen to her mouth and took a long drink. When she lowered it, she said, "Thank you. I'm hungry, too."

He dug a strip of jerky out of his pocket and handed that to her, taking back the canteen. "There you go. Are your teeth good enough to gnaw on jerky?"

"Of course." She smiled up at him, and as usual, almost immediately he became too embarrassed to look at her.

Meanwhile, Cobey had resumed pacing around in anger. Chambers watched him for a few minutes and then asked, "What are we going to do now?"

Cobey paused. "This don't change anything. We're still goin' after that treasure, as soon as Arnie or George get back and tell us which way those bastards went."

"Has it occurred to you that it may well have been our quarry who took the wagons?"

Cobey turned sharply toward the professor. "You mean Preacher and his bunch?"

"They had to transport that treasure out of there in some way," Chambers pointed out. "Once they escaped, however, it would be much easier to carry the relics and the gold, especially the gold, in wagons. Perhaps some of them circled back here, took the wagons, and then rejoined the others."

Cobey balled his right hand into a fist and smacked it into his left palm with a sound like a gunshot. "By God, you're right! That's the only explanation that makes sense. It's all Preacher's doin'!"

Chambers just smiled.

Cobey resumed his stalking back and forth. "That's just one more reason to want the son of a bitch dead! He's got to learn to stop messin' with me, and the best way to teach him is to kill him!"

Juanita shuddered a little as she listened to Cobey ranting.

She knew that Preacher could take care of himself, but Cobey's hatred was so strong, so fierce, that it was almost like a thing alive, a powerful force that would not be denied.

Beside her, Wick said quietly, "You know, I done heard some o' them things Cobey said to you whilst we was ridin' back down here. I didn't like 'em."

"Neither did I," she told him gravely.

"Cobey's my friend, but he shouldn't talk that way to a lady. Especially not a pretty lady like you, Miss Juanita."

"Thank you, Wick." She smiled at him again, and this time he didn't look away.

"It sorta hurts my head, but I reckon I'm gonna have to do some thinkin'," he mused. "This whole thing, it's startin' to seem more and more like it ain't right."

For the first time in a while, Juanita began to feel hope growing inside her again. She still believed that Preacher and Esteban would come for her, but if she could work Wick around to being on her side, as well . . .

There was a chance she might come out of this alive after all, she told herself. But in the end, her fate might depend on a giant of a man with the mind of a child.

Dog had settled down on the ground beside the rock where Preacher sat. It was still a good while before dawn when the big cur suddenly lifted his head and growled low in his throat. Preacher reached down and rested a hand on the ruff of fur around Dog's neck, silencing the angry rumble from the dog. He felt the tension in Dog's muscles.

Preacher was a mite tense himself. Dog could have smelled some animal close by, but it was doubtful the scent of a varmint would have caused him to react like that. It was much more likely Dog had smelled a human.

And the chances of anybody wandering around out here who wasn't an enemy were pretty darned small.

Preacher listened intently, and a moment later he heard the sound of hoofbeats. Two riders, he thought. They were coming from the direction of the ledge.

Two of Cobey's men, or maybe the boss hard case himself. Nobody else would be on that ledge. Preacher came to his feet and cat-footed through the darkness to Esteban's side. He went to a knee next to the young man and reached out to clap a hand over Esteban's mouth. Esteban woke up, startled by the unexpected touch, and began to thrash around. Preacher stilled him by leaning over and hissing in his ear, "Shhh! It's just me. We got company."

After a moment, when he was sure Esteban wouldn't yell out, Preacher took his hand away. Esteban whispered, "Who is it?"

"Don't know. Couple of riders. Bound to be some o' Cobey's men. They followed us along the ledge."

"What are we going to do?"

"Just sit still and be quiet," Preacher told him. "We'll see what they do and where they go."

He stood up and motioned for Dog to follow him as he slipped deeper into the darkness under the trees. The sound of hoofbeats came closer.

Preacher debated whether to jump the two men or let them go and hope that they didn't discover him and Esteban. It was always tempting to cut down the odds by disposing of a couple of enemies. But that might involve shooting, and the sound of gunfire could travel a long way. That might just announce to the others where Preacher and Esteban were and pull more trouble down on them before they had a chance to catch up to Father Hortensio and recover the treasure.

It was likely that the two men would rejoin the rest of their bunch sooner or later. Preacher considered letting them go, following them, and trying to get Juanita away from her captors. More than once in the past, he had stolen into an Indian camp and rescued prisoners. This situation was much the same, except Cobey's bunch was smaller and likely not as alert as a war party.

If he attempted that, however, Father Hortensio was going to have more time to get away with the treasure. But which was more important, the treasure or Juanita's life? Preacher didn't even have to think about the answer to that question. Juanita was more important, of course—except to a fanatic like Father Hortensio.

The two men on horseback were close now. Preacher heard them talking. One of them said, "How we gonna tell where they went while it's dark, Arnie?"

"We'll have to wait for sunup," the other man replied. Preacher recognized his voice. It belonged to the fat man with whom he had parleyed in the canyon. "We might as well get down and rest the horses for a spell." Both men reined in and dismounted.

Preacher stood tensely in the darkness, no more than twenty feet from them. So the two thieves were going to wait for dawn, too, and they were going to do it in the same spot as Preacher and Esteban.

That was a mighty interesting development.

26

Juanita lay down on the big rock, curling on her side and pillowing her head on her arms as best she could. Her ankles were tied now, too, so that she couldn't run away. She was exhausted, but the uncomfortable position and the fright she felt made it almost impossible to sleep. Every sound in the night made her jump and catch her breath, fearful that something was about to happen.

Wick sat nearby with his back against a tree, but he had not had any trouble dozing off and now was sound asleep, with loud snores emanating from him. Juanita didn't know what it would take to wake him up. Nor did she know how he would react if one of the other men tried to bother her.

A footstep somewhere close by made her sit up sharply. She gasped and looked around wildly.

"Easy, Señorita," Professor Chambers said quietly. "I mean you no harm. I just thought perhaps we could talk for a moment."

"Professor. You frightened me."

"My apologies. I wish there was some way this entire situation could be made better for you, Señorita."

Juanita glanced toward the sleeping Wick. Quietly, she said to Chambers, "You could untie me. I would be very grateful."

Chambers laughed softly. "I'm afraid that's not possible. You'd try to escape, and then Larson would kill me for allowing that to happen. He already plans to get rid of me."

She frowned at him in the darkness and said, "You know this, and yet you still aid him?"

"Of course. I'm not a fool. The man despises me, simply because I'm not an unlettered lout like he is. He has no intention of sharing the treasure with me, even though without me he would have no idea of its existence."

"What are you going to do?"

"Wait for the proper time, and then show Mr. Larson that he isn't the only one who can double-cross his allies." Chambers leaned closer to her. "I'm telling you this for only one reason, Señorita. I want your help."

"Why would I help you? You hold me prisoner as surely as the others do."

"I can protect you," he said. "The fact that Cobey wants to trade you for the treasure is the only reason you're still unharmed. Join forces with me and I'll do my best to see that you stay that way."

Juanita didn't believe him. She had seen the way he looked at her. He wanted her just as much as the others did. But if she played along with him, that might increase her chances of coming out of this alive.

"What would I need to do?" she asked.

Chambers's voice was barely a whisper now. "When the time comes, I'll slip you a weapon and cut you loose. Help me kill the others, and I'll let you go."

"How can we do that? There are too many of them! A woman and . . . a civilized man such as yourself . . . against half-a-dozen barbarians . . ."

"Who won't be expecting anything," Chambers said. "The element of surprise will be entirely on our side. Besides, we should have one other ally."

"Who?"

Chambers inclined his head toward the sleeping giant. "Wick. Everyone can see that he follows you around like a puppy, and he adores you like a puppy adores its mistress, too."

"He follows me because the one called Cobey has ordered him to guard me. Wick would never turn against him."

"I think you're wrong. In fact, you could say that I'm gambling my life on it."

Perhaps he was right. Juanita had to admit that having Wick on their side would go a long way toward evening up the odds. He could probably knock at least two men out of a fight before they knew what was going on.

"There's something else to consider, too," Chambers went on. "By the time we're ready to make our move, the odds against us may not be so high. I'm sure we can handle Preacher when we recover the treasure, but some of Cobey's men may be killed or hurt in the process." He shrugged. "What it comes down to, Señorita, is that the only chance either one of us really has is to work together. Can you deny that?"

Juanita hesitated before answering, but finally, she had to whisper, "No. I cannot deny it."

"You'll see," Chambers said. "Everything will be—"

"Who's that?" Cobey Larson's harsh voice came from somewhere nearby. Wick snorted and snuffled as he woke up. Cobey stalked out of the darkness before Professor Chambers could slip away and demanded, "What the hell are you doin' here?"

"Just checking on the prisoner," Chambers said easily. "Your so-called guard was sound asleep. The señorita might have gotten away if not for me."

Cobey grabbed Juanita's wrists and shook them, then did the same with her ankles. "She's still tied up good. She ain't goin' anywhere, not unless she wants to crawl on her belly. And I don't reckon she'd get very far that way." He chuckled. "But I got to admit, the idea of a high-toned señorita like her crawlin' on her belly is a mite appealin'."

Juanita shuddered at the man's coarseness.

"Better move on, Professor," Cobey went on. "You ain't needed here."

"What do you intend to do?" Chambers asked.

"None o' your damn business." Cobey cupped Juanita's chin. "Whatever happens, it's just between me an' the pretty little señorita."

She wanted to jerk her head away from his touch, but she forced herself to remain still as she said, "Señor, I ask of you . . . do not dishonor me."

"It's a little late for you to be worryin' about honor, ain't it? Your brother ran off and left you with us. He don't give a damn what happens to you, so why should I?"

"Please . . ."

Cobey's hand closed roughly on one of her breasts. "Beg some more," he hissed between clenched teeth. "I like it."

"Larson—" the professor began.

Cobey turned on him, letting go of Juanita and moving his hand to the butt of the pistol stuck behind his belt. "Are you still here, damn it?"

Juanita waited tensely to see if Chambers would defend her. She wasn't surprised when he said, "All right, Cobey. I'm leaving."

"Damn right you are."

Chambers shuffled off into the darkness. Cobey turned back to Juanita and reached for her again. "You and me gonna have some fun, Señorita," he said.

"Cobey."

The voice came from behind him. When he glanced over his shoulder, he saw Wick rising from the ground like a mountain in miniature erupting from the earth.

"Go back to sleep, Wick," Cobey ordered. "This don't concern you."

"I don't think you should be botherin' the señorita, Cobey," Wick said stubbornly.

With a savage snarl, Cobey said, "I told you, this don't concern you."

"Yeah, but it does. You said for me to keep Miss Juanita safe."

"I told you not to let her run off."

"You said to keep her safe," Wick insisted. "That's what I figure on doin'."

Impatient and frustrated, Cobey stepped over to confront Wick. "Well, now I'm tellin' you to leave me the hell alone! Can you understand that, or are you too damn dumb?"

Wick drew back as if Cobey had slapped him. "You never called me dumb before," he said. "Ever'body else did, but you never did, Cobey."

"Then stop actin' dumb. What I'm gonna do to the gal ain't gonna hurt her—"

"It will, Wick," Juanita cut in. "It will hurt me very badly."

Cobey twisted toward her. His hand flashed up and cracked across her face, knocking her sprawling back on the rock. "Shut up, you greaser bitch!" he roared. Juanita whimpered in pain and shock.

And then, as Cobey swung back around toward Wick, the giant rumbled in rage and fell on him like the mountain he so resembled.

Preacher glided noiselessly through the shadows and knelt beside Esteban again. "It's two o' Cobey's men, like I thought," he whispered to the young man. "And they're gonna camp here until sunup, so they can see which way the padre went."

"They're staying here?" Esteban whispered back.

Preacher grimaced in the darkness. "Yep. They're about twenty yards over yonder."

"But will they not discover us?"

"Maybe, maybe not. It all depends—"

That was when one of the men's mounts must have caught Horse's scent, because a shrill whinny ripped through the night. Preacher came up from his crouch and clapped a hand over Horse's nose to prevent the stallion from answering.

Even without that, though, Arnie and the other hard case realized something was wrong. Preacher heard Arnie's exclamation. "Must be somebody else around here, George! Come on! Hit 'em hard!"

The two men flung themselves back on their horses and charged toward Preacher and Esteban. "Split up!" Preacher snapped at Esteban as he darted to the right. Esteban rolled over, came to his feet, and went to the left.

The two hard cases on horseback charged between them. Preacher saw a stray beam of moonlight reflect off a gun barrel.

"Dog!" he said.

With a growl, the big cur launched himself off the ground and grabbed one of the riders by the arm. The man screamed as Dog's teeth tore into his flesh. The impact of the heavy beast knocked him out of the saddle. He fell to the ground with a heavy thud. Dog landed on top of him and continued savaging his arm, snarling and snapping. The man screamed and tried to scuttle away.

At the same time, Preacher leaped toward the second man, who was trying to wheel his horse around. Reversing his rifle, Preacher drove the weapon's butt into the man's stomach. The man slewed sideways but managed to remain mounted. Preacher had to jump out of the way to avoid being trampled by the man's horse. He saw the pistol swinging toward him and rolled to the side as the gun roared. The heavy lead ball smacked into the ground where Preacher had been an instant earlier.

Preacher yanked one of his pistols from behind his belt and cocked it as he raised it. Aiming in bad light like this was always a chancy proposition, but he tried for the man's shoulder. He didn't want to kill the hard case, but wanted to wound him instead, taking him alive so that he could be questioned.

Unfortunately, just as Preacher pulled the trigger, the man's horse, spooked by the previous shot, danced skittishly to the side. Preacher saw the man's hat leap into the air as the shot caught him squarely in the face and blew off a large chunk of his head.

"Damn it!" Preacher growled as the man's limp body hit the ground like a sack of potatoes. Preacher stood up and turned toward Dog and the other man.

Only they weren't there anymore. The big cur's snarling had stopped, and Preacher didn't see any sign of him or the man he had gone after.

"Dog!"

There was no response.

"Esteban! You here?"

Nothing. The night was quiet except for a few faintly fading echoes of the two shots.

Preacher hurried toward the spot where he had last seen Dog. His foot hit something soft and yielding in the darkness, and he almost fell. Catching his balance, he lowered himself to a knee and reached out. His hand touched thick fur. With worry stretching his nerves taut, Preacher explored along the bundle of fur and muscles until he came to Dog's head. His fingers encountered a sticky, swollen lump. A moment later he found a strong pulse beating in the animal's neck. Dog was all right, just knocked out. The man he had been fighting with must have clouted him with a gun barrel. Even as Preacher prodded around on him, searching for other, more serious wounds, Dog began to stir. He whimpered, lifted his head, and moved his legs. Preacher helped him roll onto his belly.

"You all right, Dog?" he asked.

Dog raised his head even more and licked Preacher in the

face. Relief flooded through the mountain man. Dog had been his friend as long as any human had been, and a better friend than most, at that.

But there was still the question of Esteban's disappearance. Preacher told Dog to stay where he was and stood up. Calling Esteban's name a couple of times still produced no results. He looked around. The moon was lower in the sky by now, with the approach of dawn, but there was still enough light for Preacher to see. He quickly came to the conclusion that Esteban was gone.

And that led to another conclusion that was pretty troublesome. Preacher checked the body of the man he had killed. He thought maybe it had belonged to one of the men who had been with Professor Chambers at the old mission, the two so-called guides. It was hard to be sure because of the damage the pistol ball had done to his face. But he wasn't fat, which meant that it was Arnie who had gotten away.

Preacher recalled how deceptively dangerous Arnie was in a fight. The fat man must have stumbled into Esteban in the darkness after knocking out Dog, and even injured, he had been able to take the young man with him as he fled, either knocking Esteban unconscious, too, or simply forcing him to go along at gunpoint. The dead man's horse was still here, but Arnie's mount wasn't. Chances were, the fat man was on his way back to join Cobey and the others right now.

Only he wasn't alone. Preacher's enemies now had two hostages instead of one, as both of the Alvarez siblings were now their prisoners.

27

Juanita cried out again as Wick's rush knocked Cobey back onto the rock against her. "I said leave her alone!" Wick roared, sounding like a grizzly bear. He looked sort of like a grizzly bear, too, as he loomed over Cobey for a second and then lunged down on him, wrapping his big hands around Cobey's throat.

Cobey fought back desperately, bringing a knee up into Wick's groin and hammering punches to his head. Wick didn't seem to feel the punches, but the knee made him grunt in pain and relax his grip on Cobey's throat. Though Cobey was considerably smaller than the giant, he was still a big, powerful man, and when he clubbed his hands together and drove them hard against Wick's jaw, he was able to knock the larger man to the side.

Wick shook off that blow in a hurry, though, and a backhanded cuff to Cobey's head packed enough of an impact to knock Cobey into Juanita again. Both of them slid off the rock and fell to the ground beside it. Cobey landed on top of Juanita. His weight knocked the breath out of her and made it difficult for her to drag more air into her lungs. Panic went through her at the thought that she might suffocate underneath him.

He wasn't there long enough for that, however. Still yelling incoherently, Wick reached down, grabbed the front of Cobey's buckskin shirt, and jerked him upright again. Gratefully, Juanita gasped for breath. Several smaller rocks dug painfully into her body where she had fallen on them, but she ignored that.

Wick shook Cobey like a terrier shaking a rat. "You shouldn't'a hit her!" he bellowed. "You shouldn't'a done it!"

"H-help!" Cobey shouted. "He's g-gone crazy!"

Juanita rolled over and became aware that Bert McDermott and Chuck Stilson had rushed up, drawn by Wick's yelling and the sounds of the fight. Professor Chambers was there, too, but he hung back, obviously reluctant to take a hand in the struggle.

Bert and Stilson were not so hesitant. They both leaped at Wick from behind, Bert grabbing him around the shoulders while Stilson tackled him around the waist. Again reminiscent of a bear, Wick simply shrugged them off and sent them flying through the air while he continued shaking Cobey.

Juanita found herself hoping that in his rage, Wick would kill the gang's leader. Without Cobey around, it would be that much easier for Preacher and Esteban to rescue her later on. And if Wick killed Cobey for trying to molest her, it would insure that the others would all be too afraid to bother her as long as she was under the giant's protection. As she watched Cobey's head loll violently back and forth, she hoped that his neck snapped.

That wasn't to be. Bert surged back to his feet, drew his pistol, and slammed the weapon against Wick's head with all the strength in his wiry body. Stilson followed suit, crashing a blow on Wick's head with his pistol. The two men took turns hammering on Wick's skull with their weapons, and after a moment, Wick's grip on Cobey's shirt relaxed and Cobey slipped free. He dropped to the ground, half-conscious at best.

Wick tried to turn toward Bert and Stilson. He stumbled as they hit him again. Juanita's heart went out to him as he fell to his knees. Bert kicked him in the face, but that just made him lean backward. As he straightened, Stilson hit him again, on top of the head this time. Wick pawed feebly at the two men. He let out a rumble of pain and confusion, and then he pitched forward on his face. After twitching a couple of times, he lay still. For a second Juanita was afraid that he was dead, and she knew that if he was gone, her chances of surviving had just dropped dramatically. But then she heard the harsh sound of his breathing and knew that he was still alive. Even though he had been dealt an incredible amount of damage, his massive frame and thick skull had been able to absorb it.

Juanita turned her head toward Chambers, thinking that this might be the perfect time for the professor to strike. He could kill Cobey while the man was helpless and probably cow Bert and Stilson into cooperating with him.

Chambers, however, wasn't making a move to do any such thing, and Juanita thought she knew why. Chambers didn't want to turn on his supposed allies until they had their hands on the treasure. It might take all of them to get the gold and silver and the old relics away from Preacher. Everyone was waiting, using the others and stringing them along, until they had obtained what they had come here to the Sangre de Cristos to steal. Then it might well be every man for himself.

"Son of a bitch!" Bert said. "It was like tryin' to knock down a damn mountain!"

Stilson cocked his pistol and pointed it at Wick's head. "I'll blow his damn brains out!"

Bert grabbed the gun barrel and forced it to the side. "Don't be a fool!" he snapped. "Once Wick wakes up, he'll be calmed down again. We may need him 'fore this is all over."

"Are you crazy?" Stilson argued. "If I don't kill him, Cobey's gonna as soon as he wakes up."

"Don't be so sure about that. Gimme a hand." Bert knelt next to Cobey and started to lift him to a sitting position. He glanced at Chambers and went on. "Professor, see about gettin' the señorita off the ground."

"Of course," Chambers said, stepping forward at last. He got hold of Juanita and lifted her onto her feet. She couldn't walk because her ankles were bound, but with Chambers's help she was able to get back onto the flat rock where she had been lying earlier. She sat on it now and watched as Bert and Stilson lifted Cobey and held him up, kneeling on either side of him as he sat on the ground.

Bert slapped Cobey's face lightly and said, "Hey. Hey, Cobey. You all right?"

Groggily, Cobey shook his head and groaned. He pawed at his face and said thickly, "Wha . . . wha . . . happened?"

"Wick tore into you," Bert said. "I ain't quite sure why. Chuck and me didn't know what was goin' on until Wick had hold of you and was treatin' you like a mama grizz goin' after somebody who'd bothered her cubs."

"Yeah . . . yeah, I remember. . . ." Cobey looked around. "Where is he?"

"Layin' over there on the ground. He's knocked out, but I don't reckon he's hurt too bad. Chuck and me walloped him a bunch of times with our pistols, but you know how thick that big bastard's skull is. Prob'ly didn't even put a dent in it."

"Want me to kill him, Cobey?" Stilson asked.

"What?" Cobey said. "Kill who? Wick? Hell, no!"

Stilson was a little taken aback. "I figured after what he did—"

"He lost his head," Cobey cut in harshly, "and I'll have a talk with him about it. But he's too valuable to us to just kill him."

Bert looked at Stilson as if he were saying that he'd told him as much.

"Help me up," Cobey went on. "I just want to get back to my bedroll and lay down for a while. Then one of you stand guard over the señorita, since Wick's out cold."

"Sure, Cobey," Bert said. Together, the two men helped Cobey to his feet.

Juanita heaved a sigh of relief. Cobey was too shaken up to bother her again, at least for the rest of this night.

But there was no way of knowing what new ordeals morning would bring.

Preacher saddled Horse and got ready to ride. Then he hunkered on his heels and gnawed on a strip of jerky from his possibles bag while he waited for the gray of dawn to advance across the sky. As soon as it was light enough to see even a little bit, he stood up and started looking around, his keen eyes examining the ground intently.

It didn't take him long to find what he was looking for. The wheels of a pair of wagons had left definite marks on the ground, heading east, while a single horse had pounded off to the west.

He stood there for a long moment staring at the wagon tracks. It seemed unlikely that there would be a pair of wagons in the Sangre de Cristos other than the ones brought up here by the Alvarez party. Not impossible, of course, but certainly unlikely. The day before, those wagons had been in the hands of Cobey Larson, Professor Chambers, and the rest of that bunch. Preacher didn't think that Cobey and the others would have brought the wagons back along here. The fact that Arnie had taken off in the opposite direction with Esteban added to the strength of that theory.

That left only one good explanation. Once Father Hortensio and the two Yaquis had reached the bottom of the ledge,

Pablo and Joaquin had left the padre here with the treasure and gone to steal back the wagons. It had probably still been daylight then, and Father Hortensio would have known that Cobey, Chambers, and the others were likely to be up on the shelf, trying to trade Juanita for the treasure. They might have left someone down below to guard the wagons, but chances were they hadn't.

That priest was tricky enough to have thought of all that, Preacher decided. And it was the only thing that really made sense. The Yaquis had brought the wagons back here, loaded the treasure on them, and then they and Father Hortensio had lit a shuck back the way the party had come in the first place, heading out of the mountains as fast as they could push the teams.

Father Hortensio was taking the treasure back where it belonged, to Mission Santo Domingo.

But that still left Juanita Alvarez and now her brother Esteban as prisoners.

Preacher wasn't given to agonizing over decisions. He looked at a situation, weighed all the angles quickly but carefully, and then made up his mind. Now, he swung up into his saddle and rode west, following the tracks left by the fleeing Arnie Ross. He knew where to find Father Hortensio and the treasure when the time came; for now he had to see about getting Esteban and Juanita out of the hands of the hard cases who had captured them.

While the sun was still just peeking over the eastern horizon, Preacher reached the Purgatoire River. Not surprisingly, the tracks he had been following turned to parallel the river. The fat man was running back to his comrades as fast as he could. Preacher rode along the river, too, but he veered away from it until he was a couple of hundred yards away from the stream. He didn't want to run head-on into Cobey's bunch. Chances were, as soon as they heard about Arnie's encounter with Preacher and Esteban, they would backtrack the fat man and try to pick up the trail of the treasure where the fight had taken place. By now they would know that the wagons were gone, and both Cobey and Chambers were cunning enough to figure out what had happened to them.

Preacher had only gone a mile or so when the skin on the back of his neck began to prickle. It was an instinctive reaction, and one that he had experienced many times in the past. He considered it a sort of alarm system.

Somebody was watching him.

Without slowing Horse or being too obvious about it, Preacher looked around, searching for any signs of whoever was following him. He didn't see anything, which didn't mean they weren't there. It just meant that they were good at what they were doing.

The valley of the Purgatoire was about half a mile wide along here. Steep bluffs rose on both sides, and the mountains climbed above them. A few miles ahead, the valley narrowed down more, and that was where the twisting canyon leading up to the shelf where the treasure had been hidden was located. The landscape where Preacher rode was hilly and dotted with thick stands of pine. Plenty of places to hide, in other words. He might be riding right into an ambush.

Somehow, though, he didn't believe that was the case. It felt more like he was being trailed.

He didn't have any friends up here except Esteban, and if the young man had gotten away from Arnie somehow, he wouldn't follow Preacher and not announce himself. Preacher had to assume that whoever was dogging his trail wished him harm.

He was going to have to do something about that, before he got around to dealing with Cobey and the others.

He rode up a hill into some pines with Dog padding along beside him and Horse. At the top of the slope the land flattened out into a long level stretch, but the trees still grew thickly. Preacher said quietly, "Keep goin', Horse. You, too,

Dog." Then he reached up, grasped a branch, and pulled himself out of the saddle. He hung there for only an instant before climbing agilely into the tree where the dense foliage shielded him from view. The pine needles pricked him, but he ignored the discomfort. Down below, Horse and Dog moved on through the trees just as Preacher had ordered.

He waited with the patience of a true frontiersman, who knew that the ability to stay still and quiet was sometimes all that saved a man's life. He could still hear Horse's hoofbeats, which was good. That meant whoever was following him could hear them, too.

Sure enough, a couple of minutes later, Preacher heard another horse coming through the trees. He waited, motionless, until the horse came into view. It was an Indian pony, and that was somewhat surprising. So was the man who rode it. He was a strong-faced warrior with thick black hair pulled back in a couple of braids, and the distinctive markings on the buckskins he wore identified him as a Crow. He was a long way from home. The Crow hunting grounds were hundreds of miles to the north of here. Preacher had had run-ins with members of that tribe in the past, but unlike the Blackfoot, who were almost universally hostile to white men, some Crows got along with the whites. It was impossible to know how this one felt, but the fact that he had been trailing Preacher in such a stealthy manner didn't bode well.

When in doubt, ask, Preacher told himself. The next moment, as the Indian rode beneath the tree where Preacher was perched, the mountain man dropped suddenly on him, tackling him and driving him off the back of the pony.

Both men crashed to the ground. Preacher landed on top, knocking the breath out of the Crow warrior. He planted a knee in the Indian's belly, locked his left forearm across the Crow's throat like a bar of iron, and used his right hand to pull the heavy-bladed hunting knife from the sheath at his belt. Preacher held the tip of the keen blade against the

Crow's throat and grated, "Move and I'll slice you open, mister. Now, how come you're followin' me?"

Under the circumstances, the Crow was going to have a hard time answering the question. But before Preacher could relax the pressure of his forearm and let his prisoner speak, a gun barrel prodded the back of the mountain man's neck and a deep voice said, "Let him go. The last thing I want to do is kill you."

28

It was not yet dawn when Juanita heard the horse coming. The swift rataplan of hoofbeats was loud in the night and roused her from the uneasy half sleep into which she had drifted as she lay on the big, flat rock.

The noise alerted the rest of the party, too, except for Wick, who had not regained consciousness. From the way he was snoring again, however, Juanita thought the giant had passed from being knocked out to simply being asleep.

Cobey, Chambers, Bert McDermott, and Chuck Stilson all sprang up and reached for their guns. McDermott had been sitting on a log close to the rock where Juanita lay, standing guard over her as Cobey had ordered. He said quietly to her, "Take it easy, Señorita. Don't yell out or anything until we know who's comin'."

All four of the men were ready to fight if they found themselves under attack. But a moment later a loud hail came to them, and they knew that wasn't the case.

"Cobey! Cobey, it's me! Don't shoot!"

"That's Arnie!" Cobey exclaimed. "Hold your fire!"

Although it was awkward because of the way she was tied, Juanita managed to push herself up onto an elbow so that she could see better. The running horse slowed. Arnie

Ross rode into the camp. There was just enough light in the graying sky so that Juanita could see he had someone with him, riding double on the same horse. The man was in front of Arnie, leaning forward over the neck of the horse, and seemed to be either hurt or unconscious. Juanita supposed it was George Worthy, who had gone with Arnie to find out where that ledge led.

From the way Arnie shoved the man off the horse, though, and let him fall limply to the ground, it didn't seem likely the man was an ally. That was confirmed a second later when Arnie said, "Better tie him up. It's the Alvarez kid."

Fear shot through Juanita. She twisted herself into a sitting position and cried out, "No! Esteban!"

"Bert, keep an eye on her," Cobey snapped as he bent over the man Arnie had dumped on the ground. "It's Alvarez, all right. Chuck, help me tie him up."

Juanita's heart pounded so hard in her chest, it seemed as if it were about to burst out of her body. She wondered wildly what had happened, how Esteban had gotten captured by Arnie Ross. What was going to happen to them now?

And where was Preacher?

Cobey and Stilson quickly lashed Esteban's ankles and wrists together. Then Cobey dragged him over to the rock where Juanita sat and dumped him in front of her. Even though she couldn't see the sneer on Cobey's face, she could hear it in his voice as he said, "I reckon your lovin' brother just couldn't stay away from you, Señorita."

"Please," she begged. "Do not hurt him."

"Long as he behaves himself, he'll keep on livin' . . . for a while." With that chilling statement, Cobey swung toward Arnie and demanded, "What the hell happened? Where's Worthy?"

"Preacher killed him," Arnie said bluntly. "Blew half his head off with a pistol. And that damn dog of his about chewed my arm off." Arnie held up his left arm. The sleeve of his shirt was shredded and dark with dried blood. "If I hadn't got lucky and walloped the critter with my gun, he'd have worked his way up to tearin' out my throat."

"Where'd you run into Preacher and the Alvarez kid?"

"At the other end of that ledge. We followed the trail along it until it sloped down into the valley again. One place looked like it had been blocked by a rock slide, but we were able to get through. I reckon Preacher must have cleared the slide away."

"What about the priest and those Yaquis? And the treasure?"

Arnie shook his head. "Didn't see hide nor hair of the priest or them Injuns. I think Preacher and Alvarez were by themselves." He looked around. "Hey! Where in blazes are the wagons?"

Cobey gave a disgusted grunt. "They were gone when we got back down here. Best guess is that the Yaquis slipped back here and stole 'em."

Arnie nodded slowly and said, "Yeah, I reckon that makes sense. As much sense as anything, anyway."

"I don't understand how come Preacher and the kid weren't with the others, though."

Chambers spoke up. "It's quite evident that the good padre prevailed on his swarthy sycophants to assist him in appropriating the treasure."

"What?" Cobey asked. He sounded irritated.

Chambers sighed. "Father Hortensio and the Yaquis betrayed Preacher and young Alvarez and stole the loot. I suppose Father Hortensio knew that Preacher intended to trade the treasure for Señorita Alvarez, and he wanted to prevent that at all costs."

Juanita frowned as she listened to the exchange. Could Father Hortensio have really done such a thing? It would explain a great deal. The priest and his Yaqui servants could have taken the treasure and left before Preacher reached the shelf again after negotiating the exchange with Arnie

Ross. Esteban would have tried to stop them, and it was possible that one of the Yaquis, acting on Father Hortensio's
command, might have knocked him unconscious or inca-
pacitated him in some other way. Then, when Preacher
found Esteban and discovered that Father Hortensio and the
Yaquis were gone and had taken the treasure with them,
Preacher and Esteban would have gone after them. . . .

It all fit, but Juanita took no satisfaction in piecing the
puzzle together. All that really mattered was that she and Esteban were both now the prisoners of these desperate men,
and the treasure they sought was gone, spirited away by
Father Hortensio. That left her and Esteban to whatever fate
awaited them at the hands of their captors.

Except for the fact that Preacher was still out there somewhere, loose and able to cause trouble.

Juanita sensed that there was no more dangerous wild
card in this deadly game than the man called Preacher.

"What do we do now, Cobey?" Arnie asked.

"It'll be gettin' light soon," Cobey said. "Can you find
your way back to the place where you ran into Preacher and
Alvarez?"

Arnie nodded. "I reckon I can."

"If we've got everything figured right, that'll be the same
spot the priest and the Injuns started from after they loaded
the treasure in the wagons. We'll pick up their trail there."

"So we're still goin' after 'em?"

Cobey gave a harsh, humorless laugh. "Damn right we're
goin' after 'em. You didn't think I was gonna give up on that
treasure, did you?" He raised a hand and clenched it into a
fist. "That loot's gonna be ours, and I don't care who has to
die along the way."

Preacher didn't move when the gun barrel poked the back
of his neck. He kept the knife at the Crow's throat and said

to the unseen man who had threatened him, "I don't want you to kill me, neither. But I reckon even if you pull the trigger, I'll still have time to shove this knife right through the Injun's neck."

The man with the gun hesitated a second before saying, "I suppose you might, at that. There's a heartbeat of time between the firing of the priming charge and the ignition of the main charge in the barrel. That might be enough of an interval for a man with sufficiently swift reflexes to carry out such a threat."

"So we've got us a standoff," Preacher said. "You could call it a Nuevo Mexican standoff."

"If you wanted to make a play on words," the other agreed. "I think we can bring it to a satisfactory conclusion, however. You are the man called Preacher, aren't you?"

It surprised Preacher that this fella, whoever he was, knew his name. But he said, "That's right."

"Then I don't see any reason why we can't be friends. To prove it, I'll take my rifle away from your neck. You can reciprocate by removing your knife from my companion's neck."

"You're askin' me to trust you," Preacher pointed out. "You can move that rifle and still shoot me with it."

"The alternative is to wait here all day and see who tires first. I doubt if you want that."

"Damn right I don't," Preacher said. He took a deep breath and then nodded. "All right. It's a deal."

The rifle barrel went away from the back of his neck. Preacher lowered his knife and pushed himself up off the Crow. So far, the Indian hadn't made a sound, and no expression had crossed his impassive face. But now he reached up and touched the tiny spot of blood where the tip of Preacher's blade had pricked his neck. He looked at the smear of crimson on his fingertip and said, "Ummm."

Keeping the knife in his hand, Preacher turned toward the man with the rifle. He planned to flip the knife underhand if he thought the fella intended to shoot him. Preacher's eyes narrowed, though, and he stiffened in surprise as he got his first good look at the man.

The gent wore buckskins and a coonskin cap, marking him as a typical frontiersman. There was nothing else typical about him. He was only about three and a half feet tall, the size of a child. His heavily muscled torso, short legs, and bearded face told Preacher that he wasn't a child. He was full-growed, as much as he ever would be.

"Son of a bitch," Preacher said.

"Indeed." The man tucked his rifle under his arm. The barrel had been cut down some so that it would be easier for him to handle, but the pistol tucked behind the man's belt was full size, and so was the sheathed hunting knife at his waist and the tomahawk that he carried behind his belt as well.

Preacher heard the Crow getting up, and moved a little so that he could keep an eye on both of them. "Who are you boys?" he asked.

"My name is Audie," the little man said. He nodded toward the Crow. "This is Nighthawk."

"Ummm," the Crow said.

"We've seen you around at Rendezvous," Audie went on, "but we've never been introduced."

"You're fur trappers?" Preacher asked.

"That's right. If Jeb Law or Dupre were here, they would vouch for us, I assure you."

Those names carried some weight with Preacher. Jeb Law and Dupre were good friends of his. But anybody could throw out their names as Audie had just done. That didn't really mean anything.

"I wish ol' Jeb *was* here," Preacher said. "I could use a hand right about now."

"If you have a problem, Nighthawk and I would be glad to assist you. I realize we got off on the wrong foot, so to speak—"

"You mean the way the two of you were trailin' me like you meant to cause trouble for me?"

"We were simply curious," Audie explained. "We saw you riding along, and Nighthawk said that he thought he recognized you. Isn't that right, Nighthawk?"

"Ummm."

"So it's true that we followed you," Audie continued, "but we meant you no harm, Preacher."

Preacher was still dubious. "If the two of you are trappers, what're you doin' off down here instead o' bein' further north where the pelts are better?"

Audie smiled and said, "Wanderlust, pure and simple. We'd heard about this country and wanted to see it for ourselves. I must say, it's rather enchanting."

Something jogged in Preacher's memory, and he said, "I recollect hearin' about a fella named Audie. Story went that he was some sort o' teacher back East before he came to the mountains."

"That would be me. I was an instructor at a school in Pennsylvania before I decided to follow my restless nature."

"Fella who told me about you didn't say nothin' about . . . well . . ."

"About me being a midget, you mean?" Audie grinned. "Well, that was certainly an important element of the story to leave out, wasn't it? But I assure you, I am the man you've heard about."

Preacher was beginning to believe him. His instincts were telling him, too, that Audie spoke the truth about wanting to help him. Preacher had lived as long as he had by relying on his hunches, as well as his ability to judge a man's character. In the case of Audie and Nighthawk, he sensed that both of them would do to ride the river with.

He slipped his knife back in its sheath and then held out his hand. "All right," he said. "I'm pleased to meet you boys, and if you ain't got somewheres else you need to be right now, I could sure use your help."

Audie reached up to clasp Preacher's hand. His grip was sure and strong. So was Nighthawk's when Preacher shook hands with the Crow.

"Tell us about it," Audie suggested.

Preacher quickly sketched in everything that had happened over the past week or so. Audie's eyes lit up at the mention of the treasure, but not with greed or avarice.

"Fascinating," he murmured. "Such artifacts must have great historical value, in addition to their intrinsic worth."

"They mean a whole heap to Father Hortensio, that's for sure," Preacher said. "He was willin' to leave the señorita in the hands of those no-good bastards rather than try to trade the loot for her."

"Ummm," Nighthawk said, and he managed to convey a considerable amount of disapproval with the grunt.

"The one who really angers me is this Professor Chambers you mentioned," Audie said. "Imagine, a scholar, a man who should be devoted to learning, a man who once inhabited the ivy-covered halls of Harvard, stooping to such ruthless behavior. He sounds like a disgrace to the entire teaching profession."

"He's pretty disgraceful, all right," Preacher agreed.

"So what we have to do is extricate the young señor and señorita from their captivity and then perhaps give some thought to recovering the treasure."

"The treasure's already recovered," Preacher pointed out. "It was goin' back to the Church anyway, except for what Esteban and Juanita had comin' to 'em for helpin' out. Since Father Hortensio's got the loot and seems to be headin' back to the old mission, I don't reckon we have to do anything about that." Preacher paused and then added, "Much as I'd like to pay him back for what he did to those kids."

"Even with the lead he's established, won't it take the father several days to get back to Mission Santo Domingo?"

Preacher nodded. "I reckon it will. Loaded down like they will be, those wagons can't move too fast."

"So it's possible that this gang of thieves, once they figure out what's going on, will pursue the wagons and make another effort to steal the treasure?"

"I'd say it's mighty likely," Preacher agreed grimly.

Audie frowned. "And they'll bring the two young people with them, to use as hostages if necessary."

"That's what I'm hopin'. That'll give us a chance to snatch 'em back."

"And of course there's a good likelihood we'll also have to protect the treasure along the way."

"Yep." Preacher chuckled. "That's all."

Audie rubbed his hands together and said, "Well, we've certainly got our work cut out for us. Perhaps we should give some thought to—"

"Ummm," Nighthawk said.

"Yeah, I hear it, too," Preacher said. "Hoofbeats. Here they come now."

29

As soon as it was light enough to see where they were going, Cobey ordered McDermott and Stilson to saddle the horses. Stilson muttered something about not getting any breakfast, and Cobey snapped at him, "Gnaw some jerky while you ride."

Then Cobey strode over to where Wick Jimpson still lay snoring. He prodded the big man in the side with his foot and said sharply, "Wick. Time to get up."

Wick didn't budge, and his stentorian snores continued. Cobey nudged him again, harder this time. "Wake up, damn it."

"He could be suffering from some sort of concussive cranial damage, considering how your men struck him repeatedly over the head with their weapons."

Cobey turned to glare at Professor Chambers, who had made the comment as he leaned casually against a tree trunk.

"If they hadn't, he'd have probably killed me. That wouldn't'a broke your heart, though, now would it, Professor?"

"I've been a faithful ally, Cobey," Chambers insisted. "I've done everything you've suggested."

"Yeah, but takin' orders from a gent like me sticks in your craw, don't it?"

"You haven't been giving me orders," Chambers said quietly. "We're partners, remember?"

Cobey's scornful grunt made it clear how he felt about that. He turned back to Wick and prodded his shoulder again. "Dadblast it, you big ox! Wake up!"

From where she sat on the rock, Juanita watched the brief confrontation between Cobey and Chambers and didn't know what to hope for. If the two men had a falling-out, one of them might kill the other, meaning that there would be one less man for her and Esteban to escape from. But if that happened, the chances were it would be Chambers who died and Cobey who lived, and Chambers might represent their best chance of getting away. She would help him when he tried his double cross of the others—she had nothing to lose by doing so, as far as she could see—but she certainly didn't trust him when he said that he would let them go. He was just as big a danger, in his own way.

The exchange of words between Cobey and Chambers didn't go any farther, because Cobey was now ignoring the professor and continuing his efforts to rouse Wick from slumber. The giant finally stirred. After moving around a little, he lifted his shaggy head and peered around, blinking in confusion. Then he looked up and said, "Oh. Mornin', Cobey. Is it time to get up?"

"Yeah, it is," Cobey growled, making an obvious effort not to lose his temper with Wick. "We got places to go and things to do."

"All right." Wick pushed himself to his feet, stretched, and then shook his head. He winced and reached up to touch his skull. "Huh. My head hurts a mite, and I got lumps all over it. What you reckon happened to me, Cobey?"

"I don't know. You be able to ride?"

"Oh, yeah, sure. It don't matter if my head hurts a little."

Chambers drifted over closer to Juanita and Esteban and said quietly, "Fascinating. He doesn't even remember what happened last night. Perhaps the blows to the head caused that. Or perhaps he's simply too mentally deficient to retain an unpleasant memory."

Juanita knew that wasn't true. Wick had told her about the incident that had led to him being thrown in jail for killing a man with one punch. She didn't bother correcting Chambers, though. She was more concerned with Esteban, who had not yet regained consciousness himself.

"Professor," she said, "could you check on my brother?"

"What? Oh, certainly. Your brother." Chambers knelt beside Esteban, felt in his neck for a pulse, and then rolled both eyelids back to look at his eyes. Esteban stirred slightly. Chambers looked up at Juanita and said, "His pulse is strong, and his eyes look all right. I think he should be waking up soon."

Juanita had heard Cobey and Arnie talking and knew that the fat man had literally run into Esteban when he was trying to flee from Preacher's dog. Arnie had struck the young man with his pistol just as he had the big cur, grabbed his horse, and thrown Esteban over the animal's back before vaulting into the saddle and galloping away. It had been sheer bad luck that had allowed Esteban to be taken prisoner.

True to the professor's prediction, Esteban opened his eyes a few minutes later, while the men were still saddling the horses. Bound hand and foot like Juanita, he had to struggle to sit up. When he did, he saw her sitting there on the rock and his eyes widened in surprise.

"Juanita!" he exclaimed. He looked around, and his face grew grim as he recognized the men moving around the camp and realized that he was a captive. Instinctively, he strained against his bonds for a moment before giving up. The rawhide thongs weren't going to loosen enough for him to get free.

"What happened?" he asked, so quietly that only she could hear. "The last thing I remember, I was with Preacher. . . ."

She leaned closer to him and equally quietly answered,

"The fat man, the one called Arnie, and another man attacked you and Preacher. Preacher killed the other man, but Arnie captured you and got away."

Esteban nodded, wincing a little from the pain in his head caused by the movement. "I remember now. . . . Juanita, *mi hermana*, are you all right?"

"They have not harmed me," she assured him, adding to herself, *Though not for lack of trying.*

"What happened to Preacher?"

She shook her head. "I do not know. He is still out there somewhere."

"Then there is still hope," Esteban breathed.

"Esteban . . . what about the treasure, and Father Hortensio?"

His face hardened even more. "Father Hortensio betrayed me. When I said that I was going to trade the treasure for your safety, he ordered one of the Yaquis to strike me down. Then they took the treasure and escaped. Preacher came back and found me, and we went after them."

Juanita nodded and said, "That is what these men decided must have happened. The wagons are gone, and they think the Yaquis came and took them while we were all up at the top of the canyon."

"I can believe that," Esteban said. "Father Hortensio has been one step ahead of all of us, doing everything he can to protect the treasure for the Church."

"Esteban," she said softly, "what else would you have him do? It is his calling. We decided ourselves, before we ever came up here to Nuevo Mexico, that the treasure must go back to the Church."

"Not at the cost of your life. That changed everything."

"Not to Father Hortensio."

He didn't say anything for a moment. He was sitting close enough to her so that he could lean over and rest his head against her knee for a second. She reached out with her bound hands and stroked his dark hair, which was now sticky with dried blood where Arnie had pistol-whipped him.

"Oh, Esteban," she murmured as Cobey ordered the men to put the prisoners on a couple of horses and then mount up. "What are we going to do?"

"Have faith," he grated. "It is all that is left to us."

"Faith in El Señor Dios?"

"In El Señor Dios . . . and in Preacher."

Lying at the top of a hill, screened by heavy brush, Preacher, Audie, and Nighthawk peered down at the Purgatoire River and the trail that ran beside it. Dog lay next to Preacher, tongue lolling from his mouth and his eyes alert. The mountain man had an arm looped around the big cur's neck. Waiting farther back were Horse, Nighthawk's spotted pony, and the sturdy, short-legged mount that Audie rode.

The three men watched intently as the party of riders came into sight. Beside Preacher, Dog let out a growl as he recognized the men. Preacher felt a mite like growling, too. Cobey and his bunch of thieves and killers provoked such a reaction in him.

Cobey was in the lead, as usual, and he had Juanita Alvarez on the back of his horse with him, riding in front of the saddle with Cobey's left arm around her waist. Just slightly behind them came Arnie, riding double with Esteban. Preacher was relieved to see that the youngster looked all right. He had been banged up and probably knocked out a couple of times, but he was tough, especially considering his privileged upbringing in Mexico City.

Professor Chambers rode next to the massive Wick Jimpson, and the other two men brought up the rear. All of them were looking around as they rode, watchful for any sign of trouble.

"Six of them and three of us," Audie said. "That's only

two to one odds, and there's a good chance we could even them up with one volley from our rifles."

"We probably could," Preacher agreed, "but with those Alvarez youngsters ridin' with Cobey and Arnie, we couldn't risk shootin' them. We'd have to go for three o' the others, and that'd leave Esteban and Juanita at the mercy o' those two bastards. I wouldn't put it past Cobey and Arnie to kill 'em right away if any shootin' was to start."

"Ummm," Nighthawk said.

Audie nodded. "I agree. If they did that, they'd be throwing away their own shields. Surely they wouldn't do such a thing."

Preacher's eyes narrowed as he said, "You're askin' a couple o' kill-crazy, gold-hungry skunks to act reasonable-like. That's a chance I ain't willin' to take, not when the lives o' those two kids are on the line, too."

"Of course," Audie said without hesitation. "It's your decision to make, Preacher. You've dealt with those men, and you know them. Nighthawk and I don't."

Preacher watched the group of riders as they trotted along the river and went around a bend out of sight. "We'll follow 'em," he said. "Wait for a better chance to grab Esteban and Juanita."

He backed down the hill, waiting until he was sure he was out of sight of the river before standing up. Audie and Nighthawk did likewise. They faded back into the trees, got their horses, and mounted up.

One thing about it—they all knew where they were going. The treasure was bound for Mission Santo Domingo, and so were the two groups of men following it. Nobody was likely to get lost.

Preacher and his two companions stayed well out of sight of the party they were trailing. The sun rose higher in the sky and the air grew warmer. Audie looked around at the wooded hills and the majestic mountains and the arching blue sky and the clear, bubbling creeks that flowed down to join the river, and the little man exclaimed, "My God, this is a beautiful country!"

"What's it like where you come from?" Preacher asked.

"Oh, it has its beauties, too," Audie replied. "But nothing really to compare with this. I enjoyed my life back there, I suppose, but I've never been happier than I am out here on the frontier, in the midst of all this magnificence." He paused, and when he went on a moment later, his tone was more reflective. "It's not just the landscape, of course. It's the freedom, and the knowledge that I'll be judged on what I do, not what I look like or how tall I am."

Preacher grunted. "How else would anybody be judged, except on what they do with their life?"

"Oh, ho, my newfound friend, you've been away from civilization too long."

"I been to St. Louis," Preacher said. "I even been to Philadelphia."

"Then you should be aware that back East, people are usually judged on everything but their own character and accomplishments. At one end of the spectrum, they're judged on how much money they have, and who their parents and grandparents were. At the other end, people are judged by how poor they are or sometimes by what color their skin is."

"Well, that's a damn-fool way to be," Preacher said. "A rich man ain't always worked for what he's got, and a poor man ain't always to blame for bein' born poor. Now, if he don't mind stayin' poor and don't want to work to make himself better, that's a different story. I got no use for a fella like that. As for the color of a man's skin, he ain't got no control over that."

"Speaking as one whose best friend is of a definite reddish hue, I wholeheartedly agree," Audie said.

"It ain't just redskins, though," Preacher went on. "When I was down in Louisiana, back when I was a young fella, I saw a bunch o' slaves, and they was a miserable lot, lemme tell you. But I never thought much about it until I rode a few rivers with Jim Beckwourth. Him and me went on more'n one trappin' expedition for Major Ashley."

Audie nodded. "Yes, I know Jim. He's a mulatto."

"That's a fancy way o' sayin' he's part black, ain't it? Well, to folks who keep slaves, part black's the same as all black, and once I got to know what a fine fella Jim was, it got me to wonderin' how many o' them slaves would've been just as smart and strong and full o' grit if they'd ever had the chance." Preacher shook his head. "That's why I don't hold with it."

"Some people up North are starting to feel the same way. They call themselves abolitionists, because they want to force the people in the South to give up their slaves."

"Well, one part o' the country forcin' another part o' the country to do somethin' ain't right, neither," Preacher said with a frown. He shook his head again and then chuckled dryly. "I'm mighty glad it ain't up to me to figure out what the country ought to do. I got enough on my mind right now, what with rescuin' them two youngsters and seein' that the lost treasure o' Santo Domingo don't fall into the hands o' Cobey Larson and his bunch o' murderin' desperadoes."

"Yes, as you put it earlier," Audie said, "that's all."

30

Preacher, Audie, and Nighthawk followed Cobey's bunch all day, staying well back so that they wouldn't be seen. To men such as these, getting around unseen in the wilderness was little more than child's play. They avoided the high ground, so they wouldn't be skylined if any of the men they pursued happened to look back at just the wrong moment, and they used ridges and gullies and thick stands of trees to keep themselves from being spotted when they were closer to their quarry. Preacher and Audie each had a spyglass in their possibles bag, so from time to time they stopped and the two men took turns climbing up in a tree so that they could check on the progress of the other group. Cobey kept his men moving at a brisk pace all day. Preacher hoped that wasn't too hard on the two prisoners. He and Audie and Nighthawk could have caught up just about any time they wanted to, but after talking about it they had decided that it would be better to wait until nightfall to make their attempt to rescue Esteban and Juanita.

So far there hadn't been any sign of Father Hortensio, the two Yaquis, and the treasure-laden wagons. But they had to be up ahead somewhere, Preacher knew, and the two groups following them had to be cutting into the lead that Father Hortensio and his companions held. It was just a matter of time. . . .

Spending all day in the saddle was nothing to hardened mountain men. They paused occasionally to let the horses rest, but otherwise they kept moving. Preacher shared his jerky with Audie and Nighthawk, and the Crow warrior passed around strips of pemmican from his supplies. Audie contributed some chunks of pone he had cooked a few days earlier. They washed the food down with swigs of water from their canteens.

Even though the strain of the long day wasn't felt much in Preacher's iron-hard frame, he knew it had to be telling on Esteban and Juanita. They weren't used to such things. Chances were they'd be mighty sore when Cobey finally called a halt for the night.

If he called a halt for the night, Preacher amended. It was possible the gang would press on even though darkness fell. They knew where they were going, and they had to be getting mighty anxious to get their hands on that gold and those gold and silver gem-encrusted relics.

As the sun dipped below the western peaks behind them, Audie said, "What do we do now, Preacher? If we keep moving after dark, and those men stop for the night, we're liable to stumble right into their camp."

"And if we stop and they don't, they'll have a big lead on us by mornin'," Preacher said.

Nighthawk said, "Ummm."

"You're right, it is a dilemma," Audie agreed.

Preacher considered for a moment and then said, "Way I see it, we can't risk stoppin' as long as we don't know what the others are doin'. We'll slow down a mite and hope that if they do make camp, we'll know it before we ride in on 'em. If they don't, they may gain on us a little, but we can make up that ground tomorrow."

Audie nodded. "That sounds like a workable plan to me. It's our best option, at any rate."

Shadows began to gather thickly. Preacher, Audie, and Nighthawk reined their horses back to a walk. They were close enough to the river now so that Preacher could hear the chuckling and bubbling of the stream as it flowed over its rocky bed. He said quietly, "Dog, go take a look around."

The big cur loped off ahead of the three men. Audie said, "He seems to have understood you, Preacher."

"Yeah, Dog's pretty smart. And we been together a long time, so that helps us understand each other."

"You don't think he'll give away our presence if he catches up to the others?"

Preacher shook his head. "He won't let them see him, and he won't attack or do anything else unless I give him the word. He'll just come back and let me know what he found."

"Amazing," Audie murmured. He sounded as if he didn't quite believe Preacher's claim.

A short time later, though, Dog came bounding back. He ran up to Preacher, who reined Horse to a stop. When Preacher reached down, Dog nuzzled his hand and then growled. Preacher nodded.

"I figured as much."

"Oh, come now," Audie said. "What could the creature have communicated with such simple gestures?"

"That the bunch we're after ain't far ahead of us. He wasn't gone long enough for it to mean anything else."

"Perhaps you're right. I just find it difficult to believe, that's all."

Preacher jerked a thumb toward the Crow. "I ain't heard Nighthawk do more'n grunt all day, but you seem to know what he means when he does it."

"Well, of course. We've been partners for a good while. . . . Oh, I see."

"Ummm," Nighthawk said, and Preacher thought he saw a faint suggestion of a grin on the warrior's hawklike face.

"Let's get down and walk a ways," Preacher suggested. He swung out of the saddle and Audie and Nighthawk did likewise. With rifles in one hand and their reins in the other, the men started forward. Dusk had settled down over the rugged terrain, and the stars were coming out overhead. The moon was not yet up, though, and wouldn't be for a while. This was actually one of the worst times of the day for seeing clearly. Often a man could make out more even by starlight than he could in such a thick dusk.

But even if he couldn't see very well at the moment, Preacher's nose worked just fine. He stopped abruptly, and so did his two companions. Preacher sniffed and then looked at Audie and Nighthawk, both of whom nodded. All three men had smelled the same thing: wood smoke. Dog growled, indicating that he had caught the scent, too.

"They've made camp," Audie whispered.

"Yeah, I reckon," Preacher agreed, "and not too far off. Let's leave the horses here and see how close we can get."

They tied the reins to some saplings and cat-footed forward through the gathering darkness. Nighthawk was the best at moving silently, but Preacher was almost as good and Audie was no slouch. It would have taken a mighty keen set of eyes and ears to notice the trio of grim-faced men moving through the woods.

Evidently sensing that they were close to their quarry, all three stopped at the same time and crouched behind some brush on a bluff overlooking the river. Down below was a stretch of level, relatively treeless ground next to the stream, and that was where Cobey and his men had made camp. Preacher could hear their voices as they talked among themselves. Stretching out on the ground, he crawled forward, pushing the brush aside until he could see down the steep slope in front of him. Audie and Nighthawk followed his

example. Even Dog got down on his belly and crawled up
next to Preacher.

Preacher parted the brush again and studied the camp
through the narrow gap. The men had placed rocks in a
circle and built a small fire within it. Preacher smelled food
cooking and coffee brewing. The tantalizing aromas made
his belly contract a little. He was more interested in checking on the welfare of the prisoners, though, than he was in
being hungry.

Esteban and Juanita sat side by side on a log, looking tired
and miserable. Their faces were drawn and haggard in the
dim, reddish firelight. Juanita leaned exhaustedly against
her brother's shoulder. One of the men, a tall, lanky gent in
buckskin trousers, homespun shirt, and coonskin cap, stood
near them with a rifle tucked under his arm. He was guarding them, that much was obvious. Across the camp, Cobey,
Arnie, and Professor Chambers stood together, talking quietly. The stocky man called Stilson, who had been with
Chambers at the mission, was at the fire tending to the food.

Preacher wondered where the giant was. From his vantage
point, he could see the entire camp, and there was no sign of
Wick Jimpson. Had something happened to him? Had the
others left him behind for some reason?

A sudden crashing of brush from behind Preacher, Audie,
and Nighthawk, much like the sound a grizzly bear would
make tramping through the underbrush, seemed to answer
that question.

Wick was behind them, and he was coming their way.

Juanita hadn't known that muscles could hurt so bad. In
fact, she ached where she hadn't even known it was possible
for a person to ache. Esteban had ridden more than she ever
had in the past, so he wasn't in quite as bad a shape as she
was, but he was utterly exhausted, too.

The one good thing about the way Cobey had pushed them all day was that there hadn't been time during any of their brief rest stops for him to make advances toward her. It was bad enough that she had felt his hands on her body as they rode and had been forced to listen to his occasional crude comments. However, he now seemed less interested in her as a woman. Thoughts of the treasure consumed him, and most of the time he regarded her more as a potential hostage and bargaining chip than he did as an attractive young female.

Surely he had figured out by now that Father Hortensio didn't care what happened to her and Esteban. If the priest had cared, he never would have gone off and left them behind the way he had. While she wasn't really surprised, and while they couldn't have expected Father Hortensio to do anything else under the circumstances, as she had pointed out to Esteban, his betrayal still hurt her. She had thought that the good padre felt more affection for them than that. After all, was it not the two of them who had made it possible for the treasure to be recovered in the first place?

But that meant nothing when weighed against the needs of the Church. Juanita just had to accept that.

Bert McDermott was guarding them now. Evidently Cobey no longer trusted Wick to do that job. That might make things more difficult later on. Juanita hadn't given up on the idea of turning Wick against his companions. He might not remember what had happened the night before, but he was still vulnerable to her charms. More than once during the day, she had caught the big man gazing at her in open adoration. Surely there would be a way to make use of that when the proper time came. At the moment, though, Wick had wandered off somewhere, perhaps to relieve himself in the woods.

Stilson brought over some fried salt pork and a couple of tortillas. He handed the plate to Juanita and said, "Here you go. You'll have to share with your brother. We ain't got a lot of supplies."

"These are tortillas you took from the provisions in the wagons, before you lost them," Esteban said.

Stilson sneered. "So what? You're lucky to be gettin' anything to eat at all. If'n it was up to me, I'd put a pistol ball through your head and then have me some fun with that sister o' yours, greaser."

Esteban stiffened and might have tried to get up, but Juanita told him quietly in Spanish to let it go. They had more to worry about than coarse insults. Reluctantly, Esteban nodded.

Bert jerked a thumb toward the fire. "Go on about your business, Chuck," he said to Stilson. "You ain't accomplishin' anything by harassin' these folks."

"Who appointed you their protector?" Stilson shot back.

"Cobey told me to guard 'em. I reckon that's sort of the same thing."

"The hell it is. He just don't want 'em to get away. That's all you're supposed to stop."

"I just don't want to listen to it," Bert said with a sigh.

"Fine, fine, I'm goin'." Stilson couldn't resist adding a parting shot. "You just want that señorita's pepper pot for yourself, Bert. I know what's goin' on."

Bert snorted in disgust but didn't say anything else.

On the log, Esteban tore off a small strip of the tortilla Juanita had given him. He put it in his mouth and chewed deliberately for a long moment before swallowing. When he had, he said quietly, "I am sorry, Juanita."

"For what?" she asked.

"For bringing you along with me on this accursed journey. You should be safely in our home in Mexico City."

"Do you not remember, Esteban, that it was I who insisted on accompanying you?"

He shrugged. "I am your brother, your protector. I should

have said no, regardless of any argument you made." He tore off another bit of tortilla and ate it.

"I do not blame you," Juanita said. "I knew there might be danger. I knew it was likely there would be."

An uneasy silence settled over the siblings. Neither of them really knew what Cobey intended to do when he caught up with Father Hortensio and the Yaquis. If it was possible, he would probably just slaughter them and take the treasure. In that case, Esteban would probably die a quick death, as he would no longer be of any possible use to the thieves.

Juanita, on the other hand, would take much longer to die, and she knew it.

They were just finishing their skimpy meal when Cobey sauntered toward them. Juanita saw the look in his eyes and caught her breath. She was in for trouble again.

And this time, Wick wasn't here to protect her.

31

"Don't move," Preacher hissed at Audie and Nighthawk as Wick came toward them. "Maybe he won't see us."

The three men lay utterly still and silent as Wick approached. His footsteps were heavy, and he thrust brush aside with a great deal of crackling and snapping. But as he came closer, it grew apparent that he was going to miss them. He was about twenty feet to their left as he walked to the edge of the bluff and looked down at the camp.

Preacher glanced in that direction, too, and saw that Cobey had walked over to stand in front of Esteban and Juanita. Preacher wasn't sure what was going on, but as he watched, Wick began to wave an arm above his head and called down to those in the camp below, "Hey, Cobey! Hey, Arnie! Look at me! I'm gonna jump off this cliff and see if I can fly!"

If he jumped, he sure wouldn't fly. He would drop like a rock instead, and the bluff was about thirty feet tall. Such a fall might not kill him, but he would probably wind up with a busted leg or arm, at best. If he landed wrong, the drop might even prove fatal. Preacher didn't really care what happened to Wick—he still remembered the way the giant had wanted to molest Lupita Ojeida back at the trading post—

but he didn't much like the idea of watching the behemoth throw himself off the bluff, either, simply because he was too dim-witted to know what he was doing.

But of course, he and Audie and Nighthawk couldn't try to stop Wick, either. That would mean revealing their presence and giving up any element of surprise.

Wick spread his arms like they were wings and perched on the edge of the bluff. Down below, Cobey ripped out a curse and shouted, "Damn it, Wick, stop! Don't jump!"

Wick hesitated. "But Cobey," he said, "I seen a eagle earlier, and it looked so nice, the way he was flyin' around. I done tried flappin' my arms, but I can't get off the ground. I figured I ought to jump off some high place to get in the air first, and then flap my arms."

Cobey thrust out a hand toward him, motioning him back away from the edge. "Just stay there!" he yelled. "I'll come up and get you!"

Preacher wasn't worried about Wick noticing them, but Cobey was a different story. He was a lot smarter and a lot more alert than the big man. Preacher whispered to Audie and Nighthawk, "We'd best fade away 'fore Cobey gets up here."

"Ummm," Nighthawk said, and damned if it didn't sound like a grunt of agreement, Preacher thought.

Staying on their bellies, they crawled backward until they were well away from the edge of the bluff. They could hear Cobey cussing as he made his way into the woods and circled around toward the spot where Wick waited for him. When Preacher and his two companions got to their feet, they slipped back in the other direction, working away from Cobey and Wick. Preacher had to hold onto Dog's ruff and practically drag the big cur along with them. No growls came from Dog's throat now, but Preacher could tell how eager he was to get at Cobey and rip him to pieces. Ol' Dog had always been a good judge of character.

When they could risk talking again, Audie whispered, "That was a near thing."

"It sure was," Preacher agreed. They had taken a circuitous route, but they were back at the spot where they had left their horses.

"What are we going to do now?"

"There's not enough cover around that camp to let us slip in and get close enough to grab Esteban and Juanita. I reckon we'd best just bide our time and wait for a better chance." Preacher frowned and rubbed his bearded jaw. "Waitin' sure as hell gnaws at my innards, but I don't see as we've got a choice."

Audie nodded. "Perhaps tomorrow will bring a better opportunity."

"I hope so," Preacher said. "Dog here is itchin' to tear into them sons o' bitches, and I know just how he feels."

Juanita felt like she had been given a reprieve. Cobey had not had time to do much more than walk up to her and Esteban when the giant had appeared at the top of the bluff, shouting about jumping off and flying. Cobey had been forced to go up there and bring him down, and once again— although inadvertently this time—Wick had saved her from the man's unwanted attentions.

By the time Cobey had talked Wick into giving up the idea of flying and brought him back down to the camp, Juanita had been stretched out on the ground with Esteban lying next to her, and they had both pretended to be sound asleep. Through one eye opened a mere slit, Juanita saw Cobey looking at them for a moment, and then he had turned away with an irritated shrug. The ruse had worked, and once again she was safe.

But how long, she wondered, could she keep dodging that particular fate?

Morning came much too early. It seemed to Juanita that she had just closed her eyes and gone to sleep for real when Bert McDermott said, "Time to get up, Señorita." At the same time, Bert prodded Esteban's shoulder with his boot.

Juanita let out an unladylike groan as she sat up. Her muscles were almost too stiff and sore to let her move. Esteban sat up without quite as much trouble, but he still looked tired, too. He managed to stand up and then said to Bert, "Help my sister to her feet, please."

Bert smiled. "Sure. I never mind helpin' a pretty lady." He bent to take hold of Juanita's arms.

As he did so, Esteban reached out quickly with his bound hands and plucked the pistol from behind Bert's belt. Stepping back quickly, he raised the gun and cocked the hammer.

"Esteban, no!" Juanita gasped.

Bert let go of her. He had lifted her about a foot from the ground, and when he released her she sat down hard, the impact jarring her. Wide-eyed with fear, Bert stared at Esteban and said quickly, "Be careful with that pistol, kid. The trigger's mighty touchy."

"Then you are the one who should be careful, Señor," Esteban grated. "I have nothing to lose."

"What about your sister?"

"I would rather she die quickly than suffer at the hands of you and your friends."

Bert licked his lips. "Listen, kid, I ain't done nothin' to you or her. Fact is, I been tryin' to look out for the two o' you—"

"Damn it!" The exclamation came from the other side of the camp, where Arnie Ross had just rolled out of his blankets. "The kid's got a gun!"

That got the attention of everyone else. Cobey came running out of the trees where he had gone to empty his bladder. He had his rifle with him, and he pointed it at Esteban as he slid to a stop.

"Drop the pistol," he ordered tersely, "or I'll blow your brains out."

"Not before I pull the trigger and kill your man," Esteban said.

"Better listen to him, Cobey," Bert said. "I think he's crazy enough to do it."

"Yeah, I reckon you're right." Cobey shifted his aim a little. "I'll give you to the count of three, Alvarez, and then I'm puttin' a ball through your sister's head."

"Esteban . . ." Juanita said.

"One."

"Give it up, kid," Bert said. "There's no way you can win this one."

"Two," Cobey said.

Esteban swallowed hard. His eyes flicked toward Juanita and took in her drawn, pale features. He sighed.

Cobey had just opened his mouth for the count of three when Esteban lowered the pistol. With the barrel pointing at the ground, he eased the hammer off cock. Bert reached out with a hand that shook just slightly and took the gun out of Esteban's grip.

As soon as Esteban was disarmed, Cobey stepped forward, reversing the rifle in his hands. He drove the butt of the weapon into Esteban's stomach in a brutal blow that made the young man cry out and double over. Cobey lifted the rifle and brought the butt down on the back of Esteban's neck, sending him to the ground. Juanita screamed.

Then, with his face contorted with hate, Cobey loomed over Esteban's fallen figure and turned the rifle again so that the barrel pointed at Esteban's head.

"You little greaser bastard," Cobey said. "I think I'll go ahead and kill you right now."

Preacher, Audie, and Nighthawk had withdrawn about half a mile the night before and made a cold camp high on the side of a hill. They had taken turns standing watch, just to make sure no one discovered them. They'd drawn lots to determine the order, and Preacher wound up with the third watch. So Audie and Nighthawk were still asleep when the sky turned gray with the approach of dawn, but Preacher was wide awake. Telling Dog to stay there, he started down toward the river, curious to see what was going on in the enemy camp.

He was about a hundred yards away from the edge of the bluff, about to belly down and crawl the rest of the way as he and his newfound friends had done the night before, when he heard Juanita scream.

The terrified sound shot through Preacher's brain, and in that instant, he knew what he had been doing wrong for days now—he had been thinking too damned much. Trying to outguess, outfigure, and outtrick his enemies hadn't accomplished anything except to get those two young'uns captured. There was a time for thought and a time for action, and as Juanita's scream died away, Preacher knew the time for action had come.

He lunged forward, gliding through the brush like the great gray wolf he sometimes resembled. His long legs covered the ground in a hurry, and as he reached the edge of the bluff, he looked down and saw that Esteban was on the ground, with Cobey standing over him and pointing a rifle at his head. Preacher snapped his own rifle to his shoulder, drew a bead in less than the blink of an eye, and pressed the trigger.

The rifle roared and kicked against his shoulder, and the heavy ball that it launched should have smashed right through Cobey Larson's evil brain. Instead, just as Preacher pressed the trigger, Arnie spotted him on the bluff and yelled, "Cobey! Look out!"

Cobey twisted instinctively in response to the shout, turning so that the rifle ball on its downward trajectory barely clipped the top of his left shoulder. The impact was still enough to knock him to his knees and make him drop his rifle. He jerked his head up and saw the tall, buckskin-clad figure at the top of the bluff. "Preacher!" he shrieked. "Kill him!"

Preacher dropped the empty rifle, yanked both pistols from behind his belt, and cocked them as he stepped off the edge and started sliding down the slope. The drop-off wasn't sheer right here, but it was steep enough so that Preacher could barely stay upright as he slid down on his heels. He saw Chambers, Stilson, and Wick off to his right, so he swung his right-hand pistol toward them and fired. The weapon was double-shotted, with a heavy charge of powder. One of the balls whined past Chambers's head and made him cry out and duck for cover. The other smashed Stilson's left thighbone and knocked his leg out from under him. Stilson went down with a hoarse cry of agony.

Preacher had time to wonder if the pendulum had swung too far and he had gone to the other extreme, from thinking too much to being a damn fool, and then he reached the base of the bluff and somehow kept his footing instead of sprawling on his face. He used his momentum to send him racing forward, toward Esteban and Juanita. Bert McDermott wheeled toward him and brought up a pistol. Preacher ducked as smoke and flame geysered from the barrel. The ball passed over his head. He threw his empty pistol, sending it spinning through the air to slam across Bert's face and knock him backward, off his feet and out of the fight, at least for a little while.

Cobey was still down, too, but Arnie was on his feet and dangerous, with a pistol in each hand. Preacher weaved to the side as Arnie fired the first one. He felt something pluck at his shirt and knew he had come that close to dying. Arnie fired the other pistol, but he rushed the shot and it missed Preacher's head by a good three inches.

Preacher kicked Cobey in the back as he went by, knocking him sprawling. Esteban seemed to be unconscious. Juanita had crawled over to her brother and thrown herself half on top of him in an obvious effort to protect him. Preacher reached their side and dropped to a knee beside her, lining his left-hand gun on Arnie as he did so. Arnie had emptied both his pistols without any luck, and now grabbed at his powder horn in an attempt to reload, but he froze as Preacher barked, "Hold it!" By striking so swiftly, he had gained a momentary advantage. Three of his enemies were down, Arnie was momentarily unarmed, Chambers looked confused, unsure of what to do. . . .

That left Wick.

And suddenly, the rising sun was blotted out and a deafening shout assaulted Preacher's ears, and when he twisted his head and brought the pistol around, the dark mass looming above him looked like an avalanche about to fall on him.

But it wasn't an avalanche, just Wick Jimpson, and he crashed down on top of Preacher with stunning force before the mountain man could pull the trigger.

32

Wick's crushing weight drove all the breath out of Preacher's lungs and made skyrockets explode through his brain. He gasped for air but couldn't get any. The pistol had been knocked out of his hand, and he couldn't reach his knife because he was pinned down so effectively by the giant. All he could get free was his right arm. It shot up, and he clamped his right hand on Wick's throat. His fingers wouldn't reach all the way around Wick's bull-like neck, but he got the best grip he could and hung on for dear life.

Wick was too close to use his long arms and immense strength effectively. He cuffed Preacher, but even though the mountain man's head was rocked from side to side by the blows, they lacked the killing power of one of Wick's normal punches. The muscles in Preacher's arm and shoulder bunched and corded as he poured all the power he could into his strangling grip. Wick's face began to turn a dark red.

Preacher didn't know what else was going on in the camp. All his attention was focused on Wick. In the back of his brain, he knew that even if he was able to escape from the big man, by now Cobey, Arnie, and the others would be ready to kill him. His only real hope was that Audie and

Nighthawk had heard the shots and would come a-runnin' to join the fray.

Wick suddenly jerked and stiffened, and Preacher heaved to the side as hard as he could. Wick rolled off him, leaving Preacher free to gulp down a huge lungful of life-giving air. Preacher rolled, too, and saw an arrow protruding from Wick's back. The feathers and the markings on the shaft identified it as a Crow arrow, so Preacher knew that Nighthawk had shown up. As he scrambled to his feet, a rifle roared on top of the bluff. The shot drove Arnie back, even though it didn't hit him. A few feet away, Preacher saw Cobey crawling toward the rifle he had dropped earlier when Preacher's shot grazed him.

Spotting the pistol that *he* had dropped, Preacher rolled toward it and snatched it off the ground. He twisted toward Cobey, expecting to trade shots, but to his surprise he saw Cobey surge onto his feet and run toward the river. Arrows whistled around his head as he ran.

Preacher pushed himself up and looked around. Arnie and Cobey were fleeing from the barrage of arrows and rifle fire laid down from the top of the bluff by Nighthawk and Audie. Chambers and Bert McDermott had hold of the wounded Stilson, one on either side of him, and they were hustling away from here as fast as they could, too. Wick still lay face-down, the arrow sticking up from his back.

The thieves reached their tethered horses and ducked behind the nervous animals, using them for cover. Cobey and Arnie jerked the reins of their mounts loose from the trees where they were tied and sprang into the saddle, ducking as lead sang around their heads. McDermott and Chambers hoisted Stilson onto another of the horses and pressed the reins into his hands, then lunged for their own mounts. Bert grunted in pain as a rifle ball clipped his arm, but he managed to make it into the saddle. He kicked his horse into a run, following Cobey and Arnie. Chambers and Stilson did likewise.

Preacher lowered his pistol, unfired. The fleeing hard cases had quickly drawn out of range. Dog chased them for a short distance, barking furiously, before turning around and trotting back to Preacher, who now knelt beside Esteban and Juanita.

The young woman was conscious and seemed to be all right. Preacher helped her up and then rolled Esteban onto his back. Pressing a couple of fingers into the young man's neck, Preacher found a strong pulse.

"I reckon he'll make it," he said reassuringly to Juanita. "Looks like he took a hard wallop."

"Si, and he would be dead now if not for you, Señor Preacher." Impulsively, Juanita threw her arms around the mountain man. *"Gracias, señor, mil gracias!"*

Even as he clumsily patted her on the back, Preacher heard hoofbeats and looked over Juanita's shoulder to see Audie and Nighthawk riding along the riverbank toward them. Nighthawk was leading Horse. The two trappers had circled around to a point where they could descend the bluff with the horses.

Preacher glanced in the other direction, where Cobey, Arnie, and the others had disappeared around a bend in the Purgatoire, back the way they had come from the day before. Although they had been forced to flee by the deadly accurate rifle and arrow fire from Audie and Nighthawk, Preacher didn't believe for a second that the hard cases had given up and would not come back. Cobey wouldn't abandon his goal of getting his hands on that treasure, and now he would be even hungrier for vengeance on Preacher and the Alvarez siblings, not to mention Preacher's newfound allies.

Gently, Preacher disengaged himself from Juanita's hug and turned to Esteban. He lightly slapped the young man's face until Esteban began to come around. "Sorry, amigo,"

Preacher said, "but we got to get movin', 'fore that bunch o' thieves and killers regroups and comes after us."

With Preacher's help, Esteban sat up and shook his head groggily. When his gaze focused on Preacher, he exclaimed in surprise. "Preacher! Where did you come from?"

Juanita said, "He came down that bluff like an angel descending from Heaven."

"First time I recollect that anybody compared me to an angel," Preacher said with a grin. He helped Esteban to his feet. "I been followin' Cobey's bunch with a couple o' fellas I ran into yesterday. That's Audie and Nighthawk." He nodded to the little man and the Crow warrior in turn.

"I'm pleased and honored to meet you, Señorita," Audie said, taking off his coonskin cap and bending low in a bow without leaving the saddle. He straightened, replaced his cap on his head, and went on. "Preacher, we'd better light a shuck out of here while we still can."

"Ummm," Nighthawk concurred.

Juanita said worriedly, "We don't have enough horses."

"I reckon Nighthawk's pony can carry double," Preacher said, "especially if you ride with him, since you're lighter. Horse is plenty strong enough to carry me and Esteban for a ways."

"Where are we going?"

Preacher looked east along the river, opposite the direction in which the hard cases had fled. "The padre and the Yaquis and them wagons are still up ahead somewheres. They'll be bound for the old mission. I reckon we ought to head for there, too."

Esteban said, "You do not intend to try to take back the treasure from Father Hortensio, do you? I am angry with him for what he did, but still, the gold and the relics belong to the Church. . . ."

"The Church is welcome to 'em," Preacher said. "What I was thinkin' was that Mission Santo Domingo might make a pretty good place to fort up when Cobey and his bunch come after us. We got to get there first, though."

Without any more delay, they mounted up, Preacher and Esteban on Horse, Juanita climbing onto Nighthawk's spotted pony in front of the stoic Crow. The riders set off at a ground-eating lope, not pushing the mounts too hard since two of them were carrying double, but not wasting any time, either. They left behind the fire, which was now dying out in its circle of stones, and the arrow-pierced body of Wick Jimpson.

Preacher and his friends were out of sight when Wick suddenly stirred. The giant groaned and tried to push himself up on hands and knees, only to fail and sprawl out again. He lay there for a while, gathering his strength. When he was ready to try to move again, he let out a yell and climbed unsteadily all the way to his feet. His broad face contorted in a grimace at the pain in his back. He reached behind him and found the arrow. His thick fingers closed around the shaft and snapped it off, which left the head buried inside his back, just under his shoulder blade. A few inches of the shaft remained attached to the arrowhead, sticking out through the blood-stained hole in the back of Wick's shirt.

He looked at the arrow, wondering where it had come from, and then threw it aside, not really caring. All that mattered was that when he looked around, he didn't see the señorita anywhere. He saw tracks, though, hoofprints that led off to the east. That must be where the señorita had gone, Wick's muddled brain decided.

He shuffled off in that direction and then broke into a shambling run. He didn't know where Juanita had gone, but he was going to find her. He didn't care if he had to run all day and all night and all the next day.

One way or another, he was going to find the señorita.

* * *

Chambers had never seen Cobey so angry. The man looked like he was going to explode with rage. Cobey had lost his hat somewhere, and as he paced back and forth he raked his fingers through his long, tangled hair.

"I'll skin him alive!" Cobey ranted, and Chambers knew who he was talking about. There was no doubt that Cobey referred to Preacher. "He's got more lives than a damned cat, but we'll see how long he makes it once I start peelin' the hide off him, one strip at a time!"

"Why don't you gimme a hand here?" Arnie suggested from where he knelt beside Chuck Stilson. He had been working on Stilson's wounded leg ever since they had stopped and Stilson had lost consciousness and toppled out of the saddle, maybe hurting himself even more.

Arnie had used a tourniquet to get the bleeding stopped and cleaned away enough of the crimson gore to see what he was dealing with. He stretched Stilson's leg out and heard the ends of the shattered bone grating against each other. Even though he was out cold, Stilson groaned loudly and shifted around, instinctively trying to get away from the pain that engulfed him.

"We need to get this leg splinted," Arnie muttered as Cobey continued to pace and rave.

"Perhaps I can help," Chambers offered. "What do you need me to do?"

Arnie looked up at the professor. "See if you can find a couple of fairly straight pieces of tree limb, about twice as big around as your thumb and maybe two feet long. I can use them as splints if you can find some like that."

"I'll see what I can do." Chambers hurried off on that errand.

"What about me?" Cobey demanded. "I'm hit, too. This shoulder hurts like blazes. Damn it, my arm ain't completely healed up from where Preacher shot me before, and now the bastard's shot me again!"

Without looking up from Stilson, Arnie said, "I'll look at you when I get a chance, Cobey. Bert got nicked, too, you know."

Bert McDermott stood to one side, calmly tying a strip of cloth around his bullet-burned upper arm, using his teeth to hold the makeshift bandage as he knotted it tight. When he was finished, he said, "Don't worry about me, Arnie. I'll be all right."

Cobey threw his hands in the air. "Ever'thing's shot to hell! It's all fallin' apart around me!"

It was true they'd had a run of bad luck . . . but some of it was Cobey's fault. They shouldn't have brought the girl and her brother with them. Either kill them or let them go, Arnie thought. Either of those things would have been better. The youngsters wouldn't have represented much of a threat, and having a pretty girl around where gents could fight over her always led to trouble sooner or later. And if they had released Esteban and Juanita unharmed, Preacher might not have come after them. . . .

That was pretty unlikely, of course. Once a man like Preacher got his dander up, he wasn't going to just go away. He would have felt like he had a score to settle, and nothing short of death would stop him.

That was still the case. Preacher had those kids back now—although there was no way of knowing what sort of shape Esteban was in after having been attacked by Cobey— but he was still a threat. For one thing, he was between Cobey and that gold, so they would have to deal with him sooner or later. Cobey wasn't going to give up the treasure.

Chambers came up carrying a couple of pine branches. "Will these do?" he asked as he held them out to Arnie.

The fat man took them and nodded. "Yeah, they look fine, Professor. Good job."

He ripped up a homespun shirt from his own possibles bag and used it as bandages, tying them as tightly as possible around the holes in Stilson's leg where the pistol ball had gone in and out. When he loosened the tourniquet, the bandages reddened a little from fresh blood, but not too much. Arnie thought there was a good chance Stilson wouldn't bleed to death, anyway.

Carefully, he laid the branches on either side of the wounded leg and tied them in place with rawhide thongs. He thought the bone was back together as best he could get it, although it was possible the ball had pulverized enough of the bone so that it would never heal properly. This leg might wind up shorter than the other, and Stilson would always have a bad limp. Better to be crippled for life, though, than dead.

Chambers watched with interest as Arnie patched up the wound, and after a few minutes he said, "Am I imagining things, or have you had some medical training, Mr. Ross?"

Arnie shrugged. "When I was younger, I thought I might be a sawbones. I apprenticed to one for a while. It never worked out, though."

"A pity. You have some definite skills in that area."

Impatiently, Cobey demanded, "You got Stilson ready to ride yet?"

Still on his knees beside the unconscious man, Arnie looked up and said, "He ain't gonna be doin' any ridin' for a while, Cobey. Not for a day or two, at least. If he does, it'll hurt like hell—"

Cobey snorted. "I don't care if he's in pain."

"And that wound will open up again and he'll bleed to death," Arnie went on doggedly.

"We're all hurt," Cobey said with a shrug. "You got your arm half gnawed off by that damn dog. The only one who ain't been hurt is the professor, for God's sake!"

"Just fortunate, I suppose," Chambers said with a smile.

Cobey ignored him and said, "So Stilson has got to ride. We have to get movin'. We can still catch up to the priest and get that treasure."

"Preacher will likely be joined up with him by then," Arnie pointed out.

"Fine with me. I want another shot at that son of a bitch."

"I know you do, but Stilson can't ride." Arnie sighed. "You and Bert and the professor can go after them, I reckon. I'll stay and take care of Chuck."

Cobey looked at him intently and asked, "You sure about that?"

"Yeah. We can't just leave him alone."

Cobey pulled his pistol, cocked it, and fired. The action was so swift and unexpected that Arnie had no chance to stop him. The ball struck Stilson in the middle of the forehead and made him jerk and arch his back off the ground as it bored on through his brain and exploded his skull. His body sagged back to the ground in death.

Cobey lowered the smoking pistol and said, "I reckon we can leave him and get after Preacher and that treasure now."

Arnie, Bert, and Chambers stared at Stilson's lifeless body and his shattered head. Finally, Arnie nodded and said in a resigned voice, "I reckon we can."

33

Horse, Nighthawk's pony, and Audie's stubby-legged mount had all had a night's rest, so they were fresh and strong. Preacher set a brisk pace that day, although he did call a halt more often than he might have otherwise, since two of the animals were carrying double and he didn't want them to get too tired.

They were low on supplies, too, and everyone was hungry as the day wore on. There was no time to stop and hunt for fresh meat, though. Preacher was certain that Cobey and the others would have regrouped by now and would be coming after them.

For a change, though, the odds were even. With Jimpson dead and Stilson badly wounded, that left just Cobey, Arnie, Chambers, and McDermott to go after the treasure. Preacher figured that he, Audie, Nighthawk, and Esteban were a match for them. Add Juanita into the mix—she had proved that she had plenty of pluck, and Preacher knew she could be counted on—and they actually outnumbered their pursuers. There were the two Yaquis to consider, too, if Preacher and his friends could catch up to the wagons before the next fracas. Preacher knew better than to be overly optimistic, but he was starting to feel like they now had a good chance of coming through this alive.

That afternoon they left the mountains behind and found themselves once again in the foothills, heading east toward the vast rolling plains. And as they descended from the mountains, Preacher's keen eyes spotted the wagons miles ahead of them, so far in the distance they were little more than dots. He called a halt to let the horses rest, and while they were doing that he got out his spyglass and trained it on the far-off vehicles.

Those were definitely the wagons from the Alvarez expedition. He couldn't see the drivers from this angle, but he was confident they were Pablo and Joaquin. Nor did he see Father Hortensio. But the padre would be there, Preacher knew. After everything that had happened, the priest wouldn't let that treasure out of his sight.

None of the others seemed to have noticed, so Preacher lowered the spyglass and pointed. "There are the wagons," he announced.

Esteban and Juanita were standing next to Nighthawk's pony. They looked up sharply at the sound of Preacher's voice and followed his pointing finger. Esteban took a step forward, excitement animating his body. "I see them," he said. "Are you sure they are the ones we seek, Preacher?"

"Certain sure," Preacher responded. "For one thing, it ain't likely there'd be another pair o' wagons out here right now. We're well west o' the Santa Fe Trail. For another thing, I recognize 'em, as well as the teams pullin' 'em."

Esteban crossed himself and murmured a prayer. "Can we catch up to them before they reach the mission?"

"Probably. Loaded down the way they are, they ain't movin' very fast."

Juanita looked around at him. "Even if we do not catch up to them before then, we know that is where they are going, do we not?"

Preacher nodded. "I reckon."

"But that bunch of brigands and highwaymen will be coming on quickly, too," Audie pointed out. "If they catch up while the wagons are still out in the open, they can pick off the mules, pin the wagons down, and make things very difficult for all of us."

"Dang right," Preacher agreed. "That's why we need to catch up and hurry the padre along with those wagons as much as we can."

A short time later, they mounted up again and rode on, and now there was an even greater urgency goading them through the foothills after the wagons.

Wick ran until he couldn't run anymore, and then he collapsed facedown on the ground. He wasn't sure where he was, wasn't even sure if he was still going the right direction. He couldn't see the tracks left by the horses.

But he heard the river and knew he had to follow it. He had trouble remembering exactly *why* he was supposed to follow the river, but he knew he was. After a while, enough of his strength came back to him so that he was able to push himself to his feet and stumble on.

Juanita. Her face filled his thoughts, and his vision of her kept him moving.

He was thinking about her when he passed out again, and this time he didn't even feel himself hit the ground.

Arnie thought it was odd when they reached the spot where Preacher had jumped them that morning and he didn't see any sign of Wick. The last time he had seen the giant before they'd been forced to flee before the withering fire of whoever Preacher had with him, Wick had been lying on the ground with an arrow protruding from his back. He had certainly looked dead, and that was how Arnie expected to find him.

The footprints told an obvious story, though. Wick's feet were huge, like the rest of him, and the tracks he had left showed him heading off to the east, the same way Preacher and the others had gone.

"Wick's a good boy," Cobey said when Arnie pointed out what he had discovered. "He's gone after those bastards."

More than likely Wick was just thinking about the señorita, Arnie mused. Regardless of that, though, he was glad that Wick wasn't dead after all.

They pushed on, with Bert leading Chuck Stilson's horse, since, of course, Stilson didn't need the mount anymore. It was past the middle of the afternoon when Cobey exclaimed, "What the hell!" and pointed to a large, shaggy shape lying on the ground up ahead.

"That's Wick!" Arnie said as he urged his horse forward. When he reached the massive form, he swung quickly out of the saddle and dropped to a knee at Wick's side.

Wick's back rose and fell as he breathed, so he was still alive. The arrow below his shoulder blade was broken off so that only a few inches of the shaft remained. A large blood-stain soaked his shirt around the wound. Arnie knew that he couldn't pull the arrowhead out; that would just do more damage. It would have to be cut out, and that would be a tricky job, requiring plenty of light and a good place to work and a lot of bandages and hot water—none of which he had here and now.

"Is he alive?" Cobey asked from horseback.

"Yeah. He's lost quite a bit of blood, though."

"Can you wake him up and get him on a horse? We've got an extra one, you know."

They had an extra mount because Cobey had murdered Chuck Stilson. But, all in all, Arnie was willing to trade Wick's life for Stilson's. He had known Wick a lot longer, and Stilson hadn't been very friendly, when you got right down to it.

"I'll try," Arnie said. "Somebody gimme a hand. I need to roll him onto his side."

"We can't take too long at this," Cobey cautioned.

"Just give me a few minutes."

"I'll help you," Chambers offered as he dismounted. Together, he and Arnie rolled Wick onto his right side. Then Arnie took out a small silver flask and uncorked it. There wasn't much in the flask, and it was the last of his whiskey, carefully horded over the past couple of weeks, but Wick needed it now. Arnie pried the big man's mouth open and poured a little of the fiery liquor in it.

Wick sputtered and snorted and opened his eyes. He tried to roll onto his back, but Chambers was there to stop him. That would have just driven the arrowhead even deeper into his body. Blinking in confusion, Wick said, "A-Arnie . . . ? Where's Cobey?"

"He's here, don't worry," Arnie assured him. "You'll be all right, Wick, but you got to get up and get on a horse we've got for you."

"I was . . . goin' after . . . the señorita . . ."

"So are we," Arnie told him. "Come with us and we'll find her."

"Oh. All right." Wick tried to push himself upright, but he gasped and slumped down again. "The world sure is . . . spinnin' around all funny . . ."

"Just take it slow and easy."

"Not slow," Cobey snapped.

The sound of his voice made Wick look at him. "Hey . . . Cobey," he said. "I'm sorry . . . I got hurt."

"Just get up and get on Stilson's horse," Cobey ordered.

"Where is . . . ol' Chuck?"

"Dead," Arnie said quietly.

"Oh. I'm sorry."

"You didn't have nothin' to do with it, Wick." Arnie glanced toward Cobey, who was clearly growing more impatient by the second. He was damned if he was going to ride off and leave Wick here to die by himself. He said, "Come on, Wick, you can do it. Help us, Professor."

Together, he and Chambers got Wick on his feet and helped him climb into the saddle on Stilson's horse. Wick's horse had run off during the fighting that morning, and they hadn't seen it since. Stilson's mount was almost as big and strong, though. It could carry Wick, at least for a while.

"Come on, let's go, let's go," Cobey urged. They set off, riding beside a long, thick clump of brush.

They hadn't yet passed the brush when the air was filled with the sound of rifles being cocked, and a strident voice ordered, *"Alto, señores!* Hands up, *por favor,* or my men will fire!"

It was almost sundown when Preacher and his companions rode down a hill, through a screen of trees, and out into a broad, open park. On the far side of the park were the two wagons. Preacher said, "Come on, Dog!" and heeled Horse into a run that carried him and Esteban swiftly across the open ground. He swung out a little to the side so that as he approached he could see Pablo and Joaquin whipping the teams mercilessly, doing their best to get more speed out of the mules and horses pulling the vehicles.

But even though Horse had to be a little tired, the big stallion seemed to enjoy stretching his legs. He ran easily, eating up the gap between him and the wagons.

Esteban rode behind Preacher, holding on to the mountain man. Over the thundering hoofbeats, he called out, "What are we going to do?"

"Stop them wagons until your sister and the others catch up!" Preacher replied. They had almost reached the rear wagon.

"Look out!" Esteban suddenly cried.

Preacher had already seen Father Hortensio poke his head out the back of the wagon. The priest had some sort of weapon in his hands. As Preacher galloped closer, he saw that it was an old blunderbuss. Smoke spurted from the barrel of the ancient gun. A touch of Preacher's heels sent Horse swerving sharply to the side. He heard a humming in the air as the heavy, slow-moving ball went past them.

Father Hortensio had claimed that he was a man of peace and could not resort to violent measures. Obviously that didn't hold true when he believed he was doing the Lord's work. But the important thing was that he didn't have time to reload before Preacher caught up to him.

"Get ready to take the saddle!" the mountain man told Esteban.

"All right, but what—"

They drew even with the rear of the wagon. Preacher vaulted out of the saddle, leaping the short distance to the wagon. He caught hold of the tailgate, and his lean muscles bunched as he pulled himself inside the vehicle. Father Hortensio was fumbling with the blunderbuss, trying to reload it, when Preacher crashed into him, knocking the gun out of his hands and driving him backward onto a stack of gold ingots. Those heavy bars with their dull sheen might look pretty, but they didn't provide a soft place to land. Father Hortensio groaned and lay there, half-stunned.

Preacher looked through the opening in the canvas cover at the front of the wagon and saw Joaquin looking back at him over his shoulder, wide-eyed with fear and surprise. Preacher pulled a pistol from behind his belt, leveled it, and ordered, "Stop this wagon—now!"

Joaquin hauled back on the reins. The wagon began to slow. Father Hortensio regained his wits and came up off the pile of gold bars to lunge at Preacher with his hands outstretched. "No!" he shouted. "You cannot have the treasure! It belongs to the Holy Mother Church!"

Preacher put his free hand on the priest's chest and held him off even as Father Hortensio flailed punches at him. A shove sent Father Hortensio stumbling back against the ingots again. As he tried to catch his balance, the wagon lurched to a halt.

Looking past Joaquin, Preacher saw that Esteban had caught up to the other wagon on Horse and managed to get Pablo to stop, too, probably at gunpoint.

"Damn it, settle down!" he snapped at Father Hortensio. "We ain't come to steal the treasure. You'd know better if you'd just stop and think about it."

"You must not take the holy relics," Father Hortensio babbled. "And the gold will rebuild the Mission Santo Domingo and do many good works—"

"That's fine," Preacher cut in. "But that won't happen unless you listen to me, Padre. Larson and his bunch are still behind us somewhere, and they still want to get their hands on that loot."

"You cannot trade it to those men for Señorita Juanita's safety. I am sorry, but—"

"They don't have the señorita anymore, blast it! She's with us now."

That finally got through to Father Hortensio. Preacher pointed, and the priest looked across the park to where Juanita, Audie, and Nighthawk were riding quickly toward them.

"A savage!" Father Hortensio exclaimed. "And . . . a child?"

"Nope. He may be little, but he's all man. That's Audie, and the redskin with him is called Nighthawk. They're friends o' mine. They helped me get Esteban and Juanita back from Larson's bunch."

Father Hortensio looked confused. "But . . . Esteban was at the cave where the treasure was stored. . . ."

"A whole heap has happened since then," Preacher said

curtly, "and I ain't got time to explain it all. Come on out for a minute, and then we'll get goin' again."

They couldn't afford much of a delay, but he wanted to be sure Father Hortensio and the two Yaquis understood the situation. When everyone was gathered beside the wagons, Preacher spoke swiftly.

"I think Larson's only got three men left who are fit to fight," he said. "So that's four o' them against seven of us, eight if you count the señorita. We got the upper hand, but not if they catch us out in the open. That's why we got to get back to the mission as fast as we can. If we can get the wagons inside what's left of the sanctuary, those old walls will give us good cover."

"You think we will have to fight those men?" Father Hortensio asked.

"I'd count on it, if I was you," Preacher replied with a grim nod. "Cobey ain't gonna give up as long as there's breath in his body. He's crazy-mad now, not just for the gold but for our scalps as well. That's why we got to fort up."

"But . . . Santo Domingo is a mission, not a fort," the priest protested. "It is a holy place. There should not be a battle fought there."

"But, Father," Esteban said, "what better place for good men to struggle with evil?"

"True, true," Father Hortensio murmured. After a moment, he nodded. "Very well. We will reach the mission as swiftly as possible and make our stand there."

"Now you're talkin'," Preacher said. "Let's get these wagons movin'. We're all on the same side again."

"The side of the angels," Father Hortensio said.

Preacher just hoped that before it was all over, the angels wouldn't be singing for *them*.

34

Cobey, Arnie, and the others sat rigidly in their saddles as a dozen men in white trousers, blue uniform jackets, and stiff black hats emerged from the brush carrying rifles. They were Mexican soldiers, members of the army of the dictator, General Santa Anna. Their leader was a slim young officer who carried a saber.

"I am Lieutenant Fernando Escobar," he announced. "We are looking for a young señor and señorita who are supposed to be in this area. Have you seen any wagons recently, Señores?"

Cobey didn't answer the question. Instead he asked one of his own. "Why are you lookin' for 'em?"

"It was reported that they might be in danger, and since they are from an old family with influence in the capital, we were sent to search for them. It was lucky my patrol was close by when the report was made by the man who owns the trading post near the pass into the Sangre de Cristos. We have been riding around here for several days, searching for Señor and Señorita Alvarez."

It was pure luck that had kept Preacher and the others from running into these Mex soldiers, Cobey knew. If they had, any hopes he had of latching onto that treasure would be gone now. As it was, though, he might be able to take advantage of this chance encounter. He remembered hearing that nearly all of the troops in Santa Anna's army were conscripts. Many of them had, in fact, been taken out of prisons in Mexico City and elsewhere and forced into service as soldiers. As he looked at them now, Cobey saw that with the exception of Lieutenant Escobar, the patrol was composed of men who might as well have been cutthroats and brigands.

Men with whom he had something in common, in other words.

"Arnie, you speak pretty good Mex," Cobey said quietly to his second in command. "Tell those soldiers that if they come to work for me, I'll make 'em all rich men. *Ricos*."

His use of that word perked up some interest among the stolid-faced troops. Escobar flushed and said, "Señor, what is this you say? These men are under my command—"

"Tell 'em, Arnie," Cobey cut in.

In a torrent of rapid Spanish, Arnie blurted out Cobey's offer. The Mexican soldiers instantly looked interested. Cobey was a gringo, which meant he was not to be trusted, but he was promising wealth, and besides, they were hundreds of miles from Mexico City and Santa Anna, as feared as he might be, could do nothing to them over a distance such as that. Cobey could practically see those thoughts going through their heads, and he saw the greed that sparked in their eyes.

"Tell you what," he said. "I'm gonna kill the lieutenant, and then they won't have to worry about him no more."

The young officer yelped in panic and began to claw at the pistol holstered at his waist.

Cobey drew, cocked, and fired before Escobar could come close to getting his own weapon out. The ball slammed into the lieutenant's chest and picked him up off his feet, driving him backward into the brush. His legs twitched a few times where they stuck out, and then he lay still.

A few of the soldiers looked surprised, but none of them seemed overly concerned about the unexpected fate of their commanding officer. Cobey smiled at them and said, "You boys work for me now. *Ricos*, each and every one of you."

Arnie translated. One of the soldiers thrust his rifle into the air above his head and shouted, *"Viva el gringo!"*

Cobey grinned. In a matter of a few minutes, this twist of fate meant that he had gone from potentially being outnumbered to having his own little army.

Preacher was sure enough in for a surprise when Cobey and his newfound troops showed up to take that treasure.

Even though the foothills were still rugged in places, the trail the wagons were following was easy enough so that Preacher decided to keep them moving, even after night fell. There was enough moonlight for him to be able to recognize the place where they were supposed to cut off away from the river and head straight across a stretch of relatively flat land toward the old mission.

He knew the chances were that Cobey and the rest of the gang of thieves would keep moving, too. It was a race now, to see if they could reach Santo Domingo before the killers caught up to them.

Juanita had climbed into one of the wagons to get some much-needed rest, and she had persuaded Esteban to come with her. The young man had been through a lot in the past few days, and Preacher told him that he needed to recuperate while he could. Nighthawk was scouting ahead, and Audie had fallen behind to keep an eye on their back trail, so that he could warn them if the pursuit approached. That left Preacher to ride alongside the wagons.

He was moving along easily beside the lead wagon when Father Hortensio climbed onto the driver's seat next to Pablo. "I must speak to you, Señor Preacher," the priest said stiffly.

"What about, Padre?"

"About what happened back there in the mountains, when I took the treasure away from Esteban."

"Yeah, I been wonderin' a mite about that," Preacher mused. "How'd you get that gold outta there?"

"We made bags out of our clothing and dragged them with the horses. It was difficult."

"I expect it was."

"But that is not what I wish to discuss," Father Hortensio said. "I want to explain to you why I did what I did."

Preacher looked over at him and said, "You don't owe me no explanations, Padre. You knew we were gonna try to trade that loot for Juanita's life, and you didn't want to risk losin' it."

"It is not loot. Those relics are holy—"

"Yeah, so I've heard."

"And the gold belongs to the Church," Father Hortensio went on stubbornly.

"You agreed that Esteban and Juanita ought to have a share of it for what they did to help."

"The archbishop agreed. I would not have. Devotion to the Church should not require a . . . a payoff, as you gringos say."

"Well, maybe not," Preacher said. "But there ain't anything wrong with bein' fair about things, neither. That ain't really any o' my business, though. I'm just here because I don't want to see a low-down polecat like that fella Cobey get what he's after. I want those young'uns to make it back home all right, too."

"As do I. I simply want to make it clear that I offer no apologies for anything I have done. I followed my conscience, that is all."

"Fine. I reckon we understand each other. Even a heathen like me can have a conscience, you know."

Father Hortensio hesitated and then said, "Perhaps I was wrong about that."

"About what?"

"About you being a heathen, Señor Preacher."

Preacher grinned. "Well, thanks . . . I reckon."

The party moved on through the night, stopping only occasionally to let the animals rest. Audie came up and reported no signs of their pursuers . . . yet. Preacher remained convinced that Cobey and the others were still back there somewhere, though.

Along toward morning, when the moon was low in the sky and the stars were losing their twinkle against the graying of the sky, Nighthawk rode back to the wagons and gave Preacher an emphatic nod as he said, "Ummm."

"You spotted the old mission?" Preacher said. Nighthawk nodded again.

That was good news, but Preacher hadn't really had time to appreciate it when the swift rataplan of hoofbeats from behind the wagons warned that Audie was approaching. The little man wouldn't be riding that fast, Preacher sensed, unless trouble was riding right behind him.

Preacher wheeled Horse around as Audie raced up out of the night's tail end. "They're back there, Preacher," he said, "and coming up fast! I thought you said there were only four or five of them."

"That's all I know about," Preacher replied as he tensed at the implications of Audie's words.

"Well, there are more than that now. There at least a dozen riders, probably more."

"Maybe it ain't Cobey's bunch. . . ." Preacher began.

But who else could it be, he asked himself as his words came to an abrupt stop. Somehow, Cobey had gone and found himself some more men, just when Preacher had started to feel good about the odds for a change.

"How far back you reckon they are?"

"Not much more than a mile."

Preacher turned to Nighthawk. "How far are we from those ruins?"

"Half mile," the Crow said, the first time Preacher had heard him utter actual words.

"Esteban! Juanita! Padre!"

Preacher's voice rang out, summoning the three he had called from the interior of the wagons. As they looked out from the covered beds of the vehicles, Preacher waved Pablo and Joaquin on.

"Keep them teams movin'!" he ordered. "Get all the speed out of 'em you can!" To the priest and the Alvarez siblings, he went on. "Those hard cases are closin' in behind us, comin' up in a hurry. We'll make a run for the old mission and try to get there before they catch up to us, but I want all the guns loaded and ready, because one way or another there's bound to be a fight! Audie and Nighthawk and me will drop back a ways and see if we can slow them down some, but don't count on that. Padre, keep them Yaquis o' yours pushin' the teams. Esteban, you and Juanita get ready to fight if you have to."

Esteban nodded, an eager look on his face in the graying light. "*Sí*, Preacher. We will be ready."

"Be careful!" Juanita called to them as they turned their horses to ride back in the direction they had come from. Preacher told Dog to stay with the wagons and waved a hand in farewell.

As they rode back along the path they had been following, Audie said to Preacher, "The señorita is quite fond of you, my friend."

"What?" Preacher said, genuinely surprised.

"I'd say she's rather smitten, in fact."

"Aw, hell, you're crazy. She's just a kid."

"On the contrary, she's a full-grown woman, and you're not more than six or seven years older than she is."

"Well, that ain't the way it seems," Preacher said. "The

way she growed up, and the way I've lived since I come to the frontier, makes for a whole lot more difference than a few years."

"I'm just saying that there was more to her admonition than a simple wish for you to be careful."

Preacher had a hard time believing that, but maybe Audie was right. It didn't really matter, though, because first they all had to live through the next few hours. If they accomplished that, then he could worry about how Juanita really felt about him, Preacher told himself.

"There they are," he said suddenly as he spotted a large group of riders coming toward them across a stretch of open ground about five hundred yards wide. Audie had been right about the number. There were about a dozen-and-a-half men in the party. The dawn light was strong enough now so that Preacher could see the white trousers and blue jackets on some of the riders. He exclaimed, "Damn it, some o' them are Mexican soldiers!"

Audie whipped out his spyglass and studied the oncoming horsemen. "You're correct about that," he said, "but I also see the one you called Cobey and several of his companions from our earlier clash, including that gigantic fellow."

"Wick's still alive?" That was as surprising as the fact that Cobey's bunch had been joined by what seemed to be a patrol of Mexican cavalry.

"He's with them," Audie confirmed. "There's no mistaking an individual of that size."

Preacher thought quickly. "Way back when all this started, I told the fella who owns the tradin' post to get word to Santa Fe and send the army up here to look for those youngsters. Maybe Cobey and the others are prisoners."

The sound of several shots rolled over the foothills, and Preacher saw distant spurts of smoke from rifle muzzles.

"That doesn't appear to be the case," Audie said dryly as

he put away his spyglass. "As a matter of fact, it looks more like Cobey is in command."

"Damn it!" Preacher grated. As if the situation hadn't been bad enough already, now they had to fight the Mex army, too. If word of that ever got back to Mexico City, he'd sure be in Dutch with ol' Santa Anna. Of course, if he lived through this mess, it was entirely possible he'd never drift down this way again. . . .

He lifted his rifle and cocked it. "We'll let 'em get a little closer and then give 'em a volley. They ain't in range yet, but if they want to waste powder and shot, that's fine with me."

Audie and Nighthawk got their rifles ready to fire, too, and the three men waited patiently as their enemies galloped closer and closer. More shots blasted out from Cobey's group, and some of the balls came close enough for Preacher to hear them. Finally, he said, "I reckon that'll do," and calmly lifted his rifle to his shoulder.

He could see Cobey, so naturally he drew his bead on the leader, announcing it so that Audie and Nighthawk could choose different targets. No more words were necessary. Preacher took a deep breath and stroked the trigger.

The rifle boomed and kicked and geysered smoke. When the gray cloud cleared, Preacher saw that two saddles had been emptied. Unfortunately, neither of them belonged to Cobey. Two of the Mexican soldiers were down. Either Preacher's shot had missed entirely, or the ball had gone past Cobey and struck one of the soldiers. Didn't really matter. Preacher was glad to have inflicted some damage on the enemy but disappointed that Cobey was still drawing breath.

He said, "Let's go," and wheeled Horse around. Audie and Nighthawk turned their mounts as well, and the three men galloped after the wagons, reloading as they rode. That was a tricky business, but they all had plenty of experience at it.

When they were ready, Preacher reined in and turned Horse again. Three more shots rang out, and another Mexican soldier hit the dirt. A second one reeled in the saddle and clutched a wounded shoulder, but he didn't fall.

"It's me, I'm afraid," Audie said with a sigh. "With its shorter barrel, this rifle of mine doesn't have quite the carrying power it needs for this fight."

"Don't worry about that," Preacher told him. "I reckon the range will be closer later."

"Undoubtedly correct. Well, we've accounted for three of them, at least."

"Yeah, and they're slowin' down. Cobey may have got those Mex troopers to work with him somehow, but right about now they're startin' to wonder if they've made a mistake."

"Ummm," Nighthawk said.

"Yeah, you're right. Let's light a shuck outta here."

They raced on toward the mission. As they came in sight of the old, tumbled-down walls, they saw the wagons rolling into the shelter of the ruined sanctuary. Remembering what had happened here before, Preacher muttered, "I hope they remember to keep their eyes open for snakes."

"The ruins are populated by serpents?" Audie asked.

"Diamondbacks. Big fat ones."

A shudder went through the little man. "I hate snakes."

"You and me, both," Preacher said.

They rode on, and minutes later entered the ruins themselves. Preacher noted with approval that the Yaquis had pulled the wagons behind the wall that had the most of it remaining. It was high enough to completely shield the vehicles.

He and Audie and Nighthawk dismounted and led their horses into a corner where they would be protected from two directions. Then Preacher walked quickly over to the wagons and found Esteban, Juanita, and Father Hortensio waiting for him. "Good job gettin' here fast like you did," he told them. "We got a chance now."

"Yes, but how much of one?" Father Hortensio said. "We're outnumbered again, are we not?"

"Yeah, but we got the fort," Preacher replied with a grin. "They got to bring the fight to us on our ground."

"On the Lord's ground," the priest corrected.

"Yeah," Preacher agreed with a glance toward the riders, who had come to a stop about three hundred yards away. "But it's liable to be a dark and bloody ground before the sun gets much higher in the sky."

35

"Damn it, don't you want to be rich, you spineless bastards?" Cobey shouted at the Mexican soldiers as they hesitated.

Arnie translated, couching the question in more diplomatic terms. One of the soldiers, a corporal named Ruiz who seemed to be their spokesman, said, "We will fight, but the gringos are dead shots, Señor."

Professor Chambers edged his horse forward. "Perhaps I can be of assistance here," he said.

Cobey glanced sharply at him. "What'd you have in mind?"

"Why don't I ride out there under a flag of truce and talk to them? Preacher struck me as being a reasonable man."

Cobey snorted in contempt. "There ain't nothin' reasonable about that mountain man! You ride out there under a white flag and he's liable to shoot you right off your horse!"

"I don't think so," Chambers replied coolly. "At any rate, it's my own life I'm risking, and since I know you don't have a very high opinion of my fighting ability, it doesn't seem to me that you'd be risking very much."

"Ain't that the truth! All right, Professor, if that's what you want to do, have at it. The rest of us will sit back here until you've got yourself killed, and then we'll go get that treasure."

"Very well." Chambers pulled out a handkerchief and tied it onto the barrel of the rifle he had been carrying, which had originally belonged to Chuck Stilson. He propped the butt of the weapon on the saddle so that the barrel stuck up in the air and heeled his horse into a walk.

Cobey watched him go and then said to Arnie, "What's he gonna say to 'em? You think this is gonna do us any good?"

Arnie shrugged. "Like the professor said, we ain't riskin' much to find out, are we?"

"One of them is coming," Audie called to Preacher, who walked over to the wall to have a look.

"Only one?"

"Yes, and he's under a flag of truce." Audie looked at Preacher. "I assume you intend to honor it?"

"I reckon," Preacher said grudgingly. He had recognized the rider by now. "Although there's a part o' me wants to blow the son of a bitch out of the saddle. That's Professor Chambers, the fella who roped Cobey and his bunch into this business in the first place."

"I see. A scholar. I'd probably enjoy a conversation with him, under different circumstances."

Chambers was about fifty feet from the ruins now. Without stepping out into view, because he didn't trust Cobey not to take a potshot at him if he did, Preacher called around the edge of the collapsed wall, "That's far enough, Professor. What do you want?"

"Just a few minutes of your time, Preacher," Chambers lifted his voice to reply. "Could you step out where I can see you better?"

"Nope."

Chambers was close enough so that Preacher heard his low laugh. "I can't say as I blame you, my friend."

"I ain't your friend," Preacher pointed out. "Now speak your piece."

"Very well. Cobey thinks that I'm here to negotiate with you, that I'll promise you something like freedom for you and your companions if you'll give us the treasure, or some such patently false proposal."

"You're sayin' Cobey don't intend to let us go no matter what we do?"

"Exactly. Nor does he intend to let me live." Chambers took a deep breath. "So I'm not negotiating, Preacher. I'm asking if you'll allow me to come in and join you."

The others had come over to the wall to listen to the conversation between Preacher and Chambers, and when the professor made his plea, Esteban exclaimed, "No!"

Juanita laid a hand on her brother's arm. "Perhaps we should consider it, Esteban. He would be one more to fight on our side."

When Preacher didn't reply immediately, Chambers went on. "I don't blame you for not trusting me. But you can ask the señorita. When she was a prisoner, she and I had begun to work out the details of an agreement. I was going to turn on Cobey and the others and help her. Ask her if that's not the case."

Juanita nodded. *"Es verdad.* The professor did promise to help me."

"Never had to see whether or not he'd have gone through with it," Preacher pointed out in a growling voice. "But I reckon it's true enough Cobey plans to double-cross him, and Chambers is smart enough to know that. And he'd be one more gun on our side, all right."

"It's up to you, Preacher," Audie said.

"Ummm," Nighthawk said.

Preacher turned back to the wall and called over it, "You realize that even if you join us, Professor, we'll still be outnumbered by two to one."

"I know," Chambers said. "But if I stay with Cobey, my

chances of surviving the day are nil. At least with you, I'd have a slim chance of living through this."

"Reckon you could look at it like that." Preacher made up his mind. "All right, Professor. Come on in. Best be quick about it, though. Once Cobey realizes you've betrayed him, he's liable to try to shoot you out o' the saddle."

"Yes, I know." Chambers eased his horse closer to the wall, aiming for an area that was only about two feet tall. "Here I come."

He jammed his heels into his horse's flanks and sent the animal lunging forward. At the same time he leaned far forward over the horse's neck, making himself as small a target as possible. Sure enough, Preacher saw several spurts of smoke as Cobey and some of the others fired at Chambers. The distant reports boomed and echoed over the rugged landscape. Rifle balls kicked up dirt around the hooves of Chambers's horse as the professor hauled back on the reins and sent his mount soaring up and over the remains of the wall.

The horse landed cleanly, and Chambers pulled him into a tight turn that carried them both behind the shelter of the higher portion of the wall. Preacher and Audie had been peering around the edge of that part, and they pulled back as rifle balls began to smack into the thick stone wall, chipping off splinters and throwing out dust, but doing no more damage than that.

With a tight grin, Preacher said, "I reckon Cobey's figured out you ain't on his side no more, Professor."

"No doubt. All I can say is that I'm glad to be here."

"Ummm!" Nighthawk warned.

"He's right, Preacher!" Audie said. "Here they come!"

"Pick your spots and pick your shots!" Preacher called in a ringing voice.

Everyone ran to positions they had picked out along the wall, even Father Hortensio. Preacher was a little surprised to see that the priest was going to join the fight, but he remembered how Father Hortensio had blazed away at him with that blunderbuss earlier. Clearly, the padre had decided that he was willing to fight for his faith, and that it was all right with El Señor Dios for him to do so.

Cobey and his men were making an all-out charge, galloping straight at the old mission. Preacher ordered, "Hold your fire! Let 'em get closer!" Chambers was a few yards to his right. Preacher said to him, "How'd Cobey wind up with the Mexican army fightin' on his side?"

"We ran into a patrol searching for the Alvarezes," the professor replied. "Cobey killed their lieutenant and appealed to the baser instincts of the soldiers. He promised to make them all rich."

"That'd likely do it all right," Preacher said, "with the sort o' scum Santa Anna forces into his army." He raised his voice again. "Little bit closer . . . *Let 'em have it!*"

Shots rang out along the ruined wall as all nine of the defenders fired. The storm of lead scythed into the onrushing attackers and swept several of them out of their saddles. Four or five of the Mexican soldiers went down, and so did a couple of their horses in a tangle of thrashing legs and hooves. Bert McDermott flipped backward off his horse, flinging his arms out to the sides as blood spurted from his chest. He hit the ground and bounced and rolled in the limp sprawl that signified death.

But Cobey and Arnie were still coming, along with five of the soldiers. Wick was far behind them, slumped over his mount's neck but trying to keep up.

With Cobey in the lead, the remaining attackers reached the wall and leaped their mounts over it, and with a mad swirl of dust and hooves and noise that made a mockery of what should have been a peaceful early morning, they were among the defenders and the battle was suddenly hand to hand, *mano a mano*.

Preacher dropped his empty rifle and yanked the two

pistols from behind his belt. He fired the left-hand gun at one of the soldiers, and at close range like this, both balls from the double-shotted weapon blew fist-sized holes through the luckless man's torso, making him fly off the back of his horse. Preacher drew a bead on Cobey with the right-hand gun, but just as he pulled the trigger one of the horses rammed him with its shoulder, throwing off his aim. The balls missed and went harmlessly into the air.

Cobey's pistol spurted flame and Joaquin went down, blood fountaining from his neck where Cobey's shot had torn it open. Pablo lunged at Arnie, reaching up to try to pull him from the saddle, but the fat man planted a foot in the Yaqui's chest and kicked him back. Pablo stumbled and fell and then screamed as Arnie rode over him, a steel-shod hoof landing in the middle of his face and shattering his skull.

Esteban reversed his rifle and clubbed one of the soldiers off his horse, breaking the weapon's stock as he did so. As the soldier landed on the ground, Esteban leaped on him and drove the shattered stock into his face again and again, smashing the life out of him.

A few yards away, one of the soldiers leaned over and grabbed Juanita, jerking her feet off the ground as she cried out in anger and fear. With a leer on his face he tried to lift her to his horse's back in front of his saddle, but he stiffened suddenly as an arrow erupted from his throat. The wound spewed blood. Nighthawk's bow had driven the shaft all the way through the man's neck from the back. He went limp and let go of Juanita. She tumbled to the ground and rolled desperately to avoid the slashing hooves of the dead man's horse.

Another soldier raced his mount after Audie, who scampered toward a pile of rocks with grass growing up between them. The Mexican slashed at the little man's head with the saber that had belonged to the patrol's lieutenant before Cobey murdered him. Audie ducked under the swipe, stopped short, and reached up to grab the man's arm. With a heave of broad, muscular shoulders, Audie pulled the man from the saddle and used his own momentum to flip him into the rocks. That was enough to stun the man momentarily, but he sprang up a second later, shrieking in horror. Several long, fat rattlesnakes hung from his arms and torso, their fangs sunk deep in his flesh. Audie had inadvertently tossed him right into a den of the rattlers. One of the diamondbacks was even attached to the soldier's neck. The man did a grotesque jig that just pumped the load of venom through his veins that much faster, and then he collapsed.

The lone surviving soldier wheeled his horse toward Esteban and Juanita. Before he could reach them, however, Chambers leaped in front of him. The professor's pocket pistol cracked wickedly. The soldier jerked back a little, but Chambers's shot had just grazed his arm. He had plenty of strength left to thrust out the rifle in his hand. The bayonet attached to the end of the barrel drove deeply into Chambers's chest. He staggered back, pawing at the blade that was still buried in his body. His eyes opened wide in horror and the realization that he was dying. He fell to his knees and then slumped forward. The butt of the rifle struck the ground and held him propped up that way, almost as if he were praying.

The soldier kept going, aiming his horse directly at Esteban and Juanita, who were now huddled together. In another moment he would have trampled them, but suddenly another rider was beside him, a huge arm lashing out in a smashing blow. At the same instant, Wick rammed his horse into the soldier's horse. The two men and their mounts went down in a welter of dust. Wick was the only one who came out of the billowing cloud, dragging a broken leg behind him. He hobbled toward Juanita, croaking, "Señorita!"

Cobey whirled his horse and charged toward them, shouting, "Wick! Get out of the way!"

Wick turned and held up his hands. "Cobey! Stop!"

The pistol in Cobey's hand exploded. Wick staggered

back as the ball struck him in the chest. "Cobey . . . ?" he whispered as blood welled from the wound.

Then he fell to the side like a massive tree toppling.

On the other side of the ruined sanctuary, Arnie left his saddle in a diving tackle that slammed into Preacher and knocked them both sprawling to the ground. Preacher rolled and came to his feet first, knife in hand, but Arnie was up only an instant later, also brandishing steel. The two men came together in a blur of thrust and parry and counterthrust, their blades ringing together loudly and throwing off sparks as they clashed. Preacher had been in knife fights before, but never had he faced such a whirlwind of steel. Arnie's knife bit and slashed him in several places, but Preacher dealt out some damage of his own, leaving bloodstains spreading in several places on Arnie's homespun shirt. Both men knew they were just about evenly matched, and the first slip, the first mistake, would likely decide this deadly match.

That slip was Preacher's, as a rock turned under his foot and threw him off balance for an instant. In that shaving of time, Arnie's blade licked out, aiming true for Preacher's throat. It took every bit of speed and instinct Preacher possessed to pull his head to the side just in time, so that Arnie's knife just ripped an ugly gash in the side of Preacher's neck.

But that missed thrust brought Arnie in too close to protect himself from Preacher's counterthrust. Preacher slammed his knife into Arnie's chest, the keen blade slicing deeper and deeper until it was buried all the way, right up to the "Green River" stamped on the hilt. Arnie stiffened and said, "Damn," and then blood trickled from his mouth and the life went out of his eyes. He sagged against Preacher, who ripped the knife free and shoved Arnie's body away from him. Preacher turned. . . .

And saw Cobey standing in front of Esteban and Juanita, both hands filled with pistols. The only thing between him and the two young people was Father Hortensio, who stood there unarmed and said, "In the name of God, I call on you to lay down your arms, henchman of Satan!"

An ugly grin stretched across Cobey's face. "God left this place a long time ago, old man. Now there's just me, and I got one pistol for you, one for the kid, and then it'll be just me and the señorita." The left-hand pistol came up toward Father Hortensio.

Preacher drew back his knife hand. It would be a long throw, but he had to make it.

Before he could let fly with the blade, a hamlike hand rose behind Cobey, grabbed the back of his shirt, and jerked him down. Cobey yelled in surprise and twisted frantically, but he couldn't escape Wick's grip. The giant closed his other hand around Cobey's throat and slammed him on the ground. Pale and bleeding heavily, Wick loomed over his former friend. Both hands were around Cobey's neck now, squeezing for all they were worth. Cobey jabbed both pistols into Wick's midsection and pulled the triggers. Wick's body muffled the twin explosions as the balls blew a huge hole all the way through him. His back arched under the impact of the shots.

But he didn't let go. His hands remained locked around Cobey's neck, and with his dying breath he lurched and heaved. Preacher was running toward them, and he heard the sharp crack as Cobey's neck broke. The muscles in Wick's arms and shoulders bunched one last time, and he tore Cobey's head right off his shoulders. As Wick slumped forward over his former friend's body, the grisly trophy slipped from his fingers and rolled to the side so that Cobey's eyes stared sightlessly toward the wagons.

Toward the lost treasure of Mission Santo Domingo, now home again at last.

36

"Well," Preacher said to Father Hortensio, "I reckon you got a good start on somethin' every church needs—a graveyard."

"Unfortunately, you are right about that, my son," the priest replied.

Along with Audie and Nighthawk, the two men stood beside the last of the numerous graves they had dug and then refilled over the course of the long day. It was nearly sunset, and it had taken that long to lay to rest everyone who had died in the early morning battle. Preacher wouldn't have minded just throwing Cobey's body in a ravine somewhere—that was more than the bastard deserved, as far as Preacher was concerned—but Father Hortensio had insisted that everyone be properly buried, even their enemies.

Somehow, Wick Jimpson didn't fall into that category anymore. Preacher hoped that somebody would put up a marker for the big man. He had a feeling Juanita would see to that.

"What are you going to do now, Padre?"

"My task is to rebuild the mission and bring the word of God to this land once again," Father Hortensio said. "With Esteban and Juanita to help me, and with the Lord's blessing, I am sure I will succeed."

"They've forgiven you for what happened up in the mountains?" Preacher asked.

Father Hortensio smiled. "Of course. God has filled them with His mercy and understanding."

"Well, I reckon I understand," Preacher said. "I ain't quite so forgivin', though."

"Then it is fortunate for me that I do not require your forgiveness, is it not?"

Preacher just grunted. Him and the padre weren't ever goin' to get along that good, but he reckoned that was all right.

He started to turn away, but he paused and looked again at the grave where Professor Rufus Chambers was buried. He supposed Chambers had redeemed himself, too, there at the end, at least a little. Preacher couldn't bring himself to feel any real regret for the man's death, though. It was Chambers's greed that had started all the trouble in motion. But in the end he had come up empty, just like Cobey and Arnie and the others. Preacher suspected that under different circumstances, Arnie wouldn't have been such a bad fella. They might have even been friends. As it was, though, all Preacher could do was feel a little grudging respect for the man.

The four of them walked back slowly toward the mission as the sun lowered toward the peaks in the west. Audie asked, "What are your plans, Preacher?"

"Mosey on back up to the Rockies and go after a good mess o' peltries, I reckon," the mountain man said with a shrug. "You and Nighthawk headin' that way, too?"

"No, I believe we've decided to stay here for a while and help see to it that Father Hortensio gets his mission rebuilt. Then I'd like to see Santa Fe before we head north again."

"Ummm," Nighthawk said.

Preacher paused and extended his hand. Horse was already saddled and ready to ride. Dog sat waiting beside the big stallion. There was some light left in the day, and Preacher wanted to use it.

"Reckon this is so long, then," he said.

"You're leaving already?" Audie asked in surprise as he clasped Preacher's hand. "Esteban and Juanita will be disappointed."

Preacher thought about what Audie had said that morning about Juanita. If she really had any romantic notions about him, it would be better for her sake if she put them out of her head.

"You can say my good-byes for me," Preacher told him. "I never was much for things like that. Rather ride on without no fuss."

"I suppose we can honor your wishes."

Preacher turned to Nighthawk and shook hands with the Crow warrior. "I got a feelin' we'll be runnin' into each other again, somewheres down the trail," he said.

Nighthawk nodded and said solemnly, "Ummm."

Preacher started toward Horse, but Father Hortensio stopped him by saying, "Wait."

Preacher turned back. "Sorry, Padre. I figured you wouldn't want to shake hands with a heathen."

"Even a priest makes mistakes from time to time," Father Hortensio said as he held out his hand. "Though I still find your name somewhat improper, you are no heathen, my son." With his other hand he brought a small pouch from somewhere inside his robes. "I want you to have this, too."

Preacher clasped the priest's hand and then took the pouch, frowning at the little clinking sounds its contents made. "Some o' the lost treasure?"

"No longer lost, thanks to you. Take it with the Church's gratitude . . . and with mine."

"Well, I wouldn't want to insult the Church's generosity," Preacher said as he slipped the bag of coins inside his buckskins. He added, "Or yours."

A moment later, he was mounted up. He turned Horse and rode north, with Dog trotting alongside. Looking back,

Preacher lifted a hand in farewell, and Father Hortensio called after him, *"Vaya con Dios!"*

Preacher smiled and rode on, heeling Horse into a ground-eating lope. By the time night fell he would be miles to the north, well on his way to somewhere else, content in the knowledge that despite what he had left behind, he had a fortune of his own in this wild, beautiful country that would forever be his home.

AFTERWORD

Notes from the Old West

In the small town where I grew up, there were two movie theaters. The Pavilion was one of those old-timey movie show palaces, built in the heyday of Mary Pickford and Charlie Chaplin—the silent era of the 1920s. By the 1950s, when I was a kid, the Pavilion was a little worn around the edges, but it was still the premier theater in town. They played all those big Technicolor biblical Cecil B. DeMille epics and corny MGM musicals. In Cinemascope, of course.

On the other side of town was the Gem, a somewhat shabby and run-down grind house with sticky floors and torn seats. Admission was a quarter. The Gem booked low-budget "B" pictures (remember the Bowery Boys?), war movies, horror flicks, and Westerns. I liked the Westerns best. I could usually be found every Saturday at the Gem, along with my best friend, Newton Trout, watching Westerns from 10 A.M. until my father came looking for me around suppertime. (Sometimes Newton's dad was dispatched to come fetch us.) One time, my dad came to get me right in the middle of *Abilene Trail*, which featured the now-forgotten Whip Wilson. My father became so engrossed in the action he sat down and watched the rest of it with us. We didn't get home until after dark, and my mother's meat loaf was a pan of gray ashes by the time we did. Though my father and I were both in the doghouse the next day, this remains one of my fondest childhood memories. There was Wild Bill Elliot, and Gene Autry, and Roy Rogers, and Tim Holt, and, a little later, Rod Cameron and Audie Murphy. Of these newcomers, I never missed an Audie Murphy Western, because Audie was sort of an antihero. Sure, he stood for law and order and was an honest man, but sometimes he had to go around the law to uphold it. If he didn't play fair, it was only because he felt hamstrung by the laws of the land. Whatever it took to get the bad guys, Audie did it. There were no finer points of law, no splitting of legal hairs. It was instant justice, devoid of long-winded lawyers, bored or biased jurors, or black-robed, often corrupt judges.

Steal a man's horse and you were the guest of honor at a necktie party.

Molest a good woman and you got a bullet in the heart or a rope around the gullet. Or at the very least, got the crap beat out of you. Rob a bank and face a hail of bullets or the hangman's noose.

Saved a lot of time and money, did frontier justice.

That's all gone now, I'm sad to say. Now you hear, "Oh, but he had a bad childhood" or "His mother didn't give him enough love" or "The homecoming queen wouldn't give him a second look and he has an inferiority complex." Or "cultural rage," as the politically correct bright boys refer to it. How many times have you heard some self-important defense attorney moan, "The poor kids were only venting their hostilities toward an uncaring society?"

Mule fritters, I say. Nowadays, you can't even call a punk a punk anymore. But don't get me started.

It was, "Howdy, m'am" time, too. The good guys, antihero or not, were always respectful to the ladies. They might shoot a bad guy five seconds after tipping their hat to a woman, but the code of the West demanded you be respectful to a lady.

Lots of things have changed since the heyday of the Wild West, haven't they? Some for the good, some for the bad.

I didn't have any idea at the time that I would someday write about the West. I just knew that I was captivated by the Old West.

When I first got the itch to write, back in the early 1970s, I didn't write Westerns. I started by writing horror and action adventure novels. After more than two dozen novels, I began thinking about developing a Western character. From those initial musing came the novel *The Last Mountain Man: Smoke Jensen*. That was followed by *Preacher: The First Mountain Man*. A few years later, I began developing the *Last Gunfighter* series. Frank Morgan is a legend in his own time, the fastest gun west of the Mississippi . . . a title and a reputation he never wanted, but can't get rid of.

The Gunfighter series is set in the waning days of the Wild West. Frank Morgan is out of time and place, but still, he is pursued by men who want to earn a reputation as the man who killed the legendary gunfighter. All Frank wants to do is live in peace. But he knows in his heart that dream will always be just that: a dream, fog and smoke and mirrors, something elusive that will never really come to fruition. He will be forced to wander the West, alone, until one day his luck runs out.

For me, and for thousands—probably millions—of other people (although many will never publicly admit it), the old Wild West will always be a magic, mysterious place: a place we love to visit through the pages of books; characters we would like to know . . . from a safe distance; events we would love to take part in, again, from a safe distance. For the old Wild West was not a place for the faint of heart. It was a hard, tough, physically demanding time. There were no police to call if one faced adversity. One faced trouble alone, and handled it alone. It was rugged individualism: something that appeals to many of us.

I am certain that is something that appeals to most readers of Westerns.

I still do on-site research (whenever possible) before starting a Western novel. I have wandered over much of the West, prowling what is left of ghost towns. Stand in the midst of the ruins of these old towns, use a little bit of imagination, and one can conjure up life as it used to be in the Wild West. The rowdy Saturday nights, the tinkling of a piano in a saloon, the laughter of cowboys and miners letting off steam after a week of hard work. Use a little more imagination and one can envision two men standing in the street, facing one another, seconds before the hook and draw of a gunfight. A moment later, one is dead and the other rides away.

The old wild untamed West.

There are still some ghost towns to visit, but they are rapidly vanishing as time and the elements take their toll. If you want to see them, make plans to do so as soon as possible, for in a few years, they will all be gone.

And so will we.

Stand in what is left of the Big Thicket country of east Texas and try to imagine how in the world the pioneers managed to get through that wild tangle. I have wondered about that many times and marveled at the courage of the men and women who slowly pushed westward, facing dangers that we can only imagine.

Let me touch briefly on a subject that is very close to me: firearms. There are some so-called historians who are now claiming that firearms played only a very insignificant part in the settlers' lives. They claim that only a few were armed. What utter, stupid nonsense! What do these so-called historians think the pioneers did for food? Do they think the early settlers rode down to the nearest supermarket and bought their meat? Or maybe they think the settlers chased down deer or buffalo on foot and beat the animals to death with a club. I have a news flash for you so-called historians: The settlers used guns to shoot their game. They used guns to defend hearth and home against Indians on the warpath. They used guns to protect themselves from outlaws. Guns are a part of Americana. And always will be.

The mountains of the West and the remains of the ghost towns that dot those areas are some of my favorite subjects to write about. I have done extensive research on the various mountain ranges of the West and go back whenever time permits. I sometimes stand surrounded by the towering mountains and wonder how in the world the pioneers ever made it through. As hard as I try and as often as I try, I simply cannot imagine the hardships those men and women endured over the hard months of their incredible journey. None of us can. It is said that on the Oregon Trail alone, there are at least two bodies in lonely, unmarked graves for every mile of that journey. Some students of the West say the number of dead is at least twice that. And nobody knows the exact number of wagons that impatiently started out alone and simply vanished on the way, along with their occupants, never to be seen or heard from again.

Just vanished.

The one-hundred-and-fifty-year-old ruts of the wagon wheels can still be seen in various places along the Oregon Trail. But if you plan to visit those places, do so quickly, for they are slowly disappearing. And when they are gone, they will be lost forever, except in the words of Western writers.

As long as I can peck away at a keyboard and find a company to publish my work, I will not let the Old West die. That I promise you.

The West will live on as long as there are writers willing to write about it, and publishers willing to publish it. Writing about the West is wide open, just like the old Wild West. Characters abound, as plentiful as the wide-open spaces, as colorful as a sunset on the Painted Desert, as restless as the ever-sighing winds. All one has to do is use a bit of imagination. Take a stroll through the cemetery at Tombstone, Arizona; read the inscriptions. Then walk the main street of that once-famous town around midnight and you might catch a glimpse of the ghosts that still wander the town. They really do. Just ask anyone who lives there. But don't be afraid of the apparitions, they won't hurt you. They're just out for a quiet stroll.

The West lives on. And as long as I am alive, it always will.